TO THE END OF THE WORLD

Colin Foreman

Edited by Lillian King

A snowstorm, a mysterious man and an adventure story, change the lives of three children forever.

Ancient, secret dangers come to life and the Battle of Pinner High School, a battle for the future of the world, begins.

I would like to thank the following people. Without their help, enthusiasm and expertise, this book would not exist. I feel proud, privileged and humbled to have worked with all of you.

Louise, Pippa, John and George at Waterstones
(Design ideas, expertise and risk taking)

Lillian King
(Editing)

Wayne Reynolds
(Cover paintings)

Fiona Campbell
(Black and white drawings)

Lee Scammacca and Craig Williams at Cree8, Kinross
(Design and typesetting)

Scotprint, Edinburgh
(Printing)

Gill Blacklock and Rosie Crawford
(Proof reading)

Les Brodie and Doug Crawford
(Wonga)

Flash Gordon
(Consultancy)

Ian Donaldson, Royal Bank of Scotland
(Overdraft)

Alan Street at Gardners
(Help and advice)

Andrea, Bob, Morag, Lisa and Sam at CHAS
(PR and enthusiasm)

CHAS

To the End of the World is dedicated to the children, parents and staff at CHAS, the Children's Hospice Association of Scotland, and all profits from the sale of this book will be gifted to them.

To the End of the World is the first part of a five book
series titled, "Keepers and Seekers."

The right of Colin Foreman to be identified as the
Author of the Work has been asserted by him in
accordance with the Copyright And Patents Act 1988

Published by Myroy Books Limited
Hillside House, Glenlomond, Kinross. KY13 9HF

This paperback edition first published in 2005
Reprinted 2005

ISBN – 0 9548 9490 1

A catalogue record for this book is available from the British Library.

Prologue
AMERA'S CAIRN
1427 BC

Gora had been running since dusk, since he had first heard about the passing, and despite the cold, sweat poured down his face. The furs he wore reeked from the great effort of travelling so far, so quickly, but the promise of riches drove him on.

Exhausted, Gora paused to look at the moon. It was full, silver and bright, the kind of moon that would signal the last days for a Stone Keeper. As his strength returned, he faced north and, through the darkness, saw the distant outline of a ribbon of pine trees, which marked the end of the land. The Stone Circle was this side of the pines and Amera's cairn lay only a short distance beyond the circle. Gora sniffed, smelled salt, and knew he was close.

Pointing his spear at the sky, he tried to imagine what it would be like to command something of such great power, such history. Then he began to run again, moving swiftly when the moonlight let him see the twists in the narrow path and slowing to a snail's pace where the rocks and trees threw their shadows across the ground.

Suddenly, the song of man was on the air and Gora stopped, turning his bearded face to trace its origin. It seemed to be coming from over the next rise. The beat of a drum, broken by rhythmic chanting, came to him like a whisper and grew louder, more distinct, as the wind caught it.

He crawled towards the cover of thick gorse bushes, which crowned the rise. He pushed into them, ignoring the thorns that ripped into his bare arms and legs. Below him the sacred earth within the Stone Circle was lit by a huge fire. Men danced, slowly, around the fire. One cried out and fell to his knees. These were Amera's people and their grief confirmed that he, the most powerful of the warrior kings of the Sea People, was dead.

Gora smiled, edged his way back out of the gorse and hurried away, keeping a safe distance from the stones and heading straight for the cairn. His spirits were high from the danger and he felt the same alertness, the same blood-pumping excitement, that he enjoyed so much on a hunt. This would be his night, his victory and, as surely as Amera's time was over, Gora's time was beginning.

Something caught Gora's eye and he slowed to look towards the ocean. A single torch shone out, yellow and bright, perhaps three hundred paces away, and its light showed the outline of a tall warrior who guarded the entrance to the burial cairn. Gora studied him, looking for any sign of weakness. The man carried a spear like his own, twelve hands long and with a sharp stone head, and nothing else.

Gora listened to the distant chanting and waited for a cloud to cover the moon. Then he moved like a stalker, behind the guard, and breathed deeply to prepare himself for the attack.

"Ten paces," he told himself, edging forward. "Run like the wolf, with cunning and silence."

The warrior turned and let out a startled, wild cry and his scream spoke of anger and terror. Gora's spear caught him mercilessly in the stomach and its shaft drove upwards. The big man fell to the ground without another sound and Gora stood over him, grinning with triumph. But later, in darkness and utter loneliness, he would curse himself for not hiding the guard's body.

Anxiously, he glanced around and, once satisfied that he was truly alone, picked up the torch and moved carefully to the entrance of the cairn. The torch revealed thick stones, which framed a dark, forbidding tunnel. Two stones ran up from the ground and held aloft a third, which had strange shapes carved into it. One was a man's skull. Gora shuddered as he ran a finger along the deep grooves, but thought again about his prize. It was here, somewhere, and he spat on the skull and entered the burial mound. It already smelled of death.

The ceiling of the tunnel was low. At first he bent double, dragging the spear and holding the torch out in front of him, but gradually the stone passage became even smaller, forcing him onto his hands and knees. Gora knew of caves, not cairns and the places of spirits, but if the stories were true he would soon be at Amera's last place of rest.

As he crawled, the torch lit only a few paces ahead and his fear increased, like that of a child in the worst of nightmares. The blackness closed behind him like a door.

He tried to comfort himself by counting the smooth, flat stones, which lined the floor of the passage. They seemed to go on forever and always down, down into the bowels of the earth, but at last

Gora stumbled into the chamber, stood upright and lifted the torch. Wonderful colours flickered and the warrior stood mesmerised as gold and yellow beams bounced off treasure and danced across cold walls. To his right, laid upon a bower of leaves and branches, was Amera. How old the mighty king looked and how peaceful. How empty of life.

Gora knelt down quickly and stabbed the torch and spear into the soft earth, to free his hands. A painted shield lay across the king's body and he tossed it aside. Tearing at Amera's furs, he saw it. Saw it at last. Tied with leather strips around the king's neck was a single ruby of great size. Gora pulled hard on the stone and it broke free.

"Amera's stone," he whispered, smiling.

He held it next to the torch and immediately the burial chamber filled with a rich, red light, strange and ghostly, and the shadows, which once protected this place of secrets, were driven away to become tongues of flame. The heart of the ruby seemed to be alive. It was eerie and beautiful, the colour of blood.

A distant *boom* shattered the silence. A drum echoed, dully, throughout the cairn and Gora thrust the stone inside his furs and grabbed the torch. Wildly he crawled back, ignoring the pain as his head struck the low ceiling.

Again the drum sounded, this time much louder than before. He glanced up the passageway at the three entrance stones. They were lit by new torches. Cold sweat poured down his back as sheer terror overcame him.

Twenty paces to the open air. He could fight out there and maybe, just maybe, escape. Gora overcame his terror and crawled on, half stumbling, half falling, every muscle, every sinew, ready for the attack.

A loud grinding noise replaced the drums. Rock ran across rock and a dark shape began to obscure the torches held by the Sea People. Gora stopped to look at the disappearing line of light and realised what was happening.

Now the drum beat was muffled as though it struggled to even enter the cairn. In desperation, he threw himself forward. The crack in the doorway was less than the width of a hand, then less than a finger, and as Gora hit the great stone with his shoulder all light from the outside world was gone. Roaring like a wild beast, he pushed with all his might against the rock that barred his way to freedom. But the stone did not move, not even a fraction.

Gora collapsed to his knees and moaned as the horror of his entombment overcame him. He took the ruby from his fur and sobbed for his lost beginning. Once again he held the jewel close to the torch and the narrow passage glowed red. His tears dripped onto Amera's stone. Through the tears, the passage seemed to be engulfed by a swirling, bloody river. Gora started to shake uncontrollably.

The torch flickered and went out.

CHAPTER ONE

Whirlwind at the Door

The old conservatory was lovely and warm. Julie Donald put her magazine down to look out at the bird table. The squirrels were back and going about their business, stealing as many of the nuts as they could carry. One scurried across the grass and another swung madly on the net that held the promise of supper. A chaffinch, perched on the lip of the table, stared down at him reproachfully and flew off across the garden fence towards the woods behind the old house.

Julie glanced up at the clock.

"Any minute now," she sighed.

Two black and white kittens started to chase each other around the floor and Julie looked back at the page *25 ideas for a great new kitchen*. She flicked through pictures of cookers and scratch-resistant work surfaces. We could certainly do with some of those, she thought and left the pictures face up for her husband to see.

Picking up her cup of tea, Julie took a sip, and looked at the clock again. Three fifteen. The sigh was bigger this time. The front door burst open and a bag was thrown on the floor.

"I'm home, Mum!" shouted a voice that shook the whole house.

"Hello, darling, did you have a nice day at school?"

"It was alright," said Laura, "but Mrs Styles was awful. She made us do a whole hour of mental maths."

"That's good."

"Mu-u-um, can I have a mobile phone?"

"When you're fourteen."

"Fourteen? Abby got one for her birthday. I'm the only one in my class who hasn't got one."

"Ben is in your class and he hasn't got one. Katie and Rebecca haven't got one either."

"Ben is a slug and wouldn't know a phone from a banana."

"You still can't have one."

"It's not fair. Peter's got one."

"Peter is four years older than you."

A tear began to form as Laura sensed defeat again.

"Why don't you ask your father?"

"Huh. I know what he'll say. 'Why don't you go and ask your mother?' He never makes a decision."

"And that's how it should be, my angel. Now go and get yourself a snack and a drink. I bought some of those seedless grapes you like."

"Can't I have some crisps?"

"What did you have for your lunch?"

"Ham salad."

"Ham salad?"

"Alright, chips."

"So, fruit it is then, dear."

Laura pulled a face and stormed off to the kitchen.

"Your room is like a bombsite," her mother called after her, "make sure it's tidy before you go to Brownies."

"It's the end of term. So there's no Brownies and no need to tidy my room."

Julie took a long intake of breath and calmed herself as the fridge door was shut with the ferocity of an earthquake.

"Hi, Mum," called out two voices together and there was the sound of more school bags being abandoned in the hall.

"Hello, darlings, you're back early. I'm in the conservatory."

Peter was tall, lean, and immaculate in his school uniform. James, younger by only a year, looked as though he had been dragged through a hedge backwards. Julie winced as she saw the grass stains on the knees of his trousers and the trail of mud that seemed to follow him everywhere.

"Did you have a good day at school?"

"School sucks," said James cheekily.

"Yes, thanks." Peter bent, as he always did, to kiss his mother on the cheek.

"Whatever, it was the last day for ages," said James and went off to raid the fridge. The phone rang and Laura came bounding down the stairs to answer it. James dived for the phone.

"It won't be for you."

"I bet it is."

"It's not." James's tone was triumphant, "It's Kylie for Peter."

"Not her again. Those two are always on the phone. Why don't they talk to each other at school?"

"Peter, it's Kylie. *Again*," yelled James at the top of his voice.

Peter took the phone from him.

"My turn for the computer," said James.

Laura made a dash for the stairs. "No it's my turn."

James rushed after her, barging past. She banged her leg and began to cry.

"Be quiet," Peter shouted. "No, not you Kylie."

In the conservatory, Julie considered the time.

"Ten minutes past three, happiness. Twenty past, misery."

How was she going to cope with the Easter holidays? Two whole weeks to find things to do with the kids.

"I'm home," called out a voice from the door.

"Daddy," cried Laura and she ran to throw her arms around her father.

"Hello, my wee chicken," said Colin Donald, "are you on holiday?"

Laura wiped a tear from her eye, beamed up at him and nodded.

"Daddy?" she asked hopefully.

"What are you after now, my chicken?"

"You know you said that if I was a good girl, then I might be able to have a little something for the holiday?"

He raised an eyebrow and sensed trouble.

"No, lass."

"You did," insisted Laura, "and do you know what Abby got for her birthday?"

"A DVD player? A gerbil? A pencil case? A music poster? New curtains? A pair of shoes? Air freshener? Hoover?"

"Stop it, Daddy. She got a mobile phone."

"That's nice."

"Yes, and I would like one too."

"I thought you wanted a horse?"

"I want a horse as well. Mummy said I can ask you for one."

"Did she now?"

"She did. So what do you think?"

8

"I think I need to speak to Mummy about it."

"Huh. You never make a decision."

Laura stamped her foot and marched up the stairs to her bedroom.

"Just like her mother," thought Colin and he chuckled to himself.

***

In front of a large bowl of spaghetti bolognese, Laura and James fought over the cheese. Peter raised his fork and began what, even by his standards, would be a particularly quick and thorough demolition of his food.

"I've got a bit of an announcement," said Colin quietly.

Julie looked at him blankly and, as usual, the children ignored him.

"An important announcement."

James stopped eating and nudged his brother. A fork heaped with spaghetti hovered in front of his gaping mouth.

"Well, now I've got your attention. Good. Mummy and I are going away for a week."

"Are we?" stammered Julie.

"Yes, it's partly work. I've booked us a hotel in Amsterdam for a few nights."

"If you get a deal, can I have a mobile phone?" asked Laura.

"When you're fourteen, my angel," Julie replied automatically.

"And what are we going to do?" demanded James.

"I thought you might like a wee break in Scotland."

"Not with Grandpa and Grandma," exclaimed Laura, "they don't even have a bloomin' computer. And they live in the middle of nowhere. It's boring."

"Nothing to do," said James.

"I knew you'd be pleased."

Colin smiled and looked at Julie.

"It won't be all work, not by a long chalk, and you could do with a bit of a break."

"I can't disagree with you there. It's just, well, all a bit sudden, that's all."

9

"Only heard this morning. Mum and Dad were really good about it and said they would get the rooms ready for the kids."

"When do we go?" asked Peter.

"You are booked on the 9.50 flight from Luton to Edinburgh."

"Tomorrow morning?" gasped Laura and James together.

Colin shuffled a piece of pasta across his plate.

"Not exactly."

"Surely not tonight?" asked Julie.

"Aye. I got a good last minute deal on the internet and it was either tonight, or at an even later time tomorrow night."

"But I won't have a chance to say goodbye to Abby and Helen," complained Laura.

"I thought of that," said Colin. "I've bought you all a phone card and I'm sure Peter will let you use his mobile."

Peter nodded. He sensed they should go, but couldn't explain why he felt like this.

"Well, that's settled then. So if you've finished your supper, you had better go and pack enough clothes for six days."

"Six days," groaned James.

"Like an adventure, isn't it?" but his words were met with more blank stares and a distinct lack of enthusiasm.

"You load the dishwasher, Colin," said Julie. "I'll help them pack, and after they've gone you can tell me what's really going on."

Apart from an argument about which music station to put on the radio, it was a sombre journey to the airport. The kids seemed to be in shock and only stirred out of it when they turned off the M1 and read a sign. *Luton 4 miles.*

Colin Donald nodded at it. "Nearly there, my chickens."

"Don't bloomin' well talk to me," said Laura, "I really don't like you at the moment."

"Will they be there to meet us?" asked Peter.

"Aye laddie, I spoke to Grandma and gave her your flight number."

Julie looked concerned. "Will they be alright on the flight?"

"The airline lady said they tend to make a fuss over unaccompanied minors."

"I'm not a miner," complained James and instantly his attention went back to the screen of his computer game.

It was dark and cold as they pulled into the short-stay car park. Colin went to get a trolley and everyone else helped to empty the boot. When the trolley was loaded with three tartan cases, it seemed to have a life of its own and wandered in any line except a straight one. The inside of the terminal building was bright, warm and busy, and they wove their way through static lines of holidaymakers. As they joined a queue, Laura looked down the line of travellers and saw a sign.

Security: please have your photo ID ready.

"Huh. I don't have a photo, so we can't go."

Colin pulled three passports from his chest pocket, grinned and waved them at her. She was still moaning when a pretty woman, in a bright orange uniform, came over.

"Hello, I'm Sally. You must be Peter, James and Laura."

James nudged his brother and whispered, "Much better looking than Kylie."

Peter raised an arm as if to hit him.

Julie grabbed his arm and said calmly, "Yes that's right, three unaccompanied *minors*."

She looked daggers at the boys. Colin handed over their passports and tickets and signed the consent form. Laura felt as though she was being handed over like a piece of baggage. The stewardess smiled at them.

"Would you like a free bag of exciting things for the flight?"

"What's in it?" asked Peter politely.

"Coloured pens, drawing books and puzzles."

James threw his head back in disgust.

"Not got Mega Death 9 on the X box, have you?"

"I might have, if I knew what it was."

She smiled again.

"Look after yourselves, my angels," and Julie hugged and kissed each of them in turn.

"Don't I get a kiss too?" asked Colin.

"No," said Laura, but she kissed him anyway.

As the children were led away into Departures, Julie turned to her husband.

"OK, so what's this all about then?"

"We have a great chance to make some money and have a wonderful time in Amsterdam."

"Couldn't the kids have come too?"

"Wouldn't you like some peace and quiet?"

"I'm not saying I wouldn't."

"Well there you are then."

As they walked in darkness to the car, Colin said softly, "Besides, the telling of the story is long overdue, for all of them."

CHAPTER TWO

Unaccompanied Minors

The engines of the Boeing 737 roared as it took off for the hour-long flight to Edinburgh, and three nervous children chattered to each other in their front row seats.

"What's in the envelope?" demanded James, "I saw Dad give it to you."

Peter pulled it from his breast pocket and tore it open.

"Thirty pounds holiday money."

"Cool," said James, "twenty quid for me and leftovers for you two wallies."

"Did you bring any money of your own, Petee?" asked Laura.

"No point, there isn't anything to spend it on in the village."

"But we might go shopping up in Perth. We did last time."

"Or get Grandpa to take us to the pictures."

Peter gave his brother one of his serious and measured looks.

"You know what Grandma and Grandpa are like, they don't let us spend any of our own money."

"Petee, can we buy some sweets?" asked Laura.

"And a drink," urged James, and they waited eagerly for the steward to push his trolley down to the front of the plane.

Stuffed full of chocolate and crisps, they listened to the pilot tell the passengers that the lights of Newcastle could be seen through the right hand windows and that there was only twenty minutes before landing.

"I'm not looking forward to this one bit," complained James. "Stuck in the middle of nowhere and no skateboarding ramps for miles."

"Grandpa *will* be at the airport to meet us, won't he?" Laura sounded anxious.

"He'll be there. Dad did seem really keen to get rid of us, didn't he?"

"Well, if he's going to work in Amsterdam, then he won't want us about. You know what *he's* like."

"Well at least he's given us thirty quid," said James.

Peter put the change back in his pocket.

Led by another lady in orange, they were the last of the passengers to descend the steps onto the tarmac. It was late, raining and cold, and the children shivered as they made their way into the Arrivals Hall.

Duncan Donald was a huge man. Tall, lean and angular, and with long brown hair that framed a friendly face that seemed to shine from an outdoor life. He was dressed in a kilt made up of squares of subtle, autumnal colours; light brown, green and ochre. His fisherman's jumper looked almost as old as he did.

"Welcome to Scotland," he boomed, "it's a real pleasure to see you bairns again."

"Hello, Grandpa," said Peter, "thank you for coming to meet us."

He held out his hand and it was shaken vigorously.

Grandpa shook hands with James, who felt as though his arm was being wrenched out of its socket.

"My, have you three no' grown."

His grandsons were handsome boys, and tall for their ages, and both had a crown of thick, brown hair. But they were very different, Peter kind and serious, while James's blue eyes twinkled mischievously, giving the impression that he was always up to something. The boys reminded Grandpa of his own sons and James was the spitting image of his brother, Hector, and the old man remembered saying goodbye, and making Hector promise to tell him everything about his new life in America. That was seventy years ago, but the memory of Hector's departure, to find fame and fortune, remained crystal clear. Looking at James was like seeing him again. Grandpa stooped, picked Laura up by the waist and kissed the small girl lovingly on the cheek.

"Come on, let's get your bags."

With his granddaughter in his arms, the old man moved swiftly to the carousel. Theirs were the last bags going round on the conveyor belt and Grandpa Donald picked them up as though they were as light as feathers.

***

The old Volvo estate chugged its way towards the Forth Road Bridge and the children began to look forward, for the first time, to their holiday.

"Have things changed much in the village since last summer?" asked Peter.

"Not at all, laddie," replied Grandpa, "we don't go in for change up here."

"That's a shame," thought James, and groaned.

Grandpa Donald heard the groan and glanced in the mirror at him.

"We leave all that change stuff to you city folk," he laughed, fumbling in the ash tray for some coins to pay the bridge toll. "I hate giving up good money just to cross a river."

"But things must change, even in Glenbowmond," persisted Peter.

"Aye, given time, lots of time," replied Grandpa in his dark voice and he seemed to drift away from them, deep in thought, as they drove under the bright lights that ran, like a ribbon, across the cold waters of the Forth.

They travelled for fifteen minutes along an empty motorway, then took a junction which led them onto dark twisting lanes. At last, they made a sharp turn and began to climb a steep hill. The road was enclosed on both sides by high banks, topped with ancient stone walls. Peter thought he recognised the twists and turns that grew suddenly bright in the car's main beam, and then disappeared in blackness behind them.

"We're nearly there then, Grandpa."

"Aye, laddie, you recognise the road?"

"Not really. I can just, well, feel it."

"What a wally," mumbled James.

Grandpa glanced across approvingly at Peter in the passenger seat.

"Supper will be waiting for you," he promised.

Laura still felt full of chocolate and began to think of the excuses she could make to get out of eating again. She felt exhausted and yawned. Grandpa gave her a knowing look.

"Of course, my *sweet*, you'll be tired after the journey and I expect you had one of those plastic meals on the plane."

She smiled back and decided that Grandpa would not be as easy to fool as her father.

The car crunched on gravel outside an old farmhouse. Whitewashed and solid, it was set apart from the other neat cottages, which made up the main part of the village. These buildings were old, but the Donalds' house gave you the impression it had been there forever. A small, good-looking woman, with silver hair, hurried out to meet them.

"Hello, my chickens," she said warmly.

"So that's where Dad gets it from," thought Laura.

"Hi, Grandma," said Peter.

He gasped as he was hugged tightly by two strong arms around his waist. Her face only came up to his chest and she smelled of apples. In that moment he felt as though he had come home. Grandma then turned on James, who winced as he received the same treatment as his brother.

"Still living in the kitchen?" James smiled at his grandmother.

"Aye, Jamie, we still live in the kitchen and the fire still burns as bright as it ever did."

From their previous stays in Glenbowmond they all knew the centre of the household, indeed the centre of the world for Grandpa and Grandma, was the kitchen. Here, meals were made and enjoyed, and close friends entertained.

"Where's Dog?" asked Laura.

"In the kitchen," replied everyone else together and they laughed as Grandma ushered them inside.

A desperate scraping noise came from the other side of the door and as it was opened a black and white sheepdog ran around them in circles, like a mad thing, and leapt up at each of the children to lick their faces.

"What a warm welcome," said Peter, and he bent down to tickle the dog's ear.

"You'll be wanting your supper?" asked Grandma.

The boys glanced at each other, not wanting to disappoint her, and Laura yawned again.

"Now what must I be thinking of," she said kindly, "and you having come all that way too."

Grandpa put their bags in their rooms and, with tall mugs of hot chocolate and plates of home-made shortbread, three weary children made their way to bed.

"Whenever we come here I feel mighty tired," yawned James.

"It's the clean air," mumbled Peter in a sleepy voice.

James looked out from his blankets at their new home.

"Just the same, it sucks," he whispered bitterly. "No telly."

Within seconds he was fast asleep but Peter lay awake for a time. The last thing he remembered, before dreaming about the hills and fields around the village, was a feeling of returning to a place that was familiar, safe and of great importance.

When he finally woke, James's bed was empty and bright sunshine streamed through the window. Dog barked excitedly and Peter heard Grandma moving pots and pans about downstairs. He yawned, rubbed his eyes and yawned again.

"First day of the holiday. Great."

He slowly made himself ready for breakfast.

"Here's sleepy head," said Grandma, and Peter realised he was last one up.

"Where are the others?"

A huge pot of lamb and barley broth simmered on a black range and Grandma bent to open one of the oven doors. She pulled out a warm plate from its belly.

"They have been out for hours, having a good look round."

She placed a great mound of bacon, eggs and sausages on the table. Peter smiled at his breakfast.

"I like it here."

"Grandpa wondered if you bairns would like to go for a walk this afternoon. It's a fine day and they are too precious to waste."

"I suppose you're right."

He remembered the feeling of space and openness that he only experienced here, away from the streets and houses of Pinner.

"I'll make you up a wee packed lunch then."

"There's nothing *wee* about any of *your* lunches," and he dropped some bacon rind on the floor for Dog.

"And don't feed that bloomin' dog. You're as bad as Grandpa."

"As bad as me?" boomed a voice and Grandpa came in and sat beside Peter. "I've drawn you a rough map and the weather forecast is excellent so you ought to be able to see many of the things you couldnae see last year."

Peter pushed his empty plate to one side and studied the map. It was hand drawn and showed the farms around the village. To the south were the waters of the loch. To the north, the far hills and high moorland.

"Follow this lane from the village. It's the old drovers' road and has been used for centuries to take sheep from the upper pastures to market. Then head off to your right, across the stile, and follow the valley up into the hills. You see this mark here?"

He pointed at three lines drawn close together. Peter nodded.

"That's the waterfall and a great place for a picnic."

"How far is it?"

"About five miles, there and back, and the hills around the waterfall mark the edge of the land we once owned. Our family used to own a lot of land."

"We used to own it?" asked Peter, but he already seemed to know the answer.

"Aye, laddie, a long time ago." Grandpa became lost in his thoughts again. "Still, even here things do change, well eventually anyway, and mostly for the better."

He got up from the table and kissed his wife.

"Making them a feast, are we?"

He nodded at a growing tower of sandwiches on the work surface. The door burst open and James and Laura bustled in.

"Nothing to bloomin' well do," exclaimed Laura. "We've been right round the village and there's nothing, not even a shop."

"Now then, my chicken, Grandpa has given Peter a map and I'm making a picnic for your walk."

"What walk?" asked James.

"Grandpa thought you might like to explore the hills around the waterfall. It's lovely up there."

"And what are you two going to do?" demanded Laura.

"We thought we might pop up to Perth and do some shopping," replied Grandpa, "we didn't have much notice of you lot coming and we need to get in supplies."

He stared down at Peter's empty plate and raised an eyebrow.

"Quite a lot of supplies by the look of things."

"Can I go too?" begged Laura, "I don't want to go on a walk."

"Yeah, can't we go and catch a movie?" asked James.

"You're going for a walk, my chickens," boomed Grandpa, in a way that left no room for argument. Then he smiled warmly at them.

"Besides we don't get days like this very often."

"Not often at all," agreed Grandma, and Peter noticed they glanced at each other as though they were sharing an old joke, or a secret.

CHAPTER THREE

A Nice Bloomin' Walk

"My feet hurt," moaned Laura and she lowered her toes back into the stream, which gurgled and spluttered away from the waterfall. "Wow, that's cold."

She stamped at the water and splashed Dog. He gave a loud *woof* and ran off excitedly to search for new smells on the hillside. Peter lay back on the heather trying to decide if he wanted to move and get another sandwich out of the rucksack. He shut his eyes and listened to the water and the bees working their way from flower to flower, then rolled onto his side to look back down the valley. Clear in bright sunshine, the path they had followed was a long, grey, winding string. Across green pastures was the loch, where the stream would end its journey in blue and still waters. More than ever Peter felt as though he was in a place that was a part of him and wondered how it had all come to be.

"Come and see this, you two," yelled James, and Peter groaned.

"I'm not going," complained Laura, "I've already walked over half of bloomin' Scotland!"

"I'll go then."

Peter called out to Dog, who bounded eagerly over to him, and together they began to climb the hill. James was waving frantically at him.

"What's up?"

"Old stones, upright and not like the others."

"They do look ancient."

James pointed at two granite pillars, each about two metres high. Another standing stone stood proudly alone a short way off.

"I saw stones like this in a picture at school. Do you think druids used to sacrifice people here?"

Dog tilted his head to one side and glanced up at them as if to say, "I don't like the sound of that."

"It's possible."

James sprinted down the hill to tell Laura what she was missing. It was a glorious day and Peter walked slowly, enjoying the sun as it warmed his shoulders. The sheepdog trotted loyally beside him, tongue hanging out.

"Why don't you go and get yourself a drink, boy?"

But Dog spotted a rabbit and decided to have some fun. Peter watched him go and went to take a look at the third stone. This massive granite slab was at least a metre taller than either of the other two and he settled himself down to rest in its shade. The view was breathtaking and he could see for miles. In the distance was a line of hills and he guessed that for most of the hard winter months they would be covered in snow. Sheep bleated in the high pastures, to warn their young ones not to stray too far away, and he gazed at one field, and then another, to count them. He gave up at a hundred.

"There must be thousands."

He smiled, for it pleased him, deep inside, to see so many, and he thought about the generations of shepherds who had worked so hard to make it possible. Then he turned his eyes away from the falling sun, and down to the grey, slate roofs of the village. On a far slope an old man, with a white beard, stooped over a low mound of stones. He placed a bunch of flowers on it, then rose, glanced across at Peter and nodded. Peter waved back and, for some reason, felt that he knew him. He looked down at his feet and tried to think where he might have seen him before. Not in the village and surely not at home in London. Peter raised his head again, but the stranger had vanished, and he leaned back against the stone. How could anyone simply disappear?

"I'm fed up now," yelled Laura.

She was followed by James who struggled under the weight of the rucksack. They dumped themselves down next to their brother and shared a cold drink out of a battered flask.

"Come on then," suggested Peter sensibly, "the sooner we go, the sooner we'll be home for supper."

He took out Grandpa's map and ran his finger along a line marking the path.

"We can go back the way we came, or cut across the fields to this lane here."

"Which way's shorter?" moaned Laura, "My feet hurt."

"The way we came sucks," said James.

"Then across the fields it is," agreed Peter, and he looked at his watch. "It's three o'clock and so we should be back by five."

"Dog," called James, and the sheepdog removed his head, reluctantly, from a rabbit hole and bolted across the grass to join them.

Peter knew that if they headed down the slope and kept the distant loch in front of them, they would eventually cross the path that led back to the village. He smiled as James and Laura squabbled over the last of the drink. Dog seemed unconcerned by it all and scouted some way ahead to find more rabbits.

Peter turned back to look at the standing stones. They stood tall, mysterious and alone, on the high pasture. Then he remembered the stranger and glanced at the low mound of rocks, but the cairn was deserted too. After a long descent, they climbed over a low wall and dropped down into the lane.

"This must be the old drovers' road," said Peter and he thought again about the generations of shepherds who had taken this route to far away markets.

Laura shivered. "Is it me, or is it getting cold?"

"It's a bit chilly," said James.

Peter had noticed the cold as well.

"I guess it's just the difference. It was lovely and warm by the waterfall and now the sun is getting pretty low."

He glanced up and was surprised to see that the sky had become totally obscured by thick, grey, angry clouds. Dog stopped in his tracks and his body pointed ahead like an arrow.

"What's up boy?" asked James.

As they went towards him, Dog walked off again, occasionally turning his head to check they were still with him. With each stride, the lane grew darker and colder.

"This is utterly weird," said James.

Snow began to fall and he watched as snowflakes landed and melted on his upturned palm.

"Well, I've heard that in Scotland you can have four seasons in one day, but this is ridiculous."

Peter began to unpack the rucksack. "Let's get our coats on."

In minutes, they couldn't see more than a few paces ahead and Peter held Laura's hand. The wind grew in strength and blew waves of thick snow into their faces.

"It isn't more than half a mile to the village," said Peter, "and as long as we stick to the lane we can't go far wrong."

Laura gripped his hand and stared down. Her shoes were already covered with snow.

"This is awful. Can you make out the path?"

"I think we're still on it," replied Peter.

"Have you ever seen snow come down this quickly?" cried James.

"No. This *is* weird."

"The dog's doing his nut again." James knelt down beside him. "What's up, mate?"

The wind whipped down the lane and ruffled Dog's fur, but he stood, unflustered, his head back and tail pointing in a straight line.

Laura's bottom lip trembled with the cold.

"Petee, perhaps he's trying to tell us which way to go."

James wrinkled his nose. "Perhaps he's just a stupid dog."

"We can't be far away," said Peter, "why don't we follow him for a bit and, if he doesn't lead us home we can always follow our footprints back here?"

James glanced back down the lane and tugged on Peter's sleeve. No more than a few metres behind them their footprints were completely hidden by a layer of fresh snow. Peter gulped and put his finger to his lips.

James ignored him. "Laura, Peter thinks were doomed."

She pushed her hands inside the pockets of her thin jacket.

"Well we can't stay here, I'm *freeeezing*!"

"Come on then. Let's trust old Dog's instincts."

Slowly, as if not to lose them, Dog trotted off and they followed. The weather was getting worse. It was dark, bitterly cold and they were utterly miserable. Peter counted his paces and reached thirty when James cried out.

"A light. I can see a light."

"Good dog," said Laura, and Dog turned back to look at them as if to say, "No problem at all."

By the time they stood, shivering, in front of the vague outline of a front door, the snow was up to their knees. A welcoming glow shone out through a tiny window and its beam brought thousands of swirling snowflakes to life.

James knocked hard, twice, and the knocks resounded like a drum inside the cottage. Dog stood on his hind legs and scraped at the door with his paws.

"Look, he's not a bit frightened," said Peter and the dog's eagerness to enter comforted them.

Laura heard footsteps.

"Someone's coming," she whispered.

The door creaked open and they blinked in the light, and stared at the cloaked silhouette of an old man. He smiled at the children through a beard that was as white as the snow they had tramped through.

"Well, this is not a night for young ones to be out in."

"I'm afraid we have got a bit lost," replied Laura, in her politest voice.

"I don't think so. It seems to me you are very much found."

Dog raced past him to settle in front of a blazing log fire.

"Don't just stand out there in the cold. Come in, come in."

He waved a hand at them, gnarled as the bark of a tree, then nodded at a low bench, which ran at an angle beside the fire. Peter thought it might have been put there specially for them.

"Sit yourselves down."

"It's lovely and warm in here," beamed Laura.

Peter looked around the room where they sheltered. There was nothing remarkable about it, except its simplicity. The most ornate thing it contained was an arched, stone fireplace, which supported an iron cauldron. Flames leapt around the cauldron and threw a comforting light into every corner. The walls were whitewashed and bare, and against the far wall was a wooden bed.

They took their coats off and shook the snow from them, and sat down by the hearth where Dog lay outstretched across the stranger's feet. They warmed their hands and felt mighty relieved to be out of the storm. The old man rolled up the sleeve of his cloak and filled a mug from a steaming ladle. He passed the mug to Laura.

"Try this. There is no better way to drive away a chill."

He dipped the ladle back into the depths of the cauldron and everyone sat with fingers held tightly around hot mugs.

"It's lamb and barley broth," said Peter and approvingly, "just like Grandma makes all the time."

The old man nodded.

"Do you mind if we stay until things clear up?" asked Laura.

"Not at all."

"I bet we're stuck here for days," complained James.

The man smiled.

"No, you'll be here no time at all."

"Are we far from the village?" asked Peter.

"Far enough, in weather like this."

"We are being very rude. I'm Peter, this is James and this is Laura."

"I know who you are, and any of the line of Donald is welcome here."

Peter noticed the old man didn't offer them his name.

"Well, now we are together, what would you like to do?"

James thought about Mega Death 9 again. The stranger smiled and shook his head knowingly.

"I could manage some more broth," said Peter to break the silence, and the old man gave him the ladle.

"How about a story?" asked Laura, "isn't that what they used to do in the olden days, before telly?"

James wrinkled his nose and the old man smiled at him again.

"How much do you know about the history of the area?"

"History sucks," thought James and the stranger's eyes flashed.

"If you do not know where you have been, you cannot know where you are going."

"I don't know much about it," replied Peter truthfully, "but Grandpa is always telling us that our family have lived around Glenbowmond for generations."

"Many, many generations," confirmed the old man, and he stared deep into the fire. It seemed to Peter that he was remembering them all.

"Still, where were we? Ah yes, a story to see us through the storm. I always begin with Gora for he has a special place in my heart and

I cannot speak of him without feeling a deep sadness for what he suffered. Even now he haunts me and it was, of course, Gora's greed that made him a prisoner of The Stone."

And he told them. They sat, silent and spellbound, and his words bewitched them, and every word touched them. It was as though they were inside the tomb with poor Gora.

"Cool," said James at last, "there were some bad dudes about in those days."

"There were indeed," replied the storyteller.

"Did he ever escape?" asked Laura.

"He did."

"Did he find another way out of the cairn?" asked Peter eagerly.

"There was no other way to leave the cairn, in fact Gora's soul would be held for over two thousand years until a young shepherd decided to give Amera's stone away."

"A shepherd?" asked Laura, a blank look on her face.

The old man peered at the window.

"Yes, a shepherd. Dougie's family, and other families like his, had enjoyed peace for many years. Even the king, the Younger, would need to be convinced that the Long Peace was over. It took a while for Dougie of Dunfermline to realise it too. But over it was and the world would never be the same again."

"How did the king, er, the Younger, know war was coming?" Peter asked.

"Three dangers, which came in one time. Murder in the High Glens, raids on the Outer Islands and the sign of the Saxon cross."

"Quite a list then," said James.

"And, just like you, children of the line of Donald, all he had to do was listen."

CHAPTER FOUR

The End of the Long Peace
Autumn 675 AD

I. THE FIRST DANGER

Borak crawled forward and, peering through the heather, studied the cottage. The sky was darkening and the attack would begin soon. He turned his head to see how his brother was coping with the horses. Tumora was struggling to keep them quiet, grabbing at their reins, trying to lead them down a ravine into the cover of a small pine wood. One of the seven beasts snorted and the warriors stiffened, and glanced anxiously at each other from their places of hiding.

Borak waited for Gath Tella's signal and saw him strike fire-stones, and blow into the base of a small leafy mound. He thought the son of the king was holding back and, taking a sip of water from his leather bottle, Borak scanned the glen below. Smoke rose lazily from a hole in the cottage roof and he grinned. That meant food. The raiding party had ridden for three days from Carn Liath and they needed to eat.

A winding path followed the line of the valley. Most of the cattle, their rich prize, were grazing off to the left. On the upper slopes was a handful of sheep and Borak could not see any dogs. Earlier, a man and two children had entered the cottage and, if there were no others, this would be an easy kill. Something caught his eye. Gath Tella was waving urgently and pointing down at the cattle. Dusk was giving way to night and Borak's eyes strained as he searched for any sign of movement. Then he too caught a glimpse of a figure moving swiftly along the path and some way yet from the cottage.

Gath Tella nodded at him, ran a finger across his throat and pointed at the figure. Borak nodded back, grasped his axe and began to run. The other Picts rose and made their way cautiously down the slope. A hundred paces from the cottage they lit their torches from Gath's.

A child of eight summers skipped down the path. She was late from her play again and thought of blaming her friends, but knew her mother would not be so easily fooled. She slowed to give herself time to think of a better excuse.

The path followed the waters of a burn, its banks dense with bracken, and where it rose above the crown of ferns, Matina was able to look down at her home. She dropped her woollen dolly and stood, open-mouthed, staring in horror at the orange glow that engulfed its walls and roof. Her puppa and little brother staggered out, then mumma with baby Morven at her breast. As they escaped the smoke and flame, their coughing and choking turned to screams as cruel men, with cruel axes, hunted them down. Matina tried to cry out, but it was as if an invisible hand held her around the throat. As if her lungs were completely empty of air. No sound came and an everlasting scream echoed inside her head.

She saw a dark shape running straight towards her. Terrified, she dived into the bracken and curled her arms around her knees, trying to make her body as small as possible. She held her breath and peered through the green stalks that formed a den right around her. The path now lay in shadow and the silence was suddenly broken by the sound of someone running. A great man, in a black kilt, dashed past and then the pounding feet stopped. She felt sick.

Borak turned on his heels and retraced his steps. He knelt to pick up the toy, looked at it, and gently parted the bracken with his axe. The little girl's mouth fell open again and her whole body shook. Borak smiled, kindly, and handed her the dolly.

"Stay here until morning comes," he whispered.

Then he left to join the others and, like Matina had done, tried to think of an excuse good enough to stand up to the questions that would surely come.

II. THE SECOND DANGER

On the western edge of the Scottish kingdom, a fisherman looked out across the Great Sea and hopefully pulled in his net. It wasn't very heavy, and it fell, sodden, onto the cluttered deck of the *Pride of Tiree*. He unfolded and untangled it and two young herring flapped about angrily.

"I'll catch you again," he promised, dropping them back into the water, "when you are the size to grace a pot."

Helden smiled at the calm waters, raised his hand and saluted respectfully.

"You have won today, my beautiful lady, but how about letting me win a little more often so a poor man can earn his living?"

It was dusk and the breeze, that often marks the end of day in coastal lands, rose to fill the craft's single sail. It billowed out and Helden steered a familiar course back to Tiree. Suddenly, the old fisherman threw the tiller to one side and the ship stalled. He ran to the bow and stared ahead at the land. Lit by the setting sun were the dark outlines of three ships, each with long keels, high prows and square sails. Their design was not known to him and he guessed they were crewed by warriors, not fisherfolk. They had already reached the entrance to Tiree Bay.

Helden dropped the sail, so it would not be seen, and let the currents carry him north to another inlet on the island. He would find a place to hide, watch and help if he could.

***

Thorgood Firebrand's crew, like those on the other ships, were working hard on the oars and with each rhythmic dip and pull made some progress. This was the fourth day without wind and their twelfth day at sea. The Norse Lord kept a meticulous record of passage and made notes on time, speed and sightings. His messengers had spoken of the islands and the rich lands to the east of them, and he knew he must quickly find a hidden anchorage on Tiree, where he could secretly assemble his fleet.

The planned invasion would not now be possible until after the Season of Storms and the Norseman thought about the terrible famine which gripped his people, and the fever that had taken his beautiful daughter. They would need to return home soon with food.

A young sailor named Olaf Adanson joined Thorgood in the tented space forward of the mast. He bristled with enthusiasm and spoke eagerly.

"We have passed the third headland and will come upon the settlement soon, as dusk falls."

Thorgood lifted his quill and placed a mark on the map by Tiree Bay and wrote, *Ulrika's Land.*

"Tell the men to approach silently, and to have torch and sword ready. Tell them to gather livestock and grain."

Olaf Adanson raised an iron helmet and put it on. In that instant the fresh-faced youth became a fierce warrior.

"Kill them all," ordered Thorgood.

Olaf kissed the hilt of his sword and ran out onto the deck.

"At last we have found new lands," said Thorgood and he tried to estimate how many longboats he could call upon, or build, during the cold months. He also wondered how long it would be before Malcolm the Younger heard about the raid and if he would guess that it was part of a greater plan.

Driven on by a fresh evening breeze, the longboats picked up speed and the oars were stowed away, and it was not long before their prows lurched and rose upwards as they hit land. The Norse Lord jumped down onto a shingle beach near the fishing village at Tiree Bay. The shingle crunched underfoot, and he watched the line of torches dart up towards the cottages.

He sat down. His body still seemed to move with the sway of the sea. He listened to the waves break on the shore and the last cries of the Scots. Thorgood shut his eyes and thought about the choices he had to save his people. But most of all he thought about his last moments with beautiful Ulrika and how cold her tiny hand had become.

Later, in darkness, Helden searched the burning remains of his village for survivors. There were none. Only yesterday morning, the quay had bustled with life and now he stood, numb, looking at the cut and broken bodies of the fallen. Despite his years, Helden's memory was excellent and vivid pictures danced through his mind of the slaughter and destruction that he had been powerless to stop. As accurate as any record made by a scribe, he held a mental note of the invaders' appearance, their ships and the strange tongue they spoke. All that night, Helden stayed close to the heat of the smouldering cottages, wondering what he should do next.

At dawn, he stood at the tiller of the *Pride of Tiree*. He could just make out the sails of the longboats, on the northern horizon, as they returned home from their terrible mission. Kind winds took him east past Coll and after two days he reached Mull, the largest and most prosperous of the Outer Islands. As the ship berthed, a young and richly-dressed lady glanced down at the fisherman. She sat on one of the many rope-stones that ran in a line along the quayside and Helden recognised her immediately.

"Margaret," he called, "I must speak with your father urgently."

"Many others wish the same," she replied coolly.

Rarely did Helden feel anger, but now it welled up inside him and he snapped back at her.

"There is death on Tiree. Fetch Murdoch now."

The Princess of the Islands was not used to being spoken to so sharply, but she knew that something bad, something like the murders on Coll, must have happened again.

A small crowd gathered in the hall of the Protector to hear Helden's story. Murdoch was grim and remained silent until it was told. At last he rose and went to stand next to the messenger.

"This is the second raid," he said softly, "and it will not be the last. My thanks to you, Helden, for warning us. This is the beginning of a dark time and your words bring news I have expected, and feared."

The fisherman waited uneasily for Murdoch's next words.

"It cannot be easy for you to be our only witness to the shadow that grows to the north, but I beg you, sail now to Oban and pass through the High Glens. Take the story to my brother. Say we are not in danger yet, but with the clear skies of spring will need his help and protection."

Helden knew he must go. It was his duty to Murdoch, but he feared the journey and the responsibility. This would be the first time he had ever travelled so far inland, away from his home and the sea. Until now the king's lowland palace, which lay many days' walk to the east of Oban, was something mentioned only in stories.

Two days later, Helden walked at an even pace up the narrow path away from Oban. It followed the line of a deep glen and seemed to twist its way forever into the distance. His brother, Kenneth, had been his normal self, gruff, but welcoming, speaking few words and kindly offering to look after the *Pride of Tiree* until he came back.

"I will tidy her up for you," he had said, which was typical of him.

Helden always felt his younger brother criticised him, but he weighed this up against Kenneth's desire for order and neatness. His beloved ship could not be in better hands.

The mountains were remote and lonely, and Helden met few people on the road. Those travellers he did pass seemed wary of him. One spoke of the need to move quickly through these lands, because of the danger posed by Black Kilts. A woman ran away when she saw him.

On the third day out of Oban, Helden continued east along a bracken-lined track that followed the banks of a cheerful stream. Its waters were clear and sweet, but his food was gone now and, reluctantly, he decided to use some of the coins Murdoch had given him to buy fresh supplies. The way rose and fell, and he passed a burnt cottage. Its charred walls brought back terrible memories of Tiree. These thoughts gripped him totally and he almost walked straight into an ancient man who was leading a family of goats along the path.

"For a wanderer, that is not a very good idea," smiled the old shepherd.

Helden smiled back, "What is?"

The old man picked up a young kid and stroked its head.

"Not looking where you are going."

"Never a truer word was spoken to a lonely traveller. Do you know where I might find shelter and food?" Helden asked.

"You have found them both." The man glanced at Helden's clothes. "You are not from the High Glens?"

"I journey from the Outer Islands to the Palace of the Younger."

"Well, the price of your stay will be a good story. I guess you have a fine one to tell."

The old man peered into Helden's eyes. "I see we both have bad memories to share."

He walked off the path and up to a rough shelter with stone walls and a heather roof. The shelter was dry and snug once a fire was lit, and the two men spoke long into the dark hours. Helden learned that the cottage he had passed had been destroyed by Black Kilts and was once home to five people, but only four bodies had been found. People now lived in fear of more Pictish raids. Helden promised that he would tell Malcolm the Younger about the breaking of the peace and watched as the ancient man divided his food in two.

"I cannot take all this," he said, looking at the bread, cheese and wind-dried meat being bundled into a cloth.

"You shall take it and I shall get more."

"Let me pay for your generosity," offered Helden, but the shepherd seemed offended and gave him a quick, sharp reply.

"My reward is the message given to the king."

At first light, Helden returned to the path and the stream he had followed east for most of his journey through the High Glens. With a low sun shining into his face, he marched on. The stream widened and by noon the path veered across the water and he had to jump, from stone to stone, to cross it.

Something made Helden turn. He glanced back along the path, which seemed deserted, and saw a crown of ferns move. He stiffened, nervously re-crossed the stream, parted the bracken and looked into two scared eyes. A pitifully thin little girl, clutching a woollen dolly, rocked back and forth. Her eyes staring blankly into space.

"What's your name?" he asked softly.

The girl rocked some more and held the dolly tightly to her chest. Gently, Helden sat down in the protective den and took out some of his bread. He bit off a chunk, made a satisfied noise and offered her some. She ignored him.

"Perhaps dolly is hungry," persisted Helden and he offered the toy a small piece too. The girl backed away.

"If she does not like bread," smiled Helden, "I have some cheese I do not mind sharing. Perhaps dolly might share some with you?"

He placed a square of cheese onto a cloth and laid it on the ground.

"Your dolly does look hungry."

Cautiously, the little girl unfolded an arm from around the doll, and snatched the cheese. An hour later, Helden took the little girl's hand and led her to the path, and they journeyed together, Helden chatting about his ship and how he fished the Great Sea, and how the king would be able to help her. Matina never spoke a word.

The queue to record their request with the king's scribe was a long one. Helden and Matina shuffled slowly forward along the line that was now a daily occurrence on the Palace Green. The little girl held his hand tightly and the sailor gasped at the magnificence of the high outer defences, the size and formidable appearance of the central tower, and the number of warriors and courtiers for whom the palace was home.

An old man with a white beard walked across the grass backwards and stumbled over, much to the amusement of the other people in the queue. Some children, who queued a few paces ahead of them, pointed at the man and giggled, but Helden's small companion showed no emotion. Apart from a tremble he felt in her hand, whenever anyone approached them, she remained silent and stony-faced.

After what seemed like an eternity, they stood in front of a wooden desk and a short, earnest looking man who was busily scribbling letters onto a long roll of parchment.

"Next," he cried.

"I am Helden of Tiree and I have a message for Malcolm from his brother, the Protector of the Outer Islands."

He raised an enquiring eyebrow.

"A message from Murdoch, you say?"

Helden placed a parchment on the desk and the scribe checked its royal seal, and read it carefully.

"The Court of Grievance will not start until tomorrow, but the king may wish to speak to you before then."

The scribe marched off towards the Great Tower and they settled themselves down and watched the other people. Many cooked over small fires and talked, some slept, and everyone seemed prepared for a long wait. But Helden didn't have to wait long. Like a hare bolting across a field, the scribe ran back at great speed.

"You are to come with me at once."

Escorted by guards, they entered the Great Hall and were led before the Younger. Malcolm sat alone upon the Ancient Stone of Kings and smiled kindly at the silent girl who clasped the messenger's hand and glanced around anxiously at her new surroundings.

Helden had never seen a hall so grand. It was many times the size of the Hall of the Protector on Mull and although they both shared the same warmth, the same smoky air, this place felt as though it had a greater history and held within its walls all the royal traditions of the Celtic kings. The spirits of Dunnerold, Donald and the Elder himself, might have been there.

"My brother is well?" asked Malcolm.

"Aye, well, but scared by the raids on the Outer Islands."

"And you saw a raid?"

"I did, Your Majesty, and I wish I hadn't."

"Tell me your story then," ordered the king.

Helden spoke about the longboats, the destruction of his village, the raids by the Black Kilts in the High Glens and, lastly, about his small companion. To begin with, Malcolm's old face remained passive, but as the tale unfolded it became lined with concern. At last he stood and, like Murdoch had done, came to stand beside him.

"This is not the first piece of ill news I have received. Indeed, ill news is all I seem to have heard these past months, but I still believe the Long Peace can be preserved, without risking a war that would surely divide our people and break the Charter of the Clans."

Helden was horrified at his king's wish to take no action and stared at him. Malcolm saw the look and ignored it.

"Most of the kingdom is unaffected and, true, my father would have sent an army to destroy them, but my first choice would be to talk, understand and reach a compromise."

"But what promise may I take to Murdoch? For the raids will surely move from Tiree to Coll, and then to Mull itself by the spring."

"I make no promises as yet," replied Malcolm, "but I shall consider your words. For now, though, I want you both to stay as my guests and to rest a while."

Malcolm glanced down at the small girl and then at Helden, who pointed a finger at his lips and shook his head. The king knelt before her and gently asked Matina her name. She buried her face into the old fisherman's shawl. Malcolm rose and left the Great Hall, abandoning them to gaze in wonder at the high painted ceiling and the rows of shields decorating the long walls.

"Now," said Malcolm, smiling as he re-entered the hall, "you both have a little more work to do. Helden, provide my scribe with a full description of the raiders."

Helden bowed, awkwardly.

"And you, my wee lady, your task is not an easy one."

The king knelt before her again, pulled a small kitten from his robe and placed it on the girl's arm.

"You are to make sure this poor beastie is named and well cared for, for she is an orphan."

The kitten snuggled into the crook of Matina's arm and purred.

"What shall we call her?" asked Helden.

"Matina," whispered Matina, and they were led from the hall to the chamber next to Malcolm's where food had been made ready for them.

By nightfall, Helden and Matina were exhausted. She had not spoken again, but seemed a little happier and played contentedly with the kitten on the bed prepared for her against a wall in a quiet corner.

Helden wrapped her in a blanket.

"Now go to sleep, my Princess," he said tenderly, and the kitten started turning in circles as she too settled down for the night.

Helden lay on a huge soft bed, in unaccustomed luxury, and wondered why the king was so reluctant to act. It would be an easy matter to send warriors to Mull, but he guessed Malcolm did not have the same desire for war as his father before him. He began to think of the words he might use to persuade him, but in seconds, like Matina, Helden of Tiree was fast asleep.

In the chamber next to theirs, Malcolm marked a parchment with his seal, addressed it to Murdoch and requested that the small girl in Helden's charge be taken as a maidservant for Margaret.

"Care for her as your own," he wrote, then stood and, as he often did, began to pace around, considering what to do next. Then the Younger stopped and stared at the floor. The stones were shimmering, like moonlight on water, and a wave of relief fell over him. The cloaked head of a man emerged through the ground and, gradually, his whole body became visible. The man drew back his hood to reveal what Malcolm believed to be the wisest face he had ever seen.

"Myroy, my dear friend, you have come back to me."

"I am here," replied the Ancient One simply.

"There is an evil rising in the High Glens and on the shores of the Outer Islands."

"There is, and from the south, from the sign of the Saxon cross, although you do not know it yet."

Malcolm looked crestfallen.

"What should I do?" he asked.

"You are the king. You will know what to do."

But Malcolm didn't know. He felt as he had done when he was being schooled by Arkinew, the most feared of Myroy's apprentices, and unable to remember the answers demanded of him.

"We *must* now find a keeper for the stone," continued Myroy. "Your father did not know of its power. That was kept from him, but you have felt it."

The king thought back to his childhood with Murdoch, playing with Amera's stone. It had been a mere trinket then, just another spoil from one of his father's wars, but now he believed in it totally. He feared and loved it.

"And you know you cannot keep it hidden. You *must* let it go," insisted Myroy.

Malcolm unclasped a brooch that contained a single ruby at its heart. He ran a finger over the stone and, at last, nodded weakly in agreement.

"But how will I choose a keeper?" he asked.

"Wait for the reluctant warrior, who turns the key, and who seeks to return home as his reward."

The king wondered what he meant, but before he could say anything Myroy raised a hand.

"I say again, the kingdom faces the challenges of *Mountain, Island and Castle*, and a darker time after them. The stone *must* be given away to be held in safety by a keeper."

"So it is as you predicted when we sealed the Charter of the Clans."

Myroy's face rarely gave away his inner feelings, but now he smiled, reassuringly, and disappeared down through the floor.

III. THE THIRD DANGER

Thomas Goodfellow, the Angle, watched the light go out in the royal chamber, and smiled into the darkness. There was no moon. His master, Cuthbert, had paid him a handsome fortune to kill Malcolm the Younger and most of it still rested in his purse.

Thomas remembered spending a whole silver coin on drinks for an old crone, the night before, and how she had boasted that once she had served the king himself. He tried to guess if he had raised any suspicion in the woman's mind, asking questions like how large and grand the palace was, where the guests stayed and, importantly, where Malcolm held his court and slept.

It was too late now anyway. He must try tonight. Once again he stared up at the high walls and began to count. The guard took fifty counts to pace the length of the battlements and at the end stopped to talk with another guard. That took one hundred counts, the same as before. They were talking more than they were watching and Thomas grinned. This would never happen at Berwick Castle and he guessed this lack of discipline was the result of the Scots enjoying almost a lifetime without war. The Long Peace had made them soft.

It would be a while longer before the wagons entered the main gate. Three had rolled through last night and four the night before that. He would make his move when they arrived. Thomas unwound the rope from his waist and recoiled it slowly, counting the number of spans between his outstretched hands. Like the number of coins he had been paid, it came to forty.

"Must be my lucky number," he whispered.

Again he counted the stones that lay, one on another, from the ground up to the sill of Malcolm's window.

He grinned as he thought about the young boy who had seen him placing his outstretched arms up the outer wall, and noting the number of stones they covered – four. The boy had asked him what he was doing and he told him he was admiring the fine stonework. Thomas checked his calculations. Forty spans of rope, each span four stones, that was one hundred and sixty stones. There were one hundred and twenty stones from Malcolm's window to the ground and the higher stones were not as wide as the lower ones. Thomas rewound the rope around his waist. He knew it was long enough.

The horse, the swiftest in the garrison, shifted its feet and looked at him. It too seemed anxious and he went across and patted his strong neck.

"Easy boy, easy," he whispered, and the chestnut calmed a little.

To pass the time, Thomas thought about his long journey north from Northumbria. He had ridden through the borderlands of heath and low lying hills, sheltered at Melrose and, at last, crossed the waters of the Forth by the ferry at Culross. His mother had been born into a Celtic village and, more than once, her teachings about their ways and language had allowed him to pass unchallenged.

Thomas stiffened. Wagons were coming down the main track that wound its way towards the palace. He glanced up at the battlements. The guards had left their positions and he took hold of the horse's reins. Silently, staying in shadow, he led the beast to the base of the wall and laid his shield upon the ground.

He tied the reins to the shield and ran towards the wagons, staying behind an avenue of dwarf birch, which edged the path. Two wagons passed him, carrying barrels. The contents of the next was hidden by a cloth. The last, pulled by an ox and driven by a woman, was piled high with baskets filled with nuts, herbs and fruit. Close up, it smelled like a room full of chopped apples.

He followed this cart up to the main gate where two warriors called the train to a halt. The men were armed with spears and they talked in a friendly way to the drivers. One of the warriors laughed as he saw the number of barrels, then the gate opened and they were waved through. Thomas crawled under the last cart and, as it creaked forward, he rolled onto his back and grasped one of the timbers on its underside. Slowly, he was dragged into the palace of the king.

He glanced down the length of his body, back towards the main gate. The guards were closing it and then they climbed stairs out of his view, and he knew they were going back to man the top of the wall. Thomas relaxed his grip and the wagon passed over him, and he sprinted towards the door of the main keep.

A single guard saw him, but too late to make any difference. Thomas's sword drove into his stomach and the guard hardly made a sound as he sank to his knees. Thomas kicked him aside and entered, closing the heavy oak door behind him and bolting it. He grabbed one of the many torches, lining the walls, and climbed up the stairs.

"Keep going. Keep quiet. Be ready for trouble," he kept telling himself.

Sweat poured into his eyes and fear made him alive to the smallest sound or movement, but he was alone and the alarm had not been raised.

The king's chamber was on the highest level and Thomas was panting as he raced silently down the dim corridor. He hesitated for a moment in front of the Younger's door and wondered why there was no guard protecting it. He glanced up and down the corridor, and placed his ear against the door. No sound. He took a deep breath and entered, and bolted this door too. His torch sent orange fingers around the richly decorated room and then, below him, muffled by stone, Thomas heard shouting. The guard he had killed had been found.

A distant *boom* came up through the floor. Then another and another. The enemy were breaking the first door down. An almighty *crack* told him they were through.

A dark shape moved and grunted on the king's bed. Thomas ran at it and, risking fire, dropped his torch to free both hands, and drove his sword down through the blankets, again and again.

Thomas picked up the torch and stared at the blood oozing through the bed clothes. Something caught his eye and he spun around. A dim figure seemed to be moving at the side of the chamber, and he heard what might have been a cat mewing. He walked across, with sword raised, and as the torch lit the small bed, Thomas found himself looking into the terrified eyes of a little girl. She ignored the calls of a kitten, who pawed her sleeve, and clasped a dolly to her chest. Together they rocked in and out of the shadow.

"Cuthbert didn't say Malcolm had a daughter."

Thomas ran back to the king's bed, and threw back the covers. He was staring at the blood stained garb of a fisherman. Fists hammered on the door and he glanced over at the girl and smiled weakly.

"Perhaps forty is not my lucky number," he muttered.

Thomas Goodfellow tied his rope around the heavy bed and climbed out the window. The bolt on the door gave way and four armed men burst in. The Younger followed. One guard ran to the window and threw his spear downwards, but the assassin was gone.

Malcolm looked down at Helden's lifeless body. He was overwhelmed by sadness and guilt for not providing his guest with proper protection. He thought about the fisherman's words, about the Black Kilts in the High Glens and the threat to the Outer Islands. Now this. Could it be the danger from the south that Myroy had spoken of?

A warrior ran into the chamber and handed him Thomas's shield. It was graced with a fine painting of a Saxon cross. Now he knew. Believed at last. After twenty three summers, the Long Peace was over. He spoke to his men.

"Bring my riders to me. We raise the clans."

Malcolm turned to see if the little girl was dead too. She rocked her dolly, back and forth, and stared into space. Matina would never speak again.

***

There was silence for a time when the storyteller finished speaking. More than anything, Laura hoped that Malcolm would care for Matina and the old man nodded reassuringly.

"The Younger was part of a truly important story. The story of how the Celtic peoples of Scotland faced their darkest hours."

He lifted himself up on a staff and walked to the window.

"No sign of the snow letting up," he muttered.

"Can we hear more about Malcolm and Murdoch and Wee Matina?" pressed Laura.

The storyteller came back to join them and smiled.

"Have your parents told you about young Dougie and the taking of the coins?"

The children glanced at each other and shook their heads.

"Are you sure they have not mentioned Dougie?"

Their blank faces told him the answer.

"Good, good, just how it should be."

The old man stretched out a thin arm and pointed at the door.

"In truth, the tale of the mountain, Carn Liath, began on a hill not far from here."

CHAPTER FIVE

The Taking of the Coins

Dougie of Dunfermline looked across the lowlands towards the far hills and sensed their power. In daydreams, he had imagined them rising high into the sky to become towering cliffs that dwarfed everything. There was something wonderful about these hills.

It had been a beautiful autumn day and the last rays of sun turned the heather on the higher slopes into a rich purple carpet. As he always did at this time, Dougie counted his sheep, the last gesture of a caring shepherd before returning to the cottage he had known since childhood.

Everything seemed so peaceful and the young man leaned back against a tall standing stone, which was his favourite resting place at day's end. His world was cocooned and safe, and he desired no other.

Yet stories about raids by the Black Kilts were increasingly told. Homes nestling in the glens to the north faced the growing threat of sheep disappearing in the dark hours. Some farmers returned home from the fields to discover their cottages burnt and looted. A few poor souls had been killed.

The Picts, or Black Kilts as they were called in this time, were said to be jealous of the fortunes of the Celtic peoples, who had prospered during the Long Peace in the years after the death of the Elder. Malcolm the Younger, the Elder's son, was said to be a good king, but what a king was, what he did, or how he dressed, were all questions Dougie could not have answered.

A look of concern flashed for a moment in his dark brown eyes and then disappeared completely as he thought about supper.

His hours on the pastures could be lonely, but Mairi and the children were never very far away, and Dougie was complete in his own company. His thoughts were like friends to him. The sun warmed his cloak and Dougie closed his eyes, letting familiar pictures race through his mind. There he was as a boy, scheming with his brother, trying to agree on the best words to use when they came back late from their play on the loch. It was always Alec who wanted to stay out, until the light faded, and explore the lands far away from the cottage.

Dougie remembered how Lissy used to scold them on their return, and warn about the dangers facing young folk when travelling alone after dark. They would bow their heads and eat supper in silence, with Alec winking mischievously at his brother. Then Lissy would sit alone by the fire, body hunched, looking as though she carried the weight of every worry in the world on her shoulders. Dougie would go over to comfort her and hold her hand, and she always asked herself the same question. How could two boys who looked so alike, like two peas in a pod, be so very different?

It came as no surprise when Alec finally left them to make his own way in life. Unlike Dougie, he was confident in his abilities and spoke often about the yearning he felt to travel upon the Great Sea.

Dougie remembered Lissy's tears as Alec prepared to go and how she made him promise to visit them each year. But it had been three summers since he had gone and not a word had been heard from him. In his heart, Dougie knew his twin was safe and well. His great sadness was that Lissy had died soon after Alec's departure, without being able to say a last goodbye to him. Lissy had loved them dearly and Dougie wondered how he would break the news of her death to Alec. She was the only family they had ever known.

Dougie yawned and stared across the fields towards the small cairn, which marked Lissy's resting place. On the gentle slope, kneeling beside the low mound of stones, was a cloaked figure. The bearded man seemed to be placing a flower upon the grave, as if recalling his own memories of the past.

He had seen the stranger many times from a distance and for as long as he could remember. Alec had rather unkindly called him the "old watcher," but Dougie had never felt threatened by him. He would have liked to talk to him, but always held back, respecting the watcher's desire for solitude. Now Dougie waved and the stranger waved back.

He called out something that sounded like, "Good fortune on your journey, Dougie."

The shepherd wondered what he meant and when he raised his head to say thank you the cairn was deserted.

In the half-light, he made his way home from the pastures. Everything was as it always was and he looked forward to a quiet evening by the fire. He crossed over a stile and followed the grassy track down to his farm. A ray of sun burst from behind a cloud and lit the far hills, and he paused for a moment to glance at them, wondering at the beauty of the land and how it had all come to be.

"There is no more worth having than this," he thought and smiled as he watched the clouds, the companions of the sky, race away to an unknown horizon.

Down the hill Dougie saw his children playing in one of the fields. Calum and Jock were fighting over a piece of old rope, and little Tanny was shouting at them to stop bloomin' arguing all the time.

"I wonder where she gets such terrible language from?" groaned Dougie, as the wee ones bickered and squabbled. He guessed his grandmother had probably thought exactly the same thing about her own boys and, as he reached the gate of his beloved garden, he pictured her tending the herbs and scolding Alec for walking on them.

His thoughts turned to Mairi and he could picture her so clearly in his mind. Long, straight black hair, crowning a pretty face, and wide hazel eyes, which lit up like a beacon when she laughed.

He remembered being pushed in front of her at a summer gathering on Arngask Farm. How nervous he had been, how clumsy when the music started, how out of place. But Mairi had floated along and encouraged him, and smiled. Her smile was to blame, the cause of everything which followed. When Mairi smiled, Dougie crumbled and muttered words he never meant to say. His heart wasn't his own anymore. Mairi could have put a rope around his neck and led him from farm to farm, like a dumb trophy. But she didn't. She had kissed him and that was that. Dougie of Dunfermline was in love. He still was.

Mairi's yell shook him out of these thoughts and he saw her running quickly to join him. She seemed upset, and this was not like her for she was remarkably even-tempered for a Scottish woman.

"Dougie …… Dougie," she called out anxiously, "someone has been in our cottage and stolen the money purse!"

His heart sank as he remembered the nine coins of silver and the years of work it had taken to earn them. He felt as though someone had stabbed him and leant with both hands against the white cottage wall.

"Our savings," he gasped.

Mairi walked over and gently ran her hand through Dougie's hair. "We were out collecting the berries and saw two Black Kilts ride from the farm."

"Is anyone harmed?"

"No, Dougie. We have been more fortunate than many."

He hugged her and went inside the cottage, and rummaged around. After a few moments, he came out and took a last look around.

"I will only be away a wee while," he promised. "Look after the wee ones for me."

"You make sure it is only a wee while, young Dougie."

Mairi kissed him and, without another word, the shepherd put an old, plain shield over his shoulder and grasped a claymore. The sword was rusty through lack of use.

The journey from the farm to the hall of the king would take over a day to walk. The paths were poorly marked and easily missed. They would wind up and down hills and cross small streams and fast-flowing rivers. Travelling alone could be dangerous, but he was so upset at the taking of the coins that no thought of this was yet in his mind.

After walking until there was no more daylight to see by, Dougie rested. He slumped onto soft turf beside a shallow pool, fed by a waterfall. He wished now he had not hurried away on his adventure, for he had not brought a thing to eat and angry grumbles came from his stomach as he lowered his mouth into the cold water and drank.

Dougie sat in darkness and listened to the comforting babble of the waterfall. He began to wonder about the king's palace and as thoughts of towers, colourful tapestries and fine gardens engulfed him, he realised he had never, ever, travelled this far from home. He was a farmer, a farmer's son, and felt no desire to visit faraway places.

The shepherd began to worry about Mairi and how she would cope alone, and cursed himself for acting so rashly. The wind started to rise with a night-time chill and, in the trees behind him, a murder of crows gathered. Like flying shadows they called to each other, demanding the most comfortable roost for the evening.

"At least *you* have some company," said Dougie mournfully and he wrapped himself into the folds of his plaid and, despite everything, fell fast asleep.

Dougie rested well and felt much refreshed in the morning. His spirits rose as the sun warmed his face and fell again as he realised how far he was from home. But he set off, purposefully, towards the north, and promised himself that the king would know what to do about his missing purse.

Later in the day, he was joined by three travellers who shared food with him. They were journeying to the palace too and had a similar story to tell. Dougie was, by nature, shy in the company of strangers, but he was relieved to walk along with a short and eager farmer named Portalla. They talked cheerfully for the remainder of the journey about crops and the seasons, and Portalla complained about his flock. It was now half its original size. He intended to join the king's army and fight the raiders who were destroying the farms in the High Glens. Although he didn't say so, Dougie had no intention of joining the army. He just wanted to see the king and get his property back.

Time passed unnoticed and the shadows lengthened to mark the coming of dusk. When this small band of determined Scots reached the top of a low hill an amazing sight stretched out before them. There, in a wide grassy plain, was the palace of the king and around its mighty walls were over a thousand heavily armed men, distinctive in their brown, green and ochre tartans.

"So an army has been raised," gasped Portalla.

"Aye," replied Dougie, "I've never seen an army before. So many people."

As they joined the ranks of warriors, Dougie saw the king himself. Malcolm sat upon a great white horse and looked magnificent. He wore the finest robes the shepherd had ever seen, for they were not woollen like those of simple folk, but silk edged with gold. He wondered at their worth and his gaze was drawn to a jewelled brooch upon the king's chest. It glinted red and yellow in the last rays of the sun.

"Warriors of the loyal clans," called out Malcolm, "Helden of Tiree, and others, have brought me news of Tella the Mac Mar, the King of the Picts. He is cruel and ambitious, and his subjects are responsible for the misfortunes we have suffered."

He paused, and a cold wind blew through his long grey hair.

"I still do not understand why the Black Kilts have broken the Long Peace and taken to stealing our animals."

There was a murmur from the clansmen.

"Or to stealing our money."

And at this there was an even bigger murmur.

"Or to killing the defenceless families who farm the land."

There was clear anger amongst the crowd.

"If we take no action, then they will see it as a sign of our weakness. The raids in the High Glens have been going on for too long and now is the time to fight back."

"Hear, hear," shouted Portalla, and then he looked embarrassed as a thousand pairs of eyes fixed on him.

"Quite so," said Malcolm kindly. "Rest now, for tomorrow we march to do battle at Carn Liath."

There was a huge cheer and the Scots waved their mighty claymores in the air. Despite this show of loyalty, Dougie sensed a feeling of deep unease amongst the warriors and it proved to be a strange, restless night. They knew they had to stand up for what they believed to be right, but the Picts had a fierce reputation. Fighting them wasn't going to be easy. How many might not return?

The old songs spoke of Malcolm the Elder. The Younger's father had taken an army to conquer these lands, but after months, of siege and battle, even his men had returned to the lowlands, weary and defeated.

Beside one of the campfires that had been lit outside the Palace walls Dougie wrapped himself up in the folds of his plaid and turned to talk to Portalla.

"I know it is our duty, but I really don't want to go."

"If you want a chance of getting your coins back, you have little choice."

"I'd rather be poor and tend the sheep, than die on a distant mountain."

"It's not about being poor, or being rich," said Portalla. "Unless we stand together, the Black Kilts will continue to break the peace."

"This isn't our fight."

"It *is* our fight."

"I've never even been to the High Glens."

"One day, Dougie, it might be your children who suffer at the hands of the Picts. How would you feel then?"

"But I'm scared. Scared of how things might go in battle."

"We all are."

Dougie nodded, yawned and tried to sleep.

Later, he awoke with a start and shuddered, half remembering a dream where a giant Black Kilt had broken his sword and chased him down a hill.

Dougie had run and run, but in the darkness the sound of the killer's menacing footsteps, grew ever louder and he knew he could not escape. Fear and helplessness overcame him.

It took the shepherd a few moments to remember where he was. The sun was rising above the hills and the palace walls were dancing with pink and orange. All around him men were stirring. A huge man called Hamish of Tain passed him a bowl of brose, a tasteless dish of oats and water, and growled.

"There we are, young Dougie, eat what you can for we have a long way to travel."

"Thank you," mumbled Dougie sleepily, "have you seen the king this morning?"

"No sign of him yet," replied Hamish and the warrior opened a mouth like a cave and spooned in a steaming heap of breakfast.

"With any luck he will have changed his mind about going to battle and we can all go home."

Portalla's head popped out of his plaid.

"Can we go home now?" he yawned and Dougie smiled.

Despite his misgivings, and night of bad dreams, Dougie felt excited. Hamish introduced him to his friends from Tain, a wild and lonely part of the country, prized for its heather ale. Dougie listened as they talked about the adventure which lay ahead. It seemed that King Malcolm's brother, Murdoch, who was fierce in battle, had been asked to bring men from the Outer Islands, the lands he ruled on behalf of the king.

"Och, no use he will be," grumbled Hamish, "he is months away, even taking the fastest ships to cross the Great Sea."

"None the less," corrected Alistair, "my guess is we shall accept any help, early or not so early, when we reach the slopes of Carn Liath."

Dougie wanted to ask them about the Outer Islands and the Great Sea, but was too nervous to break into their conversation. So he simply sat and listened as tales were told about the evil reign of Malcolm the Elder and how his son, the Younger, had won the support of the clans and secured a lasting peace.

Alistair, son of Gregor of Cadbol, appeared to be their clan leader. A tall handsome man, with long blond hair and piercing blue eyes, Dougie trusted him instinctively. He was to grow very fond of Alistair and admired, more than anything, the quiet respect held for him by the men of Tain. They were fifteen in number, uncouth and unruly, and more used to travel and fighting than shepherds.

Perhaps his nervousness was obvious to Alistair for he invited Portalla and Dougie to join them on the march to battle. Battle was the last thing Dougie wanted to march to, but he would certainly be more at ease in their company than walking without a friend to share his growing fears with.

After breakfast, Alistair asked Dougie if he would like to look around the palace grounds. He agreed readily and they set off to explore the length of the strong inner wall. This mighty stone structure was four people high and the many watchtowers more than twice this height. Every twenty paces there was a narrow slit through which archers could let fly a rain of arrows onto an enemy. Dougie was awestruck by it all.

Passing one very large tower, the friends walked onto a wide grassy area known as the Palace Green. On one side of the Green were five round-houses with many women and children. On the other side, at the edge of the grass, stood a small, wooden building. It was not round, like the others, but square and sticking out of its turf roof was something that looked like iron. The iron thing was round too and obviously hollow, for a plume of yellow smoke billowed out of it. They went to have a closer look. On one wall of the building was a window. Alistair could see right through it, into the square house, and yet it was cold and hard to the touch. He tapped it gently. Then tapped it again. What magic was this?

Dougie glanced around to see an old man, with long white hair, walking backwards towards them. Three young boys, who were playing outside a round-house, watched him too and made disrespectful signs in his direction. One of them said something, then walked backwards into the wall of the round-house, and fell over. His friends roared with laughter. The old man stiffened, but ignored their teasing. As he got closer, Dougie saw that he had a child, or creature, in a bright red jacket and with long dangly legs, sitting on his shoulder. It stared at Dougie and Alistair intently, and whispered something into the old man's ear.

Alistair tapped the window again. "This is very odd."

"So is this," said Dougie.

Alistair turned and found himself staring into the strangest, smallest and most mischievous of faces.

"Grumf," it grunted.

"Ah, visitors, good, good," said the wrinkly and bearded man, "some call me Arkinew, but you may call me Archie. Are you interested in the exciting world of alchemy?"

"I don't know," replied Dougie truthfully, "I'm not sure what it is."

"Not know what it is?" exclaimed the old man, who was still facing away from them, "not know what it is? The most important activity for the learned mind."

"Grumf," grunted the thing on the alchemist's shoulder, for as Dougie could now see it was definitely *not* a child, or a small man.

"Gangly, do you still doubt the power of the Ancient Ones?" scolded Archie.

"Grumf. Grumf."

"Do not listen to him," warned Archie, "he is the last of the Ghilly Dhus, a generally harmless race of woodland imps who can trace their ancestry to the time when there were no men. Before the time of the ice."

"Grumf," sneered Gangly.

"I am not an old fool. Have I not brought the *Guardian Shed* and *Pains of Class* into our time?"

"Grumf."

"No. I have just lost a few of my powers, that's all."

"Can you understand him?" enquired Alistair.

"Oh yes," replied Archie, "once you get used to the subtle changes in the way they speak their only word then it is very straightforward."

"They only use one word?" asked Dougie.

"Yes, yes, and that is why, of course, there are no more Ghilly Dhus."

Dougie raised an enquiring eyebrow. "How so?"

"Couldn't talk properly to each other and ended up fighting all the time."

"Weird."

"Grumf?" asked Gangly.

"No, it is not time to eat," stated Archie, "but it is time to *experident*."

"*Experident*?" questioned Dougie.

"Yes *experident*, for I have looked into the Oracle of the Ancient Ones and seen the future."

The creature winked at the two friends.

"Grumf."

"Alright, alright," said Archie, "so it is no longer a clear look, but it is a *look* and what king would not want an understanding of what is to be?"

"But, what is an *experident*?" asked Dougie.

"Come, I will show you."

Archie hobbled off backwards to the door of his *Guardian Shed*.

Alistair and Dougie followed nervously. Once inside they were astonished to see a dim room full of strange and wonderful objects, but it was the smell of rotting eggs that held their attention.

The hut stank and Dougie held his nose.

"Don't worry about the smell, it's only sulphur," said Archie.

Dougie wanted to know what sulphur was, but he did not even know yet what alchemy, *experidents* and *Pains of Class* were.

"Oh no," shouted the alchemist as he walked backwards, as quickly as he could, to a huge cauldron in the corner of the hut. He picked up a large wooden ladle and spooned out a disgusting green and slimy substance.

"Is this an *experident*?" asked Dougie.

"No," replied Archie, "this was my supper."

With a resigned look he threw the ladle into the cauldron.

"But this is."

He held up a pipe the length of a man's arm and as wide as a man's ankle.

Gangly gave another grumf.

"It is not useless," shouted the frustrated alchemist, "in years to come people will peer through these *terescopes* and see their enemies a great distance away."

"May I try it?" asked Dougie bravely.

"I am afraid not," replied Archie in a sad voice, "for the next stage of the *terescope experident* is to fit something called lenses and lenses will not be discovered for fifteen generations."

"Grumf."

"You are right, Gangly, I do not know their names."

The two friends introduced themselves and explained that they were about to leave the palace for Carn Liath and fight the Picts.

"The sun will bleach your bones on the field of battle and the crows shall feast on your eyes," shrieked Archie and his eyeballs rolled in their sockets.

Gangly's eyes rolled in their sockets too. Dougie and Alistair glanced at each other nervously.

"Your end is nigh. Your end is nigh."

Gangly ran a finger across his throat.

As the friends continued their walk along the palace walls, Alistair grinned at Dougie.

"Cheerful fellow."

"Aye. Cheerful and harmless enough."

But as Dougie spoke, the words of the alchemist rang in his ears.

***

The Scots gathered their weapons and set off. Dougie thought it was a grand sight, with so many soldiers dressed in the king's own tartan and the leaders of the clans carrying brightly coloured banners. King Malcolm and his son, Ranald, led the army towards the west. The men walked in a single file which stretched out along narrow paths for nearly three miles.

Each clan had its own crest, which was painted on the shields of their men, to make them easy to recognise in the chaos and confusion of battle. Dougie looked at the painted symbols; strange beasts, serpents and birds, and swords and castles. His own shield was plain and without allegiance to any clan.

In truth, Dougie knew very little about his parents, or the clan to which he belonged, and remembered the awkward conversations he and his brother had prompted with their grandmother when they were children …

"Please tell us about our mother and father," begged Alec.

"There is not much to tell, my angels, for they died of the fever when you were very young."

"But what were they like?"

Dougie noticed that Grandma had dropped the vegetables she was washing and was staring down at the table.

"They were fine and wonderful people." Lissy spoke softly and her eyes became distant and watery.

"And do we have no other family?" pressed Alec.

"No, no other family, but at least we have each other."

"Is there anybody we can speak to about them?"

"No, laddie."

"They must have had friends."

"Oh, they had friends, lots of friends."

"Can we not talk to even one?" asked Dougie.

"The fever claimed many."

"And have we always lived here on the farm?"

"Aye, as long as the memory goes, boys. Now run along and play for I have much work to do and precious little help to do it."

At first the soldiers sang songs and children followed, dancing and skipping along the path edge. But it began to rain and the wee ones grew tired, and returned to their homes.

Dougie had his misgivings. However, there is something in a man that encourages him to appear braver than he is, when he is with many others, so the early part of the journey proved to be a light-hearted affair despite the downpour and the dangerous times ahead of them. Dougie walked with the men of Tain and learned that Big Hamish worked with his friend Donald, who was half his size and even shorter than Portalla. They made a fine drink from barley and heather, which they sold to the leaders of the local clans.

"You won't ever get rich making heather ale," lamented Hamish, "but there are worse things you can do to make an honest living."

"Wise words," chirped Donald.

Secretly Dougie thought that tending the land was the best way to live an honest and happy life. His mind wandered back to his farm and he could clearly picture his cottage, fields and family.

Sadness must have shown on his face for Alistair nudged Hamish. The big man growled at Dougie, "You see Donald over there."

"Aye."

"He is very good to his Mum you know."

"How so?"

"Well you see, Dougie," teased Hamish, "he never goes home."

The men of Tain laughed and Donald jumped on Hamish's back and hit him on the head with his shield.

With good company, even the longest journey passes quickly and after what seemed to Dougie to be no time at all, they reached a small and well-kept village called Dalwhinnie. This was the halfway point to Carn Liath and, as the Scots settled down to a lunch of bread, cheese and cold mutton, the clouds parted and the sun came out.

"So little to keep us going," moaned Hamish, looking at the small amount of food.

"Och, if you were as good at fighting as you are at eating, we wouldnae be in this mess," said Donald.

Hamish grabbed his shoulders and lifted him so they looked eye to eye. Donald's wee legs dangled beneath him.

"Things look very different up here don't they."

Hamish growled and tossed him aside.

Dougie lay on the grass, with his shield for a pillow, and waited for his clothes to dry. He wondered what Mairi and the children were doing and wished, more than anything, that he could return to them safely. He felt as though he had let them down.

Malcolm the Younger pulled himself back onto his horse and his son reluctantly copied him.

"Time to move on," called the king and a thousand men rose for the final leg of the journey.

As they headed further west, Dougie became more and more anxious. Every step took him nearer to a fight he dreaded and as the hours went by the images of his terrible dream became clearer. He couldn't get the feeling of helplessness, of being chased by an enemy in darkness, out of his mind.

"Getting second thoughts?" asked Alistair.

"Aye, I am."

"Not to worry, Dougie," said Alistair kindly, "there is not a man here who does not feel the same way."

But, as the landscape changed, Dougie's worries and self doubts grew worse. The mood of his companions had changed too. They were now entering Pictish lands. Here the heather was sparser, the ground more broken, with large areas of rock showing through. The rounded hills and farmland, so familiar to the shepherd, were gone. Rugged, barren mountains rose up ahead of the army. As Dougie trudged along, he gradually became lost in his thoughts, totally oblivious to his new surroundings and the men of Tain. Suddenly a rock hit him on the back and he was thrown, sprawling, off the path.

"Look out," cried Portalla and the Scots ran for cover, away from a small band of Black Kilts who hurled boulders down the mountainside at them.

"Are you alright?" asked Alistair in a worried voice.

"Aye, I think so."

Dougie stared at a dent the size of a giant fist in his shield and knew he owed his life to it.

"Well one thing is certain," said Alistair.

"What's that?"

When Alistair spoke, his voice was grim. "They know we are coming."

Dougie saw a group of Scots chasing up the mountain after the Picts. Then he realised he had never seen a slope so steep, so bare of grass and heather.

"There must be a great sadness in this land for plants and birds to desert it," he thought and more than ever he wished he had stayed at home.

But even the worst days must end and, after another march and night without shelter, the menacing form of mighty Carn Liath rose up in front of them. The snows on its upper reaches could be seen clearly. It was high, barren and cold, and Dougie wondered how it had come to be.

As if reading his thoughts, Alistair said, "They say Carn Liath was created by great monsters who are long dead. They battled here and the mountain is the only evidence of their struggle."

Dougie looked up and whispered, "There must have been immense powers at work, long ago."

After yet another long march, the sun finally left the sky and the Scots made fires, and settled down for supper. As Dougie talked to Portalla about his sheep, the king walked through the camp and encouraged his men. He finally settled himself down next to Dougie.

"I wanted to speak to you," said Malcolm, looking at the dent in the shepherd's plain shield. He wondered what clan this man belonged to.

Dougie stared at the floor and felt desperately uneasy in the king's presence.

"Th-thank you," he mumbled nervously.

"I saw you hit by one of the rocks. Are you alright to go on, laddie?"

"Aye, I am, but I would rather go home."

"So why not go?"

Dougie looked the king straight in the eyes. "Because there is a Pict at the top of a mountain with my friend's sheep and my money. I have come to get them back."

He felt embarrassed for he didn't know why he said these words, but the Younger smiled, kindly, and then seemed puzzled, as if he was trying to work something out. The men of Tain remained respectfully silent. Hamish and Donald shuffled their feet.

Then Malcolm the Younger, King of the Scots and Protector of the Stone of Destiny, took Dougie's hand and shook it.

CHAPTER SIX

The Slopes of Carn Liath

Supper was a meagre affair. Dry oatcakes and stream water, and not much else, and the men of Tain shared with Dougie the little they had brought with them. Things were made worse by the hearty smell of hare stew that wafted down on them from the clansmen of Blair Atholl. These soldiers were skilled at scraping a living from the high places and two of them could still be seen in the twilight, searching the slopes for game, berries and roots.

Hamish and Donald looked across at their stew pot with envy. The Blair warriors saw them, nudged each other and slowly spooned great steaming chunks into their mouths.

"I'll not sell them any heather ale again," threatened Hamish, as he bit into a dry biscuit.

Dougie imagined himself sitting at his kitchen table with Mairi's broth in front of him. How he wished he could be there.

As dusk came, they settled down and cooked, and told more tales about the Black Kilts. Dougie gazed up at the white summit of Carn Liath. It was tall, proud and threatening, and he strained his eyes to catch any sign of the enemy. Standing defiant, upon a high shoulder of the mountain, stood the Picts' stone fortress. Its defences seemed to be surrounded by a black ring, a deep scar, which protected it on all sides. The Dark Fortress was as menacing as Carn Liath itself.

"No wonder the Elder couldn't take it," thought Dougie and he shuddered.

Back down the valley and stretching out to the far horizon, were fields and streams with silver waterfalls cascading down to feed the lower pastures. From the safety of the camp it all seemed so peaceful.

During the march they had followed long, twisting paths upwards and Dougie noticed the air was much colder up here. As the skies darkened, the chill began to reveal itself in the misty breaths of the men. Dougie shivered and rolled his plaid out, as close to the fire as he dared. The burning logs crackled and began their own journey from tall dancing flames to white ash.

All was quiet now and many tired souls tried to escape their worries by finding sleep. Dougie listened to Hamish's snoring and in the far distance a fox barked to call its own kind. As blissful sleep began to take him too, Dougie thought, half in dream, that footsteps were growing louder and reluctantly opened an eye.

A stranger had run into the camp and now stood, breathless, anxious, amongst the men of Tain. His eyes darted around and fell on the shepherd.

"Have you seen the king?" he panted.

"Aye. He left a while ago for his tent."

"Show me. I have important news."

Dougie led the man past a line of fires and ranks of sleeping soldiers. They soon reached a large tent with a brown, green and ochre banner at its head. Dougie walked forward to one of the guards who stood at the entrance. He was big, rough, muscular and looked as though he could fight anyone and beat them.

"Guard," asked Dougie respectfully, "may we see the king?"

"For what purpose?"

"This man has important news."

"What news could be more important than the king's peace?" said the man gruffly.

The messenger's words tumbled out.

"I was one of the party who chased the enemy. The Picts who attacked us with rocks. The others will be entering the camp soon and we have taken a prisoner."

The guard considered this and looked them over. Eventually he growled at the messenger.

"Place your claymore on the ground." He turned on Dougie. "Do you carry a dirk?"

The shepherd nodded, took it from his belt and handed it over.

"Follow me," and the guard led them inside the royal tent.

Malcolm glanced up from a parchment and smiled at Dougie.

"Ah, it is the brave warrior with the dented shield."

"Your Majesty," replied Dougie and the messenger together, and they bowed their heads.

Dougie noticed that the big bodyguard stood behind them, with his sword held ready.

Malcolm reassured them.

"Do not fear Angus, Thane of Tomorkin. He is strong and loyal, and has kept my safety for many summers."

The messenger told his story eagerly and Malcolm decided to go with them to see the prisoner and discover what he could about the enemy's plans. They hurried past sleeping soldiers to the edge of the camp and did not have long to wait for the line of torches that wound its way down a mountain path towards them.

A tall and surly Pict was brought before the king, dragged along on the end of a long, thick rope. The rope was tied many times around the Black Kilt's middle, pinning his waist and arms together. Dougie had never seen a more evil looking face for, down the right side, the beard was broken by an ugly white scar. The scar just missed his eye and ran all the way down to the bottom of his chin.

Malcolm studied him carefully and in a clear, quiet voice asked, "How many warriors does Tella have on Carn Liath?"

The man glowered back at him angrily and tried to kick the king. Dougie grabbed the end of the rope and pulled the Pict back, out of Malcolm's range.

"Does the Mac Mar know we are here?" continued Malcolm.

The man spat at Dougie and tried to kick him too. Dougie jumped, from one foot to the other, to avoid the prisoner's wild attempts to strike him.

"Look after our guest for a while. I need to think about the best thing to do with him."

Obediently Dougie nodded, although it was obvious to everyone that he was not at all keen on the idea. Even Angus grinned and made a noise, somewhere between a grunt and a laugh, as the Pict lowered his head, charged and drove it into Dougie's stomach.The shepherd dragged his prisoner back to the men of Tain. This was no easy task for at each step the man cursed, spat and kicked out at his keeper.

"Well, well, well," grinned Alistair, "what have we here?"

"The king's prisoner," replied Dougie, "and I got the job of looking after him!"

"Seems like a nasty piece of work to me," said Donald cheekily.

"Dangerous too," added Hamish.

"Aye, a real handful," teased Donald, "still, it is a great honour to be chosen for such an important task."

"Well, thank you … *ouch* … for your help."

Dougie yelped as the Pict's boot caught him painfully on the shin.

The men of Tain laughed heartily and Dougie was the only one who did not find his new situation funny. With much effort the Pict was eventually forced to sit quietly by the fireside and Dougie sat as far away from him as he could, whilst still holding the rope. The prisoner stared with hatred at his captor. There was a deep malice in his dark eyes and Dougie, despite the presence of so many Scots, felt nervous and fearful. The man leant forward towards the shepherd and beckoned him to listen.

"I will kill you."

There was a quiet evil in his voice.

"Thank you," said Dougie in as casual a way as he could manage.

"I *will* kill you." The Pict spat at him again.

Dougie was too nervous to sleep. The prisoner was strong and cunning, and every ten minutes he went over to check that the rope was still tight and in place. The prisoner sat like a statue and glared at him, and Dougie was left in no doubt about what he would like to do to him. It seemed like an age before Angus came, and led them back to the king's tent.

"What is your name?" asked the king.

The Pict stood before him, upright and unafraid, and gave no reply. There was a dignity about the prisoner that Dougie could not help but admire. If circumstances had been reversed, and he had been brought as a captive in front of Tella the Mac Mar, he would not have been as defiant as this warrior. Malcolm must have realised this too for he stared at him, considering his words carefully.

"From your bearing I believe you are someone of importance to the Picts."

Torik Benn did not move a muscle.

Angus growled and made a ball out of his fist and started to move towards the prisoner. Malcolm raised a hand and the Thane of Tomorkin stopped in his tracks.

"Still, there is no reason to keep you."

Dougie glanced anxiously at the king for he believed there was *every* reason to keep captive a man who had sworn to kill you.

"I want you to give Tella a message."

The Younger nodded at Angus to untie the prisoner and Torik rubbed his hands over his arms where the rope had cut deep.

"Take this to your king," continued Malcolm and he gave him a roll of parchment, tied with a black ribbon.

The Pict looked at it and then into the shepherd's eyes. He did not need to say anything for his intention was clear enough.

The words, "I *will* kill you," were burned deep into Dougie's heart.

$$***$$

Dougie yawned and peered across the camp that had been his home for just one night. It seemed like a lifetime. He remembered the scarred face of the prisoner and shivered as much through fear as the cold of early morning.

There were soldiers everywhere, running and gathering weapons and forming into large groups, which would each be led by a single clansman during the battle. Alistair ladled broth from a large pot that sat in the last embers of their fire. He passed his friend a bowl of the thick soup and Dougie ate it eagerly.

"I want you to stay with me today," said Alistair, "whatever happens."

"I will be there," promised Dougie bravely, but in his heart he wished he could be anywhere except for the slopes of Carn Liath.

"Give me your claymore, young Dougie," and Alistair took the blade, ran his finger along its edge and stared at the rust that had eaten into the iron. The leather bound hilt was worn and smooth, and in places the thin leather strips hung loose as if once it had enjoyed much use.

"How did you come by this?"

"My grandmother told me it was my father's, but he died of the fever and it has seen little use for a lifetime of summers."

"It was a fine sword in its day," said Alistair, studying it with interest. "Very fine indeed, Dougie, but it has *had* its day and I cannot allow you to face the enemy with a blade that will break on the first blow."

He reached behind him and drew out a claymore. The hilt glinted in the early sun. Dougie took it, carefully, and stared at its sharp edge. The blade was new and dull grey, the full length of an arm and heavier than any he had ever held.

"This was given to me by a friend a long time ago," continued Alistair, "and I always knew it would be given away."

He remembered being a boy and creeping in the dead of night to the balcony, overlooking the Great Hall, and overhearing his father's urgent conversation with a stranger. A sword had appeared in his hand by magic.

"I cannot take such a fine gift," said Dougie at last. "There can be few swords as well wrought and valuable as this."

"You will take it," demanded Alistair sternly, "and you will stay by my side."

This seemed like an order rather than a gift given kindly, but Alistair's face changed in an instant with a huge smile, full of care and warmth. He looked into Dougie's eyes and spoke softly.

"Please take it."

Dougie had only known Alistair for a few days and yet he would have gladly followed him anywhere. He couldn't think of anyone he would rather face the enemy with, if he had to face them at all, and certainly his old claymore would be of little use if things turned ugly. He nodded gratefully.

"It is a great gift, Alistair, and I hope one day you will allow me to repay your kindness."

"You'd better, laddie," laughed Alistair and they rose to join the men of Tain who were reluctantly being herded, along with the warriors of the other clans, into one of five groups, each over two hundred strong.

Hamish and Donald stood together and Big Hamish glanced down onto the head of his wee friend.

"I wager I kill more Picts than you," he growled.

"You're too slow and too ugly," replied Donald cheekily, "and since when were *you* an expert on killing Picts anyway?"

Hamish raised the hilt of his sword as if to bring it down on Donald's head but one glance from Alistair was enough to make him concentrate on the orders being shouted out. Malcolm and Prince

Ranald rode around the camp and spoke to the leaders of each clan.

Later, as the prince and his guards left to find a place of safety on the lower slopes, Alistair said, "More like his grandfather than his father."

"His grandfather?" asked Dougie.

"Aye, do you no get news of the wider world on your farm, laddie?"

Dougie shook his head.

"Malcolm the Elder, the king's father, was happy to let his men face the danger of battle alone. I always believed the sign of a great king was to lead in the very thick of things. The Elder was cruel but not brave, for he only fought for gain and when he was sure of victory. If Ranald has left to watch from a safe distance then we cannot have long to wait for some action."

This was not a comforting thought and Dougie's stomach tightened as more orders were shouted and they began to march. Dougie clutched his new claymore and his old shield, and gained great comfort from being alongside Alistair. The army of Scots formed a long line at the base of Carn Liath. All eyes were on the upper slopes and Dougie began to wonder if perhaps the Picts had decided to fight another day.

However, this hope was a vain one, for after only three hundred paces, great numbers of Picts arose from the ground. Fear and dismay showed on the faces of the Scots, for not only did the enemy have the advantage of the high ground, they also outnumbered them by at least two to one.

The Picts seemed to be ready for them and they hit their own shields with mighty battle axes and the noise filled the battlefield. But they did not move down the mountain. They lined up in great formations in their black kilts. Many of them had long black beards and these swayed in the wind.

Dougie's gaze fixed on a giant of a man who stood at the head of a large band of followers. Remembering his dream, a shudder ran through Dougie's bones and a feeling of dread began to overcome him.

Up the slope, Tella the Mac Mar rode forward. He glared at Malcolm and raised a parchment into the air. Slowly and deliberately he threw its black ribbon away, spat on the parchment and tore it into pieces. Malcolm showed no emotion and the Picts cheered and hit their shields again. There were now mutterings of discontent amongst the Scots. They had come so far and yet, surely, it would mean certain death to go on. The Younger rode his horse along the front of the Scots' line. He paused and looked into their eyes.

"There are those who would take the things you love. I learned as a boy that if you do not stand up for what you believe is right, then you lose more than the things you treasure. You lose your dignity."

Portalla shouted, "Hear, hear," and said to Dougie, "I don't know what this dignity thing is, but they have got my sheep and they are not getting that as well."

"Never mind your sheep, the Black Kilts have got my purse."

"Will you follow me?" roared Malcolm.

"Aye," whispered Donald, "I bet he is like his father – 'Follow me, I will be right behind you!'"

A great cheer went up from the Scots and an even louder jeer went up from the enemy.

The sun reached its high point in the sky, but gave little warmth or comfort. Dougie glanced at Alistair and there was something in his face he had not seen before. There was no laughter there now, only a hard look, shaped by anger and determination.

The Scots moved upward and the Picts moved downward.

The battle was as fierce as any that has ever been. The Black Kilts waved their axes above their heads and many young Scots fell under their crushing blows. Alistair brought his claymore down upon one of the enemy, and then another, and then another still. But there were just too many of them and, after an hour's fighting, the Scots were forced to retreat down the hill.

The Picts shouted, "Victory, victory for the Black Kilts."

At the bottom of the mountain, the remaining Scots numbered some seven hundred men and they felt a great sadness for the friends they had lost. Portalla, who had fought bravely at Dougie's side, was missing. The king's shield had three arrows embedded in it. Alistair was covered in blood.

"Alistair, are you wounded?" Dougie asked anxiously.

"No, not at all, but more than one of *them* is."

Dougie grinned for the first time that day.

Now there was a lot to do. Those who were left set about sharpening their claymores, tending the wounded and deciding on the best way to fight the Picts. The brave men of Tain were in favour of another head-on attack. Others wanted to go around the other side of the mountain, under the cover of darkness, and surprise the enemy from behind. King Malcolm listened to all the ideas with great patience and seemed to be weighing up each one in turn. Eventually he called together the High Table, the leaders of the great families who spoke for the Scottish people. They gathered beside a small stream and Malcolm rose to speak.

"If we attack again, I have no doubt we shall earn the same result."

The heads of the clans nodded and looked grave.

"A messenger has brought me news. Murdoch is still two days away and brings only fifty warriors from the Outer Islands. This means our fate is in our own hands."

A cold wind blew across the waters of the stream and the clansmen stared down at the bare earth.

There was silence for a long while and then Malcolm spoke again.

"As I see it we must do three things. Some of our number must attack the Picts from above. I need a volunteer to take a hundred men and at darkest nightfall travel to the other side of Carn Liath. They must climb the mountain, go unseen around the fortress and then come down upon the enemy."

"I will go," offered David of Blair Athol, "for my men are well used to climbing the hills around our homes."

"Secondly, we must leave the battle."

"No," cried the warriors, "we will not run away."

"Hear me," said Malcolm quickly, "we cannot attack again until David has gone around the mountain and his journey will take at least a day. We may also gain an advantage by making Tella the Mac Mar believe he has won."

"How so?" asked Robert of Inverness.

"My understanding of the Picts, is that they are a rough and ready lot who require little excuse to celebrate with the heather ale."

"Aye," agreed Robert, "and sore heads do little for the fighting man."

As the king walked away, Robert of Inverness came up to him.

"Excuse me, Your Majesty, but you said there were *three* things we had to do."

"Aye, there is something else. You are going to need my horse."

They talked quietly for some time and to Dougie the king seemed a lonely figure, as he watched Robert ride away.

There is much written about the glory of battle but, in truth, whether you win or lose, there is a great sadness that lives with you forever. Dougie didn't just feel this sadness, he could taste it.

The warriors who survived these terrible events would later remember the friends they made and the hardships they endured. However, there are some memories that must be locked away in the distant corners of the mind, hidden from all others and even themselves.

Dougie looked up. There seemed to be something going on amongst the Black Kilts and he could hear laughter coming from the top of the mountain. The sound of chopping wood could also be heard and then more cruel laughter. One of the enemy began to sing.

The giant Pict, who Dougie dreamt had chased him, was walking down the mountain towards them.

"Filthy Scots, I have a present for you," he bellowed.

Then he stopped to pull something out of a sack. It bounced like a ball down the slope and came to rest near Malcolm. The great king looked at it and Dougie saw his face drain of colour, and a single tear rolled down his cheek. It was the head of Portalla.

***

"Cool," said James.

Peter lifted his head out of his hands and glanced at Laura. She was clearly shaken by this part of the story and yet he knew that worse things were to come. He placed a reassuring hand on his little sister's and smiled.

"That is just awful," gasped Laura.

71

James had a mischievous twinkle in his eyes. "Carn Liath, never heard of it," he teased.

The storyteller shot him a questioning glance.

"You do not believe it to be true then?"

He rose to stretch his legs.

"It's the same with all these stories," insisted James, "great fun, but just made up."

"I think it's true," said Peter.

"Whatever," sighed James.

"What time is it, Petee?" asked Laura.

He looked at his watch. "It must have stopped, according to this it isn't even five o'clock yet."

"I really thought Dougie would get killed in the battle," continued Laura. She yawned and slapped an embarrassed hand over her mouth.

"So did Dougie," replied the old man.

"But I thought it was a nice touch, that you set the story around here," said James.

"A nice touch?" asked the stranger.

"I bet you did it to make us feel at home," guessed Laura.

"And do you feel at home?"

Laura yawned again and Peter glanced at the storyteller.

"I've had that feeling for a while now."

He stood up and walked over to the window. Dog raised his head and thought about getting up too, but he was too warm and comfortable, and he closed his eyes again. His legs twitched as he dreamt about chasing rabbits. Outside the cottage the snow was falling as hard as ever and banks had drifted up to the window ledge.

"It must be over a metre deep," exclaimed Peter, and the others came over to join him.

"Not more bloomin' snow," moaned Laura.

"Does this happen often, round here?" asked Peter.

"Not often, the last time was when your father was a boy."

The room went quiet and the stranger sat very still. Each of the children held their own thoughts and Peter sensed the old man was considering each of them in turn, as if making his mind up about something.

James felt restless and trapped.

"Well, we are well and truly stuck. Marooned."

Unless he was engrossed on his computer, he never sat in one place for long and now he stared, longingly, out the window at the white garden.

"I'm fed up. How about trying to find the path?"

"I'm not going out in that!" exclaimed Laura.

Peter agreed with her.

"We will only get lost again and the snow will not fall forever. My vote goes to staying put."

James ignored them and opened the door, and a cold gust of wind made the children shiver.

"Put a peg in it," yelled Laura, "it's *bloooomin' freeeezing.*"

"You put a peg in it," shouted James and he pushed his way out into the snow.

"Do you think we ought to go after him?" asked Laura.

"No need," replied the stranger, "he'll be back in a minute."

Peter began to worry about Grandma and Grandpa. They had been gone such a long time and he got his mobile out.

"A good signal," he mumbled, "I didn't expect that here."

He called them and nothing happened. Then he thought about Kylie and punched *miss u lots* into the keypad, and sent the text. He waited a couple of minutes and listened to James's moaning outside. Kylie always texted him back in seconds and so he re-sent his message.

He remembered the last time he had seen his girlfriend, on the school bus to Pinner High. They had sat together, holding hands, talking eagerly about the coming weekend, and swaying as Mr. Denver, their regular driver, took the bends too fast. Toady Thompson and Mac Mackinlay had joined them. They smelled of cigarettes and delighted in butting into the conversation.

Toady had stood up, like he always did when he wanted to annoy Mr. Denver, and the driver had yelled back angrily at him to sit down.

Mac and Toady were trouble and Peter realised that one day he would need to square up to them. If he didn't overcome his fear of what they might do then things would only get worse. Then he thought about poor Dougie, how events in the wider world had forced him to leave his family and join the Younger's army. He pictured the Black

Kilt's scarred face and remembered how the prisoner had sworn to kill the shepherd. Somehow he knew that Dougie had not heard the last of Torik Benn and wondered if the Pict would keep his promise.

"History does have a way of putting things into perspective, does it not?" asked the stranger.

Peter raised his eyebrows, nodded and sent the text again.

Another blast of icy air swirled around the cottage and James staggered through the door.

"Where were you two?" he demanded, teeth chattering.

"Trying to do the right thing," said Peter.

"You are not the only one who should decide what we do."

"But we're not the ones with wet trousers," retorted Laura, pointing at the sodden, baggy legs of her brother's jeans.

"Ah, sod it."

James pushed past them and slumped back in front of the fire. Steam rose from his trousers and he grinned. The old man grinned back.

"Well now my reluctant guest is with us again, perhaps we can move on to Dougie's unwanted guests?"

He invited Laura and Peter to sit by the fire too, where Dog's legs were still twitching.

CHAPTER SEVEN

The Chain of Death

The Younger knew that even small things can make a big difference in war. He led his men away from the battlefield and the Picts cheered, and shouted rude words at them. Little was said between Dougie and Alistair as they marched in single file past the large rocks on the lower slopes of Carn Liath. Once they were out of sight of the enemy, David of Blair Athol and his followers set off on their mission to the other side of the mountain. For the rest, it was now time for supper and it was a fine one, for a boar and a herd of deer had been caught and killed. As Malcolm told the High Table to prepare for a dawn attack, victory songs and the clinking of goblets drifted down from the Dark Fortress. These small things gave the king hope.

Dougie unwound his plaid and laid it out on the ground. He peered across the slopes. Some Scots were already asleep. Dougie could not see them, for the plaid covers all of the sleeper's body, but he could hear them. Hamish's snores filled the darkness and, in the firelight, Dougie saw the big man's plaid rise up above his body.

"The revenge of the boar," said Alistair.

Dougie giggled and fell fast asleep.

As the moon settled above the battlements of the Dark Fortress a great commotion engulfed the camp. Two Picts, fuddled with drink, accidentally strayed into the midst of the sleeping Scots. There was shouting and confusion, and the Black Kilts tried to make a run for it back up the hill.

Donald cried out, "Stop them, or they will warn Tella we have not returned home."

Hamish didn't even stir. Dougie and Alistair leapt out of their beds and grabbed their swords. They were the first of the Scots to take chase and Alistair, being taller and stronger than Dougie, was soon some way ahead. The shepherd saw that one Pict was short and stout, and Alistair was quickly on him. The warrior, who was not armed, gave little resistance, and was pinned to the ground under Alistair's claymore.

"Get the other one," he yelled and Dougie raced up the slope.

The enemy slowed and the young shepherd gained ground and, in the moonlight, he could just make out that he was a giant and more suited to fighting than running. The gap between them narrowed some more and Dougie heard the man wheezing and panting. It was even louder than Hamish's snoring. The Pict turned and drew a long dirk from his belt, and waved it in front of Dougie's face. Dougie drew his sword and brought it down. There was a loud *clang* as the two blades met and the man's dirk broke into pieces under the force of Dougie's new claymore. The Black Kilt threw the handle at his pursuer and dashed off towards a narrow, twisting path, which followed the side of the mountain.

Dougie followed the sound of pounding feet ahead of him. The Pict's menacing footsteps grew louder, as the gap between them closed, and Dougie recognised them from his dream. But, he sensed that fear and helplessness were beginning to overcome the enemy.

Then Dougie heard something else, the sound of rushing water. The Pict sprinted around a corner and was lost from sight. There was a terrible scream and Dougie stopped running.

Just ahead, the path ended suddenly. A hundred feet below, at the bottom of a sheer cliff, was a fast flowing mountain stream. He knelt down on the ledge and sucked in the cold night air.

Staring into the gloom, he saw the broken body of the giant Pict being swept away by the raging current.

He sat for many minutes, listening to the water, and realised that he had been responsible for someone's death. It was an awful thought and yet he gained some comfort from knowing Tella still believed the Younger's army had retreated to lick their wounds. A bitter wind made him shiver and Dougie retraced his steps to the camp where he was met by Alistair and an anxious king.

"Did the enemy escape?" asked Malcolm and his words tumbled out, one after another.

Dougie shook his head and told him the story. When he finished, he was surprised to find himself at the centre of a crowd of warriors. The crowd had hung on his every word.

"We have been very fortunate and I have been very stupid," admitted Malcolm. "I should have placed guards around the camp before we went to sleep and it is due to Dougie and Alistair that we have kept our presence here a secret."

It was some time before they could return to their beds, for there were many others who wanted to hear about the chase. Dougie felt relieved to finally get back to his new friends, the men of Tain. But Donald and a sleepy Hamish wanted to hear about his adventures too and it was some while before he was able to wrap himself up in the folds of his plaid and talk to Alistair.

"Well that was scary," he said.

"Aye, it certainly was," replied Alistair.

"Do you think the Pict ran because he was full of heather ale?"

"No."

"Do you think he ran because he had no axe?"

"No."

"Do you think he ran because he saw my fine claymore?"

"Definitely not." Alistair's tone was becoming agitated.

"Do you think it was my fierce appearance?"

"No, laddie, no."

"Well why did he run so?"

"Is it not obvious?"

"It is not."

"Well put yourself in his position. If a strange man chased you in the dead of night, with no plaid to cover his modesty, would you not run for your life?"

A great roar of laughter went up from the men of Tain as Dougie realised the entire chase, and the story telling after it, had been undertaken in nothing more than his shirt.

***

A great hand shook Dougie's shoulder and woke him from the deepest of sleeps.

"Time to get going again," growled Hamish, "we have a busy day ahead of us."

The first rays of sun shone up the valley. Men were running around collecting weapons and receiving their orders, in whispers, from the leaders of the clans. Unlike the morning of the first day, all was deadly quiet as the soldiers went about their business.

"I wonder if David has reached the other side of the mountain?" asked Donald.

"We must trust that he has," replied Alistair grimly.

"Look, there goes Prince Ranald again," growled Hamish and he pointed at three riders who were leaving the camp.

"Och, you cannot blame Malcolm for wanting to keep his son and heir from the fighting."

Dougie wished he too might be allowed to join the prince.

"I don't like Ranald," said Hamish, "he reminds me too much of the Elder and the guards at the palace say he has a nasty way about him."

"We are not here to serve Ranald," said Alistair in a stern voice, "Malcolm is our king and we have to be here if the Picts are to be put in their place."

A long line of warriors in their brown, green and ochre tartans started to leave the camp.

"Stay together," said Alistair and he came to stand next to Dougie.

They both smiled nervously and began to march.

***

Dark clouds scudded away to the north and Borak turned to watch the first rays of sun bathe the foothills of Carn Liath. It was going to be a glorious day.

During the night, he too had heard the celebrations of his people up at the fortress and now he felt uneasy. Bonnagh, the leader of the watch, had disappeared in the small hours and returned a while later to the lookout post with drink. Only Borak, and his brother, had stayed faithful to their task. Bonnagh and another guard had wandered off and not returned. They should have been back by now.

Borak walked to the top of the rise, as he had done many times, and scanned the lower slopes. Something was wrong and yet the mountains and glens seemed untroubled.

"They have gone," said a voice behind him.

Borak turned, saw his brother and smiled, "But, Tumora, how can you be sure?"

"The Scots are fewer than us and not even the Elder could take Carn Liath."

"I think they will return. They were ill-prepared, but the tables might yet be turned."

"The king does not think so," persisted Tumora.

"The king might be wrong."

Tumora shot his brother a warning glance.

"Men have been killed for saying words like those."

"But they need to be said, brother."

Borak lifted his spear and pointed it at the far slopes. Marching towards them was the vanguard of the Younger's army.

"How far?" gasped Tumora.

"Two hours for foot-soldiers, less for riders."

"How many?"

"Too far away to measure."

Borak ran towards the path, which led away from the lookout-post and up to the fortress.

Tumora called after him, "Have you seen Bonnagh?"

"He has gone," yelled Borak, and now he knew why the leader of the watch had failed to return.

He was not coming back.

***

Tella the Mac Mar, king of all the Pictish peoples, awoke with a headache. He had celebrated the defeat of the Scots until sleep had finally taken him and now wondered why the victory had been so easy. Easy, or not, it was a great victory and his people needed to move onto richer lands, and his power would be so much greater with the Celtic peoples paying tribute to his banner. He plunged his head into a bucket of cold water and tried to guess at the wealth that lay within the walls of Malcolm's lowland palace. Suddenly he felt alive at the prospect of leading his army east to take it.

An old and timid servant scuttled into the chamber with a tray of food. The king grabbed a hunk of bread and growled at the man, who went white and made a hasty retreat. Before he made the door, Tella roared.

"Get me my son."

"He sleeps, master," said the servant.

Tella's eyes flashed.

"I will get him, master."

The man scuttled out.

***

Borak and Tumora ran as they had never run before. The path led upwards onto level ground and then dropped down steeply towards the ravine, which protected the Dark Fortress. As they dashed over the narrow causeway, the only way across the deep scar, Borak hailed the guards who stood at the top of the battlements. The huge wooden gates opened, slowly, and they pushed their way into the inner courtyard. They were met by a tall warrior with a long white scar running down his cheek.

"What's the matter?" growled Torik.

"The Scots return," panted Tumora.

He glanced anxiously at his brother. Both of them feared this man. It was said that Tella himself was wary of Torik Benn. He was dangerous and showed no mercy to those who crossed him.

Tella had learned of Torik's love of killing and used it. One word from the king, a single name, and a disloyal or disobedient subject would be dealt with quickly, secretly and without pity. By reputation he had become a symbol of terror. The scarred warrior clasped his axe, and shouted orders to the guards to raise others from the round-houses and warn them.

"You can have the honour of telling the king himself," he sneered, and the brothers passed nervously through the inner gates.

Tella and Gath were deep in conversation when Borak and Tumora were shown inside the Royal Chamber. Instantly, father and son stopped speaking, like rowing parents who do not want to be overheard by their children, and Borak stepped forward to give them the news.

81

"Master, the Scots return to do battle," he said.

"And where is Bonnagh?" asked Tella quietly.

"I think he has been taken."

"And how was he taken?"

Borak glanced at Tumora. They would be put to death if either of them lied.

"He left the watch and wandered away in the dark hours."

"And you stayed."

"We both stayed to keep the watch," replied Borak loyally.

Tella stood and walked over to stand by them and fear ran through their bodies.

"Then, Borak, you are now in charge of the watch."

Borak nodded.

"How many men does Malcolm bring?" asked the king.

"We came to warn you as soon as we saw the leading horsemen on the lower slopes. We have less than two hours to measure them."

Tella scowled.

"Go and help the others raise the army," he commanded, and the brothers left the chamber, relieved at not falling victim to the king's rage.

When they had gone, Tella turned on his son.

"You appointed Bonnagh, didn't you?"

"I did," stammered Gath.

"One day you will be king, but you still have much to learn if you are to wield power over others."

Gath lowered his head.

"Would you like another lesson?"

His son winced.

Gath was a strong man of eighteen summers and yet in the presence of his father he felt like a child. Gath respected, feared and hated the king, and they both shared a single burning passion. To rule.

"Bring the prisoners to me at the High Ledge," roared Tella, and his son dashed from the room.

Five Scottish warriors, with bowed heads, were led up the stone stairs to the battlements above the entrance to the fortress. Their hands were bound behind their backs and they were roped together by the waist. The man at the front of the chain was pushed forward by a Black Kilt and he kicked out at his captor. The Pict struck him viciously across the face with his fist.

"Kneel before the king, you dogs," ordered the guard.

They cowered in a line before Tella, who looked at Gath.

"This is how a king gets what he wants."

Tella walked slowly along the chain of kneeling men. When he spoke his words were soft and menacing.

"How many warriors does the Younger bring to the field?"

None replied and Gath grinned at his father. Tella nodded at the guards, who prodded the prisoners with spears to make them stand.

"We do not have long to prepare," urged Gath.

Tella's eyes flashed at him.

"We do not need long."

He pointed at the first Scot, who was picked up, screaming, and thrown over the battlements.

The other four prisoners felt the rope suddenly tighten and bent their knees to counteract the weight of the man who swung below them. He was still screaming. Gath made his way carefully to the ledge and looked down. It was a terrible fall to the rocks far below. The Mac Mar moved his face to the second warrior.

"How many men?" he whispered.

The prisoner glared back at him defiantly. He too was thrown, crying, over the ledge. Tella smiled and moved on to the next man. His body trembled like a leaf in a storm.

"How many?" whispered Tella again.

The man's silence condemned him. He was grabbed by strong arms and thrown out into space.

The last two warriors fought with all their might to stop themselves falling to their death. The shrieks of the other terrified men cut through everything as they dangled on the rope and stared down into the depths of the deep scar.

The Scots on the ledge began to lose the battle against the weight that dragged them, inch by inch, towards the edge of the stone that jutted out into nothingness. Tella grinned at the leading man, whose body was leant back at a low angle. The anchor man in a deadly tug-of-war.

"How many men does the Younger bring to the field?"

The prisoner's eyes were wide with fear and he cried out.

"Seven hundred."

The Mac Mar nodded and said, "Thank you."

He kicked the man's legs from under him and the chain of Scots plummeted like a stone.

As the sun rose high upon the foothills of Carn Liath, the army of the Picts stood ready in a long formation.

"We only had two choices," Tella told Gath. "Defend the fortress, if they are many, or fight on the high slopes. We are nearly twice their number and we know this land. That is the key to victory."

Gath nodded and urged his horse forward to follow his father. Tella stopped in front of his men.

"Bring me Malcolm alive and do what you will with the others."

Amongst the king's warriors, Torik grinned and his scar twisted.

***

Alistair and the men of Tain stood proud as part of the army of the Scots. They looked up at the ranks of the Black Kilts and prepared themselves for battle. Dougie stared into the faces of the enemy, anxiously trying to see the Pict with the long white scar who had promised to kill him, but there were so many that it was impossible to pick him out from the others.

Dougie glanced at his hands. They were wet with sweat. He tried to dry them on his shirt, to get a sound grip on his new claymore, but as soon as he wiped them they became clammy again.

Dougie felt sick. He stood beside Alistair, and if his friend was nervous then he did not show it. They both stared up at the mountain and saw the Picts begin to charge. The battle raged long and hard, and the Scots, though outnumbered, fought bravely. When David of Blair Athol was seen at the top of the mountain, behind the Picts, they gave a great cheer. David's one hundred men came charging down the slope and attacked. The Black Kilts were taken completely by surprise and many fell under the claymore.

At one point Tella the Mac Mar was thrown from his horse and the men of Tain ran forward to attack him. But the Picts closed ranks around their leader and Dougie found himself fighting for his life. Donald came to help him, slashing with his sword and striking out with his shield.

Hamish lifted a warrior high above his head and hurled him, terrified, through the air into two other Picts.

A young Scot, who fought beside Dougie, fired an arrow and it struck a warrior in the knee. He fell to the ground in agony. Then the line of Black Kilts let fly hundreds of battle axes. They spun as they flew and one buried itself deep into the boy's chest.

The men of Tain charged and a screaming Pict swung his axe at Dougie. Dougie ducked and its sharp blade sliced through the air, inches above his head. He kicked out and smashed the hilt of his claymore into the man's face.

It was fierce and bloody and Alistair fought as bravely as anyone, forcing the enemy to fall back many times. The deafening roar of angry men and the smell of sweat surrounded them. Dougie's blade thrashed out wildly. It cut down with purpose, but lacked the accuracy of an experienced soldier. He loyally followed the others into the worst of the battle. But it was not courage that drove him on. It was fear. Fear of being caught alone.

As the day wore on, the superior numbers of the Picts began to prove decisive. Dougie saw Angus, Thane of Tomorkin, cut down by crushing blows from many axes. Some of the clan leaders, the High Table, were also lost. Malcolm's army was slowly, and surely, driven back down the mountain. The king himself was involved in some of the fiercest fighting and even he seemed to be losing heart as wave after wave of the enemy smashed into them.

The Scots, who were now half their original number, tried to make a last stand along the banks of a small stream, edged by grass and thistle. The Picts scowled at them. Victory would soon be theirs.

Tella called his men to be silent and shouted across at Malcolm.

"Do you wish to surrender?"

"On what terms?" asked Malcolm.

"You and the leaders of the clans leave this land forever."

"You could go and live with the Angles," added a Pict and some of the Black Kilts began to laugh.

Malcolm stared back at him grimly.

"This land is ours by right and my people are a part of it. You still have two choices, just as we do, Tella."

The king bent, wrapped his hand around a tall thistle and unearthed it.

"This is a beautiful flower," he said, pointing at it, "and we can still trade and prosper as we have done for many generations." Malcolm clasped the spines. "Or you can fight us and learn what it means to have the Scottish people as your enemy, forever."

The Younger held his arm outstretched, as though offering the Picts the plant that was to become his emblem. Blood trickled down his arm and dropped into the waters of the stream.

"Fine words," taunted Tella, "but words are all you have left now."

He got ready to lead his Black Kilts forward again.

From a long way away a strange noise could be heard. Small and distant at first, a little like a baby crying, a broken wail carried along by the wind. One of the Scots started shouting. Dougie could not understand him, not daring to hope they might be saved.

"It is Robert, Robert of Inverness."

All eyes turned to look down the valley, away from Carn Liath. It *was* Robert, riding as fast as he could towards the battle. But it was not Robert, or the bagpipes his men played, that made the soldiers freeze in their tracks. Beside Robert rode a grim-faced warrior whose appearance mirrored that of the King of the Scots. Behind him, in the distance, followed a mighty train of warriors. A small number of Picts started to run from the battlefield, dropping their axes and shields, and retreating in terror. Tella turned his horse and fled back to the safety of the fortress.

His army followed.

"Murdoch," said Malcolm.

***

At the gates of the Dark Fortress, men scattered as two riders galloped inside.

"What do we do now?" asked Gath.

The Mac Mar pulled on his reins and jumped down.

"Wait."

***

Later, in a camp swollen with people, Malcolm hugged his brother.

"I knew you would come," he said.

The Lord of the Outer Isles grinned and pointed at the hundreds of old men, women and children who had been led to Carn Liath.

"Robert of Inverness may have won us time, but the old folk will be a burden to you if the Picts realise the deception and attack again."

"We were lost," countered Malcolm, "and now we have the time to plan a next move."

"A wise move might be to return and reconsider."

They walked together to the royal tent. As they entered Malcolm spoke.

"And yet they will continue to kill our people. Tella has every intention of provoking a war at some time."

"But let us decide the place," said Murdoch, "at least deny him that."

"If we do not deal with this now, we shall regret it. Are raiders still attacking Tiree?"

"They are, and another raid last moon on Coll."

"So the threat to the Islands remains."

"It will diminish with the coming of winter and the storms."

"But it still exists."

"It does, and Myroy believes there is another, greater threat to the peace."

"From the sign of the Saxon cross."

The king shuddered as he remembered the attempt on his life and Helden's murder.

"We cannot leave this unfinished, there is simply too much to lose."

"And the foes of *mountain, island and castle* are gathering," recalled Murdoch.

"They must be faced and a *Stone Keeper* chosen, so they cannot use its power against us."

The ground shimmered and Myroy rose up through the earth. The brothers glanced at each other and then smiled at him.

"You have won time, but not the battle," said the Ancient One.

"And Tella believes we are strong and many," replied Malcolm.

"He is no fool and will know the truth as soon as we stand before him," added Murdoch.

Myroy looked at them and Malcolm felt like a pupil listening to the words of a teacher.

"Then do not stand before him," advised Myroy.

"How can we put the Picts in their place if we do not face them on the field of battle?"

"Have you not tried that already? And if you fight upon open ground can you not be sure of defeat?"

The brothers nodded.

"Then I say again, do not stand before him, attack his very heart where a smaller number might hope to win if aided by surprise."

"Enter the Dark Fortress?" gasped Malcolm.

"The fox feels safe in his lair."

"But it cannot be done."

Instantly Myroy gave them a severe glance.

"Everything you believe you cannot do, you cannot do."

"What have you seen?"

"Fire on the mountain."

"But who will burn?" said Murdoch.

Myroy sighed.

"The fox burrows deep and yet never relies on *one* tunnel for escape."

"And if we force our way inside they may be panicked enough to flee."

Myroy drew a circle on the floor with his staff and as he disappeared, they heard him say, "The fortress of Carn Liath is the key to the mountain …… turn it."

CHAPTER EIGHT

Dark Fortress

Alistair, Dougie, Hamish and wee Donald stood before their king. They had been summoned at dusk and hurried to the royal tent by armed guards. Now they waited, nervously, for Malcolm to speak. Dougie sensed that the king was choosing his words carefully.

"The Dark Fortress is the key," he said at last, "we must find a way to enter and not by the main gate. That is strongly fortified and too heavily guarded."

"And you suspect there is another way in," said Alistair.

"A way to escape in times of siege."

"It could take days to find."

Malcolm nodded and looked grave.

"I need to know tonight."

"How many men may we take?"

"A small force is more likely to remain unseen than a larger one and I only want you to find it, study it and return quickly."

"We go at once, Your Majesty," replied Alistair, and Dougie's stomach tightened.

It was tough going for they shunned the main pathways and took a circular route around the foothills of Carn Liath, always staying out of sight of the fortress. They climbed in silence and in single file, with Alistair leading. Several times Dougie stumbled in the darkness to have two great arms catch him, lift him and place him upright on the heather. Donald brought up the rear and goaded Hamish.

"If you could walk as quickly as you ate we would all be home by now."

Dougie wondered how long it would be before the big man turned on his small friend.

Some way from the summit, they crawled forward on their bellies to the top of a rise. Carn Liath has two peaks, one higher and craggier, the other more like a rounded shoulder of rock. This was where the Picts had decided to build their stronghold.

The walls were thick and formed an oval, like a giant egg. Inside it were about thirty huts. A single stone tower stood in the centre. The outer defences were surrounded by a deep ravine. It looked like a dark scar in the twilight, and ran in an unbroken, impenetrable circle around the shoulder of rock. Now they could see why the Black Kilts had chosen this place to be their home.

It could have resisted ten armies, let alone one.

They watched as a line of torches appeared at the top of the walls above the narrow causeway, which spanned the scar. Other soldiers ran across the causeway and their pace slowed as they were forced to walk two abreast. From their high vantage point, the Scots saw the gates being opened and the men pass into an inner courtyard. Then they went through a second gate and finally made their way into the inner sanctuary.

"We cannot attack this way," said Alistair.

"Wise words," chirped Donald.

"*You* can stay here with Hamish and watch for the Black Kilts entering by another gateway."

He and Dougie went to find another place of hiding where they could observe the other end of the fortress. This time the going was easier for they followed a sheep track that skirted around Carn Liath, some way below the snows of its craggy summit. Dougie glanced back anxiously for any sign of the enemy, but they seemed to be alone on the high slopes.At last, Alistair stopped and lay down, and crawled forward to peer down on the Picts, and Dougie copied him. It all seemed much as it had before. High walls and deep ditches enclosing an egg-shaped fortification, but with no gates on this side. Small ravines, cut by fast flowing streams, ran down from the slope where they hid into the long dark scar.

"Tell me what you see," invited Alistair.

"Many soldiers, preparing for war."

"And no women, or children."

"They must have sent them away, fearing a siege. They would only be more mouths to feed."

"And what else do you see?"

Dougie searched the scene below. If the Picts were ready for a siege then they would have stores of food, but these could be kept in any of the round-houses, or even in the central keep itself.

Then he turned to Alistair and smiled.

"No wells. I wonder where they get their water from?"

His friend smiled back.

"Let's go for a walk."

They made their way further along the sheep-track and Alistair glanced forward, eagerly searching for something, and then he stopped and pointed. The path was cut by a cascading stream and it headed straight down into the scar on which, on the far side, the fortress walls were built.

"I'll go first," he offered, and disappeared down into the blackest of shadows.

***

At the king's command, Robert of Inverness rolled the rug away from the floor of the royal tent, and Alistair drew an oval in the earth with his claymore.

"And how long are the walls?" asked Malcolm.

"Many thousands of paces, but no more than three times the span of the palace walls," replied Alistair.

"And how many men does Tella the Mac Mar have guarding them?"

"On this side, by the gate, thirty. Thirty more stand above the gate itself, which is actually two gates. One inner gate and an outer one. On the far side, only ten soldiers man the walls."

"And the entrance?"

Alistair looked at him and grinned.

"A stream flows off Carn Liath into the deep ravine, where it is joined by others to form a torrent that may be crossed with care. A path leads down from an arch at the base of the fortress and this is how the Picts get their water. The arch may be entered if you stoop low and it is protected by a single guard."

"So that is the key."

"And Dougie found it," said Alistair.

His friend blushed. Malcolm nodded and wondered again if this man, this shepherd, was the one that Myroy had told him to watch for.

"Alistair, you will lead my army to the arch," commanded the king, and Robert of Inverness bristled. "Your task is not an easy one for, in the darkness before dawn, you must enter and hold the walls, and the ground on that side of the fortress. Wait for a signal, arrows of fire coming over the main gate. When you see them, attack."

Dougie thought about the main keep, which stood like a granite warrior within the egg. Malcolm looked at him reassuringly.

"Tella knows that without water, his castle is lost if an enemy breaches the outer walls."

They all nodded now and Malcolm began to pace around.

"Your task is not to defeat their army, but to drive them out through the main gate. They will believe we have committed all to the attack and think they can easily escape to the high slopes, if they need to."

The king turned to Robert, who had looked aggrieved when Alistair had been given the soldiers to command.

"We must use your army in darkness too."

The Thane of Inverness grimaced as he remembered trying to get the old folk to follow his orders, and then he stood upright, proud and expectant as the king placed a hand on his shoulder.

"Tella will not be fooled on an open field of battle and so you have the most important task of all. To create another illusion!"

"An illusion?" stammered Robert.

"You are to protect me," said Malcolm, "and set the mountain ….. on fire."

***

Five hundred warriors waited for Alistair's signal at the bottom of the deep ravine. They had crossed the fast-flowing river and now peered up at the narrow pathway that led to the base of the fortress walls. It was a steep climb and from where they stood to the top of the battlements was the height of fifty men. In the depths of the dark scar they could have remained unseen for hours.

Hamish, Donald and Dougie crept forward to the arch. It, too, lay in shadow and then cut through the stone wall to form a secret tunnel some twenty paces long.

"You are too fat to get through," teased Donald, "if you ate less then you would be far more useful."

A familiar growling noise came from the depths of Hamish's chest.

Alistair was staring up at the battlements and, when the lookouts moved away, he signalled to his men.

"Time to go," whispered Dougie and wished it wasn't.

The tunnel was dry and pitch black, and Donald led them through. As they drew closer to the inside of the fortress, the gloom subsided and they heard voices. Donald raised his arm and they stopped. Dougie held his breath.

"Two warriors this time," whispered Donald, "one with axe and one with spear."

Hamish nodded.

"Wait here," he told Dougie, and the light that came through the arch on the Picts' side disappeared completely as Hamish rose. After what seemed like an age, the big man returned pulling two limp bodies.

"Get rid of them," he growled.

One at a time, Dougie dragged the Picts to the other end of the tunnel and dumped them behind some rocks. He looked down at Alistair and waved. Alistair waved back. The Scottish army rose in silence.

***

"Come along, come along, come along," ordered Robert of Inverness, "let's get these torches made."

Some of the old women glanced at each other.

"He likes the sound of his own voice, doesn't he," cackled one.

"And where's the food he promised us?" complained another.

"Fighting should be for the men folk," said another still, "and who's going to look after the cottage while I am doing their work here?"

"Now let's have less talking," ordered Robert, "and more torches made."

"What did he say?" asked a deaf one in a loud voice.

"He said he wants us to do less talking," wheezed an ancient crone, who smiled to reveal a single tooth in a sea of black gums.

"I wouldn't let my bairns talk to me like that, would you?"

"It might help if we knew what was going on. Ask him."

She pointed a gnarled, accusing finger at the Thane of Inverness.

"It would help if you told us what was going on."

"Malcolm the Younger has put me in charge, that is what is going on."

"Well, you cannot expect us to help you if we do not know what you want."

Her tone was that of a mother teaching a young child.

"That's right," agreed another old woman.

"What's that?" asked the deaf one.

"He cannot expect us to help him if we do not know what is going on."

"That's right," agreed another.

"That's right," agreed the deaf one.

Robert sensed the crowd turning against him.

"Our warriors will drive the enemy through the gates of Carn Liath. We are to beat drums and light torches, and appear as a great army in the darkness. We must make the Picts turn on the track, over there." He pointed down at the path, which came out of the fortress.

"What did he say?" asked the deaf one.

"He wants us to be a great army," replied the one-toothed crone.

"Who is he trying to fool?"

"Ask him why," demanded another.

"Why?"

"What do you mean, why? It is the wish of the king."

The one-toothed one turned to the others for support.

"I've never seen the king, have you?"

"No, I've not seen him."

"They say he's quite good looking."

"What's that?" asked the deaf one.

"They say the king is quite good looking."

"I've heard that his brother is the handsome one," added the deaf woman.

"Is he really?" swooned the one-toothed one, "is that Murdoch a bit of a looker then?"

The crowd cackled with laughter.

"We must appear as a great army," persisted Robert, exasperated, "and drive the enemy onto the path where Murdoch's warriors will be waiting."

The old crone with one tooth, hobbled over to him and poked him with a wagging, bony finger.

"Well, why didn't you say so?" she wheezed. "Come on ladies, let's make some smaller torches for the wee ones, they'll enjoy waving them about."

They shuffled past him to the great mounds of heather they had cut and dried that evening.

"Now don't get in the way, young man," shouted the deaf one.

Robert felt his authority slip through his fingers like sand.

***

Dougie stood with Hamish and Donald and the men of Tain on the battlements. They held the dead guards' spears and marched backwards and forwards, as the enemy had done. A Black Kilt on the far side waved at them and Donald waved back cheerfully. Most of the Scottish army were through the long tunnel and now stood, motionless, in a long line below them, their backs pushed against the inside of the wall and hidden in darkness.

Dougie glanced down into the oval and saw Alistair and a group of warriors creeping towards a single round-house, which stood alone at this end of the fortress. Their claymores flashed as they passed the fires that surrounded it. There were muffled cries as they entered. The Scots on top of the wall looked anxiously across at the stone keep, but the alarm was not raised. After a short while, Alistair and his men reappeared. One soldier wiped his claymore on his plaid.

All they had to do now was wait.

***

Borak stood on watch above the main gate. His brother seemed uneasy and he turned to him.

"What is it, Tumora?"

Tumora raised his spear and pointed across the narrow causeway towards the high slopes that ran down to it. To their right, ten large fires burnt, and there were many smaller fires scattered around the larger ones. Dark shapes were moving in the orange glow. Borak reassured him.

"They cannot take the fortress, and Tella will wait until they are hungry and attack again."

Tumora did not drop his spear and continued to point at one of the fires. In its flickering light he could see a group of people dancing. He thought they looked like children. Borak offered him a drink of water from his leather bottle.

"We are all a little jumpy tonight, just make sure you watch the causeway for that is where an attack will come, if it comes at all."

"It comes now," whispered Tumora.

The brothers peered down to see five Scots rushing the gate with bows and torches. Tumora threw his spear and one fell. The other Scots released their flaming arrows and they flew over the wall.

Malcolm the Younger watched his archers flee from a volley of spears that rained down onto the causeway. Their work was done and he glanced to his right. Murdoch lifted his shield and the king knew the men from the Outer Islands were ready. They lined both sides of the rocky valley and lay still, high above the narrow path, which meandered away from the fortress.

The Picts had to be driven *that* way and so all now depended on Robert deceiving Tella. If the enemy did take the path, his brother's fifty warriors, each armed with ten spears, would decimate them. They were spear fishermen and deadly accurate.

The king's horse snorted at the approach of a running man. Robert knelt before him, panting.

"Is it time?"

Malcolm shook his head and pointed at the main gate.

"When the Black Kilts are beyond the causeway. Wait for my signal."

The Thane of Inverness returned to lead his reluctant army.

"Prepare for battle," said Malcolm.

Thirty knights emerged from the gloom behind him. The riders urged their steeds forward and divided, so that half formed a line on one side of the Younger and half on the other side. Together they raised their claymores and, on the king's command, rode down the slope to join Robert.

They passed hundreds of old men and women who stood ready with unlit torches, in large groups, around the great fires that had burned throughout the night. As the High Table descended, the children pointed at them, at their horses and brightly painted shields, and Malcolm looked into the oval fortress.

Alistair's men were charging, like a swarm of bees, across the open spaces, setting fire to the round-houses, and two lines of warriors were fanning out around the tops of the walls. They were making steady progress, along both sides, towards the main gate.

Malcolm watched the battle for the far battlements. The young shepherd, to whom he had considered giving his brooch, was leading the charge with great courage. The king felt sad and scared, and knew that it was time to give the stone away.

At the first sight of the blazing arrows, a tremendous roar went up from the Scots inside the Dark Fortress. Alistair raised his claymore and led the charge forward. They passed the enemy campfires, stole torches, lit them, and threw them onto the thatched roofs of the round-houses.

The Picts awoke to utter confusion and grabbed whatever weapons they could lay their hands on.

The darkness before dawn became alive with shouting men, fire and the clash of iron upon iron.

One third of the oval was taken easily, but as they approached the stone keep a volley of arrows shot down from its battlements and many of the Scots, in the front line of the assault, fell.

Alistair saw the gate to the keep slam shut and yelled.

"Leave it. Go around and kill those outside."

The warriors divided in two and drove forward, in both directions around the base of the tower, into the main part of the Pictish army. When the roar went up from Alistair's men, a feeling of dread swept through Dougie's body.

"Here we go then," said Donald.

Hamish was already running along the top of the wall.

"Leave some for me," yelled Donald, and he chased after his friend.

Dougie raised his claymore and shield, bravely, and dashed forward to help them. A few paces ahead, Donald was fighting a huge Pict who swung his axe at the wee man's shoulder. Donald ducked and drove his claymore into the enemy's thigh. Dougie passed them as he caught up with Hamish. The big Scot lifted a screaming Black Kilt above his head and tossed him over the side into the depths of the dark ravine. Dougie was now leading the charge. Thirty paces ahead of him stood five grim warriors armed with axes.

"I am going to die," he thought helplessly, then yelled and waved his sword madly above his head.

The Picts turned and ran, and Dougie breathed a huge sigh of relief as a dozen Scottish warriors ran past him to chase the enemy towards the battlements above the main gate.

***

Tella and Gath stared in disbelief at the battle that raged below them. The Scots had taken the full length of the outer walls and the Picts army was in disarray. The main gates were open and hundreds of Black Kilts fled the fortress.

"We are safe here," said Gath.

His father slapped his face.

"This keep will become our prison if we stay." Tella snarled. "Go and prepare the horses."

The king of the Picts looked down helplessly at his army. The black mass was being herded like sheep towards the gate and across the causeway, which bridged the dark scar. A group of his men were trying to fight their way up the steps to re-take the walls, but were driven back down. One was lifted by a giant warrior and hurled like a stick onto the other soldiers who crowded around the exit.

On open ground they could slaughter these filthy Scots but, in the confined spaces of the fortress, there was little room to swing their battle axes.

Gath returned.

"Your horse is ready," he panted, and they descended the stairs to the courtyard where Tella's chieftains were already mounted.

***

"Can I light my torch now?" croaked the old crone with one tooth.

"Not until I give the command," Robert answered.

"What did he say?" asked the deaf one.

"He says we cannot light the torches."

"But we stayed up all night making them! I wish he would make his mind up."

In front of them, Malcolm the Younger looked across at the Black Kilts who streamed across the causeway. There were hundreds and they were quickly being reformed into fighting groups by their leaders. He glanced at Robert and nodded.

"Light the torches," ordered Robert.

"What did he say?" asked the deaf woman.

"He said light the torches."

"He isn't very decisive is he?"

Like the others, the woman knelt before the great fire and lit her torch. The side of the mountain glowed with a thousand fires and then the drums started.

Thud ….. Thud ….. Thud.

"Now children," instructed the crone, "don't forget what the nice man said. One *thud* and one pace down the hill."

Thud went the drums and Robert's army stepped forward.

The Picts stared up, in fear, at the fire on the mountain and the great army that had appeared from nowhere. The new regiments swayed in unison and slowly closed in on them. Tella's horse trampled through the Scottish line, mowing down anyone to reach the gate. His chieftains followed and galloped across the causeway, knocking many Picts off its edge to plummet to their doom.

Alistair saw them break through and urged his men forward, slashing out madly with his claymore at the line of warriors who stood before them. The Black Kilts saw their master desert the fortress and broke and ran for their lives. As the Picts fled through the inner courtyard, Hamish,

Donald and Dougie watched them from the top of the battlements.

"Is there no way to get at them from here?" asked Hamish.

"Only if we go a long way back along the wall and take the stairs," said Dougie.

"Then our battle is over."

Donald, sat with his legs dangling over the edge of the wall, watching the enemy dash from the inner gate to the outer one.

Hamish just growled at the Picts.

"I bet I killed more than you," jeered Donald.

Hamish picked him up, tucked him under his arm and leapt down into the horde of Black Kilts.

As Tella the Mac Mar called to his men to rally around his banner, Malcolm and the Knights of the High Table emerged like ghosts, silhouetted against a wall of fire. The Younger raised his claymore and his riders prepared to charge. Behind them, on the slopes of Carn Liath, a thousand torches burnt and a mighty army stepped closer to the beat of drums.

As the orange glow bathed the Dark Fortress, the eyes of the two kings met and Tella snarled.

The army of the Picts turned to flee along the path.

Malcolm didn't move a muscle. He didn't need to. He simply sat on his horse and waited for the screams of the enemy as they retreated down the valley.

"So, it is done," he said.

CHAPTER NINE

Alistair and Tella

Malcolm stared down the valley at the retreating Black Kilts and then across to the causeway and the high walls of the Dark Fortress. Many Scots lined the battlements. Some cheered and waved their claymores. Most stood in silence as they realised how lucky they were to have survived against a greater, more powerful, enemy.

The Younger nodded at his chieftains, the High Table, who remained like statues on their horses. The sun would rise soon and replace the red glow that bathed the slopes of Carn Liath. He glanced back and saw children dancing around the fires. The old folk sat in groups talking excitedly.

The Younger hated war and its result on his people. He knew this war was not his doing, that it was Tella's creation, and he also knew worse times lay ahead before the lines of Donald and Elder would be joined to give some hope of peace. Myroy had spoken of this future, but he had doubts about it. Malcolm was not aware of any surviving heir to the House of Donald. His father had often boasted how he had killed them all. He thought about his own son, Ranald. Could he be the one who would rule for the good? He loved him and yet, in his heart, he believed the prince would not be a king from his mould.

Ranald's ambition was as fierce as the Elder's.

The horse beside his snorted, disobediently stepped forward, and was pulled back into line. The Younger glanced again at the line of silent and respectful chieftains. The High Table had been created to give a voice to all the clans and yet not all the clans supported him. Some refused to send soldiers in times of need and Malcolm hoped this victory would help bring them together. He would need them, all of them, to defend the Outer Islands in the spring.

Within the darkness of the valley a wounded man cried out in pain. He moaned until life left him and then the quiet returned. The Younger's mind went back to his childhood, with Murdoch, and Arkinew's lessons. The alchemist had taught them both to fear Amera's stone for any warrior who held it would be invincible, but only if their heart contained anger and greed. It held no power for him. After the Charter of the Clans was sealed, to mark the beginning of the Long Peace, he had tried to destroy it. Nothing even put a scratch onto the surface of the ruby.

Myroy had kept the power of the stone a secret from Malcolm's father for he feared what the king might do with it. The Elder's tyranny was bad enough without the stone to extend his authority.

Malcolm remembered how his brother had been frightened at first by the Ancient One who appeared, like a spirit of the underworld, through the very floor of the palace. They had been knee high to him then and, even now, they felt like children whenever he chose to aid them. He had more knowledge than anyone.

Malcolm reached down and took the brooch from his robe and looked at the stone. Myroy had said that his own kind, the Ancient Ones, had been some of the first peoples to live in Caledonia.

The land was once covered by ice, which retreated as the sun's power grew. They had been so few, maybe as few as five hundred, and they had hunted and gathered across all that is now named Scotland. But out of the early peoples only four souls had lived beyond those times to become the advisors of kings.

Under Myroy's guidance, the Ancient Ones had learnt how to use the power that exists within the land itself. Malcolm remembered the story he and Murdoch held secret. Myroy's supporters had fought with Odin and Thor, who desired wealth and influence for themselves. Using the old magic, Odin created a stone of power to destroy his enemies but, after an age of battle, Myroy captured the ruby and killed Thor. The power of the land overcame the power of the sea. Myroy gifted the stone to Amera and it was buried with him. Gora, like many others, tried to steal it and now these poor souls were held prisoner within the ruby itself. Myroy guessed that one day it would be stolen from the cairn and so, after two thousand anxious years, he helped Dunnerold, a Celtic warlord, plunder Amera's tomb.

The stone was passed through marriage to the line of Donald. The Elder captured it in battle and now it lay in the Younger's hand.

Just as Gora had been a warning to Myroy to hold Amera's stone in a new place of safety, the end of the Long Peace was a warning that he could no longer trust its protection to a king. Amera's stone could only be held in the *keeping* by a quiet family, an ordinary family, a good family, out of the reach of those who were sure to seek it out.

The rim of a dawn sun burst above the foothills to the east.

"Count the fallen," ordered Malcolm and he urged his horse down the slope to claim the fortress of his greatest enemy.

***

"Bring them back," roared Tella the Mac Mar and his generals galloped off to rally the hundreds of Black Kilts who were running away in all directions.

The king glanced back down the valley. Spears, like hedgehog spines, stuck up along the path. It was strewn with bodies. On the ridges along the top of both sides of the valley were Murdoch's men and now he realised how few they really were. The new sun lit up the corpses and made the distant walls of the Dark Fortress orange. Tella's eyes searched the battlements.

"Borak, I need to know how many warriors I have to command." Borak bowed obediently and raced away.

"The men will not return to battle," warned Gath, and Tella rounded on his son.

"If any one else had said that, they would lie dead before me. Do you see Torik?"

Gath turned to look into the man's scarred face.

"Torik will kill any man, *any* man, who fails to do my bidding. Won't you Torik?"

Torik Benn smiled grimly.

Tumora sprinted down the valley towards the group of riders, who formed a circle around Tella's standard. In moments, he pushed his way past the horses and stood, breathless, before the king.

"Sire, when the Scots attacked we believed something was wrong. The army that stands upon the slopes, around the fires, is made up of no more than children and old folk."

"So, the Younger gambled and placed his true army within the fortress."

Tumora nodded.

"Bring my warriors to me. We go to take back Carn Liath."

As more of the king's guard rode off to rally the Black Kilts, Gath watched his father. He was staring at the far end of the valley, where the Scots were celebrating victory. His face became as hard as granite. The Mac Mar fingered his sword and swore.

"I will kill them. Kill them all!"

***

The surviving members of the men of Tain rested together and talked about the battle.

"If there are any spoils in the fortress then I should get more than *you*," boasted wee Donald, "I killed more Picts than *you*. All *you* did was pick them up and throw them about a bit."

Hamish's grimace was a picture, but it changed in an instant to a grin when he saw Donald's black eye.

"That's a real shiner," he growled, "and no more than you deserve."

Dougie sat down, exhausted, and began to daydream about his sheep.

"When do you think we might be able to go home?" he asked when Alistair came to sit with him.

"We have to wait for the Younger's command, and there are things we must do before leaving Carn Liath. Hamish, how many are we?"

"Seven unscathed, two with wounds that will heal and six lost."

"I am so relieved to see this day come," mumbled Dougie.

Alistair smiled at him.

"We all are," and he sensed a sombre mood amongst his followers. He winked at Hamish.

"Did Alistair not tell you, Dougie, that there will be work to do, to put right the wrongs of the Picts, before we may leave Carn Liath?" said Hamish.

"Aye, he did."

"And did I not tell you Donald and his good wife Senga do a lot of work together?"

"You did not." Dougie lifted his head to look at the others.

They were all grinning except Donald.

"Aye, laddie," continued Hamish, only the other day Donald was cleaning out his old barn, with Senga."

Donald was getting to his feet.

"Filthy, dirty and covered in cobwebs ……….. but she is good to the children!"

A great roar of laughter went up from the men of Tain as Donald jumped on Hamish.

Malcolm the Younger walked amongst his warriors and thanked them. When he heard the laughter he came over and saw Hamish and Donald rolling around on the grass.

"Your Majesty," said Alistair.

Hamish and Donald stopped fighting and went quickly to sit with their king.

"You led the charge within the fortress with great courage, Alistair."

"We both know it had to be done."

The Younger smiled and then his eyes turned on Dougie.

"I saw you lead the charge along the top of the wall."

"Hamish and Donald led the charge," muttered Dougie, "I was so scared that I just got carried along with the others."

"Dougie did as much as anyone," growled Hamish.

"And I killed more Picts than you," chirped Donald, "if Big Hamish was as good at fighting as eating and drinking then …."

Malcolm interrupted him by lifting an arm and smiling again.

"The rivalry between you two is known to me and I am grateful to all from Tain who carry the claymore. But, there is a service I need you to fulfill and it will not be a pleasant one."

Dougie looked crestfallen.

"Alistair, take your men down the valley and count the dead who lie there. We *must* know how many warriors Tella still commands."

"Aye, Your Majesty," said Alistair obediently and they rose.

"Let me know immediately if Murdoch has come to any harm."

Alistair bowed and led the men of Tain east.

***

"We were tricked into taking the valley path," snarled Tella the

Mac Mar. "Gath, take half of my force and drive along the top of the valley towards the fortress." The king pointed up at the ridge to his left. "Go that way."

"How many spearmen might we face?" asked Gath.

"There are no more than thirty Scots on each side of the valley. My guess is they have few weapons left. Ensure you make good speed and be ready to charge down upon the causeway when I arrive."

Gath raised his sword, kissed it and mounted his horse.

"Borak," commanded Tella, "gather the foot-soldiers and follow my riders. Kill anyone we miss and attack the causeway at the same moment as Gath."

Borak nodded and went to stand with Tumora.

"We are still more than the enemy," said Tella, "make sure your men know that. Tell them the Mac Mar is not defeated and will lead the horses back along the valley path. The Younger is a fool if he believes he can take our fortress from us."

"He has not been a fool so far," Borak thought and shuddered as he caught Torik's eyes.

When the generals rode away to divide the army into two, Tella turned to Torik Benn.

"You will stay with me. Kill those who threaten us."

Torik lifted his axe. It was stained with the blood of the Scots.

***

The memory of the fighting within the fortress was bad enough, but the path was truly awful. The dawn sun streamed down the valley and Dougie found himself walking between scores of dead Black Kilts. He hated being there and felt pity for those who had suffered during the retreat.

There were hundreds of bodies and the shepherd wondered how many children would be told they no longer had a father? The stench of death was wretched.

"Pile them here," suggested Alistair and Hamish dropped two Picts he held under his arms.

"I do not believe I have ever had to do such a bad thing."

Dougie knew exactly what Alistair meant. He tried to lift a large corpse and add it to the pile, which grew quickly with the labours of the men of Tain. The shepherd ended up dragging the man along the ground by his feet.

"Why not gather together the spears, young Dougie," said Alistair kindly.

***

Up on one ridge, the Protector of the Outer Islands watched the last of the enemy as they escaped from the valley. His keen eyes looked east towards the group of riders who formed a circle and he guessed that Tella had called his guard together to decide what to do next. They seemed to be breaking into two groups, mounted warriors, backed by Black Kilts, who remained on the path, and a larger army of foot-soldiers. This part of the Pictish army were marching up towards the ridge on the far side of the valley.

Murdoch went to stand with his spearmen.

"They are coming back," he said solemnly. "How many are we and how are we armed?"

"Here we are twenty and on the far ridge the same number," replied a fisherman, "and we have but one spear each on this side. All our people are poorly armed."

The Protector glanced back towards Carn Liath.

"Malcolm must be warned, Grant. Take the news to him now."

As Grant of Coll raced away, Murdoch turned to the others.

"We cannot fight so many here. We must have spears."

He looked again at the path that wound its way along the valley floor. A small band of Scottish warriors counted the fallen. One gathered spears.

"Tella leads his riders back along the path," warned an islander.

Murdoch knew his next move would decide the day and his men stood quietly as he thought things through. At last, he began to run towards the valley floor.

"Follow me to the path," he yelled, "we fight the Black Kilts there."

***

Suddenly, Alistair's face became grim and Donald shouted.

"Riders. Riders returning."

Dougie dropped an armful of spears. Hamish loomed over them.

"So the Picts want another fight do they?"

For the first time they all noticed Gath and the second army of Black Kilts, moving swiftly along the high ridge.

"They will not take long to reach the Younger," warned Donald.

"We should not be surprised," said Alistair, "Tella is a determined enemy and will not concede easily."

"Let them come," growled Hamish, "Tella started it and we will finish it."

Dougie thought about the children back at the fortress and Alistair watched his face change.

"Warn the Younger, Dougie. Tell him we are few, but will do all we can."

He pointed at a line of islanders descending the slope.

"It looks as though Murdoch is going to join us."

On the other side of the valley, more spearmen were coming to aid them. They shouted across at their master, the Protector, and some tumbled, headlong, as they hurried away from the advancing Picts.

Dougie began to run towards the fortress. Behind him a low rumble of hooves became louder. He guessed his friends would have little time to prepare for the attack and prayed they might be spared.

Tella led his horsemen on. He held his sword aloft and cried out.

"By nightfall we shall stand victorious within the Dark Fortress!"

As the king rallied his men, Torik Benn glanced up at the ridge. Gath was moving unhindered towards Carn Liath and would not be far behind them when they reached the causeway. Then he glanced ahead. Four hundred paces away the path was blocked by a wall of corpses. Behind the wall were Scots holding spears. But they held his attention for less than a second. Running towards the fortress was the man who had dared hold him prisoner. He grinned evilly, selfishly, and kicked his horse so it veered away from the others and skirted the wall of the dead.

"Stay with me, Torik," yelled Tella.

The bodyguard ignored him. He had unfinished business to attend to. His beautiful time had come.

Dougie ran as though his life depended on it and when the shouting started he did not turn. He knew Tella's riders had smashed into the men of Tain and that his duty was to warn the Younger about the danger which swarmed behind him.

The track twisted, and rose and fell. Many times he stumbled and picked himself up, ignoring the pain of each fall. Gradually the noise of battle lessened and, as it did, the sound of a rider grew louder. Dougie glanced back over his shoulder. Even from this distance he could see the warrior's scarred face. He would never forget Torik's hideous, determined smile for it said one thing.

"I *will* kill you."

Torik let out a whoop of pure pleasure and whirled his axe around his head. No one had ever escaped his vengeance and this would be a beautiful death.

Dougie gasped as the effort became too much for him. The track dipped down once more and he lost all sight of Carn Liath. Fear kept his legs moving, but as the path rose his head felt as though it would explode. In that moment the young Scot realised he would never make it. He was lost and when he heard Torik's whoop of joy, the sound ripped through his heart and he froze. Dougie stood like a statue and with a great act of will he finally turned, drew his claymore and gasped for air. He was no warrior, no assassin like this man, and sheer terror overcame him. His hands shook and his new blade shook too.

Torik Benn's horse thundered forward and fifty paces from Dougie it reared up on its hind legs and stopped in less than a stride. Dougie wondered what he was waiting for. Was he deciding on the worst way to kill him? But Torik's face had changed. He was snarling with rage.

The shepherd caught a sound behind him and spun around. He was no longer staring into the merciless face of his killer. He was looking at an army. Dougie fell to his knees and glanced up into the warm, determined eyes of a richly dressed rider with long grey hair.

And, on both sides of the Younger, the Knights of the High table raised their swords and began to charge.

***

Further along the valley, a volley of spears sliced into Tella's horsemen. Behind them, Borak urged his foot-soldiers to close the gap that had grown between them and Tella. Borak's Black Kilts charged towards the mound of corpses, which the Scots hid behind, and held their axes ready. At this pace they would join the fighting in minutes.

Gath looked down from the ridge and wondered if he should lead his men into the battle too. But his father had commanded him to be ready to drop down onto the causeway and that should remain his goal. He could clearly see the Scottish army swarm along the valley towards Tella.

"He is the Mac Mar," he said to himself, "and if he falls then I shall be king."

A Black Kilt ran to his side.

"Master, do we go to aid the others?"

Gath ignored him and continued to watch the fighting, which spilled out around both sides of the wall of corpses. Borak's warriors would soon join the fray and the Scottish army would meet them at about the same moment. He resisted the temptation to smile and thought about the times when his father had made him feel like a fool.

Tella brought his axe down onto the neck of an islander and the poor man screamed. The Men of Tain fought the riders with claymores when their spears were gone. Hamish plucked a Pict from his horse and Donald leapt on the man. Alistair and Murdoch stood back to back, fending off blows that came at them from all directions.

Suddenly, Alistair realised Tella was unguarded and scrambled over the pile of corpses, which had done so little to protect his men. Twenty paces away a horse writhed in pain and Alistair jumped down, dashed forward and pulled a spear from its flank. He threw it at the Mac Mar and the spear buried itself into Tella's shoulder.

"The king is hurt," yelled a rider and other riders came to escort their leader from the field. The others retreated back to the safety of Borak's warriors and the army of the Picts stopped two hundred paces short of Murdoch and the men of Tain.

Tella had never experienced such pain. One side of his body was numb. The other was pure agony. With every step the horse made, the spear jerked up and down and brought a new wave of torture. He passed out and Tumora caught him as he fell.

"Retreat to the ridge," ordered Borak.

His brother yanked the spear from the king's shoulder, and threw it aside. Then Tumora lifted Tella onto a horse and climbed up behind him.

"Why do we leave?" he shouted.

"We are stronger together," yelled Borak and the army climbed the slope to ally with Gath's men.

The Younger watched them go and held back his own forces.

"Shall we follow?" asked Grant of Coll.

Malcolm shook his head and looked into the eyes of the fisherman who had warned him of Tella's intentions.

"We still have too much to lose if we leave the children to the Black Kilts' mercy. Order everyone to the top of the other ridge."

The Scots moved up and away from their enemy.

As a full golden sun rose above the foothills of Carn Liath, two desperate armies faced each other across the valley. Tumora and Borak waited for their king to be tended and brought back to lead them. Gath wondered if he was dead. Secretly, he hoped he was. Malcolm and Murdoch stood in the centre of the Scottish army, which ran along the whole length of the opposite ridge. Some of the men of Tain waited patiently too and Dougie felt comforted to be with them once more.

"I wish they would get on with it," muttered Hamish.

Dougie smiled nervously and looked at Alistair, who was watching the Younger. The king walked forward and called across the valley. Amongst the line of Picts, two warriors stepped forward to hear his words.

"Hear me," shouted the Younger, "you still have two choices, just as we do."

He pulled a thistle from the earth, held it aloft and Borak nodded at him.

Gath glanced back. The Mac Mar remained still and silent as strips of cloth were pressed onto his shoulder to stop the bleeding. His skin was deathly white.

Dougie peered at the two Black Kilts. They were talking, perhaps agreeing what to do next, now their king's ambition no longer drove them on. He wished more than anything it would all end.

Silently, the Pictish army turned and disappeared behind the far ridge.

"So, it is done," said Malcolm again, but this time he was right.

"It is a trick," warned Hamish.

"You cannot trust a Pict," said Donald.

"My dear friends," said Alistair, "it is no trick, just the end of a truly awful day." To himself he said, "And the fulfilling of a promise."

Alistair had been a boy when, in the dead of night, he had heard his father talking with another man, at the far end of the Great Hall. He had thrown his bed clothes aside and crept in darkness towards the balcony that overlooked them, and listened to their conversation.

"You must do *everything* you can to protect the Charter of the Clans, Gregor," said the stranger.

"There are many who will stand against us," replied the Thane of the Black Isle.

"There are many more who will prosper and see its wisdom."

"But Myroy, the wound of the Elder is deep."

His piercing blue eyes flashed up at his son's hiding place.

"I say again, do all you can to aid the Younger. We have much to prepare for the peace will not last forever."

Myroy looked up at Alistair too.

"And you have a part to play, Alistair of the Thane's line," he continued.

Alistair went cold.

"You must protect the shepherd."

The Ancient One waved his staff at him.

A long sword, with a dull, grey blade, appeared by the boy's side and, with trembling fingers, he tried to lift it.

"Keep it safe," ordered Myroy, "and, before the battle on the mountain, place it into the hands of the shepherd with the plain shield."

Alistair found himself nodding and not understanding.

"Will you do this for me?"

"I will," replied the boy, and when he glanced back at his father he saw the stranger's head disappearing down through the floor.

"Do not fail me, Alistair," came a distant voice.

Even now he could recall every word.

"Do not fail me," mumbled Alistair.

"What are you mumbling about?" asked Donald.

Alistair of Cadbol smiled and turned to face the shepherd he had sworn to protect.

"I am so glad it's over."

"So am I," agreed Dougie, "can we go home now?"

CHAPTER TEN

A Last Gasp

As he realised that the Black Kilts had really left the field of battle, utter relief swept through Dougie. He swayed and Alistair caught his arm.

He was worn out, empty and ached all over. Dougie's heart reached out for his family. He wondered how Mairi and the children were and what he should and should not say about his time away from them. He looked down at the wall of death and the blood-soaked valley. This was no place, or life, for him and he longed to leave Carn Liath forever.

Head down, Dougie walked with Alistair and they retraced their steps along the valley path.

"Forget it, Dougie," said Alistair kindly.

"I will never forget this place."

"Given time, you may be able to."

"But it haunts me."

They crossed the causeway and entered the Dark Fortress.

"It will haunt all of us."

"So many souls lost."

"So much more would have been lost if we had not stood together."

"But why did it happen?"

The courtyard, between the outer and inner gates, contained a huge mound of bodies and men were busy carrying them out and dumping them into the depths of the dark scar.

"Anger and greed," replied Alistair and, in silence, they helped the others with their grisly task.

Later, Malcolm called his clansmen together.

"The fortress has been searched and any beasts the Picts once held have been slaughtered," he told them.

The crowd gave a low murmur.

"And there is no sign of our coins."

His warriors gave a louder murmur.

"But the enemy is truly defeated. Our lands are safe once more."

There was a great cheer.

Dougie waited for Wee Portalla to say, "Hear, hear," and then realised that he wouldn't be saying anything ever again. The king went amongst the leaders of the clans and thanked them. There were few spoils of war to share, but weapons and horses were divided equally to provide some reward. When he reached Dougie and Alistair he paused.

"Without you none of this would have been possible," he said and knelt before them.

"Alistair, a safe journey to you and your men back to Tain."

He handed Alistair his own sword.

Alistair bowed. "Thank you, Your Majesty, I shall treasure it always."

Donald nudged Hamish.

"We do all the work and he gets the sword."

Alistair gave Donald a disapproving look, but Malcolm smiled at them.

"You have *all* played your part and I thank you."

Donald and Hamish grinned back at their king and Alistair spoke for them.

"We are always at your service, Your Majesty."

"And I may be asking for that service sooner than you think, Alistair, for the field is won here, but Murdoch has told me a darker threat to our lands is rising in the west."

"I don't like the sound of that," moaned Donald.

"Neither do I," said Hamish.

Exactly the same words went through Dougie's mind.

Alistair lifted the Younger's sword and clasped it to his chest.

"The Long Peace is over and my father told me that one day it would be so. I sense Carn Liath is the first step in a very long journey."

Malcolm nodded and then beckoned his most reluctant warrior to his side.

"Dougie of Dunfermline, come forward," he commanded.

Dougie shuffled nervously towards his king.

"And how might I thank you?" he asked.

"I would like to go home," said Dougie simply.

"Perhaps there will be more to your life than tending the land," said the Younger in a soft voice.

Dougie raised his eyebrows as if to say, "But I like farming."

"This is poor reward for your bravery," added Malcolm, as he unclasped a brooch from his robes.

"This was left to me by my father and I have always prized it most highly for there is *nothing* like it in this world."

The Younger gave him his brooch and Dougie noticed that the king's hand was shaking. Dougie looked down. The gold brooch contained a single ruby at its heart.

"Do you recognise it, laddie?" asked Malcolm.

"Aye," replied the shepherd truthfully, "I saw it upon your chest the first evening I arrived at the palace."

Malcolm stared at him as if thinking carefully about what to say.

"Is that all, young Dougie?"

"I do not know what to say, Your Majesty," admitted Dougie.

"At moments like this, none of us do," said the king and without another word he mounted his horse and rode away, with Prince Ranald and his guards, to the east.

As Malcolm left he felt a strong craving to return and reclaim Amera's stone, but fought against it, praying he had chosen wisely. The future of his people would depend on it.

***

Alistair and the men of Tain were preparing to leave.

"Will I see you again?" asked Dougie.

"Aye, you will laddie," replied Alistair, "let's make a promise to meet once a year on the anniversary of the battle."

"Aye, gladly."

They shook hands on it, not knowing that greater events would upset their plans.

The hours after a battle are strange ones for those who have been a part of it. The Scots felt an unsettling mix of emotions; joy at beating a fierce enemy and protecting their lands, and intense sadness as the last of the fallen were gathered together in a great pyre and burnt, so their spirits might rest in peace for all time.

For Dougie though, the relief he had first experienced subsided and was replaced by tiredness, and an intense desire to see his children again.

"I'll wager we end up fighting the Picts again," growled Hamish. Dougie wondered if Tella would recover from his wounds and seek revenge. Donald wrinkled his nose and ran a finger across his throat.

***

Gradually, the different clans grouped together to begin the long journey home. There were many farewells, more promises to meet again, and Alistair asked Dougie if he would like to walk with them as far as Dalwhinnie.

"Aye, I would very much," said Dougie gratefully, and they set off down narrow paths through the barren foothills of Carn Liath.

Dougie kept glancing back over his shoulder. Something nagged at his senses and he felt uneasy, and comforted himself by listening to the men of Tain as they talked about how to divide the rewards they had been given.

"We could do with a new still for the heather ale," suggested Hamish.

"We could barter it and improve our ships," said a fisherman.

"I could give mine to Mairi," added Dougie.

The others gave him a long, horrified and disapproving look.

On the outskirts of Dalwhinnie, the friends shook hands and left each other. Dougie knew he would really miss their company, particularly Alistair's, so he thought about his farm and all the work that would need to be done to prepare for the long winter months. An hour later, and several miles further south, Dougie stopped to take a drink. He put his sword and battered shield down by a stream, and realised the king's brooch was not on his plaid. The shepherd felt as though he had lost an arm, or a leg, or a loved one.

Dougie cursed his luck and dropped to his knees to hunt for Amera's stone, and wondered what Mairi would say if she found out he had lost something of such great value. Her voice pounded through his mind.

"You lost the king's brooch? Oh Dougie, how could you? You went all that way and return as poor as the day you left us!"

After minutes of desperate searching, Dougie glanced up at the hills around him. They were silent, strong and majestic, and the sense of panic gradually faded. "Well, it is a warm enough day," he thought, "and the sunlight will last until I get back to Dalwhinnie."

He decided to retrace his steps until he found where he had dropped it.

But Dougie was not to get that far. He was staring intently at the earth, searching for his brooch, and not looking where he was going. He rounded a bend and walked straight into the Pict with the long white scar. Torik Benn's fist smashed into Dougie's face and he was thrown, sprawling, backwards onto the heather. The Pict raised an axe and Dougie raised his shield. The mighty weapon struck the dent in the wood and the terrible force split the old shield in two. The light iron cut into the side of Dougie's outstretched arm and Dougie squealed like a wounded pig.

Torik liked that noise.

Dougie rolled to one side and lifted his claymore, but Torik was too fast, too experienced. The axe came down squarely onto the blade and broke it. The warrior glowered at Dougie, who stood trembling and unarmed before him.

"My beautiful time has come," snarled Torik.

He threw his axe to the floor.

"I *will* kill you and with my bare hands!"

Dougie was no match for the strong Pict and blows from the killer's hard fists just kept coming.

Dougie's head swam and he began to lose consciousness. But he felt the pain. Sharp pain. Blood poured out of his nose and into his mouth.

Then Torik Benn was on him, pinning the shepherd's shoulders to the ground and squeezing his hands around his throat.

Dougie reached down for his dirk and his life passed before him as he realised he had never taken it back from Angus outside the king's tent. He looked up helplessly into the man's evil eyes and then beyond him.

The shepherd dreamed that a man with a black eye was winking at him. As a grey mist enclosed his world, Dougie's fading mind remembered a growling voice from the past say, "A real shiner."

"I *will* kill you," promised Torik.

"But … I am not … ready … to die yet!"

"I WILL KILL YOU!" screamed Torik.

"I do … not … think so."

"How so?"

His face was so close that Dougie smelled Torik's foul breath and with his last gasp spluttered, "Because of my friend, Donald."

The blade of a claymore buried itself deep into the centre of the Pict's back. Dougie rolled out from under the dead man, panting for breath, stumbling, and, when his eyes began to focus again, he saw his wee friend wiping his sword on the grass.

"Am I glad to see you," he choked.

"I came back to give you this," said Donald.

He tossed Dougie the gold brooch and it bounced off the shepherd's shaking fingers.

"You are mighty careless with the gifts of kings. First you leave it behind and then you throw it away."

Dougie picked up the Younger's brooch and stroked Amera's stone, and relief, like that of a parent finding a lost child, swept through his bones. Then he picked up Torik's axe and shuddered.

They parted company at nightfall and, for Dougie, the final leg of the journey was a lonely one, full of dark memories that he tried to fight away by thinking about the men of Tain. Alistair had promised that in time he would forget about the horrors of battle. He prayed he was right.

Here the land was greener, gentler, with many fine streams to rest beside and the weather was warm and pleasant for the walk home. Dougie began to recognise the profile of the hills and he stopped to smell the heather. It was rich, sweet and full.

He looked around and on a far slope, beside a standing stone, rested the cloaked stranger who was both known and a mystery to him. The *watcher* waved and, even from this distance, Dougie could make out that behind his white beard he was smiling. Or was the old man simply relieved to see Dougie returning home safely?

The shepherd waved back and smiled too.

At last he reached the small stand of old pines, which marked the edge of his land. He lifted Torik Benn's axe and stared at it. The blade was stronger and lighter than any weapon he had ever held. It reminded him of everything he wanted to forget and, with all his strength, he threw it away. With a sickening *thud* it buried itself into one of the pines.

He climbed over a stile into the fields, where he had played with his brother Alec, and followed the grassy track towards the farm he had known since childhood. At the top of a small hill he stopped to tighten the cloth Donald had tied around his cut arm. It was caked in dried blood. He tried to breathe in through his nose and couldn't. His nose was full of dried blood too.

He gazed down towards the cottage. Tanny, his golden-haired daughter, was playing with the chickens, and Calum and Jock were fighting over a leather bucket. Mairi was hanging some washing on the line and shouted at the boys.

"Stop bloomin' arguing all the time."

"So that's where they get it from," thought Dougie.

He grinned and walked down the hill.

"I'm home," he said.

✳✳✳

"Dougie loved his home, didn't he?" whispered Peter, and the old man nodded at him.

"Whatever," groaned James, and Peter frowned.

"I bet Dougie was relieved when Donald turned up," added James.

"I was too," replied the old man in a dark voice.

"Cool. It would make a great game on my X Box. We could have loads of Picts attacking a palace and then be Dougie and Alistair in a cool, hand to hand combat with Torik Benn and all the other bad dudes."

The storyteller raised an eyebrow and Peter shook his head.

"More broth, boys?" asked the stranger, and he whispered the words so as not to wake Laura.

She lay with her head on Peter's chest and he held her still, with his arm around her shoulder. They had sat together like that for some time, since they had heard about the terrible fate of the Scottish prisoners at Carn Liath, and then she had finally given in to sleep. Peter's arm was going numb.

The storyteller stood and very carefully covered little Laura in a tartan blanket. Then he picked her up and placed her on the bed. There was a gentleness and a strength in the way he did it and Peter wondered at his age.

"That was a good story," smirked James, "much better than the boring bits with Dougie on his farm."

"You have a strange way of paying someone a compliment," scolded Peter, and James just ignored him.

"Did Dougie have other adventures?" asked Peter at last.

"He did," said the old man.

"This sucks. Peter, go and check on the snow and let's see if we can get home."

"You check," snapped Peter, in as loud a voice as he dared.

"Who do you think you are, the King of Scotland?"

James went over to the door anyway and tried to open it. A blizzard thundered through the crack and flames danced erratically in the fire. He came back, sat down and wiped snow from his face.

"I guess we've got time for one more story then."

Laura stirred, and Peter went over to check on her.

"In the story," whispered Peter, and the old man glanced at him encouragingly, "you mentioned the Long Peace that followed the death of the Elder."

Their host nodded and smiled.

"The Elder was one of James' really *bad dudes*," he mimicked and they both smiled back at him.

"As bad as Tella the Mar *McThingy*?" asked James.

"There are few of the old stories that have survived, but his reign *was* cruel and when the Younger succeeded his father, there were many who had cause to celebrate it."

James started to feel tired as well and yawned.

"I suppose the next bit is about how the Younger became king," he mumbled.

"It is," confirmed the old man.

"And is it short?"

"Quite short."

"And has it got poor old Dougie in it?"

"It has."

"He gets about a bit, doesn't he?"

The old man grimaced and Peter quickly changed the subject.

"It really was a long time ago, wasn't it?"

"That depends how you see it."

"And how does it start?"

James yawned again, suddenly overcome by the quiet and warmth of the cottage. Peter sat upright, eager and ready to learn, and he thought about the land around the village and Dougie's descriptions of it. The storyteller watched him knowingly.

"The key to this story is Amera's stone, in fact it has been the key to many things, even war, devastating wars, and the cause of much fear and misery."

"Amera's stone?" asked James sleepily, "is that one of the standing stones we saw today?"

"No," replied Peter, "it is the ruby that Dougie had to give away, if he was to become a Keeper of the Stone and release Gora."

Then he felt foolish for he did not know why he said it. The lines around the stranger's eyes wrinkled as he smiled.

"I am glad one of you has been paying attention."

James pulled a face and poked his brother in the ribs.

"And Arkinew, I mean Archie, had great power?" added Peter.

"In his youth, the apprentice was one of the few who have an understanding of what is to be."

"And yet he lost his power."

A sad look flashed across the storyteller's face and he bent to stroke Dog.

"Listen carefully to my words, for rarely do I speak about the time before the Long Peace."

CHAPTER ELEVEN

The Rise and Fall of Elder Autumn 627 AD

Malcolm the Elder, one of the most evil men in Scotland, looked down on the battlefield and smiled. Rain bounced off the bodies that, in places, lay three deep. His warriors hunted amongst the dying and, despite the cries for mercy, drove their claymores into helpless enemy flesh. Crows gathered for a rare and easy feast.

"To me," shouted Malcolm.

His men came to gather around him. The anxious stallion on which he sat moved back at their approach and the warlord, who would be king, pulled hard on the reins. He demanded the same loyal obedience from his horse as he did from those who chose to serve him. Those who did not choose to serve him would be killed, or driven from the land. Malcolm spoke slowly and clearly.

"We have won a great victory that will be remembered in song for all the years."

His men raised sword and shield and cheered.

"Douglas of the House of Donald has fled to the fort at Dunfermline. Wealth and power to the man who brings me his head!"

The army cheered again. He slowly raised a finger and gestured towards a distant hill. The King's Seat had been the home of his sworn enemy, the Donalds, for centuries.

"Half a day's march to the fort and the crown of the Celtic people will be mine."

A strange figure emerged behind Malcolm. The tall man was clearly feared for, as he strode into the crowd, a way was quickly made for him and low whispers went from one anxious face to another. But it was not the dark cloak, long beard and staff that made them bow their heads. It was a memory of the tales of the alchemist who walked backwards and who was the source of Malcolm's great power. He *knew* of things before they happened and no enemy, no matter how strong, could face the Elder's warriors if armed with such knowledge.

Malcolm dismounted and walked a short way with the alchemist. If any of the silent soldiers had dared to look up they would have seen them nodding, exchanging a scroll and signing it. The bond between the Elder and Arkinew was now complete. By the time the king returned to his men, Arkinew had vanished.

"We are indeed fortunate. The fort is poorly defended and Douglas, his two sons and the last of the heirs to the throne, lie at our mercy."

The soldiers raised their heads and gave a roar, which rang out across the battlefield. Somehow, he always knew when the time was right to attack.

Malcolm's fastest riders stormed over the brow of Kings Seat and charged down the slope towards the fort, their hooves thundering. Women and children abandoned their sheep and cattle, and ran for their lives. Armed men appeared on the walls, but the horsemen did not attack. They seemed content to wait, circling the fort, increasing their distance as arrows were let fly at them.

"Save your arrows," commanded a man who stood above the gates.

Douglas wore the ancient Celtic crown of the Scottish kings and on his breast was a fine brooch, of gold and precious stone. It shone out, red and yellow, in the fading light. His face was grave and he turned to talk with his most trusted companion. Myroy knew he had few words of comfort to offer.

"Malcolm seems to know my every turn and weakness," said Douglas.

"It is Arkinew who knows, Your Majesty. He has the Oracle, the eyes of the Ancient Ones, and is under oath to use it for good, or for ill. He is bonded to the Elder."

"But how can I fight them?" asked the king, his face broken by deep, sad, worried lines.

"Half of your clan have fallen on the battlefield. Half are away to the north. I do not believe you can fight them. Not in this life anyway," replied Myroy.

Douglas's heart sank.

"I must leave you now to do what I can for the future. We will meet again in a better place and a happier time, old friend."

Douglas watched Myroy descend the narrow stairs, cross the grass and enter the central stone keep. He turned away and, through the sharp spikes on the wall, saw more enemy riders arrive. They now formed a complete ring around the fort. Douglas sat down to wait for the Elder and the foot-soldiers who would surely follow him.

"So the rat is in the trap."

The walls of the old fort were made of thick stone and wooden stakes. Together they were the height of only two men and Douglas knew they could not hold back the army that now swarmed towards him. Only thirty of his warriors remained and they carried weapons and rocks to the top of the wall. His sons, Stuart and David, joined him and he hugged them.

"I beg you, take horses and flee."

Stuart, his father's first born, tried to reassure him with a smile.

"The Elder will kill us here, or hunt us down later. We have as much chance either way."

David nodded and drew his claymore.

"If we are to leave this world then I would choose to leave it with my family."

"I am proud of your strength," replied Douglas, "but it gives me no comfort to have to share this moment with the ones I love."

He turned to Stuart.

"Should you not be comforting Rhona and the wee ones?"

Stuart found Rhona talking anxiously to her maid servant, Lissy. Myroy had joined them and seemed to be urging them to take some kind of action. An action they feared, or dreaded.

"It is the only way, Rhona," the Ancient One said sternly.

"My place is with my husband."

Then Rhona saw Stuart and ran, and threw her arms around him.

"Then stay, but let me take the twins, they are the very future of the House of Donald."

Myroy pointed at a cot where two contented babies slept soundly, without a care in the world.

The shouts of war and the clash of iron upon iron came loudly through the thin, deep window of the top room of the keep. Myroy spoke to Stuart.

"I offer hope for your children and one other, or no hope at all."

Rhona, weeping, kissed her husband and, in a single defiant act, threw back her long golden hair.

"I stay to carry the spear. I stay to stand by my husband."

Stuart felt useless. He could not make this awful decision. Rhona turned to face her loyal servant.

"Lissy, I have trusted everything to you and now I trust you with Alexander and Douglas, my own flesh and blood."

The cot stood upon the very ancient King's Stone, the symbol of the authority of the Scottish kings, and she went over to it and knelt. With much love and tenderness she kissed each of her boys in turn then she picked up the reed basket and handed her children to Lissy. The maid took them and began to sob.

"I now release you from my charge, Lissy, and place you in the service of Myroy. Do as he wishes and keep my children safe."

The old woman wiped her tears away and smiled bravely at the twins' innocent faces. Myroy turned to Rhona and Stuart.

"Go now, for time is not our ally."

Lissy's heart sank as their fading footsteps were overcome by the noise of desperate fighting. She clutched the basket as though it contained all the precious things of the world and looked at Myroy. He was moving his staff in a circle on the stone floor and muttering to himself. Then he put his arm through hers and forced her forward.

"In front of you are steps leading to another place."

As he spoke he tightened his grip so they were almost as one person. Lissy could only see hard floor and shot Myroy an anxious glance.

"The first step is here," he said.

Perhaps it was the confidence in his voice, or the desire of her heart to protect the children, that made her lower one foot into the stone. It disappeared and she nearly fell forward in surprise, but Myroy held her.

"And another."

She found the second step and, with increasing speed, their bodies sank through the floor into darkness.

"Where are we?" asked Lissy in a fearful voice, and one of the twins began to cry. "Hush now, my wee one," she whispered.

"We are safe for the present," replied Myroy in a reassuring voice, but he held her as tightly as he had when going down the steps. "The boys shall be raised on a farm and know nothing of their past, or destiny. There will be enemies who seek them out and our best defence against them is the children's ignorance of all that has been."

"I am not sure I can do it."

"You must." Then more softly he added, "and I will be there to watch over you."

It was like standing in the deepest of caves, without light, or warmth, and the only comfort came from the words sometimes spoken. Lissy shivered and felt cold. Myroy felt her body shake.

"Have courage Lissy. We do not have long to wait before we return to the world."

"Return to the world," she thought, "what world are we in?"

At last Myroy led her forward.

"In front of you are more steps, going upwards this time."

Lissy felt cautiously for the first step. They rose slowly back through the floor and she blinked in brilliant sunshine. As her eyes adjusted to the light, Lissy realised that they were back in the top chamber of the tower. It had never looked so well lit and she glanced up. The roof wasn't there any more and a summer sun shone down on them. The edges of the wooden beams were black and charred by fire and the King's Stone was gone.

"Whatever you see now *must* be forgotten and certainly never spoken of to Alexander and Douglas," commanded Myroy.

Lissy nodded obediently and wondered what he meant. They made their way down the stone staircase, to the great oak door of the keep, stepping around the faded blood stains that showed where the fallen had met their end so long ago. The signs of decay and destruction were all around them. The door was broken and overgrown and held to its frame by one remaining hinge.

In many places the walls had been burnt and torn down.

Even now, the abandoned tower had an atmosphere of death. Lissy felt sick. Myroy hurried her across the inner green to the gate in the outer wall. Like the door to the keep, it hung at a sad angle and creaked mournfully in the gentle, warm breeze. They were twenty paces outside the old fort and Myroy's eyes darted to catch any sign of the enemy, but this place had been left for thirty summers to fall into ruin and no living person could be seen in any direction.

Something compelled Lissy to look back.

"Don't," said Myroy in a sad voice.

But Lissy felt as though she had to look and, stubbornly, stopped in her tracks. She placed the reed basket upon the ground and one of the twins began to stir. Lissy turned and stared back.

In dreams, that turn would haunt her forever.

Driven onto the wooden stakes above the gate, as a warning to anyone who might dare to defy the new king, were four severed and grotesque heads. Even after decay and the attention of the crows, Lissy knew that two generations of the House of Donald, the kings descended from Dunnerold, had been lost forever. She fell to her knees and prayed for the souls of Douglas, Stuart, Rhona and David. And then she prayed for courage to face whatever lay ahead.

***

The King's Chamber was the finest room in the palace. It was richly decorated and carried the spoils of war. One wall alone had taken the most skilled craftsmen of the kingdom three summers of painstaking work to complete and now it told in bright colours the story of the rise of the House of Elder. The pillars of the great oak bed were carved with the animals of the forest, and gold and lace showed the magnificence of royal power. It also spoke clearly of the heavy taxes so cruelly levied upon the Scottish people.

Servants who were new to their duties would gasp as they entered the chamber for the first time and be in awe at its beauty. But none dared to linger. Every one of them lived in fear of their lord and master. However, time changes everything and in dark corners hopeful voices might be heard.

Malcolm the Elder looked at a picture of himself, sitting on a white steed, young and handsome and ambitious. He closed his eyes as if the act of remembering the past involved all his strength.

Someone moved a chair and, disturbed by the noise, he raised his hand. It was thin, wrinkled and gnarled with age. The Elder knew he did not have long to suffer in this world and his hand dropped as if it held a great weight.

His sons, Malcolm and Murdoch, knew they would always be a disappointing legacy for a man who had hoped to establish a line in his own image. Neither of them were strong, cunning and ruthless like him. He had enjoyed the power his position gave him over others and no-one questioned that the House of Elder would continue to be shaped by the will of its creator. But now the rule of the land would pass by the will of Tanis (the council of clan leaders) to Malcolm the Younger.

Father and son looked across the room and their eyes met. Neither held a grain of love, nor respect, for each other. The king wondered what he had done to deserve an heir who was so weak in his kindness for others. The Younger wondered why he had never had the love of a father.

Arkinew saw the gaze between them and moved backwards from the door to the bed. He knelt beside the king and, as if deciding that now was the right time, passed a scroll over his shoulder to his master. The old man stared at the scroll as if it held a terrible message and finally nodded at his loyal servant.

The scroll contained just two signatures. It represented a promise between ruler and servant, and bound Arkinew to do whatever the Elder commanded. But unthinking loyalty had a price.

The destruction of the parchment would mean the death of the monarch.

As told by the old laws, the bond blessed the alchemist with an ability to see further into the future. Once the promise was broken, this power would fade and become unclear. His mind would wither and he would become little more than a fool.

Arkinew reached back and took it, and remembered the terrible things he had done in the name of the Elder. The king shut his eyes as if the breaking of the bond between them had drained away all of his remaining energy. The chamber fell silent again as each of the witnesses sat respectfully for the passing.

Malcolm put his hand onto his brother's. Murdoch gave him a reassuring glance.

"I have never had a brother who was king," he whispered, and they smiled nervously at each other.

The door opened and a warrior dressed in the king's tartan beckoned Arkinew. The alchemist's eyes never left the face of the Elder as he went outside and, after a brief moment, he came back in to ask Malcolm and Murdoch to join them.

The princes shivered in the cold air of the passage and realised just how warm the chamber had been.

"News has reached us that the followers of the House of Donald have raised an army and are three days' march from the palace," said Arkinew.

"Your first test, Malcolm," added Murdoch gravely.

"The Elder still lives. He is still the king," continued Arkinew, "and his will would be to destroy them completely."

"That is the king's will, but not mine," said Malcolm and he looked at the alchemist as if seeking his help to shape the future.

They stared at each other for some time and at last Arkinew nodded at the two young men.

"Let it be so," he agreed.

Deliberately, the alchemist took the scroll from his cloak and held it in front of them. A blue flame engulfed the paper and burning fragments fell to the floor.

The heirs of Elder watched as each of the fragments gave off an orange glow, faded and turned to dust. A cold wind swept down the corridor and lifted the ashes. Like a dark shadow, the spirit of the Elder was carried past them and out of a window.

Arkinew smiled at his new masters.

"The time is now yours," he said importantly, "use it wisely."

A great commotion could be heard behind the thick oak door and Malcolm put his hand onto his brother's shoulder. They stood very still as the old man walked away, backwards.

"Long live the Younger. Long live the king," shouted Arkinew.

A servant burst from the royal chamber to give them the news they already knew.

***

Without the guard and in great haste, the two brothers rode out to meet the clans of the Donalds. When they reached the top of a low rise, they saw them below in a long, writhing formation, an army of some three hundred men. Most were on foot and all followed a small group of riders who carried the standards of each of the families who shared one purpose, the creation of a new order and the death of the Elders.

"This is madness," whispered Murdoch.

"Aye, it is," said Malcolm.

They rode slowly down to meet the enemy. The column stopped in its tracks, and shields were raised. Forty paces from the leading riders, Malcolm pulled back on the reins.

"Malcolm the Elder is no more," he called, "and we seek your help and friendship."

All eyes were on the two men and many glanced to the top of the rise behind them to see if they were supported by the warriors of their greatest foe. No-one seemed willing to speak and a tense silence fell upon the field.

"We come alone to show our intentions are not evil," continued Malcolm. "Who speaks for the clans of Donald?"

Out of the corner of his eye, Murdoch saw a small group of soldiers make their bows ready.

"We beg you not to take revenge for the past, for all the peoples of Scotland, and to join with us to make a new beginning."

"What new beginning can there be, between the Donalds and the followers of Elder, when you wear the crown of the Scottish Kings?"

It was Gregor, Thane of the Black Isle and leader of the men of Tain. Despite his years the bearded man sat tall in the saddle and his piercing blue eyes looked deep into the Younger's.

"That crown belongs on the head of a Donald."

"Let us take the crown for our own," shouted one of the warriors behind Gregor.

"Aye, it is here to take if you want it," called back Malcolm bravely, "but which of you will wear it?"

The crowd murmured at these words, for there was no appointed heir to the Donald line, only stories that one day a great king would come from the past to lead their people.

"I offer you a new beginning," insisted Malcolm, "without the cruelty of my father and with the leaders of all the clans at my table."

"A new beginning," promised Murdoch.

"Kill them. They are of Elder and not to be trusted," came a voice.

"So you kill us. Two who come alone in friendship. Then you will have to face all those who will surely seek revenge. Along that path is only war and hardship," shouted Murdoch.

Many of the warriors seemed unmoved by these words. They had suffered long and had clear memories of the wrongs done to them. A bow was lifted. Gregor, in a sharp, commanding voice, called for it to be lowered. The Thane dismounted, and from the ranks of the soldiers an old man in a dark cloak, who had remained unnoticed, joined him. A murmur ran through the men and a name was whispered in awe.

"Myroy."

Malcolm and Murdoch dismounted too and walked forward to meet them.

And so, the first Charter of the Clans was sealed. Myroy spoke of the great dangers facing the kingdom and the need for unity and just rule.

"We cannot stand alone," he said, "even now we have less than a lifetime of summers to create a High Table that can defend us from the foes of mountain, island and castle. After them are even more terrible enemies who will seek to impose their will upon us."

"And how do you know this?" asked Gregor.

"My apprentice, Arkinew, has the eye of the Ancient Ones and there are other ways of gaining an understanding of what is to be. We have no choice but to bring the clans together under Malcolm, for we are a long way from the union of the royal houses, which will surely be." Murdoch looked at Malcolm, who was thinking that every time you spoke with an Ancient One it left you with more questions than answers.

But a new beginning *was* agreed and, for a precious time, peace and prosperity were to be enjoyed by the Celtic peoples of Scotland.

CHAPTER TWELVE

Keeper of the Stone

Peter wondered at the cruelty of the Elder's reign and how all knowledge of the stone was kept from him. The storyteller rose and spoke again.

"These are the stories of the time after that beginning."

Peter sat, spellbound, in the silence of the warm cottage and guessed Dougie was one of the twins who had been rescued from the tower, but decided not to say anything. He didn't know why he should remain silent and Myroy returned his gaze and, if his eyes could speak, then they would have said, "Yes, Peter, you are of Dougie's royal line."

"Did Dougie become a Stone Keeper?" he asked at last, and smiled hopefully at his host.

"He became the first Keeper."

"And you said the Celtic peoples faced a terrible threat from the foes of Mountain *and Island and Castle*, and even greater enemies after them. Did he have other adventures?"

"He did indeed, but you must wait for another time to hear about Thorgood Firebrand and Dougie's voyage to the Outer Islands."

Laura stretched on the bed, her arms and legs reaching out to welcome the world.

"I must have dozed off," she said sleepily.

Peter pointed at James who was snoring.

"You're not the only one."

"The snow has stopped now," said the old man without even checking.

They glanced out of the window to see water dripping down the pane. It was as though someone was emptying a bucket on it.

The fire was spent and a single flame struggled to rise from the ashes. Dog rose too and stretched out like Laura. He looked up at Peter as if to say, "Is it supper time yet?" Then he barked, to make sure they all got the message. James sat up, startled.

"Did Dougie get gotted by that Torik dude?"

"Get gotted?" mused the old man.

"Whatever," mumbled James, "I could eat a giant boar."

"Thank you for sheltering us," said Peter politely, "and for the stories."

They shook hands. The moment their hands touched, a bolt of energy surged through Peter's body. It was pure and intense. Powerful, painless and crammed with sweet emotion, like opening your Christmas presents, like his first kiss with Kylie, like everything good that had ever happened to him. Myroy released his grip and Peter let out a long breath, and refilled his lungs with air. He felt as though he could live forever.

"It must be time to go bloomin' home," exclaimed Laura, and Dog leapt up from the hearth and ran about like a mad thing.

Peter bent down to tickle the sheepdog's ear.

"You're right, time for one of Grandma's special suppers."

The storyteller watched them, like a teacher preparing for his next lesson.

"Well, hurry along then," and he lifted his staff and pointed it at the door.

"Yeah, thanks for the *tall* tales," said James, "they were, er, unforgettable."

He ran out into the melting snow with Dog, Laura followed them and for a moment Peter was left alone with the old man.

"It's all true, isn't it," said Peter.

"Who is to say it is and who is to say it is not?"

Peter nodded and turned to go. Then he stopped and glanced back at his host. He was drawing a circle on the stone floor with his staff.

"Will I see you again, Myroy?" asked Peter.

"I hope so."

The Ancient One smiled, approvingly, at the heir to the line of Donald, and disappeared down through the floor. Peter ran to catch up with the others and, as he stepped onto the drover's lane, his mobile bleeped.

It was Kylie.

OK, OK, OK, I get the message – U must B the fastest texter in the world - I miss U 2!!!!!!

Peter smiled. The children rounded a bend in the lane and the sun came out, and warmed them. Within a few strides any evidence of the terrible snowfall was gone. It was going to be a beautiful evening.

"What a bloomin' place," said Laura, "one moment we're sheltering from a storm, and the next we could be in our swimming stuff."

"Whatever," mumbled James, "I bet Grandma and Grandpa are worried out of their minds."

Dog bolted off and they ran after him. In minutes they entered the village and stood in front of the old house.

"Well, I'll be a shepherd on a thistle," teased James, "we spent all that time listening to the old wrinkly and we were just around the corner."

Peter didn't rise to the bait. He didn't need to. There was an important question burning inside him and he grinned at his brother.

"I wonder what Grandpa will say?"

In the Donalds' kitchen, Laura told Grandma about their adventure.

"You wouldn't believe it, one minute sun, the next a blizzard!"

"And what did you do, my chicken?"

"Well, it was Dog really, he kind of led us to this ancient cottage, down the lane, and this ancient man gave us soup and told us some stories. I think he did it to stop James from going on about his X Box."

Grandma seemed thoroughly unconcerned and continued to peel the potatoes.

"That's nice," she said.

"But didn't you miss us?" asked Peter.

Grandma raised an eyebrow.

"You took a picnic to the waterfall and we didn't expect you back until about now anyway."

The children looked at the old clock on the windowsill. Quarter past five. Peter glanced at his watch. It read the same.

"Now then, it sounds as though you have had a nice time, so go and get yourselves washed for supper," ordered Grandma, "Grandpa will be back shortly."

***

"Why can't I get these bloomin' clothes back in this stupid case?" complained Laura. "Petee, can you give me a hand?"

Peter groaned, raised his eyebrows to the ceiling and left James, who was having the same trouble as his sister.

"I haven't had the chance to buy any new clothes, so I don't see why they won't go in."

"Perhaps your case has shrunk in the snow," yelled James from the other room.

"Perhaps it's because you haven't folded anything," said Peter sensibly, and he pulled out the things Laura had stuffed into the case, and started again.

"I didn't really want to come," admitted Laura, "but I've had a great time."

"So have I," agreed Peter, "come on, let's go and say goodbye to Grandma. You know she won't come with us to the airport."

"Get ready for the big squeeze," warned James and his brother smiled.

Laura had already been hugged and kissed, and made to promise to come back to Glenbowmond in the summer holidays. Grandma advanced on James and he stuck his tongue out as though he was having the life squashed out of him.

"Thanks, Grandma," squealed James and he winked at Peter.

Peter placed his arms, gently, around the small, silver-haired woman.

"Aye, thanks for *everything*," he whispered.

Grandma wiped a tear from her cheek and beamed at them.

"Now you make sure you call me when you get home, otherwise I shall just worry."

James was about to say that she didn't seem very worried when they were stuck in the blizzard, but Peter gave him a look and he decided to keep quiet. Grandpa gave him the same look and picked up their cases.

"Keep a hold on Dog, Ma," he ordered, and they hurried from the kitchen as the sheepdog howled mournfully.

"Can we get a dog, Petee?" asked Laura.

"I thought you wanted a horse," teased James.

"I want a dog as well. Can we Petee?"

"The kittens wouldn't like it. Besides, dogs need the fields to explore."

Suddenly he felt as though he did too.

"Get in," ordered Grandpa, as he slammed the hatch of the Volvo down. "Your flight's in two hours, so we had better get going."

After four attempts the car spluttered into life and they drove down the hill away from the village. In front of them the grey loch rippled and raindrops began to fall on the windscreen.

"I think you're going at the right time," said Grandpa, "the farming forecast is poor for the next week or so."

James mimicked his polite brother, "That probably means it will be *simply glorious*."

"Four seasons in one bloomin' day, that's twenty eight a week," said Laura, and everyone laughed.

"Have you all had a good time?" asked Grandpa, as they crossed the Forth.

It was beginning to get dark and a low moon shone through the stanchions of the great bridge. It was full, silver and bright, a Gora moon, and Grandpa knew what that meant.

"Excellent," replied Peter.

Grandpa glanced in the mirror and smiled as he saw Laura nodding, and James rocking his flat hand as if to say, "Alright, well as good as it could be with nothing to do."

They drove into the short-stay car park at Edinburgh airport and James moaned as he and Laura were sent off to fetch a trolley. Grandpa opened the boot and slowly unloaded its contents. He struggled to lift the largest bag and, in that moment, Peter thought he looked very old. They stood together and listened to James and Laura, on the far side of the car park, arguing about which trolley to take.

"Grandpa," said Peter, plucking up the courage to ask his question, "may I see it before I go?"

The old man glanced at him and smiled. It was as though they were both part of a story of great importance. It bound them together and their eyes locked.

"See it? I thought you were here to collect it!"

He put his hand into his breast pocket and pulled something out. It glittered yellow and red.

Peter took the brooch with Amera's stone at its heart. He now knew that his task was to keep it hidden, like so many of his line had done through history.

"How does it feel to be a Stone Keeper?" asked Grandpa solemnly.

"It scares me to death," admitted Peter.

"It has scared all of us. You will be *alone*. Being a Keeper can be a lonely existence even though you have family around you."
Grandpa's face became a ball of wrinkles as he stared up at Gora's moon.

"I do not think I will see you again. Not in this life anyway," he whispered.

Peter hardly caught the words, but his heart felt them.

"It's very powerful isn't it," he said quickly to change he subject.

"You don't know the half of it, laddie."

"Why have we kept it hidden for so long?"

"Thousands died taking the stone from its creators. We cannot let that happen again."

"But what is the ruby's secret?"

"Myroy will tell you when he is ready."

The old man pulled out a carrier bag from the boot. The bag contained a box of cheap jewellery.

"Put it in here for now and, if security ask you about the brooch, just say it is a present from Grandma to your mother."

Peter wrapped the box up in the plastic bag and stuffed it into a corner of his case.

"Trust you to choose a wobbly bloomin' one," cried a voice, and James came rushing towards them with a trolley. It tacked like a sailing boat, from side to side, and veered at the last minute into the wing of Grandpa's car.

"You wally," yelled Laura.

"Oops," said James, and he grinned.

Grandpa grinned too and led them into the Departures Hall.

CHAPTER THIRTEEN

Revision Blues

"Get lost, James," shouted Laura and Peter put his revision down.

It was four weeks to his exams and he had already forgotten yesterday's revision topic - glacial features. The diagram in front of him was labelled with corries, hanging valleys, eskers and drumlins. He ran his finger along the contours of a sketch map, but it wasn't sinking in and Peter felt desperate. These exams were the most important he would ever sit and time was running out. The revision planner on the wall listed all his subjects. It haunted him. The different coloured lines showed what should have been covered so far and just how far he was behind schedule. Peter felt sick with worry.

Destiny's Child blared out and Laura and Abby started to sing at the top of their voices.

Peter stared down hopelessly at the text books and files on his bedroom floor, then got up and marched to Laura's room. With the door open, the noise rose to a crescendo and he had to shout to make himself heard.

"Laura, I'm trying to revise."

"Put some bloomin' earphones on," yelled back Laura, "you're not the only one who lives here you know."

"I can't revise with *all* this noise."

"And me and Abby are dancing at Guides tonight. You're not the only one trying to learn something."

Peter turned the CD player down.

"Thank you," he said and shot the girls a menacing look.

Sitting back on his bed he pulled out some notes about volcanoes. His mobile vibrated and chimed out the theme tune to the Simpsons. He glanced at the incoming number and groaned.

"That's all I need."

"Hi, Calum."

"Hi, Peter, how's the revision going?"

"Not good. How about you?"

He already knew the answer.

"All done bar the shouting and I'm bored. Fancy a trip to the movies?"

"No chance, I've got geography to finish and then physics and then maths and then …"

"All work and no play …"

"Makes Peter a dull boy, I know."

"Well I'll ask Chris then and maybe even Kylie if she's free." Peter growled.

"She's revising too."

"Who knows? She might like a bit of a break."

"And I might just break your arms."

"Anyway, I can't spend all day talking to you, Mum is making me pay for my own phone cards."

"Thanks for nothing," replied Peter and Calum hung up.

Peter thought about Kylie, then snapped out of it, concentrating hard on a list of key words, and tested himself on their meanings. He got eleven out of twenty.

James started to play his drums. The walls shook and Peter watched his alarm clock jolt up and down with each beat. The clock staggered to the edge of the bedside table and fell off. Peter gave up and went to get a drink. He switched on the kettle and it filled the kitchen with a complaining *hisssss*.

"Nobody ever fills this thing up," he moaned and carried it over to the sink.

The lid didn't seem to want to come off and he tugged so hard that it flew through the air, and hit the fridge door. He twisted the cold tap angrily and water bounced off the element with a tremendous force, and sprayed him.

Laura and Abby danced in.

"Are you making us a drink too, Petee?"

Laura laughed and pointed a finger at her brother's soaked trousers.

"Look. He's bloomin' well wet himself."

Peter put the empty kettle down in the sink and began to cry.

***

The engines roared and the plane shot forward. Peter stared out of the thick window and watched the tarmac shoot by. He felt himself being forced back into his seat and grabbed the armrests and tightened his seatbelt. A metallic voice told him that the flight to Edinburgh would take only sixty minutes. That was too long as far as Peter was concerned. More than anything, he wanted to be with Grandpa and Grandma again and enjoy some peace, some space to study.

The huge case that his father had lent him had been hurriedly stuffed with clothes and files and text books. Now he pictured the hills around Glenbowmond and thought about Myroy, and the brooch in an old jewellery box at the bottom of the case.

Dad had talked to him about his revised revision plan on the way to Luton airport.

"With some peace and quiet, you'll be amazed at how much you can cover. Grandma is happy to have you for as long as you want to stay. She said it seems like ages since they saw you last."

"It's only three weeks," said Peter.

"But a lot can happen in three weeks. An awful lot."

"And the forecast is good, even for Scotland."

"And there is no better place to be when the sun is shining."

Peter nodded. "And I'd love to hear another story."

Colin Donald glanced across at his son.

"Don't be too disappointed if you don't hear any more. When I was young I had to wait years to see Myroy for the second telling."

"Does it matter that James and Laura aren't coming?" asked Peter.

"You are the Keeper of the Stone, not them. Even I never got that privilege."

The metallic voice jolted Peter out of his thoughts.

"Ten minutes to landing."

A fat lady, who sprawled next to him, stirred. The flight was packed and he had helped her descend, with some difficulty, into her seat. Peter found himself squashed up against the window. Then she had fallen asleep with a copy of *Woman's Own* on her lap. She snored and smelled of talcum powder.

A smiling stewardess hurried along the aisle with a black bin liner and Peter handed her an empty Coke can. The fat lady woke and started to flick through her magazine. She reached an article titled *Our top twenty calorie busting recipes* as they touched down in Edinburgh.

"Have a good flight, laddie?" asked Duncan Donald.

"Yes thanks," said Peter and they shook hands.

"Brought everything you need for your studies?"

"Aye."

"Everything?"

"Aye, *everything*."

Grandpa winked at him knowingly. He seemed to have aged ten years since Peter had last seen him. Duncan was still a huge man, but now he stooped and walked more slowly. He wore the same kilt and a fisherman's jumper with leather patches on the elbows.

"Grandma is really looking forward to seeing you."

"And I am really looking forward to some peace and quiet."

"Aye, your Dad told me your studies are not going too well."

"That's an understatement," laughed Peter and, with the case manhandled onto a trolley, they set off for the car park.

As they stepped out of the terminal building a flash of lightning welcomed Peter to Scotland and, by the time they reached the old Volvo, a downpour soaked them. The windscreen wipers laboured slowly, and seemed to leave as much water behind as they wiped away. It was like sitting inside a drum.

"The forecast was good," said Peter, ruefully.

"Och, what do they know? Black clouds have been coming in across the loch since lunchtime."

"Is it still as beautiful?"

"Aye, laddie it is."

Grandpa grumbled as he searched for some change for the crossing. Peter gave him the money and they joined a short line of cars.

Eighty pence flashed a sign beside the toll.

"Robbery, absolute robbery," muttered Grandpa.

A uniformed lady held a ready, cupped hand out of her window as Duncan crunched the car into first gear. They inched forward and Robbie Williams blared out from a radio inside the small booth. Grandpa handed over the money.

"Daylight robbery," he moaned, "I don't want to buy the bridge, just cross it."

The lady looked at him and then at the four twenty pence pieces, and shrugged her shoulders.

They skirted the loch, which seemed grey and lifeless, and then the Volvo turned sharply and chugged up a steep lane, lined on both sides with high stone walls. In minutes they were in the village of Glenbowmond and Peter felt as though he had come home.

Grandma threw her arms around him and Peter stared down at her grey hair. It was tied into a neat bun and, as she kissed him, he looked down into the prettiest of faces. She still smelled of apples.

"Thank you for having me," he gasped with the air left in his chest.

"Good to see you, Peter. My, I swear you have grown since I saw you at Easter."

"It's all the food I've not been eating."

"You'll be hungry then," she beamed.

"Aye, I could eat a giant boar."

They all laughed, Grandpa opened the kitchen door and Dog gave an almighty *woof*, and leapt up at Peter.

"Hello, boy."

He tickled the sheepdog's ear.

A huge bowl of lamb and barley broth was placed in front of him and Grandma buttered thick slices of freshly baked bread. The fire crackled and they talked about the family and life in the big city.

"You wouldnae catch me driving doon there," exclaimed Grandpa, "but they tell me it is a fine place to visit, if you like that sort of thing."

Grandma nodded.

"Mrs Simpson goes to London every year to do her Christmas shopping."

"Does she now?" asked Grandpa in a slightly disapproving tone.

"There are good shops right enough," added Peter.

"Lots of shops, people, cars and everything done in a rush."

"Now don't you go getting onto that old hobbyhorse," scolded Grandma, "everything has its place."

"Aye, and mine is here."

"No, your place is at the sink, for the dishes will not do themselves."

Duncan Donald groaned, but obediently collected up the bowls and dishes. Grandma grinned at Peter as her husband tried to pull on a pair of yellow rubber gloves.

"Why don't you go for a walk," suggested Grandma, "the weather is clearing a wee bit now."

The sheepdog cocked his head at Peter and then ran around in excited circles.

With a coat, a drink and a geography text book in his rucksack, Peter set off along the old drovers' road. Dog ran ahead excitedly and sniffed the hedgerow. It was pungent after the rain. Gorse and dwarf birch gave way to stone walls and they rounded a familiar bend, and the white cottages of the village were lost from view. It had turned out to be a beautiful day and the sun, despite being low in its arc, warmed them.

Peter thought back to his last visit and half expected it to change, in a second, to a snow storm. He didn't walk, he marched quickly, and Dog sensed his master's eagerness and barked as if to say there was no time to lose.

There was no gate into what once might have been a garden. It was terribly overgrown and the shepherd's cottage was a ruin. It had no roof and only four crumbling walls gave any sort of clue about its important past. Peter and Dog fought through tangled brambles and tall nettles, and eventually made their way inside.

Remembering what his father had said about not being too impatient to see Myroy for the second telling, Peter sighed and sat down on a stone block that had probably been a part of Dougie's chimney. Dog collapsed, panting in a shady spot, and Peter opened a battered flask, drank some blackcurrant juice, and settled down to read his geography textbook. Everything was so peaceful and he lost any sense of time as he concentrated on one page, and then another. The sheepdog snoozed and birds sang out to each other. Then the birds stopped singing.

Dog's ears pricked up and he sat bolt upright. Peter continued to read, lost in a world of lava, magma and ash cones. A cloud moved swiftly across the sun and it went dark. Peter glanced up from his book and wondered if he had been studying so hard that he hadn't noticed the coming of nightfall. The stone, on which he sat, started to vibrate and Peter stood up. It moved across the floor. The other stones started to move too and Dog came to stand beside him for comfort.

It was as though an army of invisible hands were rebuilding the cottage. Stone grated upon stone and wood creaked, like the timbers of a ship adjusting to each new wave. In seconds the walls were higher than Peter and then a roof covered them.

Logs burst into flames in the great chimney and its firelight danced around a room as welcoming and simply furnished as before. Peter sat on a low bench by the hearth and knew there would be broth in the cauldron. He put his book down and tickled Dog's ear. The floor shimmered and the head of an old man appeared. It rose slowly, through the stones, and then the cloaked figure of Myroy was with him. The ancient adviser of kings smiled and sat by the fire, and picked up Peter's book.

"A test of knowledge?" he asked.

"Exams in two weeks, and I am running out of time."

"Running out of time?"

"I've looked at it for hours and I still don't get it."

"Then look at it again, if you seek knowledge, Peter of the line of Donald."

Myroy passed him the text book and, as he took it, the Ancient One touched his shoulder.

"Tell me what you know."

He knew every word.

"So if time is no longer running away from you, perhaps we can talk about the important things."

Myroy took the book back and flicked through the pages. He stopped at a map of the Lake District.

"A fine example of radial drainage," said Peter, and then he wondered where his words had come from.

If you had asked him, what was on line twenty on page a hundred, he could have told you. But it wasn't just the sentences and words, he *understood*. The land was a jigsaw puzzle of every force that had ever acted on it and Peter knew how the pieces of the jigsaw fitted together.

Myroy nodded.

"Maps have come on a long way since the old times and perhaps it has been forgotten how powerful they are."

"Powerful?" asked Peter, surprised by his choice of word.

"The Black Kilts, who survived the battle of Carn Liath, fled across the water to the lonely island of Skye where they rebuilt an ancient fortress, the hill-fort at Deros. Tella the Mac Mar was mighty bitter at his defeat and would indeed seek revenge on Malcolm. He knew of the power of the map and planned to use it for his own advantage. It was his scribe, Denbara, who was given the task of mapping Scotland and his work changed so much."

"Can I hear about Denbara?" asked Peter.

Myroy sighed.

"Just like your Grandfather."

"Grandpa?"

"Always wanting to jump ahead. His impatience nearly lost us everything."

"He nearly lost the stone?"

"He did."

Peter took the brooch from his pocket and said, solemnly, "I want to be a good Stone Keeper."

"You are destined to be the greatest of all of them, but at a terrible price."

Peter wondered what he meant but before he could ask, a parchment appeared in the old man's hand.

"This is Denbara's map. Make a copy."

Peter made a rough copy at the back of his geography textbook and the parchment vanished.

"Now that's done, I can tell you more about the Stone's history. Not long after Amera's death, Gora tried to steal the stone. Hundreds of years later it cried out and Odin heard it, and the race to Amera's cairn began. Odin is the one to fear for he is utterly ruthless, without any compassion. He would give anything to hold the stone in his hand. I knew then it must not be *hidden*. Cairns could be plundered, but kings might hold it in *keeping*, if I was there to keep an eye on them. Then the Long Peace ended and I needed a different kind of keeper."

"Dougie," said Peter.

"This knowledge is only for a Stone Keeper. You know how the Long Peace ended and how it began. Now you must learn about the power of the stone."

"Dougie's second challenge. On the Outer Islands?"

"No. This story was a long time before that. It was when the ice retreated from the land."

A log shifted, cracked and orange sparks shot up the chimney. Dog's legs began to twitch, in a cosy dream about rabbits, as he slept at the old man's feet.

Peter took a deep breath and prepared himself for his next adventure in words.

CHAPTER FOURTEEN

The Power of the Stone
5587 BC

One family, in three canoes, braved the cold of the sea.

Myroy glanced back at his Grandfather. Speer smiled at him and lowered his paddle into the water, and pulled. They lurched forward and widened their lead on the other canoes.

"Still strong," said Speer.

"Still strong. Still ahead," laughed Myroy and they both knew that his brothers, Thor and Odin, would hate them for it.

Bright sunshine and tingly cold air raised their spirits. Every summer they made this long journey to the west, to find rich hunting grounds untroubled by other families, other hunters. Speer had told them that it was his father's father who first ventured to the lands of ice. But instead of barren lands, he had found thaw, meadow and game. For a brief time, whilst the sun was high, it was a paradise.

Myroy looked at the other canoes. In one, his mother, Frey, was breastfeeding Tirani and Thor was rowing. Blessed with physical strength, Thor was like a bull and could beat anyone he was pointed at, and it was, more often than not, Odin who did the pointing. Odin was his master.

Thor's great arms drove down, as though they wanted to punish the waves, and water splashed into his canoe. Speer lowered his own paddle and made a long, elegant, pull and, again, the gap between them grew.

"Thor rows like he eats," mumbled Speer.

In contrast to Thor, Odin could think, work things out, and everyone accepted that, one day, he would lead the family. He would love that position. Myroy shuddered at the thought of Speer's will being replaced by Odin's and not because of any jealousy he held in his own heart. Myroy knew Odin would lead for only one reason, his own advantage. He cared little for anyone else.

Myroy remembered the terrible moment, last summer, when his father had been taken from them, killed by Ghadu, the giant bear. He had been sixteen summers old then, old enough, you would think, to stand with the others and fight off the beast, which mauled at his father's body. But even with Speer, Thor and Odin at his side, they were completely powerless to stop the terrible creature. They had shouted, screamed in anger, and stabbed out with their spears. The beast ignored them and delivered a death blow to Loki.

Myroy would never forget his father's limp body being lifted up, between sharp teeth, and carried away. They all knew he would be eaten. That was the way of things and, after the grieving, they had continued their own search for food.

The canoe tilted and a loud grating noise came up through the skins.

"Use eyes," yelled Speer, as he steered carefully around the ice.

Hundreds of white icebergs dotted the way west. Some were as tall as hills. Some, the dangerous ones, were hardly visible above the waves. A bad hit on one of those could tear the canoe and result in disaster.

"Sorry," gasped Myroy and he turned to face forward.

Odin sat alone, his long blond hair lifting slightly as he pulled, rhythmically, on his paddle. He had steered the best course through the ice, and was now ahead of them. He guided his canoe, which contained the family's food and tent, into the mouth of a great river. Thor continued to splash behind them.

Myroy held his arm out to the right as an instruction for Speer to turn that way and follow Odin. Odin glanced back at Myroy and their eyes met. In that moment, Myroy knew exactly what Odin was thinking. Knew it from the merest glint in his hard, blue eyes.

"Watch me, younger brother. You might be clever, but you are no match for me. Watch me lead, brother. You are going to have to get used to it."

On land, Myroy and Thor tied poles together and threw skins over them. Speer made fire. Tirani cried out and Frey cuddled him, and kissed his nose. Odin took a spear and kept watch at the top of a rise.

The canoes were pulled further away from the riverbank and everything seemed much like it had done the year before. Except Loki was no longer with them. Myroy counted the fish they had caught, checked the strips of meat and flasks of water. The meat was rancid and stank, and he quickly tossed the strips into the river. If anything was going to warn the great bear of their arrival it was that. Ghadu could smell rotting flesh from miles away.

Myroy refilled the flasks from the river and called back. "Two days' food."

Speer nodded.

"We hunt at dawn."

"Hunt now," grunted Thor.

"Rest now," smiled Frey. "With rest, we hunt better."

"You rest."

Thor grabbed his spear, and began to walk up the slope towards Odin.

"Stay together," ordered Speer, "we are stronger together."

"You stay here. Old ones should protect baby. Leave hunt to men."

"And if Ghadu comes, who will help you?" said Myroy.

Thor stopped in his tracks and glanced up at Odin who smiled.

"Hunt tomorrow."

He wasn't ready to take over from Speer just yet. He would be patient. Something was bound to happen.

This was a good time. Some days Myroy helped his mother collect berries and roots, and these were his happiest days. Other days, when Speer needed him to flush out game, he hunted and wondered when Odin would challenge Speer. But the challenge never came and even Thor became less aggressive as his belly swelled.

Ghadu had not been seen. However, the night-fire was always tended and they all took turns to add huge pieces of driftwood, which they collected from the bank. In the dark hours, Speer talked about their ancestors and how they had struggled to survive when the land was covered in ice. They had prayed for sun and the sun had slowly grown stronger, and all creatures had become plentiful. In the firelight, Frey showed them the plants she had gathered during the day and, like she so often did, made two piles.

"These are good."

She tossed them examples. Thor ate his.

"These are bad."

These plants she held up as a warning.

"Thor can eat anything," said Myroy and his mother shot him a stern look.

Like Speer's lessons, like the two piles of plants, like Myroy's teasing of his brother's mighty appetite, it was a look they had all seen many times before. Even Odin loved her. A thin smile formed on Odin's face and disappeared quickly, as if he saw it as a sign of weakness, and he changed the subject.

"Deer tracks, half a day away. Tracks like this."

He held out a hand with his fingers fully outstretched, placed his fingers on the ground and drew around them with a stone knife. Speer raised an eyebrow.

"Raku, big deer?"

Thor licked his lips and thought about Raku's sweet flesh.

"How many?" asked Myroy.

"Six, maybe seven. A large family."

"Raku liked by Ghadu. Any sign?" asked Speer.

"No sign."

"We go now," urged Thor.

Speer sighed and Odin smiled again.

"Go with light," suggested Odin and instantly Thor nodded.

"Long way away," warned Frey.

"Myroy stay here and help Frey," suggested Odin.

"Tend baby," grunted Thor and he roared with laughter.

Tirani stirred in his furs and Frey rose to check on him.

"Together we are stronger," said Myroy.

"One Raku is three days' food. More danger from hunting three days, not one," argued Odin.

Thor licked his lips.

"Taste good."

"We go in morning," agreed Speer.

"Together we are stronger," repeated Myroy, but the others ignored him.

***

Speer, Odin and Thor lay face down in long grass, and watched the Raku graze. Even the smallest deer were taller than a man and a single, great stag was more than twice that height. Speer's experienced eyes darted around, searching for any sign of giant bears, but he saw none and they gradually relaxed into a slow crawl forward.

Speer touched Odin's shoulder and waved a hand at a small wood, of birch and willow, some five hundred paces ahead, and beyond the deer. Then he touched Thor's shoulder and pointed at a clump of gorse beside the wood. Silently, Odin and Thor crawled backwards and began the long journey around the Raku. When they arrived, Speer would stand and cry out, and the deer would run straight towards them. It was a routine they had practiced a thousand times.

The stag lifted his head and sniffed the air. Speer held his breath. Had he sensed them? Had he sensed something else? He glanced around anxiously. But they were alone and he studied the stag as if his life depended on it. The beast's nose was far better than his and if Ghadu was about then the beast would know first. The Raku began to graze again and Speer breathed out.

All three hunters knew they must act quickly. The wind was changing, beginning to blow from the wood towards Speer's place of hiding, and the Raku would flee at the merest trace of man. As Odin peeked out of the birch, Speer jumped up and cried out. He waved his spear in the sky, threw a stone at the nearest deer and the herd bolted away.

Speer danced delightedly as Thor's spear struck a young Raku and brought it down. Then he became aware of a low, deep growling noise behind him. It was the most terrifying thing he had ever heard.

***

"Where is Speer?" asked Frey and then, without an answer, she burst out crying. The baby, Tirani, began to cry too.

"Ghadu take him," said Odin.

"Ghadu tear Speer in two," grunted Thor.

Frey wailed. Myroy's head dropped as the old, hidden, image of his father's ripped body came back to fill his mind. Anger welled up inside him.

"And you did not help."

"Too far away," grunted Thor.

He lifted half a Raku carcass off his shoulders, and tossed it onto the ground.

"We would help if near," added Odin, "let us feast tonight and remember him."

"You feast," said Myroy, "I will always remember Speer."

"We will all feast," commanded Odin in an angry voice, "you will feast with us. I now lead."

"Speer good leader, you are unproven."

"We are all unproven."

Myroy got up as if to strike Odin and Thor hit him in the face.

"Odin leads now," he said.

***

162

Two moons later, Myroy looked up at the sky and gave his mother a warning.

"The sky is darkening."

Frey continued to breastfeed Tirani.

"Cold air now," she agreed.

"Must leave soon, before storms come."

He rose, and walked over to his brothers who sat huddling together by the fire.

"Must leave soon," suggested Myroy.

When Odin replied, there was a hard edge to his words.

"We go when I say we go."

"Canoes cannot survive storms," argued Myroy.

"Canoes cannot survive storms," agreed Odin.

"I take Frey and Tirani. You follow."

"Together we are stronger."

"Not stronger than ice."

Thor glared at Myroy and made his fist into a ball.

"Together we are stronger," repeated Odin. "Tomorrow we go to caves."

"What caves?" asked Myroy.

"Thor found them. Deep and warm. One day away. We live in caves."

"Caves, deep and warm," repeated Thor proudly, "I found them."

"This is madness."

"Not madness. All these lands are now mine."

"*Mine*?" asked Myroy. "We are family."

"We are family and I lead family."

"Let me take Frey and Tirani home," pleaded Myroy.

"No. You help carry food and water, tomorrow when sun rises."

"When sun rises," repeated Thor.

"How will you feel, Thor, if Frey dies from cold?"

"Caves warm," grunted Thor. "Many Raku too."

The light faded as a great black cloud drifted above them. A deep rumble came from its belly and Tirani began to cry. A snowflake floated down from the heavens and landed on Myroy's nose.

***

Thor's snoring woke Tirani and he burbled and cooed, and fingered the edge of his fur wrap. He spoke his first word.

"Mumma."

He liked that and so he said it again. Then he said it softly and then he decided to shout it out, smiling at the thought of how clever he was.

Now everyone was awake and Frey rocked Tirani in her arms, cooed back at him, told him how clever he was and kissed his nose. Odin lifted the skin flap of their tent. Everything was white. Even the air was white, as millions of snowflakes swirled to earth.

"Pack everything," ordered Odin. "But not canoes."

"This is madness," warned Myroy.

"Trust Odin," said Frey kindly, "he leads us now."

"But where does he lead us?" thought Myroy, as he tied three water flasks to his waist.

Thor swung the great bundle of furs and poles, that was their tent, up and over his shoulders, and to show off his strength to his brothers he bent his knees and stood up again, with a small jump.

"Still strong."

"Still very strong," laughed Odin.

Thor liked the compliment and did another small jump. The family set off, away from the river, with Thor guiding them and Odin at his side. For a while Myroy carried Tirani and rubbed his cheek, and the baby chatted to him with more of those clever words that no one, except perhaps Frey, could understand. The snow eased off and a weak sun lit up a beautiful landscape. The far hills and valleys looked like a rolling white sea without waves, all still, new, and silent, except for the crunching of snow underfoot and Tirani's cooing.

They trudged on for hours and when the sun reached the high point in its low arc, the family rested. Cooked strips of Raku were passed around and Thor gnawed at a thick bone. He snapped it in two, like a twig, to get at the marrow and stuck his tongue as far inside the bone as he could to get at it.

Myroy glanced around. The ice *was* coming, but this was such a beautiful place.

The next part of the journey was harder. They rose up and walked over snow covered grasslands. Then the way grew steeper as they trudged through pines and everyone became alert. Ghadu might hide here and he was sure to be hungry. At last they emerged from the pines onto a rocky, barren slope and the family pushed on to the summit of the hill. The air was colder here, but the view from the summit was breathtaking. This really was a wonderful land. So unspoilt and clean, and Myroy wondered if they were the first people to see these open blue skies.

Odin said something and Thor pointed his spear at another hill. It was slightly higher than the one they stood on and the way to it lay across a wide "u" shaped valley. A black ribbon meandered along the base of the valley and a family of Raku took water from the stream.

"There," he said.

Odin nodded.

"You now lead," he smiled.

Thor's chest swelled, and he dashed forward like an eager puppy. As the sun touched the rim of the far hills they forded the stream and began to climb again. Frey shivered.

"Getting cold," she said.

"Getting cold," agreed Myroy.

Odin had noticed it too.

"Walk quickly. Feel less cold. Light fire soon."

He glanced up and was surprised to see that the sky was totally obscured by thick, grey and angry clouds. Thor stopped in his tracks and cried out, and they all ran to join him.

"Up there." He pointed his spear at a small, distant, black hole in the hill. "Warm there."

"Good Thor," said Odin. "Now move quickly,"

They pushed on up the slope, desperate to reach it before the sun disappeared.

With a long walk still ahead of them to the cave, the heavens opened and snow fell in torrents. The wind screamed and whipped up deep drifts, which they had to skirt around. Myroy took a fur from the pack on Thor's back and wrapped it around his mother's shoulders, and everyone bent their heads as they drove themselves on into the worsening storm. The distance between Thor and Odin, and Myroy, Frey and Tirani grew and for an awful moment they lost sight of each other. Myroy cried out.

"Odin."

His words seemed to be lost in the white, gusting wind. Then Thor's body emerged, like a mighty ghost, and he lifted Frey up into his arms.

"You bring baby," he barked and Myroy followed him up the slope.

Odin stood, with his back to them, staring up at the entrance to the caves. When he turned his face was like thunder.

Thor didn't notice Odin's face and said triumphantly, "Warm in there."

He made to step forward. Odin grabbed his arm and pointed down at the ground. Partly obscured by fresh snow were Ghadu tracks. They went straight up to the cave entrance.

"Ghadu here," gasped Myroy.

"How many?" asked Frey in a terrified voice.

Odin lowered himself and placed his hand into one of the great footprints.

"Four."

They stood together, shivering, and knew they could do nothing. Ghadu would defend its winter den with all its power and aggression. They were stuck. Odin put his finger to his lips to demand silence and Myroy glanced to the west. The sun was about to fall below the far hills. Frey pointed at a gentle slope that went back down the hill and Odin nodded. The family retreated.

At a safe distance, Myroy suggested, "Get back to trees. Put up tent."

The wind howled around them and they had to shout to be heard. The snowfall was getting worse and the light faded.

"Get far away," grunted Thor.

"Must shelter."

Myroy put an arm around his mother. Even in the folds of Thor's arms, her small body shivered and any movements she made were slow, as the cold weakened her.

"Get far away."

"Rest soon."

"I lead. You follow."

"Frey needs rest. Needs warmth."

"If Ghadu wake, we all die," warned Odin.

"Against Ghadu, we may flee. Against ice, we are lost."

Odin ignored him and yelled orders at Thor. Thor squeezed Frey and trudged on. The snow was knee high. Myroy followed, as best he could, and inside his furs Tirani slept, lulled by the rise and fall of each tall step.

They climbed up again in the hope of finding some kind of shelter. No one could see more than a few paces ahead. Lost, blind, stumbling. The storm taunted them. Odin held the end of a pole, which stuck out of the tent on Thor's back, and Myroy held onto Odin's furs. They were like a line of lost ships, roped together and battling against icy waves, in complete and utter darkness.

Thor suddenly stopped and the line crunched together.

"What is it?" cried Odin.

"My feet move."

"I cannot even feel my feet," thought Myroy.

"Move feet more. Find shelter," ordered Odin.

"My feet move," repeated Thor.

Myroy wondered what he meant, then his feet began to move too. They shuddered and small shockwaves shot up through their bodies. Odin bent down and scraped the top layer of snow away. Under the snow was a layer of ice.

"We are on ice!" he yelled with fear. "Move on quickly."

Thor shuffled on and everyone tried to ignore the warning *cracks* that cut through the wind.

After a while, Odin tugged at Thor's back and the line stopped. He knelt again and scraped the snow away. Under the snow was more snow, and he grinned and cried out.

"Safe now."

An almighty *boom* sounded from the heavens and the ground beneath them disappeared. They plummeted like a stone into the bowels of the earth. Myroy felt himself spin, head over heels. Tirani protected in his arms. The dark shapes of his family, obscured by swirling snow, spun with them. Frey's body hit the floor of the underground chamber first and then Thor's great weight crushed her. Odin's body thumped down beside them and lay still. Myroy's head struck a rock with a terrible force and, as consciousness began to leave him, he saw that they were in a chamber at the base of a deep ravine.

The chamber was lined with strange rocks. Crystals which glowed and pulsed, engulfing them with light. It was like a warm blanket. A torrent of snow fell, like an avalanche, to cover them. More snow filled the ravine and compacted itself above the family's broken bodies. Myroy felt the weight of the ice above him. It pressed like heavy stones onto his chest and he couldn't breathe. He opened his mouth as if to scream. It filled with snow. The rocks glowed again and the snow turned red. Myroy closed his eyes. He felt as though he could sleep forever.

***

4356 BC

Thor's snoring woke Tirani and he burbled and cooed, and fingered the edge of his fur wrap. He spoke his favourite word. He still liked that word and so he said it again. Then he said it softly and then he decided to shout it out, smiling at the thought of how clever he was, and how his mother would cuddle him and kiss his nose.

Myroy opened his eyes and yawned, and felt cold to the core. As his lungs filled he tasted rank, stale air and he glanced up. The arched ceiling of ice rose up high above him. Everything in the chamber glowed red from the pulsating crystals lining the walls. It was a weird place and yet he felt comforted to be inside it, away from the dreadful weather up on the surface.

Myroy tried to stand, looked across at his mother, and felt sick. What he saw was not Frey but something grotesque. Black, decayed, mummified. Preserved by the ice, but empty of life. The hideous shell of what had once been his mother.

He sobbed, openly, loudly, and dived at the body and threw his arms around her. Tirani cooed some more and, with tears in his eyes, Myroy picked him up and kissed him.

"She has gone little one, gone."

He rocked his brother and sobbed some more. A great yawn cut into his grief and Thor shook his head, as if shaking away a lifetime of dreams, and then the great man stood. He looked at Myroy, rocking Tirani and grinned.

"You tend baby. You good at that."

Then he saw the blackened remains of his mother and gave out a huge roar of anguish. Odin stood too and came over to join them.

"What has happened to Frey?" he asked sadly.

"I do not know," replied Myroy. "Something terrible. The gods must be angry with us and have struck her down."

"How long have we been here?"

"Hard fall. Perhaps one night."

"One night," repeated Thor.

"Then up there," and Odin pointed up, "it is day."

"It is day here," added Thor as he ran a finger over some of the crystals that lined the walls. The brothers came over to join him and fingered the crystals too. They were cold to the touch and yet seemed to provide a reassuring warmth. An inner warmth.

"We go," suggested Myroy. "Find food. Hide from Ghadu."

"We go, when I say go," ordered Odin in a sharp voice.

"Odin leads us," agreed Thor.

"Odin leads us?"

Myroy looked down at Frey's body. He didn't need to say anything else. Tirani was hungry and wanted his milk. He began to wail to let them know and Myroy rocked him some more, and tried to comfort him.

"Find food?" asked Myroy again.

This time Odin nodded and they hunted around the chamber for a way out. With rock and crystal on the walls, and an ice ceiling high above them, they felt trapped. Thor roared with rage and wrenched a big red crystal out of the wall, and threw it up at the ceiling. An avalanch of hard snow crashed down on their heads and the prison was flooded with bright sunshine. Immediately, the crystals stopped pulsing and their glow disappeared.

"Thor did it," roared Thor.

"Thor did," said Myroy, "what next?"

They stared up at a small round hole in the ice ceiling.

"Throw again," suggested Odin and Thor threw lumps of the crystals up to dislodge more snow. As he took aim and fired, Odin collected together as many of the crystals as he could cram inside his furs. In a short while, the hole was bigger, the floor higher, and Odin was able to stand on Thor's shoulders and touch the base of the hole. Then Thor put his hands under Odin's feet and heaved him up. His eyes blinked in summer sun. Odin yelled down at them.

"No snow."

After a long wait, during which Myroy wondered if Odin had abandoned them, or been taken by Ghadu, the trunk of a long tree started to descend into the chamber.

When they were all free, they stood together and stared around. The landscape was lush, green and alive. Flowers, that none of them had seen before, grew in thick clumps. Thousands of trees crowned the hills and herds of small deer grazed below them, along the banks of a wide river.

It was gorgeous.

"We go now," ordered Odin. "Go to canoes. This place has bad magic."

"Bad magic," agreed Thor gruffly.

Myroy didn't feel as though this place was bad. Quite the opposite. He sensed a tremendous power here. Here amongst the hills.

"I stay," he said resolutely. "I stay here with Tirani."

"You go," growled Thor and he made his fists into threatening balls. "Together we are stronger."

Odin placed his hand on Thor's shoulder and shook his head.

"Let Ghadu take him. We go to rule across the water."

He pulled a red crystal from his furs.

"We rule with this."

Thor nodded and laughed.

"Let Ghadu take them."

But the Ghadu were no more.

As Myroy watched his brothers walk away, down the slope, he wondered if he was doing the right thing for Tirani. Then he imagined what life would be like with Odin's will commanding all the families across the water. He shuddered and walked in the opposite direction. His first priority was shelter, then food and water, and inside something was telling him that he knew exactly where to find them.

He walked up a steep hill, through a stand of pines, and came out of their shadows into a circular grass clearing with two, tall standing stones at its centre. Another tall stone stood some way off.

The clearing was full of people and Myroy smiled.

***

3110 BC

Myroy grew to love the Alcheri. They were some of the earliest peoples to inhabit Scotland and they adopted him as if he was one of their own. Certainly, they loved him in return and thought of him, rather embarrassingly, as some kind of Father-God. The eternal father who did not age, or die.

Twelve centuries had passed since the families' sleep in the chamber. But he and Tirani looked just the same. If there was a difference in them it was in their minds. Both found that they could remember everything they learned, everything they experienced. The baby, Tirani, could talk like an adult and reason like a sage, and had slowly grown to accept his helpless and vulnerable body.

However, Myroy never quite got used to knowing that the friends he made would someday pass away, to be replaced by their sons and daughters. With each new generation, he saw fresh faces, heard different voices and came to realise that much of what we know and hold dear, continues long after death. He learnt these lessons well and, with the wise advice he gave to the Alcheri, the villagers prospered and turned to farming.

Peace reigned and they were truly happy. The seasons rolled by, one after another, as did the years, and as a way for them to hold onto their own past they made a pilgrimage. Every summer, when the sun was at its highest, Myroy would take Tirani and visit the chamber of red crystals. The crystals pulsed and seemed to cry out, and they discovered how to use their power to see into the future.

Frey's skeleton smiled at them.

But dark clouds gathered to the north. The Sea Peoples, with whom they traded, lived in fear of the raiders who attacked their shores. They were said to be invincible and led by a great warrior, a giant of a man, who stood with a mighty hammer at the prow of his dragon ship. Myroy and Tirani knew who he was, and they knew what he commanded. They also knew how Odin had created a ruby from crystal to obey his own anger and greed.

The raids grew bolder and more frequent and it would not be long before Thor would bring every ship he had to conquer the land. Odin's power was spreading out like a forest fire. The villagers sensed it too and came to Myroy to ask for forgiveness. They had nothing to be forgiven for and a council was called to decide if help should be given to the Sea Peoples. But Thor's great fleet was already underway.

***

"He comes," said the baby Tirani.

Myroy's reply was grave.

"He does and this time he has the stone in his hammer. The power Odin has discovered will aid him. I truly fear for these people."

"Then we have no choice, but to risk death."

"We have enjoyed more life than anyone, brother, and I am now ready to make that sacrifice."

Tirani fingered his fur wrap.

"If we fail, Odin will rule all. I cannot imagine what it would be like."

"I *can* imagine."

"We have no choice," repeated Tirani.

Myroy nodded, lifted his brother into his arms and walked to the door of their hut. The villagers formed a long, silent corridor to the standing stones and seemed to sense something of the sacrifice they were making. Some of the women sobbed and one of the children spoke the words they were all thinking.

"Do not go. Do not leave us!"

Myroy stopped and smiled at them.

"Do not let fear rule your hearts. You are a free people. Together you are stronger."

He marched on and stepped inside one of the stones. With the gasps of the villagers still in their ears, Myroy stepped out of rock into the chamber of crystals. They pulsed and everything was bathed in a red glow. He gently laid Tirani next to a crystal and they both touched it. The wall opposite them turned blood-red and a picture formed. Thor was leading his ships south. He raised his hammer and struck the sea. The sea rose up ahead of him and a single wave grew to become a foaming monster a mile high. As the wave sucked in the sea around it, the waters behind it fell.

"He is going to drown his enemies," said Tirani. "So many will die."

"How much time do we have?" asked Myroy.

The baby studied the wave and shook his head.

"Then we must act now."

Tirani nodded. Thor's grinning face appeared on the wall. Behind him were hundreds of ships, all of them temporarily beached on rock, or sand. Around them all, small pools boiled as sharks broke the surface and fought each other for a meagre share of life-giving sea.

The picture changed. The brothers were now looking down at the coast of Sea Peoples Land. Hundreds of warriors stood in a long line waiting to defend their homes. Then they saw the great wave rise up like a mountain, and the line broke. They would never be able to escape it when it crashed onto the earth.

"Thor's ship is on land. You can go now," said Tirani

Myroy ran at the picture and flung himself at the rock wall. He flew up through the bottom of Thor's ship and hit his brother, hard, in the small of his back. Thor stumbled forward and his arm and hammer arched back over his shoulder. Myroy wrenched it out of his hand and dived down into the deck. His feet disappeared through the wooden planks in less than a second. Then he was beside Tirani.

"Touch the crystal," he yelled.

The baby reached out his arm. With one hand Myroy held the part of the stone, which stuck out of Thor's hammer. Then he touched a crystal with his other hand and painted a picture in his mind. His brother painted the same picture.

Smoothly, all the lands, that you now call Britain, rose up and up, and out of the sea. Huge, dripping cliffs towered high above the tidal wave that shot forward at an incredible speed towards the northern coast.

The red glow inside the chamber became intense, blinding, and the brothers felt as though every last drop of life was being sucked out of them. The wave struck the wall of rock and an immense explosion sounded around the world. Towering needles of foam and spume shot into the air and then returned to the sea.

As Tirani passed out, the wave began to reform and roll backwards. Myroy looked at his hands. They were as gnarled as bark on a tree. His head swam. With the life-sapping effort he dropped Thor's hammer, and it shattered. Odin's stone rolled free across the chamber floor.

Myroy glanced at the wall. Thor's angry face was changing. Changing to fear. His eyes bulged out and he began to shake, and he seemed to be screaming Odin's name. Then he was gone, as the sea engulfed him.

The picture faded. Most of the crystal's power was now spent and lost forever.

Myroy collapsed next to Tirani and put his arm around him, in a last act of love and protection. But his withered arms wrapped themselves around a young boy and the last thing he remembered was wondering who he was.

His eyes shut and any dreams he might have had were for the future of the peoples he had saved.

Beside him, on the floor, the ruby waited patiently for its master to come. It pulsed and the chamber became the colour of blood.

***

Suddenly, Myroy's face became sad.

"That is enough for now, you ought to go and help your Grandmother."

Peter's eyebrows rose up.

"But, please, can't I at least learn about Dougie and his adventure on the islands?"

The Ancient One ignored him.

"And when did Dougie give the stone away?"

Myroy stood. Dog stood too and barked. He wanted more supper.

"When will I see you again?" asked Peter anxiously.

"Soon." Myroy slowly descended through the floor. "Use your gift of learning wisely, Peter of the line of Donald, the age of the Celts is a rewarding area of study."

Peter fell backwards as the bench he was sitting on disappeared. Dog barked again as invisible hands tore down the cottage. When the grating and creaking stopped, Peter lay on his back, staring up at the stars.

"What a way to finish a conversation."

They made their way back through the brambles and walked along

174

the old drovers' road. It was a beautiful evening. Clear skies and a Gora moon. The lights of the village shone out and Peter thought about Odin's quest for the stone, which lay in his pocket. Was he still trying to find it?

If he was as ruthless as Myroy said he was, would he try to kill him to get what he wanted?

He lifted the latch to the front door and pushed. Nothing happened. He pushed again, harder, and it moved a little. Dog began to howl mournfully.

"Quiet," hissed Peter, "you'll wake everyone up."

He put his shoulder to the door and put all his weight behind it. The door opened enough for him to get in. He squeezed through and fell over something.

"What the?"

He pulled himself up, found the light switch and realised what he had tripped over. The new Keeper felt completely alone. It was Grandpa and his body was as cold as stone.

CHAPTER FIFTEEN

Ashes to Ashes

Niels Magnusson was efficient, neat as a pin and utterly ruthless. He stared out of the security cabin down the long, straight, approach road and tapped a red square on his screen, and the digital picture of a car appeared.

Tap. The picture zoomed onto the car's registration plate.

Tap. A man's photograph replaced the plate.

Tap. A script appeared alongside the photograph –

Paul Johnson. Age - 26. Wife - Sarah.

Children – none.

Employee of Oslo Antiques SV – confirmed.

Years employed – 3.

Location – London Office.

Title – Head of OASV Europe.

Reason for visit – monthly sales meeting with Inger.

Top 3 stated interests –

1. Crosswords.

Paul completed today's Times crossword on BA303 from Heathrow in 24 minutes.

2. Football.

Supports Charlton Athletic FC. Last score – lost one nil away to Liverpool. Steven Gerrard scored in the 30th minute.

3. Sailing.

Subscribes monthly to Yachting World. The April edition is two weeks late. His paperboy is David Wilson : Age 13.

The luxury car purred forward and stopped in front of the barrier.

"Welcome back to Norway, Paul. Is it really six weeks since you last visited us?"

"As you well know, Niels, it is four weeks. I heard you had a break-in."

"There was an *attempted* break-in," corrected Niels, "a mouse couldn't get through the systems we have here."

The two men smiled at each other and Paul waited for the second test question.

"How is Sarah?" asked Niels politely.

"She is well, we still have no children and I have been an employee for three years."

"And how are your team getting on?"

"Ruddy well lost at Anfield, but thanks for asking."

"Who scored?"

Paul faked a yawn. "Gerrard, lucky header too, in the 30th minute." The barrier rose and as he drove forward he added. "And Sarah is expecting so you'll be able to come up with some more original questions, Niels."

The guard watched him go and thought that most people could work for a lifetime, or even two, and not be able to afford a car like his.

The office foyer was magnificent. Ingrid Hellergren smiled up at him from her desk.

"I understand congratulations are in order, Paul."

"Good news travels fast, doesn't it."

Like Niels and every other employee at OASV, her English was perfect.

"Have you chosen any names yet?"

"If it's a girl and stunningly beautiful, then I thought of Ingrid."

Like a switch being thrown, Ingrid's smile disappeared.

"You are late, so you had better go down right away."

He walked past a fountain. A door clicked and opened, and he entered the long gallery. It was over two hundred metres long, floored with highly polished wood and lit by spotlights at regular intervals. Under each light were some of the world's greatest, most expensive, works of art.

"Got to be worth £500 million at least," he thought.

A red light pulsed on a camera, at the far end of the gallery, and another door clicked open. He went through and stood in front of a steel door. The lift opened and he glanced at the control panel. There were five buttons, five floors of offices to choose from, and he ignored them all and inserted a key into the panel. It swung open and he pushed the hidden button. Silently, the lift went down. When the door glided open, Paul was met by Inger, a blond-haired man, in an expensive Italian suit, who stared at him through intense blue eyes.

"You are late," he snapped.

"My apologies. I can offer no excuses that you would find acceptable."

They walked quickly past a towering wall of granite towards five men who sat around an oval table at the far side of the underground office. The whole length of the wall was covered with a relief of a Norse longship. Following the ship were sharks and terrifying sea creatures. At the prow, above a fierce dragon, stood a carving of Thor, at least three metres tall and holding a huge battle hammer.

All eyes were on Inger as they sat down.

"Let us begin the monthly sales meeting," he commanded. "United States."

The man next to Paul placed an A4 sheet of paper onto the mahogany table.

"Commission from the sale of a Monet, four million US dollars."

"Middle East."

A lean, swarthy and tough looking Turk, in an ill-fitting blue suit, leant forward.

"Sale of the artefacts from Baghdad University to private collectors, two point five million dollars."

"Far East."

"Profit from the purchase and sale of a Ming collection, on behalf of the Chinese government, one point seven million US dollars."

"Asia."

"Fabergé Egg. Search and find fee - three million dollars."

"Europe."

"Zero," replied Paul and everyone looked at him.

"Total for April, eleven point two million dollars. In the current economic climate a creditable performance. Meeting adjourned," said Inger, "Paul, I will have a word with you in private."

Paul nodded and remained seated as the others left. He watched Inger's face and tried to guess his age. Twenty four? Twenty five? That is what his handsome features and smooth skin told him. But the way he looked at you, the way he sat, the way he spoke to you, told him something very different. The lift door closed and Inger rose.

"What is it, Paul?"

"A possibility, that is all."

"For the private collection?"

Paul nodded again, "One of my people believes the family you seek lives in London. We will complete a detailed search within four weeks."

"Make it two."

"I will instruct Roberts, Johnson and Hyde to begin immediately."

Inger stared at the ship in the rock.

"Give Sarah my regards, won't you?"

"I will."

"And keep Olaf Adanson informed of progress."

Paul knew his meeting was over.

As the lift door closed behind Paul, Inger spoke to the longship.

"Open."

The great wall of rock descended into the floor to reveal a bank of TV screens. News channels reported breaking stories in all the languages of the world and Inger understood them all. In the centre of the bank of television screens were two huge screens. One showed the search page of AOL. The other showed a map of the world and it was covered in red dots. Each dot marked the known location of a descendant of the line of Donald. There were thousands. Inger took a mobile phone from his pocket.

"Olaf, London."

"London," repeated Olaf.

"You are to direct Roberts, Johnson and Hyde in their search."

"I obey, master."

"And watch out for Smith. Kill him if he gets close."

"Yes, master. What about Paul?"

"Let him join the fallen."

Inger hung up and keyed an American number into his mobile.

"Thorgood, get the next flight to Oslo. Bring your grandfather."

"I obey, master."

"We have plans to make." Inger hung up.

"London is a possibility," he thought, "although America is the obvious place for Myroy to hide them."

He typed instructions into his phone and the central AOL screen switched to Ask Jeeves. In the search box two words appeared, one letter at a time – *Amera's stone*.

Search Item Not Found flashed on the screen as it had so many times before.

"One day Myroy's luck will run out."

Like a ghost, Inger walked into the wall of screens and passed into a circular chamber on the other side. It was completely encased with rock. He waded knee high through salt water and stepped inside a standing stone, which stood alone in the centre of his dark, eternal sanctuary.

He shut his blue eyes and, as the power of the sea flowed through his body, Odin smiled. His great search was nearly over.

Paul's car purred and stopped beside the security cabin. Niels leaned out.

"Please pass on my best wishes to Sarah."

Niels watched him drive down the long approach road. He tapped the screen. A picture of the main entrance appeared. Paul went through and headed east on the Oslo road. The guard took a small metal box from a drawer, extended an aerial and pushed a button on the side of the box.

There was a flash of fire. A second later a muffled *boom* rattled the cabin windows. Black smoke rose up in the distance. Niels placed the box back in the drawer, tidied some papers and lifted a phone.

"Hello, police, I think there has been an accident."

***

Peter could feel the sadness around him. Miss McKiely, from the Post Office in Easter Malgeddie, was inconsolable and sobbed as Grandpa was lowered into the ground. Laura and James seemed to be through the worst of it all, and stood quietly, heads bowed, fiddling with their hymn books. Even Dog looked miserable and many of Grandpa's old friends wept openly.

"Ashes to ashes, dust to dust," said Reverend Collie.

He let a handful of soil fall from his hand. Like a dry rain, the soil drifted down and covered a bunch of roses. A single stone bounced up off the coffin lid and Peter watched his mother put an arm around his father. He remembered hugging Grandma and phoning his dad.

"I am so sorry …….. but Grandpa has passed away."

"It was time," Colin said, "and it was not unexpected. Let me know when we need to be there." Then Peter had heard the worst of sounds. His father crying.

Only Grandma smiled. The silver haired woman dropped a small posy of thistle flowers into the hole.

"I will not be long behind you, so look out for me, Duncan of the line of Donald."

"Page 54 everyone," said the Reverend.

They sang *There Is a Green Hill Far Away* and Peter found it hard to say some of the words.

Grandma's voice was strong. She had already passed through the sadness of her loss, long before the others, and was now ready for a life without the man she had shared so much with. In the month following the children's visit to Glenbowmond, her husband had helped her prepare for the passing. They had talked and walked together along the ancient paths that wound up to the far hills. Some days they had placed flowers on the cairn, which once marked the centre of their families' lands.

Reverend Collie began to talk about Grandpa's life. How he had always been a loyal friend, a devoted father and husband, and how there were many who might envy the quiet life he had led for one hundred and three summers.

Miss McKiely gasped at this and whispered to Laura.

"I thought Duncan was only sixty! Just goes to show what good honest toil does for you."

Standing behind the main party of family and friends, Peter noticed a stranger. He was short, stocky and bald, and wore medals on his overcoat. Peter wondered if once he had been in the army.

Five hundred metres away, Mick Roberts pressed a button on his digital camera, ducked down behind the stone wall he was hiding behind, and dashed back to his car. He copied the photos to his laptop, connected the laptop to his mobile phone and pressed *send*. The images would be with Olaf Adanson in seconds.

The mourners drifted away, through the small cemetery, and Grandma hurried amongst them, shaking hands and kissing everyone, and inviting them back to her home for supper. When she reached the bald man she lingered longer than with even her immediate family.

"Thank you for coming, Bernard," she said, "I know Duncan would have been honoured by you being here."

"Believe me, Maggie, the honour is all mine. The world is poorer now. How could I refuse an invitation written in Duncan's own hand?"

They smiled at each other and Peter saw they shared an easy way about them, as though they had known each other for many years, and needed to say little to show how they really felt.

"Bernard, may I introduce you to, Peter, Duncan's eldest grandson."

"A fine boy, Maggie, and I would guess he is much the same to look at as Duncan when he was his age."

Peter held out a hand and the old man shook it. It was strong and warm and Peter's eyes fell upon the man's medals.

"A pleasure to meet you sir," he replied politely.

"Do not be sad, young man. We aren't, are we Maggie?"

Grandma beamed at him. Peter did feel sad and wondered why they were behaving like this.

"We are a bit tight on space in the cars, could you give Peter a lift home?" Grandma asked Bernard, and he marched off through the gravestones with Peter struggling to keep up.

"This is mine. Well, mine until I return it to the rental company at the airport."

Bernard pointed at a gleaming Mercedes.

"I've never been in one of these," said Peter.

"Want to have a go?"

Peter glanced at the old man.

"I can't drive," he said sensibly.

"Can't drive? That's what your Grandfather did all the time."

"Did all the time?"

As Peter slid into the leather passenger seat. A mechanical arm lowered itself over his shoulder and offered him a seatbelt.

"A lot of the time anyway, during the war in North Africa."

"North Africa?"

Bernard chuckled. "Your Grandfather and I became good chums in Cairo."

"Cairo?"

"Cairo, Tobruk, Alexandria, El Alemain and lonely places with no name."

"And were you a driver like Grandpa?"

Bernard ignored the question.

"Funny thing," he said at last, "It was only when Monty, General Montgomery to you, started to head things up that our fortunes changed. Duncan was one of his special drivers in the Eleventh Hussars."

Peter raised an eyebrow.

"Driver, advisor and lucky mascot. Monty wouldn't go anywhere without him. He believed that, with Duncan beside him, his Desert Rats were invincible. Even after the war the big wigs asked Duncan to stay on, in quite a senior War Office job, but all he wanted to do was go back to Maggie and farming."

"I don't blame him," smiled Peter.

"I don't blame him either."

Bernard smiled back at the heir to the line of Donald.

"He could have gone far, your Grandfather. He had an almost perfect photographic memory. We used to pull his leg about it. Well, here we are, young Peter."

The Mercedes glided to a halt outside Grandma's house. Mick Robert's car pulled into the side of the lane a long way behind them. His phone vibrated and he read the text.

Colin Donald is a possibility. Book yourself onto EZY14 EDIN to LUTON tomorrow. Start at Upside Down Marketing, Curzon Street, London – photos required. Olaf.

"I think you are a generation out," thought Mick, but he called Easyjet and booked his flight, did a three point turn and drove off.

"Are you coming in, Bernard?" asked Peter.

"No, I need to catch a plane and I have already said my goodbyes. By the way, if you want to hear more about your grandad and you are ever in Corfu, why don't you look me up? Maggie's got the address. I'm retired from the security service now and would welcome the company."

"I'd really like to," said Peter.

But secretly he hoped to hear another story from a more distant past. They shook hands one last time and Peter watched thoughtfully as Bernard drove away. He remembered Myroy's words and wondered if it was in North Africa that Duncan Donald nearly lost Amera's stone.

***

The kitchen clock sounded the passage of time like a metronome and someone upstairs coughed. Peter rolled over and his feet stuck out the bottom of his blanket.

He remembered Grandma skipping between guests with hot sausage rolls and Miss McKiely bursting into tears again. He felt happy and sad, and wondered if funerals were supposed to leave you feeling this way.

After the emotions of the day he couldn't sleep. Dog snored in his basket and every few minutes his legs twitched as he dreamt about rabbits. Peter sat up and looked at the clock. It was two in the morning. He tried to get comfortable, on the folded quilt he was using as a mattress, and thought about his friends at school, about his girlfriend Kylie, about his family and Bernard. But most of all he thought about Myroy and Odin, and the time after the ice.

Peter couldn't sleep and got up to get a glass of water. Through the kitchen window he saw the far hills bathed in the light of a full moon. A Gora moon. Suddenly, he felt the need to go out and walk, for a short while at least, and so he dressed. Dog was next to him in an instant, eager and silent, as if sensing this was not a time to wake the others. Like a burglar, Peter lifted the latch on the kitchen door and went out. As they walked along the old drovers' road, Peter fingered the brooch in his pocket and felt as though he had to be out here, in the cold night air, and every step he took was shaped by a greater purpose.

It was dreamlike.

Dog's loud bark startled him and he realised he was standing outside the gate of the small garden. He smiled at the sheepdog, who ran around in excited circles, and walked past neat rows of lovingly tended peas and beans. There was no answer to his knock and he wondered what to do. Dog jumped up at the door. It opened easily and he trotted over to the fire. Peter sat down on the familiar wooden bench and carefully placed Amera's stone on his knee. As he did, the floor shimmered and Myroy appeared from the depths of the earth.

"You feel sad at the passing," said Myroy.

Peter nodded.

"Duncan was a truly brave Keeper, one of the bravest who has held the stone."

"Have there been many?"

"Yes, many. But perhaps not as many as you would think. The keepers tend to live long lives."

"Was he as brave as Dougie?"

"In their own way, they were all brave."

The Ancient One's face seemed to cloud over as if he was remembering them all.

"I felt as though I had to come," said Peter.

"I called you."

"And I am ready."

Myroy smiled and settled himself on the bench, and stared down at the ruby. Peter noticed he made no attempt to touch it and wondered if the stone held some kind of danger for the old man.

"Before I begin, you must understand that not all the enemies who threatened the peace of the Celtic peoples of Scotland were evil. Some of them were, but not all. They were dark times and the Younger was to face an even darker time once the foes of mountain, island and castle were vanquished."

"Dougie has faced the Picts on Carn Liath and now goes to the Outer islands," Peter said.

"He does. Thorgood Firebrand, the descendent of Thorfinn, knew that famine and fever would destroy his people if he left things as they were."

"So, Thorgood intended to stay in Scotland for good?"

"He had little choice," replied Myroy, "he needed to lead his warriors to richer lands to escape death. Of course, the easiest option would have been to farm the land along the shores of the ancient kingdom of the Sea Peoples. But times change and whereas these lands were rich and prosperous under Amera, in Dougie's time they were as poor as the fjords themselves. Cuthbert the Cautious was a different person altogether. He was driven by greed."

Peter raised an enquiring eyebrow and Myroy shot him a disapproving glance.

"Just like all the Donalds, wanting to hear the end before the beginning."

"But I haven't heard much about Cuthbert. Didn't he send Thomas Goodfellow to kill the Younger?"

Myroy ignored the question.

"The fleet of the dragon was coming and a power struggle was about to be settled. Thorgood Firebrand would emerge as leader of the Norsemen with terrible consequences for Dougie and the men of Tain."

Peter glanced at his brooch again.

"Do not forget their story, Peter of the Line of Donald. Your own future depends on it."

CHAPTER SIXTEEN

Fleet of the Dragon

SPRING 675 AD

The grain jar was empty.

Young Ulrika lay quietly, in her bed of straw and furs, and reached out a thin hand to her father. His great hand took it and enclosed it completely as if he was picking up a small stone. The girl began to whisper strange words and Thorgood Firebrand moved his face closer so he might understand them. They meant nothing. The fever was at its height.

The Norse Lord wiped a tear from her cheek, hugged her and pulled a woollen shawl over the trembling body. The gestures of a helpless man. The little girl began to breathe more slowly and the room became quiet once more. Thorgood remembered the times when they had played and argued, danced and feasted, and walked together to talk about the world.

The thin hand became cold and lifeless.

"Goodnight, my princess," he said and kissed her for the last time. Thorgood climbed the rocky path to the ancient coronation seat of kings, high up on the side of the mountain. It was a journey he took whenever he had the need for his own company, whenever he was troubled, or when he had a difficult decision to make. It was a journey he had taken too many times since the failed harvest.

There is a peace in solitude and he began to remember how things once were. He even dreamed of how they might be again. He lowered his head into his hands and prayed for guidance from Odin the creator, god of wisdom, war and the dead. If ever he had needed a sign about which way to lead his people it was now. His thoughts turned to the lost stone. The old stories told that, on Odin's command, Thor forged a magic stone from earth and lightning. His mighty hammer rang out for a thousand years and the stone of legend was made. The ruby was the colour of blood.

Thorgood knew the bard's teachings well. Knew every word. Any warrior who fought against Odin's Stone would be defeated and his spirit barred from entering the gates of Valhalla, a place at the eternal table denied them.

With the stone embedded in his mighty hammer, Thor had believed he was unstoppable, almighty, but Myroy captured the ruby and unleashed its great power back upon Thor, his ships and the foul creatures of the deep he commanded. Odin swore vengeance for Thor's death and began his epic search to reclaim what was stolen.

Myroy gifted the ruby to Amera, who commanded the peoples of fair lands to the south, and it was secretly buried with him. But the stone cried out and many, like Gora, heard the call and tried to take it. Even now their caged, tortured souls were held prisoner. What kind of power could overcome Thor's curse and release them?

Odin and Thorfinn Firebrand, Thorgood's grandfather, learned of the hiding place too and raced to Amera's cairn. It was as empty as Odin's heart was of pity.

"If only we had what was taken so long ago," thought Thorgood.

He looked down at the house of his fathers. The long hall sat amongst others on a thin strip of farmland, which hugged the deep waters of the fjord. To his right were the high snow-covered peaks of the Empty Lands and to his left, the open waters of a vast sea. He glanced both ways many times, as if considering one against the other, and then he bowed his head deep in thought. He had to choose.

The dark hours were the hardest to bear for the children moaned in their broken sleep, and worried parents realised just how useless they were when faced with the will of the Gods. Had Odin deserted them? Why had two harvests failed? What had they done to deserve the disease that had struck so cruelly to kill their animals?

Heavy rain began to fall and the wind rose, throwing torrents of cold water upon the earth.

Thorgood, of the line of Thorfinn Firebrand, looked up at the clouds. There were so many of them, charging in off the sea, and nothing in this world could stop them. At his feet, a leaf was lifted by the water and carried down the mountainside. He watched it go and knew it was just beginning a long journey, a great journey, towards one of the streams that fed the fjord. From there the leaf would be swept out into the mighty ocean.

"And that is where we must go too," he said to himself.

It was time for Odin's people to rise again.

By the spring of the following year, Thorgood Firebrand was in overall command of a massive Norse fleet. He looked at the dark, rugged coastline of Orkney. It wasn't dawn yet and he thought about their plan to attack three different bays at the same time.

"Are Bjorn and Olaf ready?" asked Thorgood.

Hengist Corngrinder shrugged his broad shoulders.

"Bjorn's men have already landed and drive the enemy towards the centre of the island."

"Keen, isn't he."

"Ambitious more like."

"You think he will challenge me?"

"Some time soon, old friend."

Thorgood knew he was right. "He has to survive the fight here first."

"He will, he has many times before."

"Then give the signal to Olaf Adanson. We, at least, shall attack together."

Hengist lit lamps at the prow, the mast and the stern of the longship, and three answering lights shone out at the entrance to the next headland. Thorgood raised his sword and pointed it at the shore. His crew roared, in the darkness before dawn, and the roars of the warriors aboard his other thirty ships followed. A long way away, another roar went up. The men aboard Olaf's twenty longships were ready to land as well.

"For Odin," cried Thorgood as he jumped down and waded ashore.

The invaders glanced around, looking for someone to attack, someone to win honour from, but the beach was deserted.

"Head for the centre of the island," ordered Thorgood. "Drive anyone you meet before you!"

***

Olaf Adanson waded ashore and spears thudded into his men. His torch made the iron spearheads look like silver fish, flying above the waves. One fish splashed by his thigh as it cut into the water. In the darkness he couldn't see that the sea around him was blood red.

"Put out the torches," he yelled, "we are an easy target."

All along the bay torches were doused. The line of longships, tied at anchor in shallow water, disappeared and the men of Orkney lost sight of their prey. The Orcadian warriors drew their swords and dashed down to fight the Norsemen at the water's edge.

Olaf grinned inside the helmet which completely covered his face, and slashed out with his sword. Iron hit iron. Men screamed. Shadows danced to avoid deadly blows. A warrior brought his blade down onto Olaf's shield and the force nearly broke his arm. He sliced down and cut the enemy's hand off. Blood spurted in all directions and the man fell to his knees, whimpering. Olaf swung again and severed the man's head. The vicious fighting was over in minutes. As a weak dawn sun lit the shoreline, longships bobbed up and down, and pulled against their anchor ropes, the fallen littered the beach and writhing black shapes lined the half circle of the bay. Orcadian soldiers in their hundreds were climbing up the rocky slopes.

"Chase them inland," cried Olaf, "and watch out for Bjorn and Thorgood. They are closing the other sides of the net."

***

Colfan the Fish Seeker opened an eye. His head hurt and something, some deep instinct, told him not to move. The sun was up, but all he could see was a bulging leather tunic and he wondered if the man who lay next to him was dead. Maybe he was dead too. He wiggled his toes and fingers and licked his tongue around the inside of his mouth. They all seemed to be working.

Very slowly, he lifted his head. The enemy were near the top of the slope, heading inland towards the hill fort at Bron Skara. His people would make a stand there. He lowered his head and, above the sound of the waves, heard voices behind him. In one movement he rolled over and froze.

Twenty ships lay at anchor along Half Moon Bay. Twenty invaders walked along the beach and stooped to collect weapons and anything of value from the dead.

"They've left one man to guard each ship," thought Colfan.

As he watched them he realised that he lay at the end of the line of ships. This surprised him. It had felt as though he had fought in the very heart of the battle. The enemy were combing the beach at the other end of the bay. A wounded man's leg twitched and a Norseman plunged a spear into his chest. They took fifty counts to pass from the second boat to the third. With seventeen boats to pass he knew he had some time at least to think of something.

When he thought it was safe, he crawled quickly to the water's edge. A low wave rolled in and he plunged his head and shoulders into it. Then he was swimming underwater towards the side of the nearest ship, away from the enemy. He surfaced beside it and trod water, staying as close to the wooden planks as he could. The water was bitterly cold and he blinked. Salt irritated his eyes, but that would pass.

The voices on the beach grew louder and, even though he could not understand them, they sounded cheerful. Colfan swam to the stern of the ship and, clinging to the rudder, lowered himself, so that the sea came up to his chin, and watched the shore. A group of warriors stood together and laughed. They carried armfuls of swords and spears, and one of them said something and two others left to collect driftwood. Another ran to the ship Colfan was hiding behind and clambered aboard. Then he jumped back into the water and splashed his way ashore, carrying half a sheep.

"They are going to eat," thought Colfan.

He rose and fell with each wave, and it was numbingly cold. A loud, angry shout came from the beach and two of the enemy began fighting. The rest yelled encouragement and cheered when a hard blow was landed. Spears and swords changed hands, as the bets swung from one contestant to another. Colfan counted them. All twenty accounted for.

"Time to go," he told himself.

He swam to the stern of the next ship, then the next, and eventually made it to the last longship at the end of the bay. Here the beach ended abruptly and the sea cut into hidden, rocky inlets. Colfan began to swim again and caught a wave that raced along the narrow channel. His chest scraped against a rock, which lay just under the surface, and he winced with the pain. A larger wave threw him forward onto another rock and for a moment he was stunned. The sea retreated and dragged him back. His throat filled with seawater, and he was lifted and thrown forward again. This time he was ready and kicked his legs out in front of him. As the wave thundered forward he straightened his legs, just as his father had taught him to do, and he rose out of the water and grabbed dry rock. Colfan climbed for all he was worth and, staying out of view of Half Moon Bay, made his way to Bron Skara. He would get another spear there and fight again.

***

A single dirt track led down from the round hill fort. Perched on a rocky crag it stood proud, openly defiant, above the surrounding area and Thorgood guessed the warriors who walked the thick stone walls would be able to see for miles in any direction.

One of the Norsemen, who ringed the fortress, dashed forward and threw his spear at the battlements. It landed short and thudded into the stones three quarters of the way up the wall. No arrows or spears rained down on him and Thorgood wondered if this meant they were short of arms and needed to make every effort count. Certainly, they would defend themselves with every last stone in the tower, especially if their wives and children were with them.

"Bjorn Longspear has a face like a cat who had found the cream," mumbled Hengist, "and Olaf looks like he has been fighting demons."

Thorgood ignored him and watched his two commanders leave their men and walk over to join him. Olaf was covered in blood.

"You met the enemy on the beach, Olaf?"

"They attacked us in darkness, at the water's edge, but broke soon enough once we made it ashore. I think they were waiting for us."

"And you, Bjorn, how many men have you lost?"

"Only thirty. I see that none of your men have won honour and joined the fallen."

"All my crews are ready for the *main* part of the quest. When we planned this adventure we agreed to keep losses as low as possible. We will need every sword, every spear, when we land at Oban."

"I am afraid I have lost thirty men as well," added Olaf, "so we are already five crews down out of a hundred."

Thorgood nodded.

"Bjorn, why did you attack before you saw the three lights at dawn?"

Bjorn spat on the ground.

"What does it matter? We landed and drove all before us. My men are as brave as any and will tear down the walls of the hill-fort when I raise my spear."

"I have no doubts about their courage, or yours, Bjorn, but a leader under my command will not be measured by courage alone. The decisions you make affect everyone."

"We are here as planned, aren't we?" sneered Bjorn, "and you question me, when it is you who has avoided the fight."

Hengist fingered the hilt of his sword.

"If your men faced a hopeless situation, Bjorn, would you lead them into battle?"

"Without a moment's hesitation."

"Then we need to reconsider who will command your ships to Scotland."

"Consider all you like. My men will die for me, gladly, and enter the Halls of the Gods."

"My men would follow me too, so would Olaf's. We all want a place at the eternal table, but to get there you need more than courage. You need to win."

Bjorn drove the end of his great spear into the earth, as if slicing down into the belly of an invisible enemy.

"I have always won. And if you faced a hopeless situation, would you not run away like a dog?"

"I might," agreed Thorgood, "and I would certainly find another way to achieve victory."

"These are words. Stupid words."

"Not just words. It is five ships without crews for our mission. It is sixty warriors dead when we need every one. You decided to land first, for glory, and I have no doubt that this warned the islanders, so when we landed they decided not to fight on two beaches. They concentrated their army on one. Olaf's men bore the brunt of your decision."

"So next time let Olaf go first. Let him rest. My men will do the fighting for you."

"It is not a question of going first, or second, it is a question of how we work together."

"Do we not surround the enemy? Do we not have them where we want them? Why wait? Let us kill them all."

Bjorn nodded at the fort.

"Kill them all?" questioned Thorgood. "Even the carpenters and shipbuilders?"

"If we bring the men up from the ships, we would have another one hundred men to storm the fortress."

"You would leave our ships unguarded?" asked Hengist.

Bjorn pulled his spear from the ground and pointed it at the fort.

"All their warriors are here."

"How do you know?" asked Olaf.

"Did we not sweep across the island, driving all before us?"

"Orkney is a big island," said Thorgood, "and our ships are the key to winning. Not here, but to winning the lands we need to avoid hunger."

"You talk like old women," said Bjorn, "I say we fight."

"Look at the fortress," commanded Thorgood, "what do you see?"

"It is well defended and cannot be taken without a price," warned Olaf.

"The islanders are crammed in there. In one battle we could destroy them all and Orkney would be our bridge to southern lands forever."

Thorgood nodded at Bjorn.

"So you see a fortress ready to be taken."

"Well, what do you see?" asked Bjorn Longspear.

"I see high, round, stone walls with one entrance. I see a prison that can be guarded by fifty men, whilst we gather provisions and prepare for the next leg of the journey. We can do what we want, when we want and risk little."

"You are not fit to lead. I will not tell my men to sit like gatekeepers when the blood of the enemy is ready to be spilled."

"What do you think, Olaf?" asked Hengist.

"I think we must be judged on the decisions we make."

"I agree," said Thorgood, "but which decision should we be judged against? Attack and slaughter, or hold the enemy as prisoners and exchange food for help?"

Bjorn held out a clenched fist.

"My hand goes in for the attack."

Olaf's flat hand went forward.

"My hand goes for caution now and attack at Oban."

"My hand is with Olaf," said Hengist.

Thorgood grinned. "My hand is with Bjorn."

Bjorn grinned too, as Thorgood went on, "I decide all equal votes and so we attack. Of course, Bjorn, you will be judged by this and if it fails you must agree to stand down. Your warriors will be divided between Olaf and myself."

"It will not fail," promised Bjorn and they parted.

"Get your men from the ships," yelled the Longspear over his shoulder.

Hengist looked at Thorgood. He was chuckling.

"You are as wily as a fox."

"Bjorn has set himself up to fail. Make sure he does. Go and cut the ropes on half of Bjorn's ships. The wind is from the south, so we should see them float by before we have to attack."

***

Colfan wriggled forward and looked across at Bron Skara. The enemy encircled it, but did not attack and he wondered why. His father had told him that the fortress had withstood attack from invaders many times before, but it hadn't happened in his lifetime, or his father's. He stared at the men who lined the walls. Endey was there. So was his brother. Other warriors stood beside them and Colfan didn't recognise them, which meant they were from the north of the island. He felt alone and tried to think of a way to get past the enemy, and join them on the battlements.

Four invaders stood apart from the others and seemed to be having a heated discussion. He guessed they were arguing about what to do next. They split up and returned to their men, who were formed into three fighting groups for the attack, but they still held their positions.

Two warriors from each group ran back to the sea, in three directions, and Colfan knew they were returning to their ships. He watched two men descend the path to Half Moon Bay and wriggled back to get a better view of them. A distant roar came up from the warriors who guarded the boats, as the messengers arrived. They eagerly grabbed weapons and ran back towards Bron Skara.

Colfan crawled back to the bay, all the time listening out for a warning shout from an enemy. None came. With one last, secret look at the line of ships, he realised they were truly unguarded and ran to the water's edge.

He climbed aboard the ship he had first hidden behind at dawn. It was well provisioned, but he ignored the barrels and boxes of food, the coiled ropes and oars, and concentrated on a pile of weapons. He grabbed a short sword and ran his thumb along the blade and threw it away.

He tried another. This time a line of blood appeared, and he dashed to the prow and jumped into the water. Colfan wanted to shout with delight, but resisted and ran from ship to ship, zig zagging between the bodies on the beach, cutting the ropes that held the longships to the shore.

Olaf's fleet began to drift seaward.

***

Thorgood stared ahead at the entrance to the fortress.

"Send a messenger to Bjorn and Olaf. Tell them to attack on my signal."

Two warriors hurried away. He counted to a hundred.

"Send a messenger to Bjorn and Olaf, ask them to study the defences on their side and recommend a weak point where we can all attack."

Two more warriors hurried away. He counted again and glanced at the headland off to his right. No ships.

"Send a message to Bjorn and Olaf. Why do I not have their suggestions about where to attack?"

He looked to his left. Olaf's ships, not Bjorn's, were bobbing in a circular bay.

"What is Hengist up to?"

He was tapped on the shoulder.

"Master, Bjorn's fleet drifts out into the ocean too."

"Get back to the ships," he ordered.

Bjorn watched Thorgood's men retreat.

"He is a coward," he roared.

Then one of his men pointed out to sea.

Later, as Olaf and Bjorn approached, Thorgood Firebrand hissed at Hengist.

"You did a thorough job, didn't you?"

"On Bjorn's ships, yes. On Olaf's, no. We have missed some of the islanders and should be careful."

"How many ships do I still command?" asked Thorgood.

"All of mine are recovered," said Bjorn, "except three smashed on rocks."

Olaf shook his head.

"Six ships lost, but one of these could be used for the passage to Scotland if repairs are made."

"So we are now five crews short and eight ships lost. Do you remember my words, Bjorn?"

"I do, but we still have enough. It was your indecision that lost us the day. All those stupid messengers. If we had just got on with it, the enemy would now be slain."

"Do not forget that your first decision placed Olaf's men in peril. Your second, his ships."

Olaf pointed an accusing finger at Bjorn.

"You are the one who is stupid. If you thought about tomorrow, and not the next moment, we would all be safer."

"So, the young, eager pup shows his true colours. I ought to run you through with my spear."

"Your spear is forfeit," said Thorgood, "half your men will now join me. Half will join Olaf. You will stay here, on Orkney."

"My men will follow me."

"Not if you are dead," warned Hengist.

"And a miller is going to kill me? Is he?"

"A miller will not have to," said Olaf, "I challenge you to fight to the death. Let Odin decide who is the better man."

Within an hour, Thorgood's commanders faced each other at

opposite ends of a longship. Bjorn lifted his long spear and waved it above his head. On the sands of Half Moon Bay his followers cheered and chanted.

"Longspear. Longspear. Longspear."

Olaf pulled his helmet over his face.

"The betting money is on Bjorn," said Hengist.

"Olaf is young and has all the courage of his father. His speed will trouble Bjorn."

"If they kill each other, you could end up without anyone to help you lead."

"I hope not. I have enough trouble leading you."

A hundred paces from the shore, sideways on so everyone could get a good view of the fight, the ship was secured by long ropes to two other longships at anchor. As waves rolled into the baythe craft rocked like a cradle. Standing high up on the prow and bow, Olaf and Bjorn rocked most of all.

Thorgood stepped forward and Half Moon Bay fell completely silent.

"A challenge has been made. Now Odin will decide who is fit to lead!"

"To the death," shouted the crowd.

"To the death," shouted Thorgood and he plunged his sword into the sand.

Olaf leapt down from the prow and landed on the deck. He wanted to reach the mast before Bjorn. The mast was the only thing he could hide behind and he would need all his agility to avoid the jabs from his opponent's long spear.

Bjorn took his time and walked confidently forward. His spear would keep him out of range of Olaf's sword. The pup had much to learn and he would give him such a lesson. His spear thrustforward and flashed to the right of the mast. Olaf stepped to one side. Bjorn stabbed out again and Olaf stepped the other way. A huge wave hit the side of the ship and they both stumbled over.

Olaf was quickest to rise and slashed out with his sword. It glanced off the top of Bjorn's helmet, which came off and clattered on the deck. Bjorn roared with rage and, with two hands on his spear, stabbed out, again and again. Olaf was forced back by the onslaught, caught his foot, and sprawled onto his back. Bjorn rushed him and raised his spear into the throwing position. Olaf saw it and rolled to one side. The spear missed his arched back by inches. Olaf leapt up, raised his sword and sliced the shaft of the spear in two. The iron spearhead was buried deep into the deck and over an arm's length of jagged, vibrating shaft stuck out of it. Bjorn drew a sword and brought it down onto Olaf's. Olaf struck back and the two blades smashed together, again, and again.

Both men pushed forward, as their blades sang out, and their eyes met. Bjorn brought his head down onto Olaf's face, viciously, and he cried out in pain. Another great wave hit the ship and they both sprawled on the deck, trying desperately to stand and gain an advantage.

This time Bjorn was quickest and charged at Olaf with his sword raised. Olaf leapt up, ran back to the prow, and jumped up onto the dragon's head. Bjorn's sword slashed out at his ankles. Olaf jumped and kicked Bjorn in the face. Then he grabbed the rope, which held the mast to the prow, cut one end and wrapped it around his arm and threw himself away from the ship. He swung out above the sea in a half circle and landed, elegantly, on the bow. Bjorn rose and looked for his enemy. He was gone. He spun around and saw Olaf at the far end of the ship, walking back to his position at the mast.

Bjorn roared again and whirled his sword above his head. Olaf waited and kept one arm around the mast for support. He was ready. The ship lurched sideways as another wave hit it and Bjorn was thrown to the floor. Olaf released his grip on the mast and drove at him. With both hands on the hilt, he smashed down at Bjorn, who raised his sword and with the terrific strength in his arm parried the blow.

Olaf struck down again and Bjorn held the blade away from his chest with just one hand clasped around the hilt. Then he kicked out and Olaf crashed back into the mast. Bjorn leapt up and aimed a blow at Olaf's head. Olaf ducked and Bjorn's sword bit deep into the mast. Olaf smashed the hilt of his sword into Bjorn's teeth and the warrior fell back onto the deck. This time he didn't get up.

An arm's length of cut spear stuck out of his belly. Blood oozed from his stomach and dribbled from his mouth when he snarled. He tried to lift his body off the shaft. Olaf wrenched Bjorn's sword from the mast and tossed it overboard, and stared at his opponent's blood soaked hands.

With an incredible strength of will Bjorn stood, swayed and pulled the short spear from the deck, and threw it at Olaf. It didn't even come close. Then he staggered forward, in blind rage, misty eyed, and with outstretched hands. He would wring the life out of the young pup. He would give him such a lesson.

Olaf dodged backwards and Bjorn placed his hands around the mast, and squeezed for all he was worth. The pup had a strong neck right enough, but he would break it. He had him now. He tried to laugh and only a strange gurgling sound came out.

Olaf moved, silently, behind the raving warrior and raised his sword for the last time. Bjorn's body slid down and lay, motionless, upon the deck. Olaf raised his helmet and studied a ring of blood, which stained the white pole at head height.

The mast would always bear the indents of Bjorn's fingers.

***

From a rocky crag, high above Half Moon Bay, Colfan watched and wondered why the invaders fought each other and not his own people.

***

Twenty days later, more ships arrived from Oslo fjord and an uneasy truce was brokered with the islanders. Thorgood did not want to lose any more men, or ships, and he knew the defenders in Bron Skara had few options. Their chieftains cautiously accepted an invitation to join him and feast aboard his ship. Everyone else followed, slowly, but were treated with the greatest respect by the Norse warriors. A bond was forged and Thorgood told them about the terrible famine, which drove them south to richer lands. But most of all he talked about losing his daughter.

Colfan told him that their harvest had been poor too, but they had never relied on grain alone. Their larder was the sea.

For food and freedom, the people of Orkney agreed to live in peace with the Norsemen and set about repairing their damaged ships. Thorgood's carpenters were amazed at their skill and copied them, and on the twenty fifth day after the first landing the masters of the one hundred and thirty longships were called together. They discussed the journey, how long they would be at sea, and directions, expected sightings and plans if any ships became separated from the others.

Next day, on the morning tide, Thorgood and Olaf led their ships south and Colfan watched the two groups of sails disappear.

He couldn't bring himself to say, "Good fortune," but even though he had lost friends to the warriors who came from the north, he couldn't bring himself to hold a grudge either. The Norsemen were fierce in battle. The fight at Half Moon Bay and the duel on the longship had proved that, and they were sure to return one day.

Colfan shrugged his shoulders. There wasn't a single, damn thing he could do about it and he decided to go fishing.

CHAPTER SEVENTEEN
The King's Secret Rider

Kind winds carried the Norse longships from Orkney to the barren and rocky coast of Sea Peoples Land. Never out of view of each other, the two fleets followed the coast west. Then the coastline ran southwards and Thorgood made notes about the small islands, inlets and wide bays. At noon on the third day at sea, a band of warriors shouted warnings at them from a headland. Some waved spears in a way that invited them to land and fight, but Thorgood ignored the taunts of Amera's descendants and sailed on.

That evening, Olaf Adanson joined him and they ate, and talked about the fight with Bjorn and how Bjorn's followers seemed to have accepted his new authority without question.

At dawn on the fourth day, Olaf woke Thorgood.

"Master, a single sail lies on the horizon. It heads straight for us."

An hour later the two ships drifted together and they stood at the prow, with Hengist, looking at the craft's white sail, and a black axe painted on it.

"Picts," said Olaf.

"They are said to be enemies of the Younger," added Hengist.

Thorgood nodded. "I wonder what they want."

"When one sail heads into a fleet, it is not war," said Olaf.

"Order the crew not to raise spear."

"Welcome to the waters of Skye," called a Black Kilt.

He was young, short and carried too much weight around his middle. His smile was warm and welcoming.

"I am Aglan, son of Denbara the Scribe, and the best Tongue Speaker amongst my people."

"And I am Thorgood Firebrand, Lord of the Norse Peoples."

"Well, Thorgood Firebrand, you have chosen fine weather for a sail."

Olaf smiled. The lad was fishing.

"We head south to Ulrika's Land," Thorgood told him, "where we hope to settle and prosper."

"I have sailed these waters since I was a boy and know them well.

Ulrika's Land must be many days' sail into the sun for its name is not known to me. If it is as fair as your ships, Thorgood Firebrand, I might just come with you."

Thorgood smiled as well.

"Do you need water, or provisions? My master, Tella the Mac Mar, commands Skye and great lands to the east. Perhaps you and your fine chieftains might consider feasting with him this very evening?"

Hengist glanced at Thorgood and shrugged his shoulders.

"What have we to lose? I do not believe they will try to harm us with all our warriors here."

"Lead the way, Aglan, we have barrels of ale."

The young lad laughed.

"When you are the guests of the Mac Mar at Deros, the last thing you need to bring is ale."

Next morning the Norse fleets sailed away from Skye into strong headwinds and the longships became strung out as they tacked to make any kind of progress.

"My head hurts," moaned Hengist, "and I swear I have eaten a whole pig."

"You behaved like one as well."

Tella had spoken, through Aglan, and told them that the Younger had raised a thousand men when they did battle at Carn Liath. If that was all the Scots could raise then Thorgood knew he would be at an advantage.

"What did you think of the Mac Mar?"

"I wouldn't trust him as far as I could throw him," said Hengist, "but we cannot doubt his feelings towards the Scots. He hates them with a passion. Did you see the scar on his shoulder?"

Thorgood nodded. "We must keep our presence on Tiree a secret until the very last minute. Do you think he will keep his side of the bargain?"

"He will if there is a chance of getting back the High Lands he lost to the Younger. We don't need them. We have enough high places of our own. What we need is good farmland."

Thorgood thought about the feast in the Great Hall at Deros. Tella was a very generous host and eager to forge an alliance. They had talked into the late hours with him, his son, Gath, and two of his generals, Borak and Tumora. Gath had drawn a map on the earth floor and pointed out the main paths that led away from the Younger's palace. One went south to a ferry at Culross on the Mighty Forth. One went west to Oban through the High Glens and one went north to Tain. This path passed by Dalwhinnie and skirted a long way around Carn Liath. Aglan admitted there were other paths, but if you controlled these three then the Younger could be kept in complete ignorance about anything that happened in the western half of his kingdom.

Tella's people would kill any of the Younger's messengers and stop news reaching the palace. His own son would lead the party. Then Thorgood had sent Olaf back to his ship and he brought back three bows and three quivers of arrows. Weapons of this quality were rare and Olaf had shown Gath, Borak and Tumora how to use them. By dawn the three Picts could hit a stone jar at fifty paces.

Hengist plunged his face into a bucket of water.

"What do you mean, I behaved like a pig?"

Thorgood ignored him and made notes about the passage to Tiree Bay.

***

Tumora lifted three packs, his own and one each for Gath and Borak, and staggered under their weight to the stables. He checked the provisions, set aside for him. Bread for three days, salted meat for ten, a bag of biscuits and leather flasks of water, a sword, the Norse bow and quiver, and a large sleeping blanket.

"Not much to live on for such a long adventure."

Borak and Gath joined him.

"Is that all there is?" asked Gath.

"It's all we can carry," said Borak. "It looks as though we will be living off our wits, for a while at least."

At nightfall, the three riders landed to the south of Oban and headed east. Cautiously, they crossed the Oban to Glasgow path, and headed north to join the path that ran through the High Glens to the Younger's palace.

They decided to ride only at night and camped in secret places during the day. It would take three nights to reach their positions if they really pushed along. Then they planned to take one path each and watch it for another three days before meeting up again. Their greatest fear was running into Scottish warriors in darkness, but they met no-one.

Tumora sat with his legs crossed, his bow and quiver on his lap, and stared through tall pines at the path. He felt exhausted and his eyelids began to droop. He had ridden right through the night, grabbed an hour's sleep before dawn, and now tried to concentrate on the comings and goings south of the palace. Borak had told him to watch for lone riders on the finest horses. These would most likely be the King's messengers.

So far, two carts had trundled by, full of boxes, heading south to the ferry at Culross. A young boy, leading a herd of goats had passed too, and an old man. No riders at all. Still, it was a warm day and he could have worse duties to perform in the name of the Mac Mar. He wondered how Gath and Borak were faring and glanced back into the pines to check on his horse. He knew he wasn't far from the Younger's palace, perhaps two to three miles at most. Where were all the travellers? This was supposed to be one of the main routes from the south of the Scottish kingdom.

Away to his left he saw a group of people on the path. He stiffened, then relaxed. They had no horses. There was a man, perhaps a warrior, a woman who was quite good looking for a Scot, and six children. Two boys were shouting and hitting each other with sticks. The woman screamed at them and they ignored her. She screamed at her husband and he said something. The boys ignored him too and the man shrugged his shoulders. When the family passed, Tumora fell fast asleep.

Nothing much happened on the second day either. It rained heavily and he wrapped himself up in his blanket, and shivered whilst he watched. At dawn on the third day he felt bored and useless. As the first rays of sun fell on the path, he crawled back to the edge of the pines and peered down. Twenty heavily armed riders trotted in single file northwards. All of them wore brown, green and ochre tartans, and carried huge swords. They looked like clan leaders. None spoke and they soon passed.

Ten minutes later a single rider galloped towards him. Checking that the road was empty, Tumora dashed down the slope, his bow ready. As the Younger's messenger thundered around a bend he let his arrow fly. It struck the man full in the chest and unseated him. The horse carried on at full gallop. Tumora lifted the warrior across his shoulders and carried him into the pines, then went to look for his horse. Without a rider, to urge the beast on it had soon stopped and now grazed by the side of the path. He gently took the bridle and returned to the safety of the pines. No sooner had he tied the horse to a tree, than he heard hooves again. He grabbed his bow and dashed back.

Heading south was a lone rider on a magnificent, white stallion. Tumora let an arrow fly again, it buried itself into the man's back and he let out a painful cry, but held on. Then he was gone.

Tumora went back and searched the first messenger's body. Not much in his pockets, but a fine dagger in his belt. One of the saddle bags held food. He bit into an apple and tossed another to his horse. A second bag contained a flask of water, a pipe and a parchment, and he strapped this bag to his.

***

"I killed three riders, how about you?" boasted Gath.

Borak raised an eyebrow as he looked at Gath's full quiver.

"Two for me and one put up a decent struggle."

He raised a finger to a gash on his cheek.

"I killed one," said Tumora, dropping the rider's bag beside the fire. "I may have killed another, but I cannot be sure."

"Not sure?"

"My arrow hit his back, but he galloped on and I lost him."

Gath nodded.

"On the third day I saw many finely dressed riders heading towards the palace. Twenty at least."

"I saw fifty clan leaders riding to the palace on the third day," Gath told them.

"My guess is that the High Table has been summoned from all over the Scottish kingdom," reasoned Borak, "I think something is up."

Gath rose and picked up the saddle bag.

"I will now return to talk with my father. You two watch the path to Oban. If an army heads west, send word to me at Deros."

Borak and Tumora rose too and bowed respectfully, and in darkness the son of the king rode away.

"Do you think he killed any riders?" asked Tumora.

"No idea," admitted Borak, "but there is something I really do not like about Gath."

***

"I killed six of the Younger's riders," boasted Gath and he threw a bag at Aglan the Tongue Speaker. "It is full of secret messages and warnings from the west of his kingdom. He remains in ignorance of Thorgood's progress."

Tella studied his son.

"And Borak and Tumora?"

"They have stayed to spy on anyone who takes the Oban road. They will warn us if the High Table moves west."

Aglan opened the bag and removed the pipe and parchment. The Mac Mar slapped his son on the back.

"We'll make a king out of you yet."

Gath beamed at his father.

The tongue speaker read the parchment and raised his eyebrows. It wasn't a secret message for the Younger. It was a poem, intense and beautifully crafted. He had never seen a love letter so full of desire.

***

Little Tanny was chasing the chickens again. Calum and Jock were coming to blows over a large piece of wood, and Mairi was hard at work in the kitchen preparing broth for the evening meal.

She spoke sternly to her husband.

"Do you not have work to do?"

Dougie looked up, reluctantly, from his breakfast bowl, finished it and pulled a shawl over his shoulders.

"My, we are smart today," smiled Mairi.

Dougie glanced down at the brooch he used to fasten it. The ruby shone red in the light that streamed through the small cottage window, and Dougie's mind went back to the great battle at Carn Liath the autumn before. He kissed her and went out into the garden.

Like many of his countrymen, Dougie took great care, a great pride, in growing herbs, beans and peas. Having something to eat in the hungry months depended on it. Then he headed up the grassy track to the high pastures and, as he always did, he began the day by checking his sheep.

"Thirty two, thirty three and ... thirty four. Good," counted Dougie to himself, "no Black Kilts around here last night."

He walked down to the stream, checked its level and knew there was enough water for his animals to drink. But the grass in the field by the old pines was very short, and needed to be left a while to grow back, and he spent most of the morning persuading the sheep to graze on fresh pastures.

"I should get myself a dog."

Later, he sat down by an ancient standing stone and looked around at the high pastures and far hills, feeling something deep inside. Like the sun, it warmed him.

"There is no more worth having than this."

He wondered how Alec, his twin, was getting on. Was he safe? What adventures might he have had on the Great Sea? Had he been a part of a real adventure too? Dougie glanced at his arm and ran a finger along the scar Torik Benn had given him. From now on adventures were for other people.

Last night Mairi had said that even though they had not heard from Alec it did not mean he was harmed, or lost. But Dougie knew he was well. He knew it with all the surety only a twin can have. With the children tucked in and asleep, they had talked about Dougie's time away as part of the Younger's army. He never boasted about his part in the battle, in fact he tried to avoid any of the terrible images he held in his mind. But he did talk about Alistair and the men of Tain, and rather timidly about how Malcolm had given him his brooch. It seemed a funny thing for a king to give to a shepherd, particularly as there were so many of the others who were braver, stronger and more deserving than him.

Dougie held Amera's stone in his hand. It was beautiful. No doubting it. Then he pictured Mairi's smiling face again and his inner feeling of love, of complete happiness, took hold of him. He pinned the brooch to his shawl.

"You are a great gift, but you cannot hold a candle to some things."

The stone shone out, red, and gradually faded, as if it was content to sleep in a troubled world.

As Dougie ate his oat bread he heard the far off sound of a galloping horse and got to his feet. A magnificent white stallion jumped the stile. But it was not the beautiful horse, which held Dougie's attention. It was the arrow in the rider's back.

The horse slowed to a trot then, coming to a halt, lowered its neck and began to graze. The stranger looked as though he was going to fall and Dougie caught his arm, and gently lifted him down. The arrow was unlike any he had ever seen. Strange markings were carved along its shaft. Dougie had to bend close to his face to understand him.

"Danger," whispered the man, "great danger."

The shepherd looked hastily around.

"I cannot see any."

"Great .... danger," gasped the man.

"Who are you?"

"I am .... the king's secret messenger. You are ..... to go to the Younger ...... immediately."

Dougie cradled the messenger's head in his hands.

"Why?"

"Terrible danger ..... from the islands," gasped the man, "you must .... go to Malcolm now."

"But, I cannot leave you," replied Dougie kindly.

"Promise me .... that you will go straight to the palace, for it is only when I have heard your solemn oath .... that I can rest," he pleaded.

"I give you my oath, but what about you?"

"Forget me," mumbled the dying man. "Take ..... the King's horse."

"My wife will be here soon and she has a way with the medicine."

Dougie tried to reassure him, but if Mairi did come to the high pastures, as she sometimes did, it would be too late for this poor soul.

Malcolm's secret rider closed his eyes for the last time.

Dougie covered the body with stones and mounted the stallion, and looked down towards his farm. It was only a short ride away and he should tell Mairi about his orders. But, he had made a solemn promise and Dougie turned the horse towards the north. He could not imagine what Mairi would think if she went to the field and found him gone and a rough grave there in his place. Still, the King *was* the King and if *he* had summoned him, then he simply had no choice in the matter.

He quickly reached the outer fields of the farm, crossed the stream by way of the old ford and headed for the path he had taken on foot, alone, the year before. Dougie realised that, like the last time, he had left in haste and without food.

He patted the stallion. "At least I'll get there quickly on you, boy."

At the edge of his land, he pulled back on the reins and the horse slowed. Turning in the saddle, to take one last glance at his home, Dougie found himself looking down on a cloaked stranger.

"Hello," said Dougie.

"Hello, Dougie of Dunfermline," replied the old man, who Dougie had seen from a distance so many times before.

"You know my name?"

"I have known you and Alec since you were babies."

There was a kindness in his voice that put Dougie at ease. Then his voice was grave.

"These are dark times. The enemies of the king may still be nearby so do not stop, for any reason. Go straight to the Younger and stay away from the main paths."

"But how do you know I am on the way to the palace?" asked Dougie suspiciously.

"There are many things that are known to me and many more that remain a mystery."

He lifted the hood of his cloak to cover his bearded face. Dougie thought it was the wisest face he had ever seen.

"I feel I know you so well and yet this is the first time we have ever spoken," said Dougie quickly, fearing the man was preparing to go.

"You do know me, as I knew your father and his father before him."

"You knew my father?"

"Aye Dougie, he was a fine man. Perhaps when all this is over we will be able to talk more, but go now. Malcolm suspects the threat to the kingdom comes from the Outer Islands, but make sure he knows it *will* come soon."

"The rider said the danger comes from the Islands."

"And stay close to Alistair for he is a good man."

"You know Alistair?"

"Aye, I know him," and the man began to walk away. "Mairi will need to know you are safe and on the way to the palace. I will tell her."

"Thank you," murmured Dougie, as he watched the stranger go.

Dougie turned the horse towards the north and then stopped. Looking back over his shoulder he said, "I don't even know your name."

The stranger had vanished but on the wind Dougie thought he heard a single word. "Myroy."

The great stallion was strong and swift. Importantly, it also seemed to know when to slow down, for Dougie was not an experienced rider. Many times he felt himself slipping off its back and he clasped the harness for all he was worth. Hour after hour they travelled, through farm and field and over hill and high moor, and the sun was falling in the sky when at last they reached the walls of the palace. Dougie dismounted and walked towards the great gate, which led into the central courtyard.

"Halt, who approaches the palace of the king?" yelled a huge man, guarding the entrance.

"It is I, Dougie of Dunfermline and I am here at the command of the King."

The guard eyed him suspiciously and raised his claymore so its sharp point lightly touched Dougie's chest.

"And where did you get the king's horse from?"

"From the king's messenger. He died in my arms."

"I did not know the king had sent a messenger."

"He was a secret messenger," muttered Dougie, not much liking the way the conversation was going.

For the first time, Dougie became aware of three more guards who had walked up behind him. One of them wore a fine tartan tunic and carried a long wooden staff. He seemed to be in charge of the others for he stepped forward to take a closer look at Dougie.

"And what is this?" asked the man, pointing at Dougie's gold brooch.

"It was a gift from the Younger himself."

"And how do you earn your living?"

"I tend my flock," mumbled Dougie weakly.

"And what would Malcolm the Younger, King of all the Scots and Protector of the Stone of Destiny be doing giving a humble farmer such a treasure?"

The guard ripped the brooch from Dougie's shawl.

Now, and not for the first, or last time, the shepherd was to do something he would come to regret later. He punched the man on the nose. Two pairs of strong arms seized him and forced him to his knees.

The warrior held his face. "These are troubled times, Dougie of Dunfermline. If that is truly your name."

"Aye, it is."

"Well let us see what a spell in the dungeon does for your honesty."

Dougie was dragged away kicking and shouting.

"I *am* Dougie and I *am* here at the call of the king!"

They wrestled him down a steep and narrow stone staircase. Eventually, the shepherd was thrown headfirst into a tiny cell. It was dark, cold and smelled of misery. The thick door crashed shut and a man's face appeared at a small grille. He laughed and spat at his new prisoner. The grille snapped shut.

CHAPTER EIGHTEEN

Pride of Tiree

Shivering in the cold cell, in complete darkness, and with nothing to occupy his mind, Dougie soon lost all sense of time. He thought about the *watcher's* words, but no matter how many times he went back over their conversation, he could not imagine how the man knew of him, or his father.

Eventually, Dougie crawled into a corner, made himself into a ball and went to sleep. He was woken by shouting and the sound of a key being turned. The door burst open and a deep, apologetic voice called out to him.

"My dear boy."

In the darkness Dougie struggled to see who was pulling him to his feet. The deep voice spoke again.

"I am so sorry."

Something was thrust into his hand. He recognised it instantly. The gold brooch.

"Thank you, Your Majesty."

"There is no need to give thanks to someone who has wrongfully imprisoned another."

Dougie spoke quickly. "I came as fast as I could and I bring evil news. Your messenger has been killed. But before he died he begged me to tell you that danger comes soon from the Outer Islands."

The king listened intently.

"Come on, laddie, let's get out of here."

The shepherd followed him out of the cell, up the long stairway and into bright sunshine. Dougie blinked and swayed a little on his feet. The king took his arm and they crossed the Palace Green, more as friends than as master and servant.

The great banqueting hall was full of warriors and clan leaders, and Dougie was invited to sit at Malcolm's right hand, a place normally held for guests of honour. The young prince Ranald sat to Malcolm's left and he did not smile at the new visitor. He wondered why a part of his inheritance had been gifted to a shepherd. One day he would take the brooch back.

Dougie tried to hide his embarrassment at joining the king's table by looking around the magnificent hall. At one side was a huge fireplace. Ten grown men could have stood up in it. Within its black stone grate, a blazing tree trunk, which would have kept Dougie's family warm all winter, sent dancing firelight into every dark corner.

The hall buzzed with urgent conversation and Dougie recognised some faces from his last adventure. Robert of Inverness was there and so were many of the clan leaders who made up the High Table. But there was a face Dougie searched for more than any other and at last he saw him. Sitting amongst the remaining members of the men of Tain was Alistair of Cadbol. As he gave Dougie a friendly wave, a hush fell on the hall and the Younger rose to his feet.

"Whatever lies ahead will be best faced together."

Dougie felt that if Portalla had been there he would have shouted, "Hear, hear."

"As some of you know, our messengers have been killed and little news reaches us from around the kingdom. The news we do hear is dark. We face desperate times. The Outer Islands are in trouble and need our help. The raids that began before the Season of Storms have begun again. We do not know who they are, or where they come from, but we do know their intentions are evil."

The Younger paused, all eyes were on him.

"They are burning our houses."

A low murmur went up in the Hall.

"They are taking our women and children to be slaves."

There was a louder murmur.

"And they are stealing our cattle."

"Save the women," shouted Gordon of Balgedie.

"Get the cattle back," cried the others.

"The Outer Islands are too far away to send an army to, even if we had enough ships to take us across the Great Sea. We do not even know where, or when, the next attack will be."

Robert of Inverness prayed that whatever lay ahead did not involve the old people who had helped at Carn Liath.

"As I see it," continued Malcolm impressively, "we must send a small band of our best warriors to the islands. They need to discover *who* is behind this and come back to the High Table with a plan."

There were murmurs of agreement, but no-one volunteered for such a dangerous mission.

"Robert of Inverness. Would you lead the men to the islands?"

Robert stiffened with pride.

"It would be a great honour, Your Majesty."

"Take Alistair and the men of Tain with you."

Once again Dougie was to do something he would regret later.

"May I go too?" he said.

After the banquet, Alistair and Dougie walked around the palace walls and talked about all that had happened to them since they had last been together. Alistair had been commanded to deliver a message of goodwill to the leaders of all the largest clans and he spoke about his journey to the southern borderlands and to the clans of the Great Plain, to the north of the royal palace.

"The High Table is growing," he said.

Dougie thought his own story would seem dull, commonplace, to his friend, but Alistair listened carefully about how the early rains had threatened the barley, and he asked many questions after Mairi and the children. Then he explained about Arkinew, the king's alchemist. Since the breaking of the bond with Malcolm the Elder, his previous master, the terrible powers he had once commanded had gradually faded away. Despite this, the Younger remained loyal to Archie and it saddened him to see the alchemist reduced to a figure of fun by the children at the palace. But Malcolm never forgot the wise counsel Arkinew, the greatest of Myroy's apprentices, had given him. More than anyone, even Murdoch, Arkinew had helped to widen the Charter of the Clans.

They passed the eastern watchtower and had just stepped onto the Palace Green when a deafening explosion stopped them in their tracks. Twenty paces away, Archie's *Guardian Shed* shook. Thick yellow smoke poured out of the hole where the *Pains of Class* had been. The metal thing on the roof shot up into the air and landed at their feet. Archie coughed, spluttered, and walked backwards out of the hut with Gangly on his shoulder.

The alchemist was very old, but the wrinkled face, behind his long, white beard, was as eager and curious as ever. But it was not the beard, or gnarled appearance, you noticed when you first met Archie, it was the small, mischievous looking Ghilly Dhu who sat on his shoulder. Gangly was one of the last of the imps, who in ancient times had been plentiful across the forests of Caledonia. He was dressed in a bright red jacket and had legs that were twice as long as his short and stocky body. When Archie walked backwards, Gangly's legs swayed and his eyes darted in every direction.

He whispered into his master's ear.

Without turning to look at them, Archie said, "Why, it is Alistair and Dougie, how are you both?" He reached an arm out behind his back to shake their hands.

"I must tell you about my new *experident*."

"What are you working on this time?" asked Alistair, smiling to himself.

"Grumf," grunted Gangly, and the old alchemist grimaced.

"So you still lack confidence in the power of the Ancient Ones do you?"

"Of course not," said Dougie, "it must be, well, a little difficult to work in all the smoke, that's all."

"Smoke and fire are the price we pay for progress," stated Archie importantly. "Come, let me show you."

He led them into his smelly *Guardian Shed*. It was ten paces wide and ten paces long, but inside it seemed much smaller. This was because of the great collection of glass jars, which sat upon rows and rows of shelves. Every inch of wall was covered by them and Dougie strained his eyes to see what was in them. There were many dead creatures in vinegar, all manner of precious stones and powders. In one large jar was the skull of a man, the last traces of skin clinging to the bone.

"I call them my curiosities, and there is no finer assembly of the ordinary and the mystical anywhere in the known world."

"Looks like a pile of junk to me," thought Dougie, and Gangly gave him a knowing look, but said nothing.

"This," Archie croaked, "is the future."

He clasped a long pipe in his gnarled hands. It was as long as a man is tall and had a small hole in one end.

"Looks like a pipe," said Alistair.

"Grumf," barked Gangly.

"Doubters. I am surrounded by small-minded doubters."

Archie waved the pipe over his shoulder at Alistair.

"By the eyes of the wise Ghilly Dhu, this will be the future of all wars and the king who wields this *Bartillery* will be the ruler of all lands and all peoples."

"Grumf," grunted the imp, as his little hand smacked his master in the ear.

"I am not mad," yelled Archie, "for I have looked into the Oracle of the Ancient Ones and seen death and fire coming from the mouth of these *Bartilleries*."

"Grumf."

"Say that again and I will be having Ghilly Dhu for supper tonight."

Gangly grinned mischievously. Archie grabbed the pipe and a large arrow from the table, and pushed his way past the two friends.

Outside Dougie blinked in the sunshine. Archie was striding backwards with much purpose to the centre of the Green and, on seeing him, women dashed from doorways to grab their children and drag them to safety. Archie thrust the pipe into the grass so it stood upright. He took a cow's horn from his pocket and poured something into the pipe. Then he rammed in the arrow. Dougie noticed that the arrow had a small iron box at the top and a piece of cord dangling out of a hole on one of the box's sides.

Malcolm came over to see what was going on.

"Is this wise?" asked the king.

"It is the future."

"Future or not, we agreed no more explosions."

"The work of the alchemist must go on."

Archie bent over the pipe and sent a spark from his tinder box onto the string. It began to fizzle. Then he put a spark from his tinder box to the hole at the base of pipe.

"Take cover," said Archie.

At this simple instruction Dougie was amused to see Malcolm, King of all the Scots and Protector of the Stone of Destiny, pick up his long robes and bolt towards the safety of his castle.

Dougie and Alistair stood rooted to the spot, awe-struck at the *whoosh* that came from the pipe and the speed at which the arrow shot up into the sky.

"Grumf," warned the imp.

"Yes, Gangly," agreed Archie, "it is supposed to go bang."

They watched the arrow until it was a mere speck against the clouds. It seemed to be wobbling and losing speed. Indeed it seemed to have reached the limit of its climb and was starting to fall back to earth.

"Grumf."

"What do you mean? 'Cover?' I've got my best robes on," said Archie calmly.

"Grumf, grumf."

"Yes," agreed Archie, "take cover!"

The alchemist dashed, backwards, into his shed. As if in slow motion, the arrow got bigger. It fell at an alarming speed into the iron smoke hole in the roof and exploded. Great plumes of black smoke burst out of every opening, the wooden walls were flung in all directions and the roof fell down. A man's skull shot across the green and bounced like a ball.

The two friends ran to the hut and pulled Archie from the blazing ruin.

"The *Bartillery* works, it works," shouted the alchemist excitedly as his robes smouldered.

"Grumf," coughed Gangly and a small smoke ring came out of his mouth.

"It is unfortunate though," reflected Archie sadly, "for all it needs is something called a *Guide-Ants system* and that will not be invented for many hundreds of years."

"I think we had better go now," said Alistair.

"Where are you off to this time?" Archie asked.

"On the king's business to the islands at the end of the world."

"The wailing of your loved ones shall be heard forever and your broken bones never found," shrieked Archie.

Dougie's heart sank.

"Your end is nigh, nigh you hear me, nigh," Archie shrieked again.

With a sad shake of his head, he began to collect together the few unbroken glass jars.

***

To a stranger, the men of Tain, who now numbered only nine, might appear unlikely soldiers. The youngest was sixteen and the oldest sixty. The shortest was wee Donald, with Big Hamish twice his height. A mix of farmers, fishermen and ale-makers. A more scruffy and ill-disciplined lot you might never meet, but Dougie knew their true worth.

The friends had much to catch up on and so the journey from the palace to Oban went quickly. It was a fine spring day and this was a beautiful part of the world. The paths wound up through high hills, covered in purple heather, and there were many mountain streams to drink from. Robert of Inverness rode the leading horse and seemed to enjoy the authority the Younger had given him. The men of Tain hated it.

By the first evening of the journey they had climbed steadily and reached a place known locally as the hermit's cave. It was a lovely spot, sheltered, wooded and beside a fast flowing river. They sat around their fire and discussed the next part of their journey. It would be another two days to Oban where they would stay at the house of Kenneth of Blacklock. He was said to be grumpy and miserable, but his loyalty to the crown and his ability as a seaman were without question.

Once rested, and with the morning tide, they would sail for the islands. The men of Tain knew little about them, except that the people of Mull were true Scots, who lived a lonely and isolated existence. Few of them ever journeyed to the mainland and even fewer people went to Mull. Dougie didn't think there was anything strange about this. After all, it was only last autumn when he had left his farm for the very first time. Alistair said that the islands were at the very edge of the known world and surrounded by the Great Sea.

"What is the sea like?" asked Dougie.

"Have you not seen a loch?" answered Alistair. "Well, it is like a loch, only bigger. You know it is the sea because whichever way you look, you cannot see the land."

Dougie's heart missed a beat. He didn't like the sound of that.

By morning, rain was lashing down on the camp and everyone was soaked through. They ate their brose in silence and set off quickly for Oban. This part of the journey was a miserable affair and Dougie could not help but wonder how the weather could change so greatly the appearance of the landscape and the mood of men.

However, they made good progress and before sundown the sea was in sight. How grey and angry it seemed. Tall waves crashed onto the land and the small port of Oban looked as though it was clinging helplessly to the shore.

Robert led them down a narrow lane to a small house at the edge of the village. A warm glow shone out of its window and Dougie saw a model ship on the sill. Robert knocked importantly on the old door and it was some time before they heard footsteps approaching. The door swung open and a tall, dark haired man, stood before them. Rugged, handsome and stern-faced, Dougie thought he was someone who could command great authority.

"Who are you?" the man asked gruffly.

"I am Robert of Inverness and we are a party in the service of the king."

"What do you want?"

"Are you Kenneth of Blacklock?"

"What is it to you?"

"Kenneth," interrupted Alistair, "we have news from the Younger. We need your help."

The man looked them over. Dougie started to shiver as the cold rain ran down his back.

"Well, it is a dreich night, fit for neither man nor beast, so you had better come in."

If on the outside the sailor's manners were a little rude and to the point, this was in stark contrast to his hospitality. Kenneth gave them all large tumblers of heather ale and a delicious supper of fish broth and oat bread.

They sat around a roaring fire to dry and felt mighty relieved to be indoors. Outside the wind howled and the rain pounded on the cottage roof.

"Will we be able to sail for the islands in the morning?" asked Alistair.

"Who knows?" replied Kenneth. "We shall see what we shall see at the dawn tide."

They slept soundly, despite the storm outside, and at first light they awoke to find Kenneth gone. Rain was still pouring down and when he returned his shawl dripped with water.

"Get your things together," he ordered sharply.

They collected their claymores, shields and food, and walked down the cobbled lane to the harbour. Dougie found it hard to keep up with the big man's fast pace. The *Pride of Tiree* had a single mast and no cabins for shelter. Fifty paces long, strong and with a lovingly cared for appearance, its wood newly varnished, the brass polished and the deck ordered, neat and clean, Helden wouldn't have recognised it.

The rain eased off and the ship made good speed with the help of the spring tide. Dougie, who had been very nervous going aboard, began to feel more at ease as he became familiar with the gentle rocking motion of the ship. The men of Tain were excited to be getting underway. Some of them were fishermen, like Helden had been, and were impressed with the craft's speed into the wind. Kenneth appeared to be completely at home at the tiller. As they left the shelter of Oban Sound he ordered two of the Tain fishermen to raise the sail.

Dougie started to feel more and more keenly the rising and falling of the ship before the growing waves. His head started to swim and his stomach felt as though it wanted to leave his very body. He hung on to side of the boat and was sick. Never had he experienced such misery. The sea sickness seemed to go on forever and, as there was no let up in the ferocity of the waves, there was no end to his suffering. In fact, the waves were growing to become the size of small hills.

The *Pride of Tiree* was tossed up and down, and lurched sideways as if it were a piece of driftwood. Great walls of water crashed onto the open deck and the ship tipped alarmingly to one side.

"Start bailing. Bail for *your lives*," shouted Kenneth.

The mention of "*your lives*" had a profound effect on the crew and they learned very quickly what was required. They each grabbed a bucket and scooped water over the ship's rail. After half an hour the ship returned to an even keel and all aboard were wet, cold and exhausted. Dougie noticed that he felt a bit better and committed himself to keeping busy for the rest of the voyage. Any job, no matter how small, Dougie would take it on with real determination in fear that the sickness would return. Kenneth looked on approvingly.

"You could make a seafarer," he said, but Dougie's reply was drowned by the wind.

There was little conversation and even less food taken, except by the skipper and the fishermen who seemed to gain some amusement from the suffering of their shipmates. The voyage seemed to last forever, despite the stiff breeze that helped the *Pride of Tiree* make good speed towards the islands. Dougie, who had relieved Kenneth at the tiller for the tenth time, looked at the stars through the gaps in the menacing clouds. He had never seen stars that shone so brightly, or seemed so close.

"Do not forget, laddie, to keep the North Star on your right hand, for that will keep us steered to the west." Kenneth smiled. "The sea will start to calm now. The worst of the storm is over and, in truth, we did not see the worst of it."

Dougie tried to imagine how it could ever have been worse than it had been.

When he awoke next morning, he felt hungry. The Great Sea was calmer now and as deep a blue as the sky. The mountainous waves had subsided along with the atmosphere of misery, which had gripped them. Hamish offered him a bowl of brose and he took it gratefully and ate the lot.

Dougie's brother had often talked about running away to sea, but it had never appealed to him. Alec, who was older than Dougie by just a few minutes, had left to find a different life and adventure in faraway places. Dougie often wondered about him and how he could ever have been drawn away from their farm and the known routines of tending the land, but watching the boat cut through the waves on a beautiful day, Dougie began to see some of the attraction. Then he thought about Mairi and the children. Home felt a long way away.

The sun had passed its highest point when there was a shout from the bow of the ship.

"Land, I can see land," yelled Robert excitedly.

"Do you know this shore?" asked Alistair.

"Aye," said Kenneth, "it is Mull."

"What is it like?"

"It is the nearest and largest of the Outer Islands. There is good fishing, a few fine cottages and not much else."

"How many people live here?" asked Dougie.

"Not more than a hundred."

"It must be a lonely existence."

"Aye. But some people like it that way," said Kenneth.

Under full sail, the *Pride of Tiree* sped towards the island and the skipper steered her towards a small harbour around which thirty low-lying cottages, with turf roofs, huddled together for comfort. Kenneth looked grave.

"What is the matter?" asked Dougie.

"No women, or children."

Armed warriors stood at the top of a low wall, holding spears that could be thrown at a moment's notice.

"Men of Mull," called Kenneth, "do you not know me?"

"Aye, we know *you*, but we do not know *them*," said one, pointing an accusing spear at Dougie.

"These are true Scots, Scots men like you, in the service of the king," said Kenneth with great authority. "This is not the welcome a stranger should receive."

"But these are dark times," replied the man, "how do we know you are indeed on the king's business?"

He paused, and a cool sea wind blew through his long grey hair. Dougie stepped forward and threw something up to the warrior. It caught the sun and flashed red and gold. The warrior stared at it for some time and then offered Dougie his hand, and pulled him up onto the side of the dock.

"I am mighty glad you have come."

"I am mighty glad you caught it," replied Dougie, and Murdoch, the Protector of all the peoples of the Outer Islands and brother to Malcolm the Younger, gave him back his brooch.

CHAPTER NINETEEN

To the End of the World

They were taken up a steep lane into the village and, after a signal from Murdoch, the women and children returned from their hiding places in the surrounding hills. They were led by Murdoch's daughter, Margaret, and a small girl who walked silently by her side clutching a dolly to her chest. All of them kept their distance from the visitors.

The men of Tain rested in a small cottage until Murdoch's guards called on them at sundown, and took them to the Hall of the Protector. Over a dram of heather ale, Alistair told the men of Mull about their mission and the terrible journey from Oban. Kenneth sat some way apart from the others.

Murdoch told them that there had been three raids since the beginning of spring on Tiree, the outermost isle, two attacks on Coll, which was Mull's nearest neighbour, and one raid on Mull itself.

"They come in long ships the like of which we have not seen before. They have shields along the sides and carvings of fierce dragons on their bow. Their warriors are tall and many have red beards. They all talk in a strange tongue, carry axes and are skilled archers."

He laid an arrow upon the table. Dougie looked at it. Along the shaft were the same letters he had seen written on the arrow that had killed the king's secret messenger.

"Runes," said Hamish, "these are Norse runes."

All eyes in the smoky hall turned on the big man as he examined the arrow.

"My father's father used to talk about them. Many years ago people from the north came to trade with the fishing villages along the coast where I grew up. The description you used for the boats is the same as told to me."

"Did they attack you too?" asked Murdoch.

"No they did not," said Hamish, "they came to trade furs for cloth, leather for grain, jewellery for silver. They left a carved stone on the edge of our village as a sign of friendship and it is covered in these runes."

"And did they have red beards?"

"My grandfather said so, but I have never seen one and neither had my father."

"Our experience has been very different," said Murdoch solemnly.

"I can understand that," said Hamish, "for I was told that in battle the Norsemen do not fear death. They believe there is no greater honour to their gods than to die in battle."

Dougie shivered and thought the best time to die would be counting the sheep as a very old man.

"If we want to find out more then we must go to Tiree," said Alistair. "Will you take us there, Kenneth?"

"Aye," replied the sailor simply, "first thing in the morning."

It was a pleasant evening, for the company was good, but the conversation kept returning to the threat from the north. Dougie was feeling warm and relaxed, when he noticed a man sitting in a corner away from the others. He was dressed in a woollen cloak with the black hood pulled down so no part of his face could be seen. He was a big man and Dougie wondered if he had once been a soldier, for a small axe was tattooed on the back of his left hand.

Dougie turned to speak with his companions and when he looked again the man was gone.

As the evening drew to a close, Dougie stepped out into the cool night air, and walked down to the quayside. No distant shore could be seen and he thought of his home and how far away Mairi was. He turned to go and when he reached the cottage he saw what looked like a coin on the ground. Dougie bent to pick it up and there was a loud *thwack* as an arrow smashed into the wooden door above his head.

Dougie swung round to catch a glimpse of a man in a black cloak disappearing like a shadow into the night.

He stood for many minutes looking at the arrow, his feet frozen to the floor. It had Norse runes along its shaft. He rubbed the coin between his thumb and fingers. It was thick and heavy, with the face of a bearded man on one side. On the other side was a fortress on a mountain.

"A Pictish coin, I wonder what it's doing here?" and he decided to keep it in his pocket for good fortune.

It was a fine morning and when the party reached the quay Kenneth was already busy loading food and barrels of fresh water onto the *Pride of Tiree*. Murdoch and three warriors from Mull were to come with them on the voyage. The rest of the local men were reluctant to join them for they feared leaving their island unprotected. The first stop was to be Coll, and the waters near it were reached without incident a few hours before nightfall. This island was smaller and rockier than Mull and, as their ship sailed closer, Dougie guessed that it was only a few miles wide.

Kenneth told him the main inhabitants were goats, with twenty goats for every person who lived there. It was a truly wild and lonely place, without tree or shrub. With a strong wind at their backs, they soon saw a group of a dozen houses, which lay together on Coll's eastern shore. Above them was a cloud of black smoke.

The men of Tain jumped out, with their claymores ready, and ran towards the low white buildings. They need not have run. Dougie and Kenneth made fast the boat with strong ropes and followed the others to the village. Death and fire was all around them. There were signs of a mighty battle with many dead islanders lying, still and bloody, on the ground.

"They must have come in the early hours of this morning," said Murdoch grimly.

He looked at the remains of a once fine cottage. Its roof timbers were still smouldering.

"And no sign, alive or dead, of any enemy," added Kenneth.

As the others made a pyre for the dead, Dougie and Alistair climbed to the summit of the highest hill on the island to see what could be seen. As the light faded, Alistair reached the top and stood facing the west, hands on hips, to get his breath back. Dougie joined him, panting, and stared at his friend's face. He had seen that look once before on the slopes of Carn Liath. It was shaped by anger and determination.

"What's the matter?" asked Dougie.

Alistair pointed across the water towards Tiree, alone in the Great Sea and at the end of the world. It was a fine evening and the distant island could be seen easily. The last rays of sun shone gold behind its low lying and green hills.

Around its shores were over a hundred Norse longships.

Dougie awoke on a grey and damp spring morning on Coll. Alistair and Donald snored, and Big Hamish added wood to the campfire, which had been kept going all night. Dougie shivered, for the fisherman's cottage they sheltered in had no roof, and its walls were blackened by fire.

When Alistair and Dougie returned from the hill, the night before, they explained about the Norse fleet and Robert decided to sail immediately back to Oban to warn Malcolm. Alistair suggested that one of them should stay behind on Coll to observe the enemy.

It was finally agreed that Kenneth would take Murdoch and the men of Mull home, to warn the others and prepare for the defence of the island. He would then take most of the Scots to Oban. Alistair, Donald, Hamish and Dougie would remain as the eyes and ears of the king. When Kenneth reached Oban, he would ask one of the fishermen to return to Coll and collect them.

Dougie would have liked to leave with the others and it was with fear and regret that he watched the sail of the *Pride of Tiree* get smaller and smaller.

With the rising sun, the four friends set off for the top of the hill.

"Can you make out anything?" asked Hamish.

"A lot of ships," replied Donald, "and not much else. We are too far away."

"We are the eyes and ears of the king and we cannot make out what they are up to."

"A pity Archie hasn't invented the *terescope* yet," thought Dougie.

By evening they were bored. They had swapped places so everyone spent two hours looking across at Tiree. The others killed time in the village by sharpening their swords and retelling their adventures in the Dark Fortress.

Dougie wandered along the shore and about a mile from the village made an important discovery. In a rocky cove, tied to an old wooden post, was a small boat. It could not have been used for some time, but the oars were in it and there didn't seem to be any holes in its floor.

He ran back to the others and told them about his find.

"It would be madness to go to Tiree in that," said Hamish.

"Wise words," chirped Donald, "pure madness."

"Nevertheless, two of us should go, for the more we know about the intentions of the enemy, the better prepared we shall be," said Alistair. "I suggest that at nightfall Dougie and I row across and if we are not back on the following night then you are to assume we are not coming back."

Not coming back did not sound like a good idea to Dougie. Neither did going in the first place, but when the sea and sky were at their darkest, two shadows dragged the small craft to the water's edge. Dougie was no sailor and it seemed that for every boat length they went forward, they drifted half a boat length back. Dougie sweated with the effort and his hands became blistered and sore. But they *were* getting closer and Dougie saw the outline of many ships.

"They look so much bigger from here," he gasped.

They stopped rowing and, on the breeze, could just make out strange voices in an unknown tongue.

"We are the eyes and ears of the king and we can't see what they are up to, or understand a word they are saying."

The shore was lit by many campfires and men walked in their glow.

"We cannot land here," continued Alistair, "we will have to row around to the other side of the island."

It was an hour before sunrise when they reached the far shore. They landed cautiously and decided to overturn the boat and cover it in seaweed.

"Looks just like a rock," said Alistair proudly.

"Sails like one as well," Dougie thought.

They headed inland, following the line of a low stone wall, and found a place to hide amongst some thick-growing gorse bushes. Ignoring the thorns, they made themselves as comfortable as they could and were soon asleep. Dougie awoke with a start, when the sun was high, and heard voices, not too far away. Alistair was snoring and Dougie snapped a hand across his friend's mouth.

Alistair opened his eyes and tried to call out. Dougie put a finger to his lips and whispered, "People coming."

Alistair sat up, totally alert.

"They are getting closer," whispered Dougie, "they must have found the boat."

"It won't be long before they find us, either."

And once again, Dougie did something he was to regret later.

"Find out about the invasion and get back to the others. I will lead them away."

Before Alistair could move, Dougie raced away up the hill. A Norse war party *had* discovered their boat and were searching the lands overlooking the beach. They were no more than fifty paces from Alistair's hiding place when they saw a man appear from nowhere. They gave chase and Alistair saw the front three catch up quickly with Dougie.

Thinking he had dragged them far enough away from the gorse, the shepherd turned to face his pursuers, like a cornered prey turning on the hunter. Alistair watched helplessly as one of the warriors slowly and deliberately raised a bow, and shot an arrow into his friend's chest.

Dougie fell like a rag doll to the floor and the enemy made their way to the other side of the island to report the death of their foe.

CHAPTER TWENTY

Race to Amera's Cairn

Peter was stunned by the events on Tiree, but they didn't seem right. He thought about Myroy's words. Dougie had become the first keeper. Amera's stone had been handed down through his family, the line of Donald, and he now held the brooch in his hand. The ruby pulsed a dark red.

"I am here for a reason, aren't I?"

Myroy nodded.

"To understand the future, I must understand the past."

"The passage of the stone through time is like a jigsaw."

"And I need to piece it together."

"What do you know, Peter of the line of Donald?"

"I don't know how Dougie can pass the stone on to his children if he is dead."

Myroy's eyes flashed.

"I did not ask you what you do not know."

"Four Ancient Ones discovered they did not age and you stopped Odin, your own brother, taking power by stealing the stone from Thor's ship. You hid the stone from its creators. First you gifted it to the kings of the Sea Peoples. Amera was the last and when he died, Gora tried to plunder it from his tomb. He failed and became a prisoner of the stone itself. Two thousand years later, the Donalds held it until Malcolm the Elder took the crown and killed them all."

"All?"

"Not all. You rescued Alexander and Douglas, and kept them a secret with Lissy as their guardian."

Myroy stroked Dog.

"Then Dougie became the first keeper by facing the challenges of mountain, island and castle. The stone has been in my family ever since."

"Do you have any questions?"

Peter thought for a while, then nodded.

"What happened after Gora? How did the Donalds get to hold the stone, before they were killed at King's Seat?"

"The key to the answer is a descendant of Amera, named Dunnerold, and an ancestor of Thorgood Firebrand. His grandfather, Thorfinn."

"Thorfinn?"

"When Odin discovered that the stone lay in Amera's cairn, it was Thorfinn who helped him in the race to take it."

"And my future depends on the story."

The old man sighed and, slowly, tickled Dog's ear.

"Do not be too eager to enter the future. There are lessons to learn before you do."

OSLO FJORD : SUMMER 602 AD

A boy skipped into his longhouse and shouted.

"Father, a sail approaches."

Thorfinn Firebrand grimaced at the interruption, put down the trap he was mending, and grabbed a spear. Blinking in bright sunshine, he gradually made out a crowd of excited people down by the quayside. He pushed through them and stood beside a tall, red-headed warrior.

"Who returns?" asked Thorfinn.

Magnus pointed the tip of his spear at the ship.

"It is Lars Stonehammer, four days sooner than expected."

"Well, either he has been carried by kind winds, or he carries little for the feast."

"Lars has not failed us before."

"Lars has not sailed so far before."

A woman behind them wailed loudly in Thorfinn's ear.

"Praise be to Odin. Lars is brought back to us safely."

Thorfinn wiggled a finger in his sore ear and stared at Lars who stood on the prow, waving his arms up and down.

"He looks like a bird without feathers," said Magnus.

As the longship neared the quay, ropes were tossed ashore and strong hands caught them. A young, heavily-built warrior jumped ashore and threw his arms around Thorfinn.

"Welcome home, Lars," Thorfinn looked past his friend to the ship. "Welcome home all of you."

"What a tale we have to tell," beamed Lars, "we ….."

"Look at the sea," shouted Magnus and the crowd hushed at his warning.

A tower of bubbles rose up beside the ship and a ring of water boiled. Inside the ring, a young, handsome man rose up, like a ghost rising from the bed of the sea, and as the waters calmed his blue eyes flashed.

"Odin," whispered Thorfinn and everyone fell to their knees.

"Lars, bring the slave to the quay," commanded Odin quietly.

Lars obeyed quickly. The slave, an old man, had his arms tightly bound and Lars kicked the back of his knees, and he fell to the floor. Odin nodded at Lars.

"Tell your story then."

"We raided the Sea People's village, twelve days' sail from here, and return with grain, chickens and slaves. A day from home we questioned the prisoners and asked if there was treasure to be had. Most of them refused us, but this one sang his heart out when we threatened to throw him overboard."

Odin nodded again.

"He says that inland from the village, not far inland, is a cairn, the resting place of a great king who ruled long ago. He says a ruby, a powerful ruby, lies with him."

"Prepare the ships," commanded Odin, "we leave with the next tide."

He walked across the surface of the water to stand beside them. The young god's fine robes were bone dry.

"You will lead us there, Lars."

The woman behind Thorfinn began to wail again and he put his finger back in his ear, and wiggled it.

***

"I will not marry him."

"Oh yes you will."

"Douglas Donald has got the brains and legs of a chicken."

Under the breakfast table Catriona's foot stomped on a flagstone.

Dunnerold growled. "Oh yes you will."

"Oh no I won't! Just because you are the king it doesn't mean you can always get your own way."

"Oh yes it does, and Douglas Donald is really quite clever."

"He certainly hides it well," snapped Catriona, "just give me three reasons why I should spend the rest of my life with a Donald."

"Firstly, I have no son and so my line must run through you. Secondly, Douglas is kind and, of all the tribes, the Donalds are the bravest and most trustworthy."

Behind Catriona the floor began to shimmer. Dunnerold grinned mischievously.

"And thirdly, Myroy says so."

"Huh. That old fool wouldn't say that if he had to marry a man with chicken legs."

"I probably wouldn't," agreed Myroy and Catriona nearly jumped out of her skin.

"Having trouble, Dunnerold?"

"Nothing a good spanking wouldn't solve." Dunnerold smiled at his daughter.

Catriona pulled a defiant face. "Oh no it wouldn't."

Myroy raised his hand to stop the argument.

"Odin knows where Amera's stone is hidden."

Dunnerold's smile disappeared and he rose quickly, and barked at a servant.

"Tell Brudan to gather his riders." He turned to face Myroy, "Has he set sail yet?"

"He leaves now."

"Then there is still time, old friend."

"We have a day over him and no more." Myroy looked at Catriona. "You really will be very happy. I have seen it."

"That's what you say."

"It is," said the Ancient One and touched her shoulder.

"I am going to be really happy," she said softly.

"You couldn't show me how to do that hand on the shoulder thing, could you?" asked Dunnerold, "Catriona's mother comes home tomorrow."

***

Lars Stonehammer jumped down onto a sandy beach and ran up to the Sea People's village. Odin, Thorfinn, Magnus and the slave, and a hundred warriors followed him.

"The pots are still warm," said Lars. "They must have fled moments before we landed."

Odin nodded. "Order the slave to take us to the cairn."

Magnus led the old man, on a long rope, to stand before them.

"Take us," demanded Lars.

The slave didn't move and Lars placed his sword at the man's throat.

"Shall I kill him, master?"

"Kill him and you will never find the cairn." Odin walked over to the slave, "Where is the cairn?"

The prisoner shook with fear, but remained silent and Odin touched his shoulder. The old man jumped up and ran off at an incredible speed through the village.

"This way," he shrieked.

Lars whispered to Thorfinn, "He has a way with people, doesn't he."

Thorfinn ignored the joke, but Odin heard it.

The old slave led them towards a distant line of pine trees. The sandy path rose up small hillocks, covered in ferns, coarse grasses and wild flowers. Magnus found himself being dragged along and some of the warriors laughed. It was like a child taking a pack of hounds for a walk.

Before they reached the pines, the old man veered off the path and they were forced to run in single file along a narrow avenue of gorse. Eventually, the raiding party emerged into a grass clearing. Amera's cairn lay on the far side; a long, low stone mound.

"Watch for signs of an enemy," warned Odin.

His men formed a ring around the cairn.

"The entrance is here," said Lars excitedly and Odin, Thorfinn and Magnus joined him.

A huge rock rested against the mound and warriors were summoned to help roll it aside. Rock grated across rock. At first the black gap was the width of a finger, then the width of a hand and, after a real struggle, it tumbled away and with a *thud* it fell and split in two.

Three weathered stones framed a dark, forbidding entrance. A skull was just visible on the top stone.

"Fetch torches," yelled Thorfinn.

"Lars, you go first. I will follow. Thorfinn you follow me. Magnus stay here."

As they crawled down the tunnel, Thorfinn wondered why Odin wanted this ruby. There were other rubies that could be taken more easily.

In front of him a voice said, "Because there is no ruby like this one."

Two skeletons lay side by side on a bower. Thorfinn gently touched a skull and it rolled on the floor, and fell to pieces. He sniffed the musty air. There was death here. Ancient death.

Lars held his torch above the skeletons.

"Where will it be, master?"

"The slave said a king was buried here, not two kings."

"Do you think the tomb is plundered?" asked Thorfinn.

"Not by this one," replied Odin and he kicked Gora's bones.

A cloud of dust rose up into the torchlight.

Thorfinn lifted Amera's ribcage and felt underneath. He pulled out a necklace, a dagger and a silver pin, and shook his head at Odin.

"Nothing over here either," said Lars, "and we passed no treasure in the tunnel."

A distant, muffled voice called out to them from the entrance stones.

"Go," ordered Odin and he grabbed Thorfinn's torch.

Thorfinn and Lars returned quickly and blinked as they left the darkness.

"What is it, Magnus?" demanded Lars.

"At the back of the cairn is a wider path. It goes south through the pines. Many riders came here and not long ago."

"How long ago?" asked Thorfinn.

"The hoof prints are fresh. One day, possibly two."

"I will tell the master," said Thorfinn and he took Lars's torch.

As he approached the central chamber he heard Odin shouting angrily, "You did this."

"You shall not have it," said a calm voice.

"How did you know I journeyed here?" asked Odin.

"It is enough that I knew."

"You were lucky this time. Next time, Myroy, you won't be."

"I sense your anger and greed. They are as strong now as they were when we were children. When the land was first free of the ice."

"Stronger," boasted Odin, "and when I hold the stone there will be no mercy for the Scottish peoples you hold so dear."

Thorfinn dashed forward and raised his sword. He thought he saw a head disappearing down through the floor.

"Master, are you safe?"

Odin nodded.

"Magnus has found horse tracks. Many riders came here only yesterday."

"I have waited for century after long century and I missed the stone by one day," hissed Odin and he shook with rage. "Kill Lars, he has failed us."

As Thorfinn hurried up the passage a voice called after him.

"Tell him I have a way with people."

Odin stepped out of Amera's cairn and, without batting an eyelid, stepped over Lars's body.

"Magnus, take twelve men and follow the riders. I do not care how you do it, but find their homes and return to me with that knowledge."

"I obey, master."

Magnus called out the names of the warriors who would join him.

"A place at my table, in the Halls of the Gods, if you succeed," promised Odin and the men cheered.

***

Dunnerold and Brudan crawled forward and peered through the bracken. In the far distance, longships headed out into the Cold Sea. Norse warriors came out of the pines and began to cross a wide expanse of moorland.

"How did you know they would follow us?" asked Bruden.

"I didn't know, although I should have guessed. Myroy told me," said Dunnerold. "Wait until they are far from the safety of the trees. Make sure none escape."

He held Amera's stone in the palm of his hand. Set in gold it would make a fine dowry.

"How many are they?"

"Thirteen and all on foot."

"No match for your riders, Brudan," and he ran down the slope to his horse.

Brudan followed. "Not staying to join in the fun?" he asked.

"No. I have a wedding to organise and a present to give to the Donalds."

***

"Another piece of the jigsaw, Peter of the line of Donald."

Peter felt confused. If he was a *Donald* and Dunnerold had passed the ruby to Douglas *Donald*, then could he really be descended from him?

"In some ways, the stone has come back," the old man said quickly, "but you will learn soon enough about the full history of Amera's stone. First though, I want to tell you more about Alistair and the Norsemen on Tiree."

Peter grinned and looked at Dog. He was snoring like James had done just four weeks before. That now seemed like an age ago.

CHAPTER TWENTY ONE

A Great Escape

Dougie was dead, with a Norse arrow sticking out of his chest. Alistair sat and wept, and it was a long while before he was able to pull his thoughts together. He felt as though he had failed Myroy and his father.

"I must find out what the enemy plan to do, or Dougie's brave sacrifice will have been for nothing."

He set off in the direction the enemy had taken, hoping they would lead him to their camp, and deliberately avoided Dougie's body. He wanted to remember his friend in life, not in death.

Eventually, many masts and the tops of brightly coloured canvases came into view. As he got nearer, he crawled on his hands and knees, and reached a rock where he could look down on Tiree Bay unseen. One hundred and thirty Norse ships lay at anchor and Alistair guessed each would carry at least twelve warriors. Over one thousand five hundred warriors. Tents lined the beach and one, the nearest to him, was larger and grander than the others. Two heavily armed men guarded it.

"That is where I have to go," thought Alistair and he decided to remain in hiding until nightfall. He felt hungry, lonely and sad, and passed the time by counting the number of soldiers on the beach. Whilst counting, a boat landed. It was shorter than the long ships and was made of animal skins sewn together in patches, and had a picture of a black axe on its sail. Men, with long black beards, jumped out and Alistair thought he recognised some of them. Faces from Carn Liath.

"Black Kilts," he thought, "I wonder what part they play in this?" One of the Picts, a big man, wore a dark cloak. Another, shorter, man was greeted by an older Norseman who was probably a Norse Lord. His cloak was edged with gold. They shook hands, at the water's edge, and went across to the large tent. The Picts were treated with respect. As they walked through the camp, men bowed their heads and a few raised their swords in salute.

The weather was changing and a mist drifted in from the Great Sea. At first it was thin and wispy, but gradually Alistair began to lose sight of one tent and then another. There was no wind to drive it away and, after a short while, Alistair could see no more than five paces in any direction. Under the cover of the sea mist, he crawled to the back of Thorgood's tent unseen.

"Do not worry about Malcolm," said a voice. "He is a fool."

"They say he is a great warrior," said another.

"He may be, but thanks to my son, your presence has remained undiscovered," replied the first voice. "No news has reached the palace by way of riders from the west."

"Surprise is our ally," said another voice, "and on the morning after the next full moon we will land at Oban."

"Then the highlands will be mine and the rich lowlands yours," the first man said.

"And we must have it. We had many fine summers and our numbers grew. But the last two years have seen our harvests fail and we must move south to escape famine."

"And I want revenge on Malcolm, so we seem to have a partnership made in the halls of the gods."

"Here's to us. Skol."

The toast was followed by the sound of clinking goblets.

"I've heard enough," thought Alistair.

He turned to crawl back to the stone but, after only twenty paces, an angry shout cut through the still air. The Mac Mar's eyes were red with fury. He was joined by another Black Kilt, armed with a battle axe, and together they gave chase.

Tella's shoulder still hurt him and he had enjoyed too many feasts to keep up with Alistair, but the other man could run like a hare. Alistair was stranded in the open and glanced back to see the Pict emerging from the mist just a few paces behind him. He turned and raised his claymore, but the enemy was too fast and the axe crashed down onto his blade and it shattered. The force of the blow threw the Scotsman backward onto the wet ground.

Alistair could just make out the face of his enemy. The man's eyes were fixed on him and they spoke of death. The warrior raised his axe and smiled, but he did not bring it down onto Alistair. He stood there for many seconds, the mighty blade hovering above his head. Alistair waited for the death strike, but the Pict started to shake, slowly at first, and then as if his whole body was wracked with some uncontrollable anger. He fell forward on top of Alistair, and Alistair looked up to see Dougie, standing there with blood on the end of his claymore.

"I thought you were lost," gasped Alistair.

"So did I," agreed Dougie and he reached into his pocket and tossed something across to his friend.

Alistair stared at it. The bronze coin had a picture of a bearded Tella the Mac Mar on one side. The Dark Fortress on Carn Liath was on the other side. It was deeply dented and twisted by the impact of the Norse arrow.

"Let's get out of here," urged Alistair and the two men ran as fast as they could across the fields to their boat.

They reached the beach, on the other side of the island. Luckily, the boat was bobbing in the water and tied to the shore with a single line. The enemy must have cleared away the seaweed when they had found it. As they pushed off, they saw the ghostly outline of the Norsemen, less than a hundred paces away. The two friends started rowing for their lives. Arrows struck the water, but fell short and Dougie heard the anger and frustration of the enemy on the shore. They felt a little safer, after a time, and though they continued to row out into the sea mist, they did so more slowly.

"We must start to go to the east soon," said Alistair.

"But which way is east?" asked Dougie, trying to catch a glimpse of the sun.

Their clothes were damp and cold as the low cloud settled upon them, and their spirits began to fall. Dougie imagined himself lost forever, heading out into the Great Sea towards the very end of the world.

They stopped rowing and the small boat rose and fell with each wave. It could have been a day, or an hour, before the wind got up and the mist thinned. The sun could just be seen as a hazy orange ball, low in the sky, and so they began to row away from it to the east. Dougie strained his eyes to catch a glimpse of the land and instead saw strange shapes all around them.

"Monsters," shouted Dougie.

"Quiet," hissed Alistair.

"Monsters all around us," whispered Dougie, pointing at the fierce heads of dragons, which rose up out of the sea in all directions.

They heard voices in a strange tongue.

"They do not sound like monsters," said Alistair, and at the same time the two friends realised they had drifted around Tiree and right into the middle of the Norse fleet.

They rowed away as quickly as they could, but now the fog was clearing and they were seen. Oars were dropped into the sea. Loud shouts of command came from one of the largest of the long ships and Dougie's heart sank as he saw its great sail raised. One boat was in pursuit and it was clearly enough.

"We cannot outrun them," said Dougie, fear in his voice.

"But we can make it more difficult," said Alistair resolutely.

They were less than two hundred paces from the enemy, who gained on them with each second, their banks of oars thrusting them forward. There was a small patch of mist left behind them.

"Go that way," shouted Alistair, "it is our only hope."

They pulled on the heavy oars with all their might. Dougie's head felt as though it would explode. He was exhausted, but he kept rowing. Every muscle in his body screamed out with the effort and both men kept their eyes fixed on the Norse ship. It had already halved the distance between them.

They entered the fog bank and Dougie knew it was not dense enough to hide them for long. They stopped rowing, panted for air, and waited for the inevitable. The great head of a dragon emerged like a ghost and raced toward them at a fantastic speed. The mighty prow cut through the water like a knife. Then there was a mighty crash, the sound of splintering wood and screaming men. A Norse helmet flew through the air and landed in the boat at Alistair's feet.

"Look," cried Dougie, "it is Kenneth."

Gliding through the sea, between the two broken halves of the longship, was the *Pride of Tiree*.

A huge muscular arm reached down like a crane and grabbed Dougie's shawl.

"Up you come, laddie," boomed Hamish.

Ignoring the cries of the Norsemen in the water, Kenneth threw the tiller over and the *Pride of Tiree* turned. The sail billowed out and they began to run east.

"Murdoch has taken his people to Oban for safety," Donald told them, "and Kenneth says Robert is going straight to the king with news of the fleet."

Alistair nodded.

"The only things we do not know are *when* they plan to invade and *where*," growled Hamish.

"I know," said Alistair, "they intend to land at Oban the morning after the next full moon."

"Only six days," gasped Dougie.

"Murdoch will ride south from Oban and raise the clans who are loyal to the crown. His guess is that Malcolm will head to somewhere on the coast and muster as many men as he can on the way," said Donald.

"We must reach Malcolm and tell him to defend Oban," said Alistair gravely, "if the enemy are allowed to land and hold a strong defensive position, then there may be no stopping them."

Kenneth spoke for the first time. "So, it is just a race."

"A race?" asked Dougie.

The seafarer pointed back over the stern at two distant sails. They were being hunted. The five Scotsmen were silent for the rest of the day. The *Pride of Tiree* held its lead ahead of the longships, which stayed, menacingly, on the horizon. They passed the shadowy outline of Coll during the night and steered a course past the southern tip of Mull.

"Do they never give up?" asked Dougie, staring back at two faraway lights, which marked the positions of the Norsemen.

"They know we know," replied Alistair, "and will do all in their power to stop us passing the message on."

"And how many warriors might they have?"

Alistair grinned. "Twenty to thirty, but they have got to catch us first."

At dawn, Donald held the tiller whilst the others slept. Hamish was snoring and he tried to think of something funny to say about it when his friend awoke. He looked back and the ocean was bathed by a low orange sun. The enemy sails were nowhere to be seen.

Later, Hamish mumbled, "I do not believe they have given up."

"Neither do I," replied Kenneth, "the breeze now comes from the south west and they may have tacked south to get a long run with the wind full in their sails."

"How far are we from Oban?" asked Dougie.

"We will sight land after noon tomorrow," replied the skipper.

Like many days at sea, this day was uneventful. Hamish and Donald sharpened their claymores and Dougie eagerly helped Kenneth with even the smallest of tasks. As the sun passed its high point, a line of hills was spotted and their spirits rose. Then Alistair called them over to the ship's rail and pointed south. The Norse longships had returned and were on a course to intercept them before they made Oban.

"They know how to sail," said Kenneth.

He eased the tiller over to match the Norsemen's course and the *Pride of Tiree* cut through the waves more quickly as the wind came square on behind them.

The coastline was now tantalisingly close, but so were the enemy. Dougie saw their warriors clearly, saw their determined faces, and shouted to Alistair.

"They carry horses on the second ship."

The men of Tain ran to him and stared across. The first longship was less than five hundred paces away and the other was only a short distance behind it.

"Four horses," growled Hamish.

"And they are gaining on us," added Alistair, "Kenneth, it is now or never, turn her to land."

The *Pride of Tiree* lurched towards a shingle beach.

"Not there," said Alistair, "drop us near rocks where their horses cannot follow."

The boat lurched again.

"Are you coming with us?" asked Dougie, and Kenneth shook his head.

"Good luck, young Dougie. They are not interested in me and there is no advantage in leaving them another ship, which they would surely use against us."

The two men shook hands. Alistair, Donald and Hamish tied their claymores to their backs and Dougie copied them. The ship passed a headland and Alistair dived overboard. He made the shore easily and the others followed. Dougie was not a strong swimmer and Donald helped him, cold and spluttering, onto the rocks.

Alistair led them up a steep slope, covered by coarse grass. At the top of the headland was a large open area and they stopped to get their breath back, and to look down. Nine of the enemy had swum ashore and the second boat was searching for a beach where they could land their horses.

"We must split up," said Alistair, "get to Malcolm with all speed."

Hamish and Donald ran off.

"This way, Dougie," Alistair ordered, and they sprinted towards a line of trees, which followed the contours of the coast.

Donald pushed Hamish into a sandy hollow and the big man snarled and raised a fist. The wee man put a finger to his lips and they lay hidden as the head of the leading Norseman appeared over the top of the grassy slope. The man shouted something in a strange tongue and pointed at Alistair and Dougie, who were running like men possessed towards the wood. The Norsemen gave chase and Donald grinned at his friend.

"They would have caught us in no time with all the food you carry in your stomach."

Hamish growled again and they lay on their backs in their comfortable place of hiding, and waited for the afternoon sun to dry their clothes.

"The trees are too close together for the horses to follow," panted Dougie, as he pushed his way through the dense undergrowth.

"But we make the way easier for the foot-soldiers," retorted Alistair.

"Should we split up too?"

"No, stay with me."

They came out into a bright clearing, where a twisting path led towards more trees on the far side.

Dougie found it hard to keep up with Alistair, but fear of the enemy drove him on. They moved from sunshine into darkness the instant they re-entered the wood and Dougie tripped over a root. He crashed to the ground heavily and all his remaining air was knocked out of him. Alistair ran back and helped him stand.

"I need ….. to rest," whispered Dougie, gasping for breath.

His friend glanced around, frantically, and led him off the track and through a stand of birch where they hid behind some moss covered rocks.

"We'll be alright here, for a while at least," said Alistair, "the path is stony and we left few marks where we turned off it."

As they lay, Dougie heard his heart beat like a drum and then he heard another sound, running feet. He peered around the side of the rock and saw three Norse warriors sprint past. He glanced at Alistair and held up three fingers, and his friend nodded. In moments the other Norse foot-soldiers followed and they heard horses. Four riders galloped down the track.

"Get up, Dougie. That's all of them."

They ran back to the path, crossed the sunny clearing and searched for a better hiding place in the wood they had first entered.

"Where are we?" asked Dougie, after a while.

"Less than half a days' walk, to the north of Oban."

"Do you know this country?"

Alistair shook his head.

"What should we do?"

"Get some sleep and travel by night. In darkness we have a good chance of getting past them."

They settled down, in the dappled shade, and began to doze.

Olaf Adanson's horse was the first to leave the forest and he pulled back on the reins. He looked down the path, which cut through open fields and wound its way up to the bare slopes of high mountains. He studied the scene, inch by inch, like an eagle searching for prey. Three riders joined him and he pointed ahead.

"We have been fooled," he said angrily, and they returned to the trees. His foot-soldiers came back into view and Olaf called his steed to a halt.

"Fan out," he yelled, "they are here somewhere!"

Hamish and Donald found the coastal path to Oban easily. It hugged the headlands and bays, and they made swift progress. Well before sundown, they sighted the small harbour below them, full of fishing vessels and they guessed most of these had been used by Murdoch to evacuate his people from Mull. As the track entered the outskirts of Oban, a band of kilted warriors watched them approach and raised their spears.

"We serve the Younger," boomed Hamish and he brushed one of the men out of his way.

They seemed wary and followed at a distance, and soon the party was standing at the quay, from where the two friends had departed for Mull. One of the guards ran off and returned with more men and a tall, lean and handsome youth, who appeared to be their leader.

"We seek Murdoch, urgently," said Donald.

"He has ridden south to raise the clans. I am Stuart, Thane of Coll since my father's murder, and the Protector has left me to hold Oban."

"Alistair of Cadbol, in the service of the Younger, has learnt that the Norse fleet intends to land *here* the morning after the next full moon," said Donald.

"And how does he know this?" asked Stuart.

"By risking his life," growled Hamish. "As we speak, Alistair is heading here pursued by Norse riders and foot-soldiers."

The crowd started to murmur at these words and Stuart asked, "How many are there?"

"Four mounted warriors and nine on foot. I need your help to get our message to the Younger, with great speed, and to help our friends."

"I shall consider your words," promised Stuart.

"Consider them now," boomed Hamish, "or risk the deaths of two loyal Scots on your conscience."

Stuart stood before Hamish and looked up into his eyes.

"I do not know you, or your friend, and the last thing I want is the death of anyone on my conscience. But, if your story is false, and we rally the clans here, then the enemy may land somewhere else without hindrance, and at a great cost to us later."

Donald wondered if Hamish would pick the youth up by the scruff of his neck and throw him into the sea. But, the big man took his claymore and gave the hilt to Stuart.

"I speak the truth," he said simply.

A way was being made through the crowd and a lady appeared, with a small, silent maidservant following behind her.

"I know these warriors," Margaret said, "they came to help my father and arrived on Mull aboard the *Pride of Tiree*."

"Kenneth has sailed north to escape the enemy," Donald told her. The Thane of Coll gave Hamish back his sword.

***

"Come on, Dougie," yelled Alistair and they splashed across a river towards cover. An arrow bounced off a stone and flew up past Dougie's face.

They had been dodging the Norsemen all afternoon and were completely exhausted.

"Run that way," ordered Alistair, pointing along a path that followed the bank upstream, and he hid behind a large boulder at the water's edge. Dougie glanced at him and Alistair hissed through his teeth.

"Go on."

Dougie ran out of the range of the archer and glanced back. The man splashed across the river and, as he leapt for the bank, Alistair's claymore slashed out from behind the rock and the enemy's body fell backwards into the water. Alistair grabbed the man's bow and quiver, and dived behind the rock again. Another Norseman ran across the river, but only made halfway. An arrow struck him in the chest.

Alistair dropped the bow, dashed over to Dougie and drew his dirk.

"Going to kill me too?" teased Dougie, relief flooding through his body, and his friend shot him a dark look.

Alistair cut a strip from his plaid, dropped it on the upstream path, then they retraced their steps in the opposite direction and sprinted along the path that led downstream. There always seemed to be men shouting around them, but now their cries faded into the distance and they eased the pace a little.

"Find another place to hide up in," panted Alistair, "the sun will fall soon and then we can rest."

Dougie moved off to the left, following a smaller path, and cried out. His friend was at his side in a moment. Below them the trees ended and at the bottom of a grassy slope was the main track to Oban.

"Shall we chance it?" asked Dougie, and Alistair nodded.

Olaf Adanson ordered his foot-soldiers to sweep through the forest and he and his riders galloped along the main path searching for the Scots.

"At some time they must take it if they are to warn their people," he reasoned.

From the cries of his men in the trees, he knew two of his warriors lay dead by a stream. The enemy could not be far away. Olaf looked across at the mountains and glens to the east. They were lit by a low sun, and green and rich, just as Thorgood had promised they would be. The land reminded him of home, but with great swathes of high pasture, and each glen carried many more animals than even he had hoped for. After they had killed the Scotsmen, he would order his men to slaughter some sheep and return to the ship with honour and provisions.

He glanced back at the sun. It was touching the sea. Olaf drove his heels into the horse's flanks and it bolted forward. He galloped around a bend in the track and a rider came into view.

"Any sign, Inger?" he yelled, and the man shook his head.
Another horseman joined Inger and they waved frantically to him, and he urged his steed on again.

"We have them," cried Inger, as Olaf approached, and his eyes followed theirs.

Running down the main track to Oban, in open countryside, were two kilted men. Olaf Adanson smiled.

"Bring the others to me," and Inger rode off to fetch the fourth rider and the foot-soldiers.

Alistair knew they had taken a huge gamble, taking this path in low sun. It rose up and down foothills that sloped down to the sea, off to their right. The grass on both sides of the track was broken by small clumps of wild flowers and low lying broom.

"You couldnae hide a wren here," he thought, and prayed the enemy were too busy in the forest to notice their escape.

The path led steeply upwards and Dougie's legs felt as though they would collapse at any moment. His chest hurt and he stopped running, put his hands on his hips, stared up at the sky and sucked in the early evening air. Alistair, who was now a way ahead, sensed his friend had stopped and turned to check on him. Galloping along the path, and only a few minutes away, were enemy riders.

"Run, Dougie, run," he yelled.

The slope seemed to go on forever. Up and up. Nearing the top, Dougie's legs were like lead. Alistair disappeared over the crest and Dougie lost all hope. Then he heard galloping hooves and the jubilant shouts of the Norsemen as they prepared to kill their prey. His head became dizzy with the terrible effort and he fell onto his hands and knees. He glanced up at Alistair. His friend stood upright, armed with claymore, waiting bravely to defend him. As the noise of the enemy overwhelmed them, Dougie collapsed with exhaustion. Would he ever see his family again?

As the Norse riders reached full gallop, the distance between them and their foot-soldiers widened. The enemy were in clear view and Inger glanced across at his chieftain. Olaf was trying desperately to lead the charge. He wanted to be first to deliver a death-blow with his sword. They rode on up the slope and it was obvious that their foe was weak and faltering.

"Kill them," roared Olaf, and they thundered over the crest of the hill.

Ahead of them, one of the Scots was dragging the other off the path. Beyond them stood Stuart of Coll and a line of fifty horsemen, armed with spears.

"Prepare to enter Valhalla," yelled Olaf and, without a second's hesitation, he led his men on to fight the enemy.

The kilted riders raced forward too and the horses reared up as the two lines smashed together. Inger was cut down and Olaf drove his sword down onto one of the Scots.

He did not feel the first spear pierce his body, nor the second. It was joyous and sacred, and what he had been born to do. He, Olaf Adanson, was going to join the bravest warriors who had ever been. In the Halls of the Gods.

CHAPTER TWENTY TWO

Tricked

Dougie and Alistair stood, shoulder to shoulder, on the high-ground overlooking Oban Sound. Beside them were the men of Tain. To their left were three hundred Scots dressed in their earthy brown, green and ochre tartans, all armed with shield and claymore, and to their right another thousand warriors.

The wind blew through Malcolm's long, grey hair as he studied his army. They were stronger now than when they had faced the Picts, and he knew their success on Carn Liath had swollen his numbers. Many clans had sent more of their men and some of the shields were not known to him. This meant some clans were supporting him for the first time.

The Younger's eyes, like Murdoch's and everyone else's, became fixed on the masts of the great fleet, which drifted towards them. His horse swished its white tail impatiently, as though it wanted to get something over with. Two hundred paces from the shore the Norsemen stopped rowing and stared at the army of the Scots. A single boat made its way forward and Thorgood stood at the prow. He rested his arm upon the carving of a huge and ugly dragon's head.

"Are you Malcolm?" he shouted across the water.

"I am," he called back and their eyes met.

An anxious silence surrounded them and Malcolm remembered Helden's words, *"But what promise may I take to Murdoch? For the raids will surely move from Tiree to Coll, and then to Mull itself by the spring."*

He had been right. Now they were here.

Thorgood knew he must lead his people to new lands, but he had lost his main advantage, a surprise attack that would allow his soldiers enough time to establish a strong fortress. He felt a long way from home. The Norse Warlord stared along the shores at the determined and ready enemy who stood before him. He considered his chances of winning in battle and glanced back at Malcolm. There was iron in the eyes of the Scottish king.

Then Thorgood looked back along the line of the Scots. There was a glint of bright red and he stared at Dougie, and the stone upon his chest. The words of the old stories raced through his mind, "*Any army who fights against the stone of legends shall fall and none of them may enter Valhalla.*" Yet he could not be sure this was *the* stone. The sun caught it and the ruby lit up. It cried out. The stone was the colour of wounded flesh.

"Maybe we will meet again in happier times?" the Warlord said.

"I hope so," replied Malcolm.

The great fleet turned towards the open sea.

***

Thorgood sat, quietly, in the tented area by the mast.

"He knew we were coming."

"Perhaps the Mac Mar warned him," said Hengist Corngrinder.

"I do not believe so. I can see no reason why he would risk plans that might return lands to him. But the Younger *did* know, somehow, and did you see a flash of blood-red light from one of the Scottish warriors?"

Hengist shrugged his shoulders.

"It is a possibility that the Younger commands Odin's stone," said Thorgood. "The old stories say Myroy took it South to richer lands."

"I don't believe it. Not after all this time."

"Time will make no difference to its power."

"Do you think Olaf's death was caused by the stone?"

"Who knows?" replied Thorgood. "But if they do command the ruby, we have no chance of beating them in battle."

"Then let's sail south and take the lands we need there."

"And risk Odin's wrath? If we have any chance of discovering his ruby's hiding place we *must* take it."

"I suppose we head north then."

"If you were the Younger, which way would you expect us to sail?"

"South. He knows we know the lands from here to Orkney offer few rewards for a starving people."

"And so he will keep his army together for a while. Until food runs short and discontent spreads. All the time waiting for news of us marching up from the south."

"I am glad I don't have to do all this thinking. North, south, what does it matter?"

"It matters if you want to win. Order the fleet to go south, past the southern tip of Mull. We will then turn north and go around Tiree. Tell the ship masters we return to Sea Peoples Land."

"But we have just come from there."

Thorgood ignored him. "And tell them, on the way, we may drop in and see our old friend, the Mac Mar."

***

On the seashore at Oban, the men of Tain sat around their campfire and moaned about the lack of food. Dougie felt relieved to have been spared another battle. He glanced at his ration, a single oat cake, dreamt about lamb and barley broth, and Mairi. Alistair smiled as he saw the shepherd's downcast face and winked at Hamish, and the big man turned to face Dougie.

"Do you remember the path we took from the palace to Oban?"

"I do," said Dougie.

"And did I tell you that I saw Donald driving down that very path some years ago?"

"No."

"Aye," continued Hamish, "I said to Donald, 'do you know your wife fell off the back of your cart three miles ago?' and he said, 'thank heavens for that.'"

Dougie smiled and glanced at Donald who knew what was coming.

"Aye," growled Hamish, "and he said, 'I thought I had gone deaf.'"

When the shield came down onto Hamish's head, the men of Tain laughed until they cried.

Later, Dougie was listening to his friends when, out the corner of his eye, he saw Kenneth. He had sat apart from everyone else and was now preparing to leave. Dougie followed him in the darkness and called out.

"Kenneth."

The sailor turned and looked at Dougie kindly.

"I just wanted to say thank you."

Kenneth nodded. "I still think you would make a fine sailor."

"My heart lies elsewhere. I wanted to ask if you have heard of, or seen, my brother, Alec? He is of my age and much the same to look at as me."

Kenneth shook his head. "No laddie, but I shall ask after him for you."

The two men shook hands and Kenneth of Blacklock left without saying another word.

***

Late spring brought welcome relief to the fields, for it had been a wet and cold lambing. On his return from the adventure, Dougie had found his farm well cared for by Mairi and the children. They had been given food when needed by the watcher who walked the hills, but some of the lambs had been lost in the hardest days, and he now prayed for fair weather and fresh grass as the latest young ones stumbled on uneasy legs.

"I should get myself a dog," muttered Dougie, as he had many times before.

He was working so hard that he did not notice the daylight hours pass and the sun fall below the summits of the far hills.

"Is it not time for you to be making your way home?" asked a familiar voice.

Dougie turned quickly to see the cloaked stranger, sitting on a stone, one of many slabs of granite scattered around the high pastures. He glanced up at the darkening sky and smiled.

"Aye it is."

Dougie put down the lamb he had been comforting.

"This poor wee thing lost its mother to the fox last night and it needs a bit of a helping hand."

The man looked at him knowingly, but did not speak.

"You once said you knew my father," continued Dougie, eager to discover anything about the family he had never known.

"I did, but that is not why I am here, young Dougie. I thought we had nearly lost you on the island when the Norseman shot his arrow at your chest."

"How do you know about that? Have you spoken to Alistair?"

The stranger shook his head.

"I have not spoken to Alistair, but the important thing is you still have the stone."

Dougie clasped the ruby and eyed him suspiciously.

"I do not want it, Dougie of Dunfermline, so fear not. Indeed it is nearly yours by right and, for the moment, yours to do with as you please."

Dougie relaxed.

"I need to thank you, for Mairi told me you gave her help and food whilst I was away."

"I was pleased to provide that small service, but now I need you to listen carefully to my words. Keep the stone safe, but be willing to let it go when you must. Poor souls, like Gora, are waiting."

"Who is Gora?" asked Dougie.

Myroy ignored his question.

"A great challenge lies ahead of you to the south. True, it is a time away yet, but there are lost souls who are depending on you. So enjoy the beauty of the stone and tell yourself that one day it must be given up with a glad heart."

Dougie did not have a clue about the meaning of the old man's words and yet they were spoken with such belief that he knew they held a great significance for him.

"I face another challenge and to the south?"

The man nodded gravely.

Dougie's heart seemed to miss a beat.

"Can I not just be a farmer?"

"You are a farmer, but the path which stretches out before you is not an easy one, and many of its turns are unknown to me. There are brave deeds to be done, young Dougie, and a destiny to fulfil."

"A destiny?" asked Dougie.

"The destiny denied to your father."

"I don't even know your name," said Dougie, but the stranger had gone and any answer he may have given was lost on the wind.

***

A few months later, the land around Dougie's farm was beautiful and the fields of barley looked like a golden sea as the breeze made waves of the ripening crop.

As the sun rose to its highest point in the sky, Dougie sat down by the standing stones to eat his oat bread. He tilted his head back to catch the warm rays of the sun, dozed happily and imagined he could hear the distant sound of a galloping horse. His mind, as it often did, went back to his adventures and the friends he had shared them with.

The sound of horse's hooves grew louder and Dougie thought he must be dreaming. A fly buzzed around his ear and he raised a hand to drive it away. As he did so, he glanced across at the stile and saw a magnificent white stallion jump over it.

"Not again," he groaned.

The rider was dressed in a tartan shawl and his huge belly made him look as wide as he was tall.

As the horse slowed and trotted towards him, Dougie stood and his attention was no longer on the fine beast, but on the man's stomach. It seemed to have a life of its own for it was moving up and down, and jerking from side to side.

The stranger pulled back on the ropes tied around the horse's neck.

"Are you Dougie of Dunfermline?" he asked.

"Aye, I am."

The fat rider looked down at him.

"I am the king's messenger," he said importantly. "I offer you words of thanks from Malcolm the Younger, King of all the Scots and Protector of the Stone of Destiny."

Dougie nodded and smiled.

"Dougie of Dunfermline, by order of the king and for services to the kingdom, I bring you a token of friendship and gratitude."

The rider lifted his shawl to his chest, to reveal a black and white puppy. He handed it down and the puppy eagerly licked his new master's face.

"Malcolm says he is not named."

"I shall call him Dog," replied Dougie.

"And you are to take good care of him for he is from a litter of the finest sheepdogs that you might find anywhere in the land."

"I will," promised Dougie, a huge grin on his face as the puppy licked him again.

"Do you not have a message for the king?" asked the man.

"Aye, tell him that I still do not know what to say at times like this," and the stranger raised his eyebrows.

As the man rode away Dougie said to himself, "There is no more worth having than this," and he walked with Dog down the hill to tell Mairi.

***

Peter looked into the heart of the fire and thought about the invasion fleet off the shores of Tiree. He knew Dougie and Alistair had been lucky to discover Thorgood's plans, and that history had been changed by the slimmest of chances, the slimmest of coins. Then Peter felt hungry and realised there was no broth.

The Ancient One nodded at the fire and an iron cauldron appeared. Myroy held out his hand and a mug appeared too. Then he dipped a ladle into the broth and filled the mug in a single pour.

"The Norsemen would, of course, return," he said at last.

"They had no choice," agreed Peter, "they needed to avoid hunger."

"You *always* have a choice," corrected Myroy. "Always."

Peter sensed he was being given a warning.

"But Thorgood did suspect that one of the Younger's warriors carried the stone. He meant to have it and use its power."

"But, like the other Norsemen, he fears it."

"He did fear it and with good reason."

"And so Thorgood would try to find Dougie and take it."

Myroy shook his head.

"He certainly would have liked to and that is why he turned North. To stay near Scottish soil. From Sea Peoples Land he would invade Tain. But Odin searched for centuries and could not find it. How might Thorgood? Unless Dougie went with the Younger to fight him in Tain."

Peter thought about this.

"You let him return to Mairi and his farm, didn't you? You kept him away from the fighting this time. Did Dougie ever find out about the defence of Tain?"

"Later on he did. Alistair told him after they escaped from the clutches of Cuthbert the Cautious, Baron of Berwick. I sensed he was mighty glad to be spared the battle."

Peter smiled. Dougie would be glad to avoid *any* battle.

"Still, there is no point in waiting before telling you. The Younger suspected Thorgood would come back, and he knew other enemies would try to destroy him."

"Tella the Mac Mar?" asked Peter.

"The Mac Mar, yes, and also Cuthbert. The sign of the Saxon cross would prove to be Dougie's greatest challenge. With so many enemies poised to attack at once, the Younger believed he must win an ally."

"But who can he turn to?" asked Peter. "Thorgood and his warriors came from the North. Tella holds lands to the west. Cuthbert's Angles hold the south."

Myroy lifted himself off the bench, stretched and walked to the cottage window.

"I never had this trouble when the stone was held by kings. Peter, if you listened as much as you talked then you might find out."

CHAPTER TWENTY THREE
The Defence of Tain

After Dougie left to walk home, the Younger ordered the High Table to split up and take men to watch the coast to the south. A larger force was sent to protect Glasgow. But after ten days no word of warning was received from any of them, and the Scottish army drifted away from the high ground above Oban.

"Thorgood could well have sailed far to the south," said Murdoch, trying to understand why they had no news of the fleet's whereabouts.

"He will come back. Myroy warned us that he would and we must be ready."

Malcolm stared out of a window at the *Guardian Shed* on the Palace Green. Archie had rebuilt it and now it seemed to be shaking. The Younger groaned.

"He can land anywhere, at any time. How can we be ready?" asked Murdoch.

"I do not know. I wonder what our father would have done?"

"The Elder would probably have gathered together every ship he had and attacked Norse lands across the Cold Sea."

"He probably would, but we know other enemies will make their move at some time. We cannot leave our lands undefended."

"Has Myroy told you anything more about the danger from the Saxon cross?"

"No, and he is not likely to."

"So, our fate is in our own hands."

"We have no choice, but to wait and keep watch. At some time news will come to us. We must then act quickly."

"Is there nothing we can do?"

"There is much we can do. There always is. But how much of it will do any good, I don't know."

"You have something in mind, brother, I can tell," said Murdoch.

"We are not strong enough to face the foes of *Mountain, Island and Castle* alone. Any one of them would test the courage and spirit of our people."

"Surely, you are not thinking of forging an alliance with the Mac Mar?" gasped Murdoch.

"No, not the Mac Mar. Tella cannot be trusted to honour his word."

"He might if there was something in it for him."

"What is in it for him is revenge. No brother, I think we need to search for friends across the sea."

***

The leaky ship smelled of fish and rolled along like a barrel, and Holke was quite the most boring man Alistair had ever met. "The *Crab* isn't the *Pride of Tiree*, that's for certain," he thought. Still, it was the only ship which could be hired for the trip to Belfast at short notice.

"Go to Patrick Three Eggs with all speed," the Younger had commanded, "alone and in secret." Now, here he was, one day from port, counting down every second, and Alistair stared ahead trying to get his first ever sight of Irish soil. He felt apprehensive. So much depended on him making a good impression. The *Crab* lurched and he grabbed the ship's rail. It was as rough as old boots and hadn't seen a lick of paint in years.

He glanced back at the young, earnest sailor who steered their course. That was a mistake. Holke of Oban took the glance as an act of encouragement, waved at him and tied a rope to the tiller, and strode across the deck. Alistair's very soul cried out for peace.

"Sir, not long to go, sir," blurted Holke, with one of the shortest sentences he had ever used.

"Good," replied Alistair, but not too eagerly.

"It's grand out here, isn't it, sir, well grand of course in fine weather like this; not so nice of course when the clouds gather and the waves rise. You don't like bad weather, do you, sir? Nasty. Why, I've seen waves you simply would not believe, sir. Great towering monsters the size of cottages. No, bigger than cottages, bigger than the hills themselves, sir."

Alistair wondered if Holke had stopped to refill his lungs.

"Really," he mumbled.

"Really, sir, yes, really. Quite frightening they are too. Are you going to Belfast to do some trade?"

Alistair's lips hardly moved.

"You can't beat a good bit of trade, sir, don't you agree, sir. Why, where would the world be without the peoples of different lands sharing the good things they have to sell? The world would be a poorer place, sir. A much poorer place and that's for sure. My uncle was a one for the trade, sir. Travelled all around the kingdom he did. Bartering something here, bartering something there and always with an eye for a good deal. Do you like a good deal, sir? I know my wife does. She goes off for food every day and you should see the things she comes back with, sir. One day I sent her off for some eggs and she came back with apples. Apples, sir, can you believe it? What use are they when there is bacon a sizzling in the pan? I ask you that!"

Not having any eggs clearly had significance to Holke and Alistair nodded weakly.

"Sir, yes, we'll soon be there, sir, so have you got all your things together? I know I have. Well, I don't have a lot of things, you understand, sir, being just a humble sailor and all. Now, I bet the Younger has a lot of things, sir, don't you? Why, I bet the palace is full of all sorts of wonderful objects. You ever been to the palace, sir?"

"No, no I haven't," lied Alistair.

"My cousin has, sir. Been there lots of times with the trade, sir. He says there are tapestries on the walls as big as sails, bigger than sails, and more shields on the walls than could be carried by an army. What do you think of that, sir?"

Alistair felt his eyelids droop.

"Well, thanks very much for your company, sir, I had better be getting back to the tiller. I can't stand here talking to you all day, even though I'd like to, sir. You understand me, sir? Work to be done. We aren't far from land now. Just you keep looking ahead, sir, and let me know if you see anything, wont you, sir."

Holke didn't wait for a reply and went away to the stern, and Alistair called after him.

"Do you spend a lot of time on your own, Holke?"

"That I do, sir, a terrible amount of time."

"Doesn't surprise me," thought Alistair.

"Talking of time, sir, did I tell you about the time I sailed with my

274

grandfather, down to the Land of the Welsh Kings. What a time that was, sir. What a time. You've never seen sheep like they've got down there, sir. Do you like sheep, sir?"

Alistair lowered his head and contemplated jumping overboard. If the Younger's messenger had arrived, as planned, then Alistair would be met by Seamus, Prince of all Ireland and Patrick Three Eggs' son and heir.

As Holke talked about how to cook real fish broth, Alistair wondered what a king's envoy should say. Holke threw the tiller over and Alistair nearly jumped out of his skin.

"Well, there we are. Nice quiet journey, wasn't it, sir? That'll be four silver coins, sir."

Alistair nodded and handed him the money. He felt like he had after the battle at Carn Liath. Totally drained. He grabbed a rope, jumped ashore and secured the boat, glancing around the quay. People bustled around many kinds of ships, which were tied in a long line to the shore. Fishing boats and larger traders competed for space, and the whole scene was backed by pretty, brightly coloured cottages. Three riders trotted down the quay towards them, one leading another horse behind him.

"Welcome to Ireland," said Seamus, as he dismounted, "I look forward to escorting you to the royal court at Mountjoy."

They shook hands.

"Thank you, Seamus," replied Alistair politely, "and I bring you warm greetings from Malcolm the Younger, the Protector of the Stone of Destiny and ruler of all the Scottish peoples."

"Has the Younger fallen on hard times? Most visitors arrive in something a bit grander."

Seamus nodded cheekily at the *Crab*. It looked more like a giant bucket than a boat. Luckily Holke missed the comment and carried on coiling a rope.

"Quiet fellow, is he?" asked Seamus.

"Hardly says a word," said Alistair.

Alistair couldn't help but like this man. Perhaps twenty years old, he was tall, cheerful and dressed in fine clothes.

"Is it far to Mountjoy?"

"Half a day, if you can stay on." The prince nodded at Alistair's steed. "You do have horses in Scotland, don't you?"

"Aye, we do, but rarely have I seen beasts as fine as these."

"Oh, horses are one of my father's passions and let me tell you he has *many* passions. He doesn't do *anything* in moderation."

Alistair nodded and watched two of Seamus's bodyguards, who began to argue about which one of them should carry his bag from the ship. They dismounted and began punching each other.

Seamus chuckled. "Now don't you go worrying about Declan and Michael. They have their own way of settling little disagreements."

"I wasn't," grinned Alistair, "I was worried about my bag."

He went back on board to say goodbye to Holke, and that was a huge mistake.

***

Half of the Norse invasion fleet held their positions fifty paces from the shore of Sea Peoples Land.

"I can't see Niels Magnusson," said Hengist Corngrinder, "do you think he will be as reliable as Olaf?"

"He will be here soon," replied Thorgood, "and then we attack."

"Everyone is ready for the fight, even those who are new to battle. They want the chance to blood their swords."

"And blood them they will. We cannot allow any of the enemy to escape and cause trouble later. With the summer ahead of us, we can at least make the land pay its way and send food home."

"Is there any news from Oslo fjord?" asked Hengist.

Thorgood shook his head and then stiffened and stood bolt upright on the prow, his eyes searching the pine trees, which ran in an unbroken ribbon along the coast. Something was moving in the trees behind the enemy who stood on the shore.

"Niels has completed his journey unseen. Get ready, old friend, the time for words is over."

As Niels' men emerged from the pines, Amera's descendants spun around and looked in fear at the Norse warriors who blocked their retreat. Thorgood lifted his sword and waved it at the fleet.

"For Odin." he yelled.

The crews yelled back.

"For Odin."

The anchors were raised, oars dropped and the longships sped towards the shore.

"Kill them all," roared Thorgood.

***

"How many of the enemy escaped?" Thorgood asked later.

"Not more than twenty," said Hengist.

"I want them hunted down. We must keep our landing a secret for as long as possible."

"My men are searching the pines. We will get them," promised Niels.

"And how many men have we lost?"

"Seventy are fallen, five will not last the night and five have wounds that will heal."

"Praise be to Odin. We are still strong in number. May he bless the fallen with a place at his table," said Thorgood.

"Praise be to Odin," repeated Niels and Hengist together.

"And now the hard work begins. Niels, take fifty men and explore the coast to the south. Look for any headland, which can be defended easily, with shelter for the fleet nearby. Hengist you search the coast to the north. Return no later than two days from now."

"And what are you going to do?" asked Hengist.

"I am going to search the Sea People's village and take what I can to make our stay here as pleasant as possible."

As Hengist and Niels left him, to gather their search parties together, Thorgood said to himself, "And I might just visit a cairn and pray for the soul of Thorfinn Firebrand."

***

Yashus ripped a handful of plants from the sandy soil, chewed them and stuck them onto his cut arm. The medicine stung terribly, but would help to stop the bleeding. The loss of blood had made him light headed and he needed to rest. He also needed time to think.

In one battle his people had been destroyed, his friends killed, his family enslaved. Now he was being hunted by the warriors who came in the dragon ships. He glanced around the pines and saw that there were few places to hide. He glanced up through the canopy of branches. The sun was high in its arc and nightfall, blessed darkness, would be a long time away.

Yashus crawled into a small hollow, protected by a fallen tree, and waited for his strength to return. Men with swords and spears were shouting, some way off, but getting closer. He was unarmed and not strong enough to climb up into the branches. Sweat poured down his back. The voices grew louder, but no nearer. Yashus risked peeking out from his hiding place. The enemy had unearthed someone else and a man zigzagged through the pines with spears thudding into the earth at his feet.

Yashus didn't wait to see what happened to him and ran, as fast as his legs would carry him, away from his pursuers. His arm started to bleed again.

Seven days later, weak and dishevelled, he stumbled into a village. His body was exhausted from dodging the enemy and lack of food. But his mind was even wearier and it wandered, helplessly, from the desperate struggle on the beach to the words he might use to beg for mercy.

A little girl came out of a round house and looked at him. She screamed and dived back inside. Yashus wandered on, muttering to himself, and oblivious to the silent crowd of people who gathered with spears around him.

He had to find someone. Tell them his story and ask for help. If only someone would help him. He stumbled again and a villager raised his sword. Some of the womenfolk took a step back and grabbed their children.

A huge warrior stepped out of the Great Hall, at the far end of the village, tossed a bone onto the ground, and wiped his face on his sleeve. He watched the stranger stagger from side to side and, more often than not, in his direction. Yashus mumbled something and stumbled on, and bumped into his great chest.

"Can I help you, laddie?" asked Hamish.

A deep ditch, backed by a bank of earth, ran in a line along the full two hundred paces where the headland narrowed. Buried into the bank, firm, upright and rising high above it, were thick pine trunks. Thorgood surveyed his new home with a sense of satisfaction. His people had sweated for this. From the base of the ditch to the top of the tree trunks was the height of four men. With a bit more work the Younger could never take it back. They were here to stay.

The Norse Lord walked down the bank towards twenty long, narrow houses. Some were finished, their stone walls topped by thatch. Most of them, though, were in varying stages of completion and all around him men carried stones, sawed wood, or cooked. None rested. In twenty days they had built a village.

He looked around. The headland was surrounded on three sides by the sea and on the other side by their defences. The fleet bobbed up and down in a small bay beside the headland, and a sandy path had been cut by the passage of men carrying stores from the bay to the houses. Some of the longships were away taking slaves and grain to Oslo, and they should return soon with the women and children. It would feel more like a home when they arrived.

"How long have we got?" asked Hengist.

Thorgood sighed. "How long for what?"

"Before the Younger finds out that we are here, on his soil."

"I would be very surprised if he does not know already."

"Will he come to fight us?" continued Hengist.

"From what Tella has told us, I do not think so. He faces other, more powerful, enemies than us. I think he will want to agree a peace, to free up the High Table to fight the Angles."

"And do we want peace?"

"At the moment we do. We need to establish ourselves before we take on the full might of the Younger's army."

"We could hold him off here."

"We could hold him off, yes. We could even survive a long siege as our ships can bring in supplies easily enough. But he can stop us farming the land and that *is* what all this is about."

Thorgood and Hengist watched a group of men lift two large wooden beams on top of a stone wall. They were lashed together to form the beginning of a new roof.

"Niels says that three days' march to the southeast there are fine lands, which could be farmed for grain, cattle and sheep. Whilst the Scots are weak, I think we should take them, hold them and then sue for peace," continued Thorgood.

"And the lands here are no richer than those at home," said Hengist.

"Tomorrow, you will gather one in three of our warriors and go with Niels to take them."

"And do these new lands have a name?"

"Niels says the Scots call the lands *Tain*."

***

"I can't see anything, can you?" asked Hengist.

Niels Magnusson strained his eyes and shook his head.

"No. No movement anyway. Let's wait a while longer, just to be sure."

"Let's get on with it. We've been sitting here, watching, for an age and my men are hungry for food and the roar of battle."

Niels rolled onto his side to face him.

"Thorgood would advise caution."

"He isn't here. He would want us to take the initiative. Anyway, it's only a river. A river that can be no more than fifty paces wide. We could wade across in no time *and* we haven't seen a single sign of the enemy all day."

"That's what worries me."

Hengist rolled on his back and looked up at the leaves in the trees.

"Olaf Adanson would have conquered the whole of Scotland by now."

"Olaf is fallen."

"And no doubt looking down on us, from his seat at the eternal table, and saying to himself 'What in the name of Odin are those two doing?' I find myself asking the same question."

"Ask all you like. My hand goes in for caution."

"You might be right. There is movement on the other bank."

Almost directly opposite them, a shape moved down to the water's edge. As the shape came out of the dappled shade, out of the trees, they both grinned. A small girl knelt down and filled a pot with water, and left.

Hengist glanced at Niels, who nodded. They rose, and five hundred Norse warriors rose too, and made their way down to the river. They entered the water together, in a long line, with swords held at the ready and everyone alert, staring at the far bank.

They got half way. A volley of arrows and spears flew out of the dappled shade, and cut into them. Most of the Norsemen fell immediately.

Hengist saw Niels struck in the chest and his body floating downstream. The line turned and splashed its way back to safety. More arrows shot out of the shade and thudded into their backs. The river became choked full of bodies.

"Get into the trees," screamed Hengist, as he made the bank, and then he stopped dead in his tracks.

Two Scottish warriors, one huge the other tiny, were waiting for him. The big one picked Hengist up and tossed him back into the river. He spluttered his way to the surface and tried to find his sword. It was lost and he grabbed an axe from the back of a floating body.

Someone cried out, "For Odin," and was cut down. A line of horsemen emerged from their hiding places in the trees and charged into the last of the Norsemen with long spears. The enemy foot-soldiers began to hack down anyone who was left standing. Hengist dropped the axe and pulled the floating body back towards him. He froze and tried to play dead, but Hamish dashed into the river and, grabbing him by the scruff of his neck, dragged him ashore and dumped him, without ceremony, in front of Malcolm the Younger.

Hengist looked up into the king's eyes, which were firm and wise, and not without pity. When the king spoke, his words were in the Old Norse, which Arkinew had taught him.

"Tell Thorgood that, from this day, Sea Peoples Land is gifted to him. Tell him I expect peace in return. Tell him my people *will* be watching. Tell him of my hope for a *true* peace, for in my heart I know we can live together and prosper. But if the peace fails, you can expect more of what you have lived through today."

"I will tell him," promised Hengist.

Malcolm smiled at the miller.

"Tell Thorgood, of the line of Thorfinn Firebrand, we *will* meet again in happier times."

Hengist stared at the line of the dead along the river.

"I hope so."

"Tell Thorgood a place at the High Table is offered too."

The Younger turned his horse to lead the knights of the High Table south. As he passed Donald, he nodded gratefully.

"Please tell your daughter I thought she was very brave. Many children would not have gone down to the river."

"And did you see that I killed more of the enemy than Big Hamish?" said Donald.

Malcolm smiled, kicked his heels into the flanks of his steed and knew Tain was in safe hands.

Hengist began his long walk back to Sea Peoples Land. He felt ashamed and empty, and tried to string together the words he would use when he met Thorgood.

***

Peter thought about the defence of Tain and knew that Thorgood Firebrand would not give up his claim to it so easily. He looked at Myroy and sensed that this story was over.

"When will I see you again?"

"When you are ready."

"I thought I might visit Bernard in Corfu one day and ask him about Grandpa."

"Do you not think that keeping the stone has some advantages, young Peter?"

"Advantages? I only know I should live quietly and guard it until I am able to pass it on to my children."

Myroy rose and began to draw a circle on the cottage floor with his staff.

"You have already been gifted two powers, although you may not have realised it yet. Long life, earned by Dougie's courage at Carn Liath. The ability to learn, earned by Dougie's good fortune and loyalty to a friend on Tiree. You owe your third power to the shepherd too."

"One power for each of the challenges of mountain, island and castle," said Peter. "I am not sure I want any powers."

He was suddenly afraid.

"It would be unwise to let you hold Amera's stone without them."

Myroy walked back to the bench, and held his hand out, as if to place it on his pupil's shoulder. With a sudden panic, Peter leant back, away from Myroy's hand, but when the old man touched him he felt no different, no pain, no flood of energy through his body like the last time, and Myroy turned away from him.

"Will you tell me about Grandpa and Bernard and the war?" asked Peter quickly.

"No."

"I feel as though I must know more, just as I have to learn about Dougie, Grandpa and all of the Donalds, who have kept the stone before me."

"You do," agreed Myroy, as he began to disappear through the floor.

"But I might not be able to go to Corfu for ages," stammered Peter, fearing this was his last chance to get an answer.

From the bowels of the earth, Myroy's reply was muffled and Peter did not believe he heard his last words correctly.

"Why not ask your Grandfather?"

In the neat garden, it was as dark and cold as it had been when they had first arrived, and Peter's fingers trembled as he pressed the light on his watch. It was two thirty in the morning. Dog bounded across to the gate and Peter followed him onto the old drovers' road. Then the sheepdog barked and Peter turned to see that Dougie's cottage had become an ancient ruin once more.

"I'm still not a bit sleepy," said Peter and Dog looked up at him as if to say, "Me neither, let's go for walk."

They headed for the standing stones on the high pastures. A Gora moon lit up the far hills and Peter sensed their beauty and power. These were the same hills Dougie had seen, had worked on, and been so fond of. They had been a part of the shepherd and were now a part of Peter too and, like the brooch, a strong link to a past most people had forgotten.

At last they came to the cairn, which Peter guessed marked Lissy's grave. This was a truly peaceful place and he sat beside the stones to rest and to look at the loch, and the shapes made by the moonlight on its rippling surface. The effort of the climb had warmed him and he yawned, as sleep called to him at last, and he whistled to Dog so they might return home together. Respectfully, he nodded at the cairn and walked back down the slope.

"I wish I could speak to Grandpa," thought Peter.

"You will, laddie, one day," replied Grandpa.

In fear, Peter spun around and his anxious eyes searched for ghosts. Dog bounded over to him and they stood together on the deserted hillside. With his companion beside him Peter did not feel frightened anymore. He simply thought about his ancestors, all of them, and wondered how it might be possible to ask them for help if ever he needed it.

"Let's hope we never need it," he said to Dog and they set off towards the old drovers' road.

In his heart, Peter felt he should tell Grandma about what he had heard.

But it was something she already knew.

CHAPTER TWENTY FOUR

Mr Smith

Peter awoke from a terrible dream about fierce armies, hopeless battles, dungeons and dragon ships as his plane touched down in Luton. He remembered the walk back from the standing stones to Grandma's. It had been slow and weary, and even Dog's tail had drooped between his legs. They needed sleep, but every step was crammed full of memories, conjured up by Myroy's words.

After the funeral, his family had returned to Pinner and he had revised in the shepherd's cottage, every day, in the hope of seeing the storyteller again. But the rest of his stay in Glenbowmond had been uneventful. He studied hard, without interruption, and now felt much more confident about his exams. Peter didn't want to be overconfident, or cocky. That just wasn't his nature. But every text book he read he remembered and understood. Something he couldn't explain had happened when the Ancient One had touched his shoulder and his new abilities scared him.

Lost in his thoughts, Peter walked to the carousel to collect his bags. Why did Odin seek the stone? What was the danger from the Saxon cross? What dangers would Dougie face during his third challenge? He recalled the old man's warning about learning from the shepherd's story.

Why did his own future depend on it?

His father would be waiting for him in the Arrivals Hall. *He* knew the story, well most of it anyway, but he could not ask him to break his promise of secrecy with Myroy. But he *needed* to know. The new term would start in a week and Peter decided to find out if any written evidence had survived from the period. That, at least, might give him a clue.

***

The tube train was packed and Peter counted down the stations from Pinner to King's Cross. He was surrounded by passengers who read newspapers, or who stared into space. Peter guessed that many of them made this journey every weekday, silent and immersed in their own private worlds. The carriage lurched and he lost his balance and grabbed out at one of the plastic straps which hung down from the ceiling. Peter swung round and his face plunged into a businessman's armpit.

"Sorry," apologised Peter.

The man ignored him and continued to read the paper he held in his free hand. He smelled of roll-on deodorant.

The Reading Room of the British Library was peaceful and gave off a reassuring odour of cleaning fluid and old book. The neat lines of desks and reading lights were quickly being occupied by eager students and Peter felt that all the knowledge of the world might be hidden around its walls. He shuddered at the prospect of finding anything in the labyrinth of bookshelves and decided to ask for help. He walked quietly to a desk which stood apart from the others. A sign read, *Miss Dickson, Day Librarian, Enquiries Welcome.*

Miss Dickson was a thin, eager lady with the biggest glasses Peter had ever seen. She placed her coffee mug down onto a coaster, ordered some papers and arranged two pencils so they lay exactly parallel to the papers. She glanced up at Peter and smiled. Her glasses magnified her eyes so they looked like they belonged on a face that was twice as big as her own.

"May I help you?" she asked in a squeaky voice.

Peter smiled back, "Yes please, it's my first time here."

"Well, welcome, young man, what are you working on?"

"Personal interest. The history of Scotland, the age of the Celtic kings and particularly the reign of Malcolm the Younger."

"Follow me," ordered the librarian and she dashed off, with Peter struggling to keep up.

They twisted through rows of high shelving and past piles of books, waiting to be returned to their proper place of rest. In minutes they stood in-front of a section marked –

History/Scotland/Post-Romanic/Celts.

"Do you know where everything is?" asked Peter, impressed by Miss Dickson's ability.

"Not at all," she replied in her squeaky voice, "it's just a coincidence."

"A coincidence?"

"Only yesterday a Mr Smith asked me the same question and it took us a while to find what he wanted. Once I know where something is, I don't forget it."

With Miss Dickson's guidance, Peter soon sat at a reading desk and thumbed his way through huge volumes of historical information. Much of it was conjecture. Only scraps of writing had survived from the time before the first recognised Scottish king, Kenneth MacAlpin, and Peter guessed that the Younger had lived many years before Kenneth, and he began to lose heart.

A huge shadow fell over his desk and Peter lifted his head. He stared up into a face. A face hidden by a huge black beard.

"Are you going to be long, laddie?" asked the man rudely.

"I don't know," replied Peter.

"I want this one," demanded the man.

He pointed at a book near the bottom of the pile called, *Early Celtic Writings and their Meanings*.

"I could read it next and give it to you," offered Peter.

"Get on with it then," he barked, "I haven't got all day."

The shadow went away and Peter felt relieved because he sensed the man had wanted to just take what he wanted. Peter closed the book he had been reading and dug out *Early Celtic Writings and their Meanings*. He became lost in its words in the quiet Reading Room. At last, he came to a chapter called *The legends of the Celtic Kings of Scotland*. There was a short reference to a ruler called the Elder, who was as ambitious as he was cruel. One of the most powerful of all the clan chieftains. It said his death was followed by a long period of peace and just rule under his heir, Malcolm the Younger.

Peter read on ...

Although few songs or stories have survived, it is thought that the Younger was killed in battle by his own son, Ranald the Betrayer. In many ways, Malcolm's death signalled the end of the Charter of the Clans, which had bound the majority of the peoples of Scotland together for a generation. More importantly, it marked a major transition from what might be thought of as the Old Ways, the ancient Celtic traditions, to darker times and the threat of further invasions by the Norse Peoples.

Peter's head sank into his hands and he cried out.

"No. No. No."

A sea of heads lifted as their concentration was broken and Miss Dickson shot him a severe, disapproving glance. Mr Smith stared at Peter, snapped a pencil in two and decided to follow him home.

A week later, Trevor Smith walked into the staff room of Pinner High and checked his watch. O7:14. His dark eyes darted around the walls and ageing chairs, and settled on the notice board. He read the latest teachers' bulletin. "Any instances of bullying must be reported to Mr Sweeney, (Deputy Head of P.E.), and logged in the school anti-bullying register on the same day."

Smith spat on the floor, glanced at his watch and moved to the first of two steel cabinets, with double doors, that stood side by side. He passed a sink, which overflowed with unwashed coffee mugs, and a poster praising the virtues of renewable energy sources. Smith tried to wrench the first cabinet open and the handles came off in his hands. He stepped back and kicked the doors and the metallic *clang* made him jump. Smith prised the dented doors apart and found himself looking at a huge pile of risk assessment forms and a biscuit tin with a hand-written label sellotaped to the side. It read PHYSICS BISCUITS – KEEP OUT! He opened the tin and bit into a stale garibaldi.

Mr Smith glanced at his watch again and attacked the second cupboard. He thumped it with his fists and cursed, then realised it wasn't locked and pulled the handles gently. The metal doors swung open to reveal a stack of class registers. He began at class 1S and moved to 1R, then 1B and finally to class 1G. His fingers ran down the names of the children, an Archer, a Broderick, three Baxters, two Beeches and a Cob. Then a huge grin shot from behind the black beard.

"So, Peter has a younger sister."

A door slammed in a distant corridor, and Smith's grin disappeared. He threw the register back with the others and ran to the door. An old caretaker, in a brown coat and carrying a bucket, was walking towards him.

Smith hurried back across the staff room and pushed the metal bar of the fire exit. Outside he breathed heavily, and cold, white steam came out of his mouth. He ran along the line of classroom windows and passed the gym. Smith began to wheeze and his lungs hurt, but after a lifetime of searching, he wasn't going to give up now.

He approached the school gates and slowed to catch his breath. A car came around the corner of New Hope Drive and Smith dived behind one of the tall pillars which marked the school entrance. The car sped past and parked in a reserved space.

Smith took another deep breath, tucked his shirt into his trousers and straightened his tie. Casually he walked over to the car and reached it as a rather tubby lady with silver hair got out. She clasped a leather briefcase that overflowed with papers.

"I don't mean to startle you," said Smith politely, "but I have just arrived for my first day."

"You're very keen aren't you," smiled the lady.

"I think it's important to create a good first impression."

"First class … and you are?"

"Trevor Smith, I'm here on supply to cover for Miss Grenoski."

"Ah yes, Sheila will be on maternity leave for another twelve weeks."

"Long enough," thought Smith.

"I'm Mrs Bold, the Head Teacher."

"A pleasure to meet you, Mrs Bold."

Smith held out a hand like a piece of fish.

"I teach history to A level, but prefer the wee ones."

"Miss Grenoski's form was 1G, you can start with them."

"Perfect, just perfect."

"Where did you do your teacher training?" asked the Head.

"Dundee. My degree was in ancient history. Scottish history."

"Do you know I have always been fascinated by archaeology and particularly the Celts in Britain. They say they could never explain why the Pictish peoples vanished."

"There is much that is not known, even to scholars."

"Perhaps we can discuss it sometime?"

"It would be my pleasure."

The school doors burst open and an old man with a bucket burst out.

"Mrs Bold," said Crickly, "the vandals are back."

"Oh dear, much damage?"

"A cabinet kicked to bits."

"There goes the repair budget."

"Can I be of any help?" asked Smith.

"I don't think so," smiled Mrs Bold. "Anyway, I hope you enjoy your time at Pinner High."

"I am sure I will," agreed Smith and they walked off together to inspect the damage.

***

"Mum," shouted James, "I can't find my PE kit."

Julie Donald glanced up from her bowl of Fruit and Bran Crunch and sighed.

"I'm surprised you can find anything in your room," she mumbled.

"Mum," shrieked another voice, "can I have two pounds for lunch?"

"What's happened to your allowance?" asked Julie calmly.

"I've spent it," said Laura as she rushed into the kitchen. "Why can't I have the same as bloomin' James?"

She threw her empty bowl into the sink and filled a glass with orange juice. Most of it spilled onto the work-surface.

"You can have the same as James when you are the same age as James."

"That's typical. I have to spend the same on food as him, you know."

"You have more than enough for school dinners."

"But how am I supposed to pay for my phone cards? They don't grow on trees."

"When we bought your mobile we agreed it was up to *you* to manage things, that's why we give you an allowance."

Laura stomped off to get the money from her Dad.

"Mum," asked Peter quietly, "could you run me over to Kylie's after school? We want to revise together."

At that moment the kitchen door burst open and James shouted.

"Has anyone seen my PE kit?"

"Where did you last see it?" asked Julie.

"I put it where I always put it."

"You mean you threw it into the cupboard under the stairs."

"Whatever," said James, "but it's not there now."

Julie sighed and went to the cupboard under the stairs. James's PE kit was festering behind the ironing board.

"Haven't you washed it?" he asked.

"I have washed and ironed everything that was in the washing basket."

"You mean everyone's except mine."

Julie tried to keep her temper.

"Other people, James Donald, help me by placing their dirty clothes in the *wash basket*."

James smiled back at her with his *who me?* look.

"Time for the bus," he said.

Colin Donald came out of his study and kissed his wife.

"Laura said that you said it would be OK to give her extra dinner money."

Laura picked up her school bag and dashed to the front door.

"Laura," yelled Julie.

"See you tonight, Mum," yelled back a voice, which shook the house to its foundations.

"Bye, Laura," said Daddy, "Bye, James, have a good day at school."

"Whatever," grinned James.

"Don't forget you're taking me over to Kylie's after school," called back Peter.

"Come home on the bus and I'll take you over," offered Daddy.

"Thanks," said Peter, closing the door behind him.

Julie stared at her new kitchen. She remembered the picture in the brochure and the wonderful feeling of newness, sparkle and order when the workmen had finished. It looked as though a hurricane had hit it.

***

"Old Crickly told Katie that Miss Grenoski has had a boy and called it Beckham," said Abby.

The school bus lurched away and everyone lurched back and then forward.

"What do you think of that?"

292

"I think Mr Denver thinks he's a bloomin' racing driver."

"No, about Miss Grenoski calling her son Beckham."

"Bloomin' Beckham," muttered Laura as she concentrated on the approach of the next bend.

"Beckham," repeated Abby. "Her boyfriend is a mad keen United fan."

"Mad and not keen on decent names," said Laura, "I wonder who will take History?"

"I hope it's not one of those students we get sometimes."

"Yeah, the last one took us through the Industrial Revolution and Mum says it's not even on the curriculum."

The muffled theme tune to Eastenders came out of her bag and she grabbed at it eagerly and glanced at the number.

"It's a text from Helen."

"What does she want?" asked Abby,

"She says Miss G has called her boy Becks."

The school bus lurched again as it entered New Hope Drive. A large poster by the bus stop proclaimed, "THE BIG ONE! England V Scotland at Highbury, coming soon!"

"Tell her we know. Perhaps we could make her a card in Art, we've got two periods after History."

***

Mr Smith scoured the Monday morning faces of class 1G. His eyes rested on a golden haired girl who sat three rows back and he smiled. Abby thought he looked like a werewolf.

"Now then," said Smith in a friendly voice, "I'm Mr Smith and I shall be filling in for Miss Grenoski. Can anyone tell me where you have got to in your studies?"

The lesson was an enjoyable one and the time passed quickly. They talked about why the Romans had invaded England and the problems they might have faced crossing the Channel. At one point Mr Smith passed around a bag of coins and asked how old they might be.

Laura answered, "About two thousand years."

The teacher smiled at her again and said, "Well done, Laura, they are very ancient and part of the evidence we have for the Roman occupation."

Laura glowed with appreciation and Abby whispered, "He's a bit of a creep."

1G were putting their things away when Smith asked them to look at a picture. He placed an acetate on the overhead projector and beamed at his audience.

"I have always loved history," he said in a sincere voice, "in many ways the past is the key to the future and it is relics, like the coins we saw, that really bring the past to life."

He paused for effect and pointed at the drawing of a brooch up on the screen.

"Some relics have a fantastic story to tell and some, like this, like Amera's stone, have stories very few can remember. It is such a shame we cannot share their secrets together."

In row three Laura's hand shot up.

"I have seen it," she said.

"Have you really, Laura? What wonderful news."

"I could bring it in tomorrow."

"Excellent," said Smith, "bring it in and we'll see if we can bring the past to life. You have all been so helpful today that I am not going to give you any homework for a week."

Everyone beamed, like Mr Smith, and 1G left to go to Art.

CHAPTER TWENTY FIVE

A Very Special Assembly

"Ah, Laura, did you remember to bring in the brooch?" asked Mr Smith.

"I did, although I don't know what Petee will say when he finds out."

"Need, er, *Petee* know?"

"I suppose not. I just didn't like taking it without permission."

"Never mind, it will be a real treat for the class to hear its story."

Laura smiled and reached into the bottom of her bag. Smith felt every nerve in his body tingle with excitement. The door of the history classroom opened and Mrs Bold waddled in. Laura took her hand out of her bag and Smith clenched his teeth.

"Good morning, Mr Smith," she said brightly, "I wanted to let you know there will be a special assembly at three o'clock. County have asked all the schools in the area to invite the police in to talk to the children about the dangers of drugs."

"The police," replied Smith.

"Yes, the police. We do not get the whole school together very often and I wondered if you have any experience pulling together an anti-drugs policy."

"I do," lied Smith, "in fact I still have my notes from Kinross High School. They have an excellent track record of working with parents and the local community to address the problem."

"First class. Would you like to open the session and address the school?"

"I would be delighted to help," offered Smith, "we'll make it the most special of all assemblies."

"First class," repeated Mrs Bold and then she turned to Laura. "Lessons start in a minute, shouldn't you be somewhere else?"

"Yes, Miss," said Laura in her politest voice.

"Well, off you go then."

Mrs Bold walked her out of the classroom. Behind their backs Mr Smith snarled.

***

Toady Thompson and Mac Mackinlay smelled of cigarettes and stood with their heads bowed in front of Mr Freeman and Mr Smith.

"I caught these two smoking behind the bicycle sheds. This is the second time I have had to speak to them and we have only been back at school a day and a bit," said Mike Freeman.

Toady grinned at Mac and Mr Smith's face became stern.

"So you think it is funny do you?" he snapped.

They bowed their heads again. They knew how to deal with Freeman, they just ignored him, but this new master was different. There was more than a hint of danger in his voice.

"Anyway, I have to go and prepare for my geography lesson with 4S. We are looking at Continental Drift today. Very exciting. Could you deal with them for me?"

"It would be my pleasure," said Smith and his eyes never left Freeman until he left the room.

"You are not sorry, are you?" whispered Smith.

Toady and Mac glanced at each other, but said nothing.

"And if I was honest," continued Smith, "I don't see why you should be. Why should that idiot Freeman tell you what to do?"

The boys glanced at each other and smiled cautiously.

"If you want a fag, what harm are you doing to anyone else? I mean, it's not as if you are smoking in the classrooms, is it?"

They both nodded.

"Still, I can't let you go unpunished, can I?"

Toady and Mac's cautious smiles faded.

"But I am a good judge of character and my guess is you can both keep a secret."

They nodded again.

"Do you know the Donald children?"

Mac scowled.

"You don't like them do you?"

"They give bad kids a bad name," mumbled Toady.

"And do you like money?" asked Smith, a huge grin appearing behind his beard.

"Yeah," said Toady and Mac together.

Smith took a wallet from his back pocket and pulled out a thick stack of notes.

"Fifty for you, Toady," he offered, "and fifty for you."

He handed it over and the boys beamed at each other.

"What do you want us to do?" asked Toady.

"A simple job of mugging."

Toady and Mac's faces lit up.

"And you both get fifty more when it's done," and Smith showed them an acetate of a brooch.

***

"That's the worst bloomin' art lesson I've ever had," complained Laura.

"Mrs Hotter stinks," said Helen.

"Why can't she give us something interesting to do? All we do is look at old pictures and paint," moaned Abby.

"And because it's not raining we have to go and stand outside in the bloomin' cold."

"Let's see if we can find Charlotte, we can tell her about the sleepover on Saturday night."

The three of them skipped off.

"There they are," said Mac and he pointed at the girls who huddled around their mobile phones.

Helen saw him pointing at them.

"Don't look now, but Mac and Toady are watching us."

"Just ignore them," urged Abby.

"Yeah, they can bog off," said Laura.

The bell rang to sound the end of break and hundreds of pupils shuffled towards the entrance. Mac and Toady began to run and barged their way towards the girls.

"You've got my bag!" shouted Toady tugging at Laura's bag.

"It's mine, you dip-stick," shrieked Laura.

Mac pushed Abby over and Toady hit Laura in the face.

***

"I don't know why Mrs Bold got the job," said Barry Sweeney in an angry voice. His words were filled with pent-up resentment that came from every boring lesson he had taken, every failed career move and all the worthless changes in teaching practice forced onto him.

"My dear boy," said Thomas Greacher, the Head of English, "you would have my vote any day. I simply cannot imagine why they passed you over for that woman. *She* has been nothing but trouble since she arrived. I simply do not know why we stand for it."

"Why do you stand for it?" asked a soft voice and they both turned in their chairs to see Smith taking a plastic container out of the staffroom fridge.

"What can we do?" grumbled Greacher. "Teaching is ruined as a profession. It is not respected. Why, I had friends around for dinner, only last week, and they could not believe what we have to put up with. It makes me so cross."

"And what about this risk assessment nonsense," added Sweeney, "you can't hear a kid blow off without filling in a form."

"It isn't right, is it?" said Smith.

"It isn't right. If I was Head there would be some changes around here I can tell you."

Smith pulled back the lapel of his jacket to reveal a brooch.

"And I bet they would be changes for the better."

"Why, you can't even hit a child any more. Simply nonsense," growled Greacher. "No discipline, that's the trouble."

"No discipline," repeated the other teachers in the staffroom.

"But who is to blame?" asked Smith.

"I'll show you who is to blame!"

Sweeney leapt up from his armchair and strode to the notice board.

"Look at this crap, fill in this form for bullying, don't feed the kids in case the sweets you give them contain bloody nuts, the National Union of Teachers (and what have they ever done for us?) are in talks with the government about Performance Related Pay. Can you believe it? Performance Related Pay?"

His colleagues nodded angrily.

"As if we do not perform already," said Smith.

"And we have to beg the parents for money to buy books," added Miss Tag, Deputy Head of Biology.

"Its cuts, cuts, cuts. Everyone knows we are understaffed," said Sweeney.

"And underpaid."

"Why do we stand for it?"

"Why do you?" asked Smith.

Greacher slammed his fist down on the table.

"What can we do?"

"Kill Mrs Bold," cried Sweeney.

"Kill them all," shouted Miss Tag.

"And we should wait until we are ready," whispered Smith.

"Wait until ready," repeated the teachers.

"Until the assembly," whispered Smith.

"The assembly," repeated the mob.

Mr Smith sat down in the armchair vacated by Barry Sweeney, lowered the lapel on his jacket, and took a cheese and pickle sandwich from his lunchbox.

***

"Good afternoon, everyone," said Mrs Bold.

"Good afternoon, Mrs Bold," replied eight hundred voices.

At the side of the stage in the gym, Toady nudged Mac.

"This is going to be good," he said.

"I would like to introduce you to Sergeant Bernie Wagg of the North London Anti Drugs and Community Affairs Unit," continued the Head Teacher.

Sergeant Wagg got up from his chair and nodded at the sea of faces. James thought he looked a bit old and portly to be a policeman, and wondered if school lecturing was what you did when you were too slow to chase the bad guys. Wagg sat down again.

Peter stood next to Kylie and knew that something was wrong. He glanced across at Mr Sweeney. His face looked like thunder. Then he saw Laura. She was holding a blood-stained hanky to her nose.

The two periods of Biology after lunch had been awful. Miss Tag had refused, point blank, to teach them and insisted that school was a complete waste of time. He asked her about the kind of questions they might get in their exams. She had slapped his face.

Peter didn't know what to do. Miss Tag had always been an excellent teacher. He would speak to his Mum about it when he got home. Peter smiled nervously at Kylie and she ran a finger down her cheek and then pointed at his red cheek.

"Tell you later," he whispered out of the corner of his mouth.

"And our special assembly, about the terrible threat we face from illegal substances, will be opened by Mr Smith our new History teacher," continued Mrs Bold.

Smith nodded at her reassuringly.

"Some of you may not have had the chance to meet Mr Smith, but I can assure you all of the high quality of his teaching. He brings a wealth of experience, in the field of education, to Pinner High."

Mackinlay yawned. Laura lowered her hanky and beamed up at her new teacher.

"And so to introduce the assembly I would like to invite Mr Smith to the podium."

Smith rose and shook hands with Mrs Bold as she sat down. He took his speaker notes from his breast pocket, laid them on the ledge of the lectern, raised his head and smiled at his audience. Then he picked up his notes and slowly tore them into pieces. Peter gasped as he recognised the shadow from the British Library and felt sick when he saw his brooch on the teacher's jacket. It shone red. An angry red.

"Friends," began Smith, "can anyone here say they are truly happy?"

Peter noticed that most of the teachers were nodding in agreement. Something bad was going to happen. He could feel it.

"We live in a world that has lost its sense of priorities," continued Smith, "teaching has been reduced to a figure of fun by the government. Not only do they refuse to invest in children, our future."

He paused to see many of the pupils nodding too. Mrs Bold was squirming in her chair.

"They create unnecessary rules, which take away the very thing education must be built on. The freedom to act. We all have a right to be treated as adults and to use our initiative. There are many rules that destroy our freedoms."

Smith paused again.

"Like having to spend our time form filling, rather than teaching."

Miss Tag and Greacher said, "Yes," together. Barry Sweeney looked downright nasty.

"Like not being allowed to use mobile phones in class."

The mood of the pupils changed to anger.

"Now we all know we need rules," said Smith.

"We all need rules," mumbled the assembly.

"But why can't we make them?"

"Why can't we make them?"

Mrs Bold got up from her seat and walked to the podium.

"That's quite enough of that sort of talk," she ordered.

"And who wants to impose their will on us?" asked Smith.

Peter sensed a growing rage amongst the crowd. Many were his friends and this wasn't like them. Nothing was as it should be and he watched, frozen, as Toady and Mac came from the side of the stage and threw a rope around Mrs Bold. They manhandled her back into her chair and tied her to it. Smith unclipped the brooch and held it above his head. A deep red glow filled the gym and the crowd began to chant.

"Kill her. Kill her. Kill her."

"Why should we not be listened to?" whispered Smith.

"We must be heard," chanted the crowd.

"We must be heard," whispered Smith.

"We must be heard," repeated the teachers and pupils.

"We *will* be heard!" cried Smith.

"We will be heard. We will be heard. We will be heard."

Peter glanced at Laura. She was chanting like her friends. So was Kylie and he searched the room for anyone who had resisted the power of the stone. James had a bewildered look on his face, and he caught his eye. His brother circled his finger around his temple, to show he thought everyone had gone mad, and Peter nodded at a fire exit at the back of the hall.

"What shall we do with the person who has ruined our lives?"

Smith went to stand next to Mrs Bold. Patches of sweat were appearing under her arms and staining her maroon blouse black.

"Hang her," screeched Greacher.

"She could be useful," whispered Smith.

"She could be useful," chanted the mob.

"We could take her as a hostage," whispered Smith.

"Take her as our hostage," chanted the mob.

James and Peter made it to the fire escape without attracting any unwanted attention. It had already been pushed open and Mike Freeman stood on the path, which led to the school entrance.

He seemed bewildered and kept muttering, "I've never seen anything like it. Not in twenty years as a teacher."

Shouts and crashing noises came out of the gym and they stared back in. Everyone was smashing the furniture to pieces. Making weapons.

"Let's get out of here," urged Mr Freeman.

"Hold on a second," said Peter as he watched Sergeant Wagg organise the mob into fighting groups. He was barking out orders and waving his truncheon about.

Then Kylie saw them and shouted, "They are not with us."

"Let's get out of here," said James and they ran around the corner of the gym and onto the school car park.

"I think we will be alright," panted Mr Freeman.

Bricks and broken chairs crashed down around them and two hundred angry pupils chased them through the gates of Pinner High.

***

Julie Donald sat glued to the Six O'clock News. A reporter in a thick black coat held a microphone and stood beside a sign that read New Hope Drive. He spoke in an urgent voice.

"The local authorities are completely baffled as to why the staff and pupils of Pinner High School have barricaded themselves inside the school grounds. There is a huge police presence in the area, over thirty squad cars, and I can confirm an attempt was made earlier to enter the main school building.

It was beaten back by a hail of missiles, thrown by those inside. Chief Inspector Morgan has denied that a Police sergeant is helping to lead the mob and that some of the men, involved in the first assault, have joined with the rebels. A spokesman for the Ministry of Education has confirmed it is extremely unlikely that the revolt at Pinner High has anything to do with the government's policy to establish Performance Related Pay in the teaching profession.

And now back to the studio."

Julie was worried sick about little Laura. Her boys had made it home and had spent most of the afternoon giving statements to police officers. They made them tell the story four times and the policemen drank six cups of tea in her new kitchen.

"Don't worry, Mum," reassured Peter, "it will all work out OK."

"It doesn't look OK," replied Julie as she watched the reporter in the black coat appear on the screen again.

"News just in that thirty schools in North London have followed the lead of the protestors at Pinner. Harrow School, amongst many others, has been occupied by angry mobs.

And news just breaking here. Literally, just breaking now."

The reporter was passed a slip of paper.

"The police surrounding the school have joined with the protestors. They have joined with the protestors and more police from outside the constabulary are on the way to reason with them.

Well, quite incredible scenes here in Pinner and now back to the studio."

The front door opened and Colin Donald called out, "It's me."

Julie ran to her husband and threw her arms around him.

"Have you heard the news?"

"Aye, I have, lass. Are the bairns all safe and home?"

"Laura is still missing."

Colin Donald's heart sank and they went over to the TV.

"I could do with a cup of tea," he said and Julie went out.

He looked at Peter who nodded slowly.

"They have the stone."

***

The Donalds stood in the cold, on the wrong side of a red and white plastic ribbon, which divided New Hope Drive in two, and stared at the blue flashing lights that ringed Pinner High.

"Is there any news of the children?" Julie asked a policewoman for the third time.

"No news, but we have over five hundred officers on the scene now. Things will be fine, I'm sure."

In front of them, lit by huge spotlights, were the world's press. The cameramen jostled for position and reporters talked constantly into microphones, or mobile phones. One cameraman was high in the sky, perched on the end of a crane. Then pandemonium broke out. The long blue line, facing the school gates, turned and charged at the press. They beat them with truncheons, cuffed them and smashed their equipment.

Behind them all, Mr Smith smiled and wondered what his first target should be. The crown jewels? The gold deposits of the Bank of England? The diamond stocks at DeBeers? He held up Amera's stone and a blood red beam shot out in a fork. One beam sliced into a BBC Outside Broadcast lorry. All over the country television sets, tuned to its signal, glowed red and exploded. The other fork hit the crane and it rocked, alarmingly, before crashing down onto the BBC lorry. It cut it in two. Smith pointed the stone at an electricity pylon. Its wires glowed like crimson worms and every light in London went out.

"We had better make ourselves scarce," said Colin.

In darkness, they ran back down the drive and passed a police incident wagon. James heard one of the officers inside shout into a microphone.

"Yes, you heard me. I want the army here now."

***

In the quiet of his bedroom, Peter looked at his battery-powered alarm clock. It was one of the few things working in the house and read 02:16. He couldn't sleep and, once again, he reached under the bed to find a shoebox. He lifted the lid and took out a plastic carrier bag. It was still empty.

How on earth had Mr Smith got the brooch? Mum had been in all morning and so he couldn't have stolen it. Peter lay back on the bed and closed his eyes. He felt as though he had let down everyone who had ever kept Amera's stone hidden through all those long centuries. He created a picture of Myroy's face in his mind. The bedroom floor began to shimmer.

Odin watched the bank of TV screens and lifted his mobile.

"Olaf, the stone cries out. Order all our people to London."

"I obey, master," said Olaf Adanson. "What about Smith?"

"Make sure he suffers."

Odin hung up, tapped a new instruction into his phone and *Pinner High School* appeared in the search line on Ask Jeeves. The ancient one read the new screen and committed each word to memory.

"Close."

A wall of rock rose up silently to hide the screens. The rock graced the entire length of his underground office and he went to stand beside the great carving of a Norse longship. He raised a hand and, affectionately, stroked the foot of a warrior who stood at the prow.

"My dear brother, Myroy's luck has run out."

CHAPTER TWENTY SIX

Battle of Pinner High

Peter closed his eyes and waited to be scolded. "I have been such a fool," admitted Myroy, "I watched the obvious and forgot about Smith."

"Laura's new teacher? Is Mr Smith Odin?"

Myroy raised an eyebrow. "No, Smith is not Odin. He is not even one of Odin's people and I dread to think what will happen to him now the location of the stone is known."

"I'm scared," said Peter.

"You should be. Very scared."

"And I worry about Laura."

"I worry about *all* the children under Smith's control, for his power will grow quickly now and, even in your time, there is little anyone can do about it."

"You stole the ruby once, from Thor and his followers, can we take it again?"

"We have no choice but to try, and I pray Odin's people fail him."

"Are Odin's people on the way here?" asked Peter in a frightened voice.

The Ancient One nodded.

"How will we recognise them?"

"You will know them when you see them. To understand what will be, you *must* think about the true power of the stone."

"But the police are calling in the army and Laura is still at school. We can't wait."

Myroy looked fierce.

"Tell me, Peter of the line of Donald, what can you do? Smith holds the ruby and his heart is full of greed. Now, in this moment, in Pinner High School, you can feel *some* of its terrible power. But not all of it! You have been a *Keeper* for one moon and what do you know about the stone's history? That Gora tried to steal it. That Dunnerold beat Odin to Amera's cairn by one day. That Dougie faced three challenges to become the first *Keeper*. Is this knowledge enough to guide your actions?"

Peter felt himself shrink inside. Then Myroy's face changed. It became warm and full of concern.

"Listen to me, Stone Keeper. Your future, everyone's future, hangs in the balance. *Listen* to me."

He glanced down at his hands, rubbed them together and studied the veins and wrinkles, and remembered the scenes of his long life, since becoming an Ancient One.

"What do we do?" asked Peter.

"What do *we* do?"

"Smith holds Odin's Stone and his power is growing."

"It is," said Myroy.

"But what shall we do?"

Myroy gave him a hard look.

"Have I not taught you anything, Peter of the line of Donald?"

Peter put his head in his hands and thought about the story. There wasn't anything he could do, on his own anyway, and he lifted his face and smiled.

"Together we are stronger."

Myroy nodded and rose, and made a circle on the floor with his staff. Then Peter was alone and he dressed and went to get his brother. He would need to be in on it too.

James opened an eye and hissed, "Get lost, you dip-stick," and shut his eye again.

Peter shook his shoulder.

"Come on. We've got work to do. Get some warm clothes on and keep quiet."

"Whatever," said James sleepily, but he got dressed and followed his brother.

As Peter opened his bedroom door an awful, musty, unwashed smell attacked his senses. James held his nose and Peter stuck his head inside his room. The blade of a claymore came up and out of the shadows, and hovered below his throat. Then a hand grabbed his fleece and lifted him, and threw him across the room onto his bed. James gasped as the same hand grabbed him, and tossed him onto the bed too.

Two shapes stood over them and one said something in a language they couldn't understand. It was rough and guttural, but not threatening. One of the men laughed. Peter tried to stand and the claymore swung down to rest on his chest. Peter grinned, as his eyes became used to the dark again, and he raised his hands above his head.

"Don't kill us. We are on the same side!"

The blade lowered and Peter stood.

James whispered, "Who the hell are these guys?"

Peter went over to his bedside table, took out a box of matches, struck one and lit a candle.

One of the kilted strangers stepped back in fear as he struck the match.

They were older than Peter by about three or four years and yet they were small. Even James was taller than these warriors. Peter went over to the shorter of the two men and, in the candlelight, studied him. Thick brown hair crowned a handsome, sincere and outdoor kind of face. He held out a hand and the shepherd took it.

"I am so glad you have come."

Dougie glanced at Alistair and shook his head. They couldn't understand a word he said either.

"It's not the people out of the old wrinkley's story is it?" asked James.

"It is."

Then the bedroom floor began to shimmer, like moonlight on water. In seconds, Myroy came up though the floor with his arms linked to two more warriors. One was the same height as Peter and the other was half his height. They stank as well. Myroy made a circle with his staff and then he was gone.

"We could be here all night."

The men of Tain stared at James and wondered what he had said. The floor shimmered and the children sat on the bed to make some space for Myroy's return. Peter wondered if he intended to bring him the whole of the High Table.

This time though, the Ancient One brought him only one extra guest. The man was tall, strong, and lean, and his face was as sun burnt as a fig. But it was his army uniform that held Peter's attention. The short-sleeved shirt, long shorts, backpack and round helmet were all the colour of sand. His long rifle was tipped with an evil looking bayonet. Unmistakable. He could have been no more than thirty.

Peter shouted, "Grandpa," and ran and threw his arms around him. A cloud of dust came off Grandpa's uniform.

"Easy, Laddie," he boomed, "I haven't had any children yet!"

"Cool," said James.

"Well, I think some introductions are in order."

Myroy tapped his staff on the floor.

"Peter and James of the line of Donald, may I introduce you to Alistair of Cadbol."

Alistair gave a small, polite bow.

"To Hamish and Donald of Tain."

Hamish growled and Donald said, "Don't take any notice of him, he can hardly put two words together."

"And this," continued Myroy, "is Dougie of Dunfermline, First Stone Keeper, Friend of Kings and Hero of Battles."

Dougie shuffled his feet and looked embarrassed.

"You said you needed our help, Myroy," boomed Grandpa.

"Aye, what has happened in this time?" asked Alistair.

"The Keeper has lost the stone."

It was Peter's turn to feel embarrassed.

"The filthy Picts haven't got it, have they?" asked Donald.

"A descendent of Tella the Mac Mar has it," confirmed the Ancient One. "His named is Smith and he holds it in a place of learning."

"Is it a terrible fortress?" asked Dougie.

"No," said Myroy, "but that makes our task none the easier. Smith has many followers and their numbers grow as his greed nourishes the stone."

"How many followers and how are they armed?" Hamish asked.

"Ten hundred, all armed in some way, and many of them are children who we must not harm."

The bedroom fell silent and Peter was asked by Myroy to draw a map of Pinner High School. They talked about where Smith might hold the stone and finally agreed on a plan of attack. The sun came up and flooded the bedroom with light. Hamish rubbed his great belly.

"I'm hungry. No warrior should fight on an empty stomach."

"We have lost the advantage of darkness," considered Alistair, "we may as well feast before battle."

Dougie raised an eyebrow at the word battle.

"Cool," said James.

Myroy sighed.

"We must leave quietly. Peter, will you lead the way?"

Peter rose from the bed and crept to the door, then led them down stairs and out of the front door. He closed the latch quietly and ran to the front of the line.

James winked at him. "Nice to be out in the fresh air."

A paperboy stopped his bike and watched them. "Off to a fancy dress party, are we?" he shouted.

"Off to the football," said Peter. "We're the tartan army."

"More like the barmy army," laughed the paperboy.

Hamish growled at him and he fell off his bike.

After fifteen minutes of snaking though the leafy back roads, they came out onto Pinner High Street.

"I never liked London," said Grandpa as he strode along with his rifle in front of him. But the men of Tain were dumbstruck at the pavement, the lines of parked cars and the streetlights. The street lights came on and Donald wanted to climb up and touch them.

"Power's back on," mumbled Peter, "I wonder if it means anything?"

"It means we might get a burger," said James.

"A burger?" asked Dougie, "is that a warrior who might aid us?"

"No," laughed James, "it's food."

"Don't mention food," warned Donald, "we will never get to Smith if Hamish stops for breakfast."

They walked past Boots, Marks and Spencer, and an estate agent's window. It had a red, neon sign, which flashed *House Bargain of the Week*.

"What a lot of nonsense," criticised Grandpa, but Dougie couldn't stop himself staring at it.

"Hey, this is McDonalds," said James.

"Is this the house of the burger?" asked Dougie.

"The McDonalds are loyal to the Younger," chirped Donald and he walked in.

Peter dashed ahead of him and pointed at a table.

"Better leave the ordering to me."

He pulled some money from his back pocket, and walked up to the counter where a thin, spotty youth was eyeing up his first customers of the day. His nose twitched.

"Eight Big Mac meals," said Peter.

"What drinks would you like with them?" asked the youth cautiously.

"Make mine a diet cola," yelled James.

"Better have one diet cola and seven strawberry milk-shakes," suggested Peter and the youth tapped something into his screen.

Hamish loomed up behind Peter.

"I'll help you carry the feast."

"Would you like to go large?" asked the spotty youth.

"He's large enough" said Donald.

Peter nodded and paid, and noticed that the men of Tain didn't offer to help pay. Hamish squeezed beside Myroy and looked at the carton, which contained his burger. He bit it and spat it out.

Peter opened the carton and handed him the burger. In four bites it was gone and so he started on the fries.

Donald's face was turning the same colour as his strawberry milkshake, as he tried to suck it up through his straw, and all the time the youth stared at them. Peter saw his stare.

"We're off to the football. Should be a good game."

The youth nodded slowly and continued to stare at their claymores and Grandpa's rifle. He wondered if he should call the police and decided against it. He wasn't going to be a hero and, anyway, the world had gone mad since the start of the riots at the school.

Dougie of Dunfermline tried some of James's cola and the bubbles shot up his nose. He sneezed and James grinned. Donald ripped the lid off his shake and drank greedily, and poured most of it down his chin. Grandpa couldn't open his sachet of Mild Mustard Sauce and sliced it in two with his bayonet. The youth groaned and left the counter to use a phone. Myroy raised his staff and the lad froze like a statue.

"Are we less hungry now?" he asked in an agitated voice.

Hamish shoved the last of his fries into his mouth and mumbled something like, "Not really."

Myroy nodded at the big man and they all rose.

"I need the loo," said James.

"The loo?" asked Alistair.

"How do I explain this one?"

Peter shrugged his shoulders and Grandpa boomed, "It's where we go to relieve ourselves."

The men of Tain nodded, knowingly.

"Why not just go at the side of the path?" asked Donald.

"We don't do that sort of thing," corrected Peter, "much more hygienic to go to the loo."

"I've got to see this," said Alistair and the kilted warriors followed James.

With a little instruction, the five urinals were approached and four kilts lifted.

"I like this," said Donald and then he jumped backwards as unseen hands squirted water out of a pipe and down around the bowl. His back set the hand drier off and it *whooshed* like a demon. Hamish brought the hilt of his claymore down onto the drier and it *whooshed* no more. The lights went out and orange sparks from the dangling drier lit the loo.

"There is evil here," warned Dougie.

At last, they were walking again down Pinner High Street. There were more people about now and they all stared at them suspiciously. James clapped his hands together and shouted, "Scotland, Scotland," to make them think they were football fans.

"Do the Angles not hate our war cry?" asked Dougie.

"We don't fight each other anymore," said James.

"And where's the fun in that?" asked Donald.

They turned down New Hope Drive and approached the school gates, and ducked down behind the wreck of a BBC Outside Broadcast lorry. The gates were half open and guarded by four policemen with truncheons, three teachers with chair legs, and five pupils.

"Get the children away from the gate," ordered Alistair.

James ran up to the gate and shouted.

"Come on then, you wallies. If you think you're hard enough."

He slapped a boy on the face and dashed off shouting, "Come on then!"

The pupils chased him along New Hope Drive and the policemen slammed the gates shut, and padlocked them. Grandpa stood and took his backpack off, and pulled out a smaller canvas bag.

"Give me ten seconds and keep your heads down."

He ran and yanked a pin out of a grenade and thrust it back with the others. Chair legs crashed around him and he tossed the bag at the base of the gates. Then he was sprinting back to them like a rabbit.

The men of Tain watched in awe as the gates of Pinner High flew up into the air.

***

Sergeant Bernie Wagg led his advance party south through Harrow on the Hill towards Wembley. Two tanks barged parked cars out the way and ten police cars, with flashing lights, followed them, sirens screaming. A mob, five hundred strong, looted any shops they passed. Wagg waved his truncheon at a group of policemen who were manhandling a washing machine out of Dixons.

"Leave it, you fools. There are richer pickings in London. Tell the others to head straight for the Houses of Parliament."

A soldier in a camouflage jacket popped out of a hatch on one of the tanks.

"Enough fuel for fifty miles."

Wagg considered this and nodded. A red glow pulsed out from Smith in Pinner High School and engulfed them.

"Fire three rounds into central London," ordered Wagg. "If they don't think we are serious, then now is the time to show them we are."

***

Barry Sweeney and Thomas Greacher, the Head of English, followed Smith about like devoted puppies. First they checked the School Gym. Toady Thomson sat on the stage looking down contemptuously at a dozen disloyal pupils.

Laura sat beside Kylie. They had been forced to fold their arms and cross their legs, and were hungry, tired and stiff as boards. When they thought they could get away with it, they talked in whispers.

After the assembly, the girls had woken up from a dream. The power which gripped them had eased and now they felt awful. They knew they had helped Smith and his followers to prepare for the march on London, and regretted it. The other pupils were possessed and seemed to hate them as much as they wanted to escape. Smith had called them the 'disloyal' and Toady had slapped their faces. Toady got up as his master entered the hall.

"Any problems?" asked Smith.

"That one," he said, pointing at Laura, "tried to run out the fire escape an hour ago. We're OK now. Even the reporters are feeling more at home."

He pointed at three men who were tied with thick ropes to the bars of a climbing frame. Smith looked approvingly at Laura's red cheek and nodded, and marched off to the Headmistress's Study, with Sweeney and Greacher following at a respectful distance.

Mac Mackinlay smelled of cigarettes and grinned at them. He waved a shotgun at Mrs Bold, who was tied to a chair beside the school trophy cabinet.

"Any problems?" asked Smith.

"No," grunted Mac and he placed the end of the barrels under Mrs Bold's chin. She winced.

Smith continued his rounds to the staff room. Greacher jumped ahead and opened the door for his leader. A mixture of policemen, teachers and reporters tracked the progress of their army on a large map of central London. Miss Tag, Deputy Head of Biology, pushed a model tank forward across the North Circular Road.

"Any problems?" asked Smith.

"We'll be in Trafalgar Square in less than an hour," she squeaked proudly.

***

The Emergency Committee for Civil Unrest sat around a long mahogany table in the basement of Whitehall.

"I can't believe this has been caused by our policies for the introduction of Performance Related Pay into the teaching profession," said the Prime Minister.

John Prescott, Minister for Education, nodded.

"I doubt it very much, Tony."

"Then what the devil is this all about?"

Sir William De Villiars, Senior Civil Servant, lifted his face from his hands.

"I think, Prime Minister, you should talk to the nation."

A hopeful look shot across the PM's face.

"Are the television channels working?"

"No," replied John.

General Sir Martin Arthur cut in.

"The only form of civil communication still operating is Radio 4 on long wave. Everything else, including mobile phones and land lines, is static. Just static."

"Are they terrorists?" asked Tony.

John Prescott grimaced.

"Worse than that. They are teachers."

"Do you think a foreign power is behind it?" asked Tony.

"I don't believe a group of teachers have the technology to cripple the nation and turn everyone who tries to fight them onto their side," said John.

"Is it the Russians?"

Sir Martin shook his head.

"Since the last summit we've been getting on rather well with Moscow."

Tony Blair thumped the table. "Then who is behind it? Will someone give me a straight answer!"

The committee fell silent.

"Well can anyone give me some options?"

The earth seemed to shake around them and a chunk of ceiling fell onto the table as a round from Wagg's tank ripped into the side of Whitehall.

Without batting an eyelid, Sir Martin Arthur stood up.

"We have two divisions of light infantry moving south from Catterick and Royal Marines are being flown up from Lympston in Devon."

"I hope they will do better than the tanks you sent in," said John coldly.

317

"That's the point. I don't think they will."

Tony raised an eyebrow. Sir William De Villiars coughed, apologetically, pulled a bright yellow handkerchief from his pocket, and wiped his brow.

"I must advise caution. The best thing might be to fly the Royal Family to Balmoral Castle. We all need to leave London until things settle down."

"We certainly need time to consider if we bomb Pinner," added Sir Martin.

"I am not going to be remembered as the Prime Minister who nuked his own people."

"I wasn't suggesting a nuclear device," countered the General. "All the intelligence we have (and God knows there isn't a lot of it) suggests this all started in Pinner High School. Whatever is spreading around the country, is spreading out from there."

"Have we had any demands for money, or changes to Government policy?" asked John.

Sir Martin shook his head.

"As a purely precautionary matter, I have asked RAF Leuchars to fly a tornado down to Pinner. It contains enough conventional explosives to obliterate the school."

"How many children are in the school?" asked Tony.

"The Pinner High role lists eight hundred," mumbled Prescott.

"Eight hundred," yelled Tony, "get the Tornado back to Leuchars immediately."

Sir Martin groaned and lifted a green telephone.

"Get me RAF Leuchars at once."

Someone said something and General Sir Martin Arthur raised an eyebrow.

"It would seem that we have lost all contact with the outside world. Nothing, not even the military COM's link, is working."

***

Smith looked up at the sky and barked, "Go and find out where Wagg has got to."

Thomas Greacher sprinted off.

The RAF Tornado circled at two thousand feet above the school. Its engines roared as the pilot banked to come around again.

"Five miles from Trafalgar Square," yelled Greacher.

Smith lifted Odin's Stone and a red beam shot up at the fighter plane. Immediately it dived, screaming as it raced towards the earth. Then it levelled out and shot off towards the south-east.

Four minutes later it dropped its bombs onto Tower Bridge.

***

Just outside of Oslo, in Odin's underground office, every television screen died and he tuned a radio to BBC Radio 4. London was in complete chaos. His ruby cried out. He walked through the screens into the rock lined chamber and stepped inside a standing stone. He would need to use the power of the sea to talk with Olaf Adanson.

Olaf and his men were outside Pinner High School, watching the entrance through telescopic sights. The gates had just been blown to smithereens.

***

Grandma sat at her kitchen table and listened to Radio 4. Dog sat, mournfully, beside her and had hardly moved all morning.

She prayed for her family, "I hope they are alright."

"Maggie, they are fine," said Grandpa's voice. "We are going in now to get back what was taken."

Grandma nodded and stood. "And Peter cannot stay in London."

"Why not give Bernard a call? Lines to Corfu might be working. Do you have a passport?"

"Of course I have a passport, you old fool," she said in an anxious, irritable voice.

"Don't call me an old fool," said Grandpa, "Myroy will collect you shortly. Be ready."

Grandma made her call and put Dog on his lead. He didn't like that and seemed to sense what it meant.

After a short walk to the Post Office at Easter Malgeddie, Grandma tied the sheepdog to a hook outside the shop. The bell tinkled as she went in and Miss McKiely said, "Hello Maggie, I'm afraid we haven't got any papers today. Everything seems to be in a bit of a pickle."

Maggie smiled. "I'm afraid I'm not here to buy anything. I am after a bit of a favour."

"Certainly, Maggie. What can I help you with?"

"Could you look after Dog for me?"

"And how long are you going to be away?"

Grandma put on a brave smile. "I really don't know," she said and burst into tears.

***

Hamish sprinted forward and lifted a policeman above his head, and tossed him at a teacher.

"Leave some for me," said Donald and he jumped onto a teacher's back.

Peter and Dougie ran past them and began to fend off chair legs that swung down viciously at their heads. Alistair and Grandpa joined them and after a few minutes most of the enemy were down. James came sprinting back along New Hope Drive, chased by five bigger boys.

"Come on you wallies," he yelled and he ran to stand beside Myroy.

A policeman hit Donald on the shoulder with his truncheon and he cried out. Hamish slashed out with his claymore and cut the man's arm off. Donald grabbed it and tossed it at James's pursuers. Blood spurted out, the fingers curled and the pupils ran away. James grinned at the curling fingers.

"Cool."

"When we are inside, split into two," ordered Myroy.

Alistair nodded and led Dougie and Peter through the school entrance. A set of double doors blocked the way along the corridor. An intercom lay beside it. Peter pressed the button and asked, politely, "May we come in?"

A thin fourth-former lifted his head above the glass in the reception room and looked them over.

"Not a chance," he scoffed.

Like a herd of buffalo, Hamish and Grandpa dashed past Peter and the doors were smashed off their hinges. The fourth-former's head sank back below the glass. James and Donald followed Hamish and Grandpa towards the school gym. Myroy and the others turned down another corridor and headed straight for Mrs Bold's office.

The Battle of Pinner High was about to begin.

***

Olaf Adanson crouched with Roberts, Johnson and Hyde in the bay window of number eight New Hope Drive. They had a clear view of the gates of Pinner High and watched, silently, as the men of Tain fought their way in. Mick Roberts put his revolver down and pressed a button on his digital camera.

"Just for the record," he said.

"What do we do now?" asked Hyde, as he stroked the telescopic sight on his rifle.

"Wait," ordered Olaf.

"Wouldn't it be better to follow them in and kill them when they take the master's stone?" asked Johnson.

"Wait," repeated Olaf.

Hyde got up. "This isn't what I have been paid to do."

He walked to the door.

Olaf swivelled around and shot him, twice, in the back.

"Anyone else wish to join the fallen?"

Johnson and Roberts glanced at each other.

"I think we should wait," said Mick.

***

Twenty staff and pupils had raised a barricade across the gym corridor. Tables, chairs and fire extinguishers barred the way and, as James approached it, the defenders launched a hail of missiles. A blackboard rubber glanced off his forehead and blood dripped down onto his shirt.

He retreated around a bend in the corridor to stand with the others. Then he stuck his head around the bend and tugged at his stained shirt.

"That cost me sixty quid!"

"What are we going to do about them?" asked Grandpa, sticking his thumb around the bend.

"They are weak," said Hamish, "and strong defences are never made of wood."

"Have you any of those magic fires?" asked Donald.

Grandpa took a box of matches from his breast pocket and shook them.

"Collect tinder," ordered Hamish and they dashed in and out of classrooms collecting waste paper bins and paper.

Grandpa dived around the corner and fired three shots above the barricade. The others ran forward with flaming buckets and emptied them amongst the chairs.

"This is great fun," whooped James, as the barricade began to catch fire.

Donald grinned and nodded. Then his face went white.

"How will the children get away?"

"Oh, they will probably go through the gym to the fire exit," said James.

"Come on then," ordered Grandpa, "that's our way in."

They ran back to the school entrance, across the playground and along the path behind the classrooms.

A door burst open at the back of the gym where thirty to forty armed teachers and pupils staggered out. As they coughed and spluttered, the men of Tain hit the teachers and sent them sprawling. James and Grandpa barged their way inside.

Toady Thompson still sat in judgement on the stage above his captives. He would stay there until his master told him otherwise. He would burn if necessary. They would all burn. Smoke billowed into the gym from the corridor and, through the mist, James saw Laura. As Grandpa untied the three reporters, James ran to save his sister. He lifted her up and saw the red handprint on her cheek.

"Come on, all of you, get up and get out."

The girls stood and helped each other, unsteadily, towards the fire exit.

Toady leapt down from the stage and punched James.

"Sit back down."

Some of the girls sat back down. Laura and Kylie came back and tried to help them stand. Toady punched Laura too. Something snapped inside James and he drove his head into the bigger boy's belly. As he doubled over, James brought his knee up into his face. Then he was on top of him.

"No-one," yelled James and he punched him in the nose. "No-one hits my sister without my permission."

For good measure, he hit Toady again. Grandpa lifted James up by the scruff of his neck.

"Time to get going," he said and he grabbed Toady's limp body and carried them both out into clean air.

The three newsmen stared at James and grabbed their cameras and recording equipment. In the sunshine Grandpa dropped Toady and turned on James.

"We're going to help the others. Stick to the plan. Get the girls out of the school."

James nodded and rounded them all up. The reporters followed as he led them through the gates of Pinner High and a cameraman snapped picture after picture. The sound recordist held a microphone next to James's mouth.

"Are we linked up to Radio 4?" asked the interviewer.

"We're live now," replied the soundman.

The interviewer cleared his throat.

"Welcome to the incredible scenes here, outside troubled Pinner High School. I am joined by a very brave young man, who has helped rescue some of the hostages. For our many millions of listeners, may I ask your name?"

"Whatever," said James.

"We saw you fight off one of the rebels who held the girls hostage. How does it feel to be a hero?"

"Don't know."

"And did you see their leader? Can you give us a name and a description of the man who is holding the country to ransom?"

"I can."

There was an uneasy silence and the interviewer thought, "I've interviewed pop stars and politicians, and none of them gave me trouble like this."

He nodded at James to encourage him to speak. James stopped in his tracks and grinned at the sound recordist.

"His name is Smith."

"And what does he look like?"

"He's got big cheeks and a thick black beard."

Julie and Colin Donald sat in their conservatory, listening to every word their son spoke on the radio.

"Oh James, no," whispered Julie.

In her kitchen in Glenbowmond, Grandma was listening as well. She grinned for the first time in days.

"Yeah," said James, "the dudes got a face like a badger's arse."

***

Myroy's dark cloak flowed behind him as he marched down the school's main corridor.

"The girls should be out by now," said Dougie.

"I hope so," mumbled Myroy, "we cannot face Smith if he can still threaten them."

Peter pointed at another corridor, branching off to their left. It had pale yellow walls and a long display of children's writings, pinned on string with clothes pegs. A huge banner above them proclaimed, *The Poems of Peace.*

Alistair drew his claymore and Dougie did the same, and they took up their positions on either side of a heavy looking door. A sign read –

Mrs Bold. Headmistress.
Please knock before entering.

Peter knocked politely and Mac called out, "Yeah?"

"A message from Smith," lied Peter.

"What is it?" yelled back Mac, suspiciously.

"Smith says everyone is to join him in the staff room. London has fallen."

Inside Mrs Bold's office, came the sound of a chair being moved. A key turned in the lock and the door opened slowly. When the crack was the width of a hand, Peter kicked the door and Mac cried out in pain. Myroy entered first and stared at Mrs Bold. She was tied to a chair and gagged, and she nodded frantically at Mac. He was scrambling across the floor towards his gun.

The Ancient One ignored the warning and walked over to untie her. Mac stood, a hideous smile on his face, and fired both barrels at Myroy. The shots passed through his body and the school trophy cabinet exploded into a million pieces. Shattered glass peppered the wall behind the cabinet.

Peter gasped. But it wasn't as big a gasp as Mac gave. His mouth was like the Channel Tunnel and Peter walked over, and took away the shotgun.

"I don't think you are going to need this. Dangerous things, guns."

He hit Mac over the head with the butt. Unconcerned, Myroy continued to untie Mrs Bold and she stood, trembling, not daring to hope that her ordeal was over. Then she stared down at Mac's limp body and then at Peter.

"First class."

"Make your way to the school entrance," ordered Alistair, from the doorway, "you will get help there."

Mrs Bold looked at his kilt and claymore.

"First class," she repeated.

"Come on," said Dougie. "We have to meet up with the others."

They dashed back past *The Poems of Peace* and marched through the library, which had been completely vandalised, and into the school restaurant. The kitchen was filthy and smelled of rotting vegetables. Then they were past the ranks of low tables and chairs, and out into the science corridor. Dougie glanced at the posters of space and sea exploration and wondered at them. Three teachers barred their way and ran off as soon as Alistair charged at them with his claymore.

"Catch them," said Myroy, "or they will warn Smith."

They chased the men past physics, biology and chemistry, and Peter rugby-tackled one as he turned into the corridor, which led to the staff room. The teacher cried out and grabbed Peter's throat.

"Sorry, Mr Mead," said Peter and he slammed his French teacher's head onto the floor.

Dougie helped Peter up.

"That's no way to treat a scribe."

"Come on, Dougie," urged Alistair and they ran on.

Hamish, Donald and Grandpa rounded a bend at the far end of the corridor and chased a teacher towards them. He dived into the staff room at about the same time as the other teachers, that Alistair was chasing, dived inside too.

The door was locked and barricaded with two metal filing cabinets.

"What do we do now?" asked Dougie.

"Break the door down," boomed Grandpa and Hamish.

"Not yet. Wait here," said Myroy and he disappeared down through the floor.

***

The Ancient One rose out of a conservatory floor.

"Colin of the Line of Donald."

Colin sat bolt upright and Julie dropped her cup of tea.

"Bring your car to the entrance of Pinner High. Make sure you have petrol to reach Luton airport. Pack a bag and a passport for Peter. Book him onto the next flight to Corfu. The Keeper cannot stay here."

Then he was gone. Julie Donald stared at the shimmering floor and then at her husband. He was twiddling his fingers.

"Is there something you want to tell me?"

***

"Got any more grenades?" asked Peter.

Grandpa shook his head. "Just brute force."

"We have to be in and out in fifteen minutes," said Myroy, as he came back to them.

"All rooms have a fire exit," suggested Peter, "shall we go round and see if it's open?"

Before anyone could answer, they heard the sound of metal scraping across the staffroom floor. The filing cabinets were being pulled away.

"They go on the attack," warned Alistair.

"Get back," cried Grandpa and they dived away from the door as bullets ripped it apart.

Someone inside yanked it open and Greacher and Sweeney jumped out, armed with pistols.

Grandpa shot Barry Sweeney and he fell. Greacher shot Dougie and his body spun around before hitting the floor. Hamish grabbed Greacher and threw him into the corridor wall. He slid down the wall as if in slow motion. Peter grabbed Greacher's pistol and fired two shots into the staffroom.

"Go," yelled Alistair and they charged in.

Sitting in an old armchair, smiling at them, was Smith. He held Amera's stone in his hands and it glowed a greedy red. Behind him were twenty heavily armed policemen and teachers. By the windows, Miss Tag was pushing a model tank across a map; out of Trafalgar Square and along the Embankment.

"A little later than expected," said Smith, "but you're here now. Here at the time of my ultimate triumph."

Peter stepped forward. "I think you have got something of mine." Smith laughed and lit a cigarette. "It was so easy to steal from you. I might as well give it back for safe *keeping*. I could certainly take it back whenever I wanted."

The mob behind him burst out laughing.

"Wagg is outside the Tower of London. Can I order him to fire?" screeched Miss Tag excitedly.

"Fire," agreed Smith lazily and then, almost as an afterthought, "I wonder how much the Crown Jewels are worth?"

Peter stepped forward again and the barrel of a rifle was thrust into his chest. He took the change from McDonalds out of his pocket, and threw it at Smith.

"Is this what it was all about?"

Smith shrugged his shoulders. "I like money."

Peter's blood began to boil. "You mean you took my sister and my girlfriend hostage for the sake of money."

Smith walked over to the map.

"And why not? This stone is the key to incredible riches. Why shouldn't I have them? I am the new *Keeper*, not you."

Peter glanced over his shoulder at Dougie and pure anger pulsed through his veins. The shepherd lay, still, in a pool of blood next to Barry Sweeney.

"And you killed Dougie. After all he went through!"

"He doesn't matter," said Smith quietly. "You no longer matter."

He pointed the ruby at Peter.

Myroy stepped back and made a signal to Hamish, Donald, Alistair and Grandpa to do the same. They crept out of the staffroom. A red beam shot out of Amera's stone at Peter and Smith laughed.

Peter fought with every ounce of anger he could muster and the beam curved around him, and turned on Smith. Smith wasn't laughing now, and when the beam struck his body he glowed red.

Peter jumped forward and took the stone. His stone. The staffroom filled with a rich, red glow and all the policemen and teachers collapsed on the floor.

Smith's body exploded.

Outside the Tower of London, Sergeant Wagg fell to the ground and a tank swerved into a gift shop. Its engine stalled and became silent.

Myroy dashed in and grabbed Peter.

"Come on. It isn't over yet."

He dragged him down the corridor, with the others following.

"What about Smith's followers?" asked Grandpa.

"Leave them to the police. We must get out of here. Odin's people will not be far away."

As they ran back through the school restaurant, Peter glanced at the warrior beside him. Dougie clutched a wound on his shoulder.

"I thought you were dead," gasped Peter.

"Myroy told me to make it look that way," said Dougie, sheepishly, and Peter realised that he had been tricked into feeling so angry.

"It had to be," said Myroy, "and now I think you know a little more about the stone."

Peter nodded and continued to run, and thought, "Odin poured his soul into the ruby and his anger is greater than his greed."

They burst out into brilliant noon sunshine. The twisted school gates lay thirty feet apart and a car waited, engine running, outside the entrance to New Hope Drive.

"Get in, Peter," yelled Colin Donald and the car sped away.

"What about the others?" asked Peter.

But he only had to look out the rear window to know the answer. Myroy had taken Hamish and Donald, his first passengers, down through the tarmac. Back through time.

***

"Shall I kill them?" asked Johnson, and Mick Roberts took the safety catch off his revolver.

Olaf Adanson shook his head and the Donalds' car sped past their bay window.

"Did you do what I asked?"

"Easiest job in the world. They weren't looking at me," replied Mick.

"Then it is done," muttered Olaf. "Get the car."

***

Colin Donald drove at break-neck speed up the M1 towards Luton airport.

"Did you get it, Peter?"

"I did, although I shouldn't have lost it in the first place."

"I'm afraid it's all my fault," said Laura sheepishly. "Smith asked me to bring the ruby into school, to show the rest of the class. I bloomin' fell for it, hook, line and sinker."

"Oh Laura, how could you?" snapped Julie, and Laura's bottom lip began to tremble. Peter put a reassuring arm around his sister.

"It was very brave of you to say that."

"Yeah, don't cry," said James, "it was the biggest giggle I've had in ages and we got to meet all these weirdos out of the old man's stories."

"They aren't weirdos," shouted Colin Donald, "they are our ancestors."

"Whatever," chirped James, "and I'm going to be on the front page

329

of all the newspapers tomorrow. I can just see it. *Handsome Hero Rescues Dumb Sister*."

Laura burst into tears.

"Stop that at once," ordered Julie.

"We have to get you away, Peter," added Colin quickly. "Give him his stuff, Laura."

Laura sniffed and handed Peter a holdall, a passport and a piece of paper with instructions on it.

"That's Bernard's address on Corfu in case you get separated from Grandma," said Julie calmly.

"Corfu? Grandma?" stammered Peter.

"Bernard is going to hide you away until things settle down. Grandma is going to keep you company."

"Can't Kylie keep me company?"

"No," barked Colin, "and whatever you do, don't try and contact her. Or us. Odin's people will know who we are by now. Don't phone, don't write and especially don't e-mail."

Peter nodded grimly. "And where is Grandma?"

"Myroy will be dropping her off in the ladies' loo, in Departures, about now," said James, "I think he's a bit on the kinky side."

"James," snapped Julie, and James gave her one of his, *who me*? looks.

The car slowed as they approached the airport drop-off zone.

"You have the stone?" checked Colin and Peter felt it in his pocket.

"Put it in the jewellery case, in your bag."

"Aren't you coming in?" asked Peter.

"They are bound to know our car and the sooner we go, the safer we will all be."

Julie undid her seat belt and swivelled round, and kissed him.

"I still don't know what this is all about, but when it's over I want you home. Home, you hear me." She kissed him again.

James grinned.

"Don't I get a kiss for saving your daughter?"

"No," said Julie. "You're helping to make the tea and telling me what on earth you've been up to."

James shrugged his shoulders.

"Go," ordered Colin and, as soon as Peter was out, the car sped away.

Julie stuck her head out the window.

"We'll wave from the car park at the end of the runway."

Peter picked up his holdall and went through a revolving door. Grandma grabbed his arm, without a word of introduction, and led him to the last call at desk twenty two. A lady in an orange uniform glared at him.

"Cutting it a bit fine aren't we?"

"Sorry," stammered Peter.

"Photo ID?"

Peter handed her his passport.

"Have you got any bags?"

Peter held up his holdall.

"Well, that's something. That can go as hand-baggage. You had better go straight through to the departure lounge. Boarding at Gate Six in ten minutes."

"Thank you," mumbled Peter and Grandma grabbed his arm again.

***

Peter sat by the window and felt his body forced back into his seat as the engines roared.

"I've never been to Corfu."

"I've never been abroad," beamed Grandma, excited by the take-off. "Where will they be?"

"Down there. It's where they always wave from when we fly up to see you."

Grandma pointed out the window.

"There they are."

As clear as day, James and Laura stood up through the rear sunroof. Mum and dad waved frantically out of the front sunroof.

Peter waved back and mouthed, "Bye."

In his ancient chamber, Myroy touched a crystal and whispered, "Oh no."

At exactly the same moment, Grandpa said the same words.

"Oh no."

Grandma's face creased and went white. Peter smiled and held her hand.

"Don't worry. Flying is very safe these days," and he glanced out the window to get a last glimpse of his family.

There was a blinding flash and the Donalds' car was hurled skywards. It crashed back to earth and became a fireball. A metal tomb engulfed by flame. Grandma's head fell into her hands as their plane sailed, effortlessly, up into a cloak of clouds.

A metallic voice sang out.

"Ladies and gentlemen, please keep your seatbelts fastened until the captain turns off the seatbelt signs. Our flight time to Corfu will be four hours and we will shortly be serving you with a range of drinks and snacks. So please relax and enjoy the flight."

But Peter didn't hear the voice. He felt numb. Then he thought about his family and Myroy's warning.

But, only one part of the terrible price had been paid.

Peter and the men of Tain will return in their next thrilling adventure, "Killer in the Dark," in which Alistair of Cadbol is under sentence of death in the bowels of Berwick Castle and Odin's secret agents arrive in Corfu.

Tella the Mac Mar forges a secret and terrible alliance to destroy the Younger and the Celtic peoples of Scotland. Only one man stands in Tella's way and he is a young shepherd, and his name is Dougie of Dunfermline.

The battle of the "light iron" is about to begin.

If you would like to read the start of the next book then please visit –

www.myroybooks.com